By Dean Murray

Reborn

Dean Murray

Reborn is a work of fiction. Names, characters, places and incidents are the products of the author's imagination or are used fictitiously. Any resemblance to actual events, locales, or persons, living or dead, is entirely coincidental.

Published by Fir'shan Publishing

ISBN 978-1-9393635-1-0

www.FirshanPublishing.com

First Edition

For Ms. Thompson

Thanks for taking a chance on a shy kid who failed the test to get into the 'smart' math class.

There are a few events I can point to which contributed to my feeling that I could achieve most anything I put my mind to.

Your classes were one of them.

Chapter 1

"You should be more careful, Selene. One of these times you're going to get hurt—you know, if you don't pay attention to where you're going."

The words were said with a sugary sweetness that adults ate up, but which always made me want to vomit. It was hard to believe that the teachers were all stupid enough to believe Sandra's act, but then again she never did anything really nasty unless it was just you and her.

Shoving me into the red and black lockers a few seconds earlier was the perfect example. School had been over for more than an hour so the halls were empty—other than the two of us and her clique. Sandra wasn't just mean, she was a coward. If anyone else had been around she would have left me alone, but I'd had the misfortune of having to wait for my little sister to get done with drama practice before I could drive the two of us home.

"Thanks, Sandra. I hope you get hit by a bus on the way home today."

We'd hated each other for as long as I could remember. Sometimes I could get her mad enough to drop the act, but not today, not given that someone was approaching the corner ahead of us. She just smirked at me before turning and heading towards the exterior door.

I adjusted my backpack and followed along behind her. I was going to have a bruise on my right shoulder—I could already feel a dull ache setting in. The more I thought about it, the more convinced I became that being hit by a bus was too good for her. Actually, I was having a hard time coming up with something suitable. Leprosy was too slow and a heart attack was too fast.

The footsteps turned out to belong to somebody I'd never seen before, which was novel given that the state of the local economy meant that recently all of the moves were *out* of town rather than the other way around.

The new arrival was a guy...a tall, built guy with wavy blond hair and a chin that looked like it had been carved out of marble. My heart started going a hundred miles an hour as soon as I saw him. I usually barely noticed guys, but something about this one was different. He wasn't just gorgeous, he was out-of-this-world gorgeous.

I wasn't the only one who registered that fact—not that I should have been surprised by that. Sandra shot him a smoldering look before turning and exiting the building, but he hardly noticed.

It was pretty rare for guys to realize just how much of a total witch Sandra has always been—at least not until after she'd treated them like crap for a couple of months—so normally I'd be all for a guy blowing her off, but this time there was a complication.

He smiled at me, and it wasn't just any smile. It was one of those slightly lopsided, lazy smiles that only the hottest guys can pull off without looking like an idiot. Even worse, Sandra looked back to see what kind of effect she'd had on him just in time to see him look at me.

Crap. That was the last thing I needed. Sandra and I already hated each other, but things could always get worse. She already had a boyfriend, there was no reason for her to fixate on this new guy—no other reason than that he'd had the temerity to ignore her and smile at me instead.

She was going to find a way to make my life even worse.

Maybe that would have been okay if Mr. Hot-Stuff had actually been interested in dating me, but he wasn't. I knew the type—granted none anywhere near as hot—guys who knew that they made girls' hearts go pitter-patter every time they walked by. There was just something about being hot that seemed to make people want to take advantage of their good looks. He probably smiled at anything in a skirt—regardless of whether or not he was interested—just because he liked seeing girls walk into walls because they were so focused on him.

I frowned at Mr. Hot-Stuff, which earned me a confused look—he obviously wasn't used to his charm failing like that. He started to hold the door open for me—doubtlessly a reflexive action. The fact that I wasn't impressed apparently hadn't made it to the pea-sized organ that he used for a brain.

I pushed past him, opening the other door for myself, and headed towards my car without looking back to see what kind of a response my rudeness had triggered.

Ari, my younger sister, claims that I'm incapable of being rude, that doing so leaves me in physical pain. She's also prone to gross exaggeration. I'm as capable of rudeness as anyone else, I just don't *enjoy* being rude. Unlike, say Sandra.

Actually I was already feeling bad about not letting him hold the door open for me...and for frowning at him...and for thinking that he had stunted cognitive abilities. None of that had been fair of me.

Don't get me wrong, any boy who was that hot was probably a self-centered jerk, but you were supposed to give people the benefit of the doubt before you start acting on those kinds of assumptions. Besides, even if Mr. Hot-

Stuff *was* an egotistical, narcissistic waste of skin he was probably just a product of his environment.

I wanted to turn around and apologize, but my only hope of weathering the nastiness that Sandra had in store for me was for Mr. Hot-Stuff to leave me alone and decide he had a sudden, compelling interest in Sandra. I couldn't do anything about the second half of that equation, but being rude was a good start towards making sure of the first half.

As long as Sandra felt like she'd ultimately come out on top where Mr. Hot-Stuff was concerned, she wouldn't feel the need to put me in my place. It was a crappy way to treat people, but I was just one girl. As long as Sandra's dad owned the tile factory that was the main employer in our town, I had exactly zero chance of upsetting the pecking order and instituting something more equitable.

I was so focused on not turning back to apologize to the blond guy that I almost didn't notice my tires. They were flat. Not just a little low, they were rims-on-the-blacktop flat. I did a slow circuit around my car, but I knew what I was going to find even before the last tire came into view. All four of them were flat.

I wanted to scream. Or maybe cry—it was hard to say. The only thing I was certain of was that if I opened my mouth I was going to regret it. There wasn't any need to guess who'd sabotaged my car; I could hear giggling from across the parking lot.

More than anything else in the world I wanted to walk over and key her shiny blue Lexus. I wanted to score the paint from one end to the other and then find a rock and bash in her headlights.

I closed my eyes and forced myself to take deep, slow breaths. As much as I wanted to pay Sandra back for the last twelve years of brutality, acting on the urge wasn't an option. Anything I did would eventually make it back to my dad, and that was the one consequence that I couldn't live with.

My dad worked at the tile factory. One word from Sandra to her father and my dad would be out of work. I was stuck between a rock and a hard spot with no exit visible until I graduated from high school and left home.

I sank down to the asphalt and put my back against the side of my Nissan. My car hid me from the view of Sandra and her friends, but I wasn't under any illusions. I was giving them the satisfaction of knowing that they'd gotten to me. I just didn't have enough fight left in me to care.

Hadn't someone done an experiment some-where involving tormenting animals and the ones that weren't allowed to fight back died in short order? That's how I felt. If I'd been allowed to fight back I could have endured two more years of this, but I wasn't sure I could make it if things continued on like they were now.

I let my mind drift away to a world where I wasn't a social pariah, a world where I could smile back at a cute guy instead of worrying about what his attention was going to make Sandra do.

The sound of approaching footsteps snapped me out of my reverie.

There were only two sets, which meant that Sandra had left one of her friends back at her car. I couldn't take all three of them, but there was a chance that I could put Sandra down with my rusty karate skills before her friend could intervene, and I lunged to my feet intending on doing just that—only it wasn't Sandra.

Mr. Hot-Stuff was back, but this time he was accompanied by a tiny girl who was every bit as attractive as he was. She had fine golden hair that was cut in a stylish bob, flawless white skin and a body that had slender curves in all of the right places. Had someone started making size negative one jeans?

"Are you okay?"

It took me a second to realize that the girl was talking to me. It just seemed wrong for a girl like that to even acknowledge my existence. Up until that point my experience with attractive people had been restricted to my school, where everyone paid homage to Sandra.

"No, I'm most certainly not okay."

"Oh, your tires are flat. I didn't even know it was possible for two tires to go flat like that at the same time."

"Then this is going to really blow your mind—all *four* of my tires are flat."

Her forehead creased in thought. "Someone did this to you, didn't they? Was it those girls over there by the blue car?"

Another biting response quivered on the tip of my tongue, anxious to launch itself at her. This time it was something about her being brains and beauty—the whole package and then some—but I just couldn't bring myself to say it.

Sarcasm had been the only thing to get me through the last few years of Sandra's tormenting, but this girl didn't deserve that. She actually seemed to be trying to help. I deflated.

"Yeah, Sandra let the air out of my tires."

"Did you do something to her? It seems like a pretty severe reaction..."

I shrugged. "That's the funny thing about Sandra. She doesn't actually need a reason. We were in the same kindergarten class and she took an instant dislike to me on the first day of school. She's spent practically every day since then making sure that she 'got' me *before* I could get her. By now it wouldn't matter what I did to her I still couldn't come out ahead on points."

The new girl gave me a sad smile. "You never know what the future holds, but for now we should see about getting you mobile. Jace, do something manly and re-inflate her tires."

Mr. Hot-Stuff—Jace apparently—held his hands up in a 'slow down' gesture. "My knowledge of cars ends at the gas pedal. I'm useless at this kind of stuff."

The girl rolled her eyes at him. "That's not the only way that you're useless." She held out her hand. "My name is Katrina, but everyone just calls me Kat. This hot mess is my brother Jace. He's not completely hopeless, but rather than waiting around in the hopes that he figures out which end of the tire iron goes on the lug wrench, we should probably just give you a ride."

Her characterization of her brother drew a smile out of me. "I'm Selene. I appreciate the offer, but I don't want to be any trouble. Besides, if Sandra sees you helping me she'll just be nasty to you too. The last girl who tried to stand up to her was sorry. Sandra got her dad fired from the tile factory and then they were forced to move to another town."

Kat shrugged. "We don't have any ties to the tile factory and if Sandra tries to screw with us she'll be the one who ends up regretting it. Seriously, you won't be any trouble at all."

"I was going to go pick up my sister from the junior high and then go home—we're all the way out on the west side of town. Are you sure you don't mind?"

Jace shook his head. "How come I have a feeling that this is all just a really convoluted plan designed to help you get your hands on my car keys?"

"Because you're not completely hopeless, Jace. Seriously, aren't you paying any attention at all? Come on, Selene. I've been dying to drive Jace's Viper again—you're not an imposition, you're my personal golden ticket."

I found myself liking Kat almost in spite of myself. I took half a step towards her, but stopped as I registered what she'd just said.

"Wait, a Viper? Is there even room for all four of us in one of those?"

"Nope, which is why my suddenly chivalrous brother will be staying here to fix your car. Don't worry though, he's secretly been hoping to find a damsel in distress to rescue—that's the only reason he's willing to part, even temporarily, with his faithful steed."

Jace rolled his eyes at Kat. "You sound like you were born sixteen hundred years ago."

"Better sixteen hundred years ago than sounding like I was born yesterday, infant. Now hand over those keys."

"How exactly do you expect me to fix Selene's tires?"

"I don't know—call that roadside assistance company that you pay an obscene amount of money to every month, or walk up to the road and show a little leg—it's about time you used that hunky body you spend so much time on for something worthwhile. The keys. Now. Oh, and Selene is going to be wearing your jacket home—it's getting cold and she's starting to shiver."

I opened my mouth to protest, but right at that instant a colder than usual gust of wind tore across the parking lot and I did shiver. Jace sighed as he pulled a set of keys out of his back pocket.

"Fine, but if you put even so much as a scratch on it, I'll—"

"Please. If I drive it into the side of a building you'll just use it as an excuse to buy something even more expensive. Come on, Selene. If we don't get on our way now Jace will still be trying to figure out how to get your tires fixed when the first bell rings tomorrow. Trust me when I say that you don't want to see Jace when he's gone without his beauty sleep—it's the kind of thing that could scar you forever."

I still wasn't convinced. For all of my earlier rudeness, I suddenly found myself not wanting to do anything that might make Jace dislike me. He had an easy smile and wasn't so uptight that he couldn't put up with some ribbing from his sister. I couldn't imagine any of the hot guys Sandra dated being willing to have anyone give them that kind of crap.

Jace looked away from my tires for long enough to make a shooing motion at me. "You'd better just go, Selene. Kat is insufferable if she doesn't get what she wants. It's a good thing she's usually pretty reasonable or else I'd have to kill her and hide the body. Don't worry, I'll get your wheels working again and leave your car at your house—just leave your keys with me and they'll be waiting in the ignition when you wake up tomorrow."

My inherent distrust of people tried to claw its way up to the surface, but for once I wasn't inclined to give it its head. Something about the easy give and take between Jace and Kat felt comfortable. I'd spent most of my life avoiding other people as much as possible, but seeing them joke with each other had awoken a hunger that I hadn't even realized I had. I *really* wanted to get to know the both of them better.

I handed Jace my keys, and then Kat reached out and grabbed my hand. "Hurry, we need to get to the car before he changes his mind."

The Viper was parked in the back section of the parking lot, where hardly anyone parked anymore. Back before the economy had taken a turn for the worse, the school board had ap-proved an expansion to the school to prepare for the growth that the city had been projecting, but then the tile factory had started laying people off and the student body had dropped by twenty percent over the course of three months.

The back parking lot now went unused just like more than a third of the new classrooms. There was even talk of moving the junior-high kids into the high school and trying to sell the junior high. It was just talk though. My dad said that there wasn't anybody stupid enough to buy a twenty-year-old school building in a town where property values had dropped fifty percent over the last five years.

We arrived at Jace's car breathless and giggling, and even I had to shake my head in amazement at the sheer perfection of the black paint job and chrome rims. If Jace had parked it in the main parking lot there would *still* be a huge crowd of people standing around rubbernecking.

"Wow...just wow."

Kat smiled at me. "I know, right? Don't let on to Jace how amazing it is though. The last thing he needs is for this particular bad habit to be reinforced. If I didn't give him so much crap about the Viper he would have already replaced it with something even more ostentatious."

The car chirped as Kat unlocked it. I climbed into the passenger seat and shook my head again at the black leather interior as I buckled my seatbelt. Kat pushed the start button and the engine roared to life with a throaty growl that shook my entire body.

Kat returned my smile with one of her own. "That's nothing, watch this."

She stepped on the gas at the same time she let off of the clutch and cranked the steering wheel to the left. We shot forward with a squeal of overheated rubber and smoke, slewing around

.and then shooting towards the exit. My knuckles went white as I held onto the door with one hand and the edge of the seat with the other.

The road was approaching at an insane clip and I opened my mouth to warn Kat about the speed bumps, but she threw the car to the right at the last second, driving over the grass and skirting around the speed bump with only inches to spare before swerving back onto the asphalt. The car was still fishtailing as she jerked the wheel to the right and sent us screeching onto the main road that went past the school.

I should have been scared out of my mind; with anyone else I would have been furious, but somehow the fact that it was Kat short-circuited my normal responses. I was still scared, but I felt alive in a way that I'd never felt before. It helped that Kat seemed to have complete control over the car. Her hands were rock-steady on the wheel, and when she made a correction it always seemed to be exactly the right amount of turn to put the car exactly where she wanted it.

Kat brought the Viper to a roaring ninety miles per hour before coming off of the accelerator and letting our speed drop back down to a relatively sedate ten over the speed limit.

"Where is the junior high?"

"Seriously, you don't know?"

Kat shrugged. "We just arrived in town this afternoon. We didn't even bother going to classes today—we were only at the high school so we could get registered for tomorrow."

"Take a left at the stop light and then take a right at the old newspaper building. You can't miss it. You might want to slow down a little though—we're probably going to pass a cop at some point along Main Street."

Kat took her eyes off of the road for just long enough to throw me a pout. "You sound like Jace. Seriously you have to wonder about a guy like that. Why buy a car with this much horsepower if you're never going to open it up and see what it can really do?"

"I don't know. Bragging rights?"

"Yeah, I guess." Kat shrugged as though it didn't really matter and then turned right. "So what's your sister's name?"

"Ari. She's a freshman and she's the only reason I was still at school that late. Starting this week, she's helping out with making the sets for her school's production of *Romeo and Juliet*. We don't have internet at home so I thought I'd take advantage of the school's Wi-Fi since I had to stay in town anyway. I guess I'll have to start going to the junior high and waiting there for her."

"Oh, I don't know. I think we can probably find something else for you to do instead of just hanging out at the school for an hour. Knowing Jace, he'll be full of ideas even in a small town like Cold Springs. Assuming of course that you're willing to hang out with us."

I started to answer and then stopped as I realized that I had no idea what I was going to say. Despite all of his efforts to get his schedule swapped around to working days, my dad currently worked swing shift at the factory, which meant that he usually left for work forty-five minutes after we got home from school.

Given that Ari and I were now stuck in town for an extra hour every day, we were embarking on an extended block of time during which we were only going to see him on the weekends. Assuming I could get Ari to keep her mouth shut, there was nothing saying that we couldn't spend all evening away from home.

"I don't know—I guess it depends on what you guys have in mind..."

Kat gave me a knowing look. "You're not expecting us to ever hang out, are you?"

"Honestly?"

"Always, Selene."

"Well, if I'm going to be honest, once you've had a chance to get the lie of the land I fully expect you'll drop me like the radioactive social waste I am. The fact that you and Jace don't have any tie to the factory means that you don't have to bow down to Sandra, but if you don't play nice with her you're not going to have anyone else to hang out with. People around here have learned that they have to keep Sandra happy."

"Not even you, Selene? Are you going to give her what she wants?"

"It would be a lot easier." My response came out as a whisper.

"It's always easier to give a bully what they want in the short term, Selene."

"I know. The problem is that sometimes fighting back hurts other people."

Kat shrugged. "Not fighting back hurts *you*. Give it some thought. Jace and I aren't going anywhere and it's not like we're going to give that spoiled princess what she wants, so we'll be around if you change your mind."

She downshifted and then grabbed the emergency brake as she spun the wheel to the left. The back end of the car broke loose from the road and came whipping around us. A second later we skidded to a stop facing back the way we'd come, parked within inches of the curb. I was pretty sure that I'd left my stomach back on the road somewhere.

I looked back and confirmed that there were only three feet between the back of our car and the front of the next car, and felt myself start to shake as the adrenaline finally hit my system. I opened my mouth, but I didn't know what to say.

Kat winked at me. "Careful, Selene. If you keep hanging out with me you might decide you like living on the edge."

"I have a feeling that being your friend might reduce my life expectancy."

"Maybe, but you'll never know until you try."

Kat pushed a button on the dash and the hard top above us started to retract. With all of the near-death terror, I hadn't been paying very much attention to the front of the school, but as the car finished making the switch to a convertible, I realized that what I was hearing was cheers. A second later Ari was standing up against the car and shaking her head.

"That was awesome. You must be some kind of pro right? I don't know how else you could both drive like that and have afforded to have Hennessey put a Venom conversion on this thing."

Kat gave Ari a perky smile. "Nope, no pros here—I'm just a gifted amateur. You must be Ari. My name is Katrina, but everyone calls me Kat. Some moody skank let all of the air out of your sister's tires so I'm giving you both a ride home."

Ari's smile got even wider for a second. I frowned at her. "Did you even hear the first half of what she said, runt? I've got four flats. For all I know all four tires are ruined at this point."

"Yeah, I heard, but you're only kind of freaking out, so that probably means that the tire situation is under control. Besides, we're about to drive off in a Viper Venom and the whole drama club is here to see it, which means by this time tomorrow the entire school will know I got to sit in one of the sweetest muscle cars known to mankind. We could get hit by a meteor on the way home tonight and I'd still die happy."

"Well, based on what I've seen so far, with Kat driving you just might get your wish, but it will probably be us hitting the meteor rather than the other way around."

Kat stuck her tongue out at me. "I think I'm going to like you, Ari. Your sister didn't tell me that you were a gearhead. Unlike me, you can probably fix all of the stuff that I'm planning on breaking over the next few days. You'll have to excuse Selene, she's still trying to recover from being forced to be something other than dull."

I was still trying to come up with a response as Kat reached back between the seats and grabbed a heavy, black leather jacket.

"Here, Selene. It looks like Ari was smart enough to wear a jacket to fight off the chill of driving very fast down a road with the top down, but you weren't, so you're going to need Jace's jacket. Put it on so we can get out of here."

I accepted the jacket and put it on with a frown. "You're planning on Ari and I sharing a seat, aren't you?"

Kat batted her eyes at me. "Unless you want me to let Ari drive, in which case you and I can share a seat."

I held a hand up before Ari could jump all over that idea. "No, there is no way Ari is driving this thing."

"But, Selene—"

"No, and that's final. There is no way we could afford to fix this thing if you wrecked it.

Kat is driving, but..." I gave Kat my best stern look. "You are going to need to take things more sedately with Ari in the car."

Kat gave me a wide-eyed, innocent look. "Why, Selene, I never would have even considered putting your sister in danger. I'll drive like a sixty-year-old grandma on her way to Sunday school. Scout's honor."

I shook my head at her, but Ari opened the passenger door and plopped down on my lap. "Okay, let's go. Are you sure you can't squeal the tires a little as we leave? It would do a lot for my street cred..."

The car dropped into gear with a click that was only barely audible over the engine, and then Kat let the clutch out and spun the tires in one long squeal. I opened my mouth to yell at her, but was assaulted by the smell of burning rubber.

I got a lungful and started coughing. Kat once again gave me her best innocent look. "Would you believe I meant a sixty-year-old grandma with an especially grabby clutch?"

Ari looked back at me and nodded, face full of mock seriousness. "She's right, Selene. They have to upgrade the clutch on these things. If Kat hadn't given it a little extra gas it would have died. "

I rolled my eyes at her, still coughing too hard to get a word in edgewise. By the time my coughing finally subsided to the point where I could give the two of them a piece of my mind,

Kat had been driving sedately for nearly five minutes.

"How did you ever end up as such a gearhead, little sister?"

Kat raised her hand. "I'll bet there was a boy involved. Am I right or am I right?"

Ari smiled. "Yep, you're right. Two years ago I had a crush on Jack Samuelson, but he barely registered the presence of anything that didn't have headlights and a gearshift so I had to become con-ver-sant in car speak in order to get his attention."

I thought the way she'd stretched conversant out like that was juvenile, but Kat just made a fist and pounded it against my sister's knuckles.

"I knew it. And then by the time you decided that Jacky boy wasn't worth your time you realized that you liked cars. I swear, ninety percent of everything we girls do ends up coming down to boys in some way or another."

Ari turned even further so that she could look at both of us at the same time. "I don't know about you, Selene, but I think Kat and I are going to be great friends."

Kat's look of innocence had been replaced by one that was pure mischief. "I'll bet you're starting to reconsider your desire not to hang out with us, aren't you, Selene?"

"Yeah, I'm starting to realize that leaving you and Ari alone with each other would be a very bad idea."

Chapter 2

Kat dropped us off at home and then left with a jaunty wave before I realized I was still wearing Jace's jacket. That meant I was going to have to track him down tomorrow in order to give it back to him. At least he'd seemed fairly normal—surprisingly so in comparison to Kat.

I shook my head as I followed Ari into the house. I never would have guessed when I woke up that morning that I was going to end up getting a ride home in a sports car from a crazy person.

Dad had turned the thermostat down again which meant two things. First that the house was downright cold, and second that he'd had a bad day at work yesterday and had been more worried about his job than he usually was when he got home. The thermostat had become the perfect barometer of how Dad was doing professionally, and finding out that he'd lowered it again put a damper on my mood faster than anything else could have.

Ari hadn't put two and two together yet, but it was only a matter of time. For now she just complained as she went about cooking dinner for us. At least she'd realized that the thermostat was a big deal, even if she hadn't figured out why yet. She would spend the evening complaining, but that was all she would do.

It was cold enough that I didn't even think of taking off my jacket until we'd finished eating, and even then I probably wouldn't have realized I was still wearing it if I hadn't had to wash the dishes. I pulled it off and hung it over the back of my chair and immediately felt a sense of loss.

It was the smell that did it more than anything else. It smelled like leather, cologne, and sunshine, like someone had packaged all of the best things about boys and then slathered it over the jacket, working the scent deep into the leather.

It was the kind of jacket that you sometimes saw in old movies, a jacket that was made to withstand decades of use, a jacket you could wear on a motorcycle and know that it would protect you from the pavement if you dumped the bike over doing sixty-five. The black leather had been somehow doing more than just protecting me from the cold air inside our house. It had been cushioning me from all of the worries you expect a seventeen-year-old girl with no mother, no social life, and an over-worked father to suffer from.

For a little while I'd been living wholly in the moment rather than worrying about what might be barreling towards us with all of the momentum of a freight train. It had been nice.

I finished the dishes in record time, hoping that I'd be able to recapture that feeling by putting Jace's jacket back on, but I had no such luck. The jacket still smelled like a little piece of heaven, and it felt almost like I had Jace's arms wrapped around me, but that wasn't enough to distract me from all of my worries.

Ari didn't comment about the jacket until later that night. I'd finished up the last of my homework and was slowly pulling it off so that I could change into my pajamas when she broke the easy silence between us.

"So Kat's brother must really be something…"

"What makes you say that, runt?"

She stuck her tongue out at me, but didn't let the much-hated nickname sidetrack her as she followed me into the bathroom.

"Oh nothing much, just the fact that you've worn his jacket all night, the fact that you're obviously wishing you could get away with wearing it to bed…"

"I am not!"

"Yes, you are, but there's no need to get so defensive. There isn't anything wrong with liking a boy."

"It's comments like those that prove it's a good thing I'm around to keep you from getting swept up in some torrid romance that leaves you in Las Vegas divorced before the one-week anniversary of your marriage, runt. I don't have the time and we don't have the money for me to start mooning after Jace or any other boy."

I squirted a little toothpaste onto my toothbrush and tossed the tube to Ari with more force than I usually used. She easily plucked it out of the air and rolled her eyes at me.

"Isn't that the point of having a boyfriend? Don't they pay for everything?"

"Maybe in the movies that's the way it works, but these days it's more like fifty-fifty."

"You don't know that."

She was right. It wasn't like I had any experience dating, and I didn't have any close friends—female or otherwise—to live vicariously through, but it sure seemed like the girls I watched from afar spent a lot of time and money chasing the objects of their affection.

For once being speechless turned out to work in my favor. Ari sighed. "You're right. Damn feminists. They should have stopped pushing so hard a couple of decades ago."

"What, you'd rather live back in the days when women couldn't vote?"

"Nope, after women got the vote, but before men stopped being chivalrous."

I finished washing my face and used a towel to pat my face dry. "I'm not sure there was ever any such time period."

"Sure there was. I have it on good authority that there was a block of three whole years where everything was perfect. Mom told me all about it—she called it the golden age."

There was one thing that was guaranteed to instantly shut down any conversation around our house. Mom. Dad and I had gotten really good at not mentioning her, but Ari still sometimes forgot the unspoken rule.

She realized what she'd said almost as soon as she'd said it, but by then it was too late. "I'm sorry, Selene. I wasn't thinking."

I shrugged. "It's okay. It's not like you don't miss her too."

Ari followed me to our cramped little bedroom and dropped down onto her bed. "Sometimes I wonder what things would have been like if she never had cancer. No medical debts, no second mortgage, Dad working more reasonable hours."

I tried to blink the impending tears away. It didn't seem to be working. I turned off the lights so she wouldn't be able to see me and made my cautious way over to my bed.

"We wouldn't still be living in Cold Springs. Without all of the debt Mom would have been able to convince Dad to go get a job somewhere else."

REBORN

It was a seductive vision. A world where we weren't beyond broke, a world where Sandra was a non-issue in my life, a world where my mom was still around to have some of the awkward conversations that dads weren't very well-equipped to have with their daughters.

I felt the tears break free and trickle down onto my pillow. I would have been happy to just let the conversation die right there. I needed the barrier of silence to shelter me while I tried to put myself back together.

Ari, on the other hand, seemed to have a deep, ongoing need to talk about what had happened, a need that neither Dad nor I had been willing—or able—to fulfill. Apparently she felt like the conversation so far meant that all of the usual rules were off.

"It's been almost five years. I still remember what she looks like because I sometimes sneak into Dad's bedroom and go through the picture albums hidden in the back of his closet. I don't remember what she sounded like though. Do you remember, Selene?"

There was a pleading note to Ari's voice that made me want to say yes, but I couldn't bring myself to lie to her. Not now, not after so many years of always trying to be honest with my little sister about what had happened to our mother and what it was going to mean for us.

My voice came out rough. "I'm sorry, I don't. I don't really even remember what she looked like anymore. All I remember is the way she made me feel. No matter where we went, as long as Mom was there, it always felt like we were home."

Chapter 3

I'd basically killed the conversation with my last response. Ari went to sleep half an hour later without saying anything else, but I tossed and turned for an hour and a half before my hand finally ended up touching Jace's jacket where it was resting on the chair next to my bed.

I ended up pulling the sleeve up onto my bed, near my face where I could smell it. I felt more than a little stupid—especially given that Ari was going to give me an even worse time if she saw it—but by that point I was exhausted enough to try anything.

I held the warm, smooth leather up to my nose and within a few breaths my anxiety started to melt away. Five minutes later I was asleep and dreaming of a white-sand beach that stretched on for miles.

Given how long it had taken me to fall asleep, I expected to wake up exhausted when my alarm finally went off the next morning. Surprisingly, I felt the most rested I had in weeks. Even better, at some point during the night I'd pushed the sleeve of Jace's jacket off of my bed, so there wasn't anything for Ari to tease me about.

I showered and ate breakfast at record speed, which left me with more time to apply the finishing touches to my hair and makeup. I didn't usually wear a lot of makeup—partially because of the expense and partially because dressing to the nines just invited more unwelcome attention from Sandra and her clique—but that didn't mean that I didn't know how.

Ari was just finishing up her breakfast as I came back downstairs. Her eyes lit up as she took in my appearance. The makeup would have been enough all by itself to alert her to the fact that it wasn't just another day, the fact that I was wearing my skinny jeans and my best sweater just sealed the deal.

I could see the war going on inside of her head. She wanted to gloat so much she was practically bouncing in her chair, but she wanted to hang out with Kat again even more and she knew that I was stubborn enough to avoid Jace and his sister if that was what it took to make my point.

Actually, that wasn't true. With a normal guy I would have been capable of avoiding him in order to prove Ari wrong, but I wasn't so sure that was going to be the case with Jace.

I'd gone to sleep thinking about him and then spent the whole night with him on the beaches from my dreams. I hadn't been able to stop thinking about him all morning, and I was obviously infatuated enough with him that I was willing to risk Sandra's displeasure.

I managed to get a glass of orange juice poured before Ari stopped fighting against the urge to crow.

"I knew it!"

"Knew what?"

Dad had left his room so quietly that I didn't even realize he was up until he started down the stairs and by then it was too late to warn Ari against saying anything. Ari blanched as she realized that she might have just blown everything. Dad's experiences at work had left him with a severe distrust of wealthy people.

I quickly pulled on the neckline of my sweater, adjusting it so that both of my shoulders were covered and the slack in the neckline hung down my back. Ari and I did our own laundry, so Dad still didn't know that I owned a sweater that hung off my shoulders. I'd kept its existence a secret so far mostly by virtue of the fact that I never wore it, but I should have thought about the fact that I was going to need a jacket to cover it up if I wanted to make it out of the house without Dad seeing it.

I was so worried about my sweater that I didn't have a chance to come up with a believable lie where Jace's jacket was concerned. Luckily Ari was even faster on her feet than normal.

"Selene kept claiming that she wasn't cold yesterday, but she's wearing a sweater today, so obviously she was full of it when she told me that she didn't need to borrow my friend's jacket."

I looked down and realized that I was holding Jace's jacket in my free hand. I didn't even remember picking it up. It was like the stupid thing had grafted itself onto me when I wasn't looking.

Dad tiredly ran his hands through his hair as he took in the jacket that I was very carefully not trying to hide behind me. It was just a jacket, it wasn't like he'd caught me walking around with Jace's boxers.

As soon as I thought that, my face heated up. Dad's eyes narrowed slightly.

"Selene, is there something going on with this boy that I should know about?"

I scrambled for an answer that would keep him from forbidding me from hanging out with Jace and Kat.

"I've only met him the one time, you have nothing to worry about. Besides, Daddy, you can't really think that I would date one of Ari's friends."

Apparently I was believable, because he turned back to Ari. "What about you? Are you crushing on this guy?"

Ari rolled her eyes at him. "I'm way more interested in spending time with his sister than I am in getting to know him, Dad. Boys are icky."

Ari had always been a much better liar than me. She never would have gotten away with telling those kinds of whoppers if Mom had still been around, but my relative lack of interest in boys up until now had somehow convinced Dad that girls didn't actually become interested in boys until after they'd left junior high.

Dad nodded and yawned. "Well, I'm glad that's all settled. By the way, I *did* notice that your car wasn't in the driveway last night, I just decided against waking the two of you up to find out what happened. So what happened and how long do I have until I need to drive the two of you to school?"

I felt like slamming my head into the nearest wall. I was literally too stupid to have a social life. I'd been so distracted by thoughts of Jace to even try to put together a cover story for when Dad asked me about the car. I should have realized that I was headed into trouble back at school when Jace had first said that he'd bring my car back to my house after he got it fixed.

"Oh, that. Well, I waited at my school for an hour until Ari was done with her drama stuff and then I headed over to her school, but once I arrived over there her friend pointed out that I had a flat tire."

Ari was wide-eyed with nervousness that I was going to screw this up, but so far I was actually managing to avoid my normal, mid-lie stutter.

"So you two got a ride home with someone else and I need to make a trip to the junior high later today and get your flat tire repaired?"

I wouldn't have said it was possible for Ari's eyes to get any wider, but they did. I forced my face to remain relaxed despite my inner alarm. This was the problem with lying, all it took was one unanticipated development to call your whole story into question. If Dad went in to town and saw that my car *wasn't* at the junior-high building I was going to be in real trouble.

"Actually, we were hoping to save you a trip, Dad. Ari's friend Jace swapped the flat out for the donut and then we drove to the tire store and asked them to fix the flat."

"It was cold and we were standing around for a while, so Jace loaned Selene his jacket..."

I suppressed the urge to shoot Ari a nasty look. Her lie fit in well with the rest of the story I was weaving so far, but the last thing I needed was for her to start elaborating—I was having a hard enough time fitting my lie in around the things that actually *had* happened. I didn't need her making the process even more complicated.

"Getting a hole patched shouldn't have taken you any more than twenty minutes. Why is the car still at the tire shop? Did you drive on the flat and ruin the tire?"

"No, nothing like that, Daddy. They were getting ready to close by the time we arrived, and the guy behind the counter said nobody was going to be able to stay late to take care of us. He lives out this direction though so he offered to drop us off."

That earned me a frown. "I don't approve of the two of you getting in a car with some random guy who works at the Tire Shack."

"I know, Daddy, but by that time you were already at work and we didn't want to make you come get us."

Ari jumped back in again with an innocent expression that was easily a match for the one that Kat had flashed last night.

"We're sorry, Dad, we didn't know what else to do. Jace followed us out to the Tire Shack. He offered to drive us home instead, but Selene and I didn't think you'd like us getting into a car with someone who had just barely gotten his license. He's not even supposed to have passengers in the car with him yet, so we decided the best option was for us to go back with the guy from the Tire Shack, but make sure that Jace knew we'd left with him so if we wound up missing someone would know what had happened."

Dad gave us a suspicious look. "What was the name of this guy who brought my daughters home last night?"

"Jack—."

"Jake."

It was the classic mistake you saw characters on sitcoms make. We'd both offered up a different name at the same time. I thought we were screwed, but Ari just laughed.

"I guess it's a good thing that Jace wrote the guy's name down before we left. We wouldn't make very good eye-witnesses."

Dad wasn't fully convinced. "Well, I guess I can have a long conversation with the manager of the Tire Shack when I go in to pick up your car this morning. Next time, just go ahead and drive home on the donut and we'll get the flat fixed the next day. Since I have to take you in to school this morning anyway it's not like it saved me a trip."

Ari was looking at me again, her self-satisfied look replaced by one of nervousness. I still didn't appreciate her jumping in and out of my story, but she was right, if Dad went to the Tire Shack it was only going to take thirty seconds for our lie to fall apart.

"Actually, the Jack-Jake guy said that he was coming in early this morning to try to make up some hours. He was going to try to drop off the car here this morning so that you wouldn't have to drive us in. Sorry, Daddy, we really were just trying to save you a bunch of unnecessary trips into town."

Dad grunted noncommittally. "Let's go see if Jack/Jake came through for you so I know whether I need to change into some jeans."

Dad was obviously waiting for the two of us to lead the way, but I couldn't do that without giving him a clear look at my back and the generous helping of skin that my sweater was currently displaying. Ari looked over at me as though confused over the fact that I hadn't already started moving towards the door.

I pointed at the door with my chin and gave her a pleading look, which finally made things click for her. She jumped to her feet, leaving her bowl and glass on the table, and grabbed Dad's arm as she hurried towards the door.

I waited until they were both headed away from me and then I slipped on Jace's jacket, which was more of an undertaking than it sounded because I had to adjust the neckline of my sweater as I went.

"I'll grab the dishes and be right out."

It took me only a second to drop Ari's bowl and cup into the sink and then I grabbed my backpack and hurried after Ari and Dad. They were both standing next to the car—my car—and some of my lie-induced stress melted away as I realized that there was a good chance that Ari and I were home free now.

Dad had probably come in after two or three in the morning—he was working a lot of overtime—so more than anything he just wanted to go back to bed right now, and once that happened he would naturally revert back to his normal schedule. In spite of every intention of doing so, he probably wouldn't ever make it to the Tire Shack.

"How early did you say that kid was going to drop this car off?"

Ari looked at me questioningly, obviously unsure where Dad was going with this particular line of questioning. It's hard to tell an effective lie if you don't know what the other person is really after.

"I'm not sure. I don't think he said a specific time, just that he would have it to our house well before we needed to go to school."

"He can't have dropped it off in the last few minutes or I would have heard it pull into the driveway, but I just don't get why he would have gone to all that trouble and then dropped it off so early that he wouldn't have any chance of seeing the two of you…"

"Daddy, not every guy who is nice to us has ulterior motives. I think he really just felt bad about not being able to get our tire fixed last night."

"It's sweet that you think so, Selene, but as the resident male I'm the only one in the family qualified to speak to the motivations of my gender. Trust me, that kid had only one thing on his mind. I'm just glad that you have enough sense not to get involved with any guys your age. Keep doing what you're doing. You can start dating when you turn thirty. By then at least *some* of the guys your age will have matured enough to be worthy of you."

Ari rolled her eyes at Dad behind his back, but I almost didn't notice because I'd just spied a white envelope resting on the driver's seat. It was hard to see because of the tinted windows, but it was definitely there, and if Dad got close enough to my car to see Jace's message I was back to being screwed.

"If you're done planning out the next decade of my life, Ari and I need to get to school and you need to go back upstairs and get some more sleep."

"What's the rush? Usually you drag out of here at the last possible second. You're the last person in the world to be rushing off to school."

I casually stepped between him and the car, blocking his view of Jace's note with my body. "I'm not in a hurry to get to school, I'm in a hurry to get away from here before you decide to launch into 'the talk' again—out here in the middle of the driveway, no less."

That shut Dad up instantly. He went bright red and looked like he wished he could jump into a hole and pull it closed behind him. I felt bad—those conversations weren't any less awkward for him than they were for us—but he was the parent so we had extra right to be grossed out by them.

Ari stood up on her tiptoes to give Dad a hug and a kiss on the cheek, and then ran back inside. "I need my book bag, I'll be right back."

"I don't mean to make you uncomfortable, Selene, I just don't want you to get into trouble. That kind of thing can change the entire course of your life."

"I know, Dad. You're just going to have to trust in the fact that I'm levelheaded and antisocial enough not to get swept off of my feet by the first smooth-talking guy who shows the slightest bit of interest in me."

Dad looked at the ground, obviously unsure of how to respond to that, and I took him by the arm, gently pulling him toward the house. "Please go back inside and get some more sleep. Ari and I worry about you—if you let work run you down you'll end up sick again. With the way they've cut back your salary, you've been using up all of your vacation days to bring in enough money to keep ahead of the bills, so you can't afford to get sick."

"How did you know that?"

"I do all of the shopping, Dad, remember? You gave me access to the bank statements so I can make sure the checkbook balances. I know how much you make, and there's been extra money coming into our account with every paycheck for a couple months now. It wasn't hard to guess how you were coming up with the extra."

"Have you told Ari?"

"No, she doesn't need to know."

"Good. I wish I'd thought to make sure you wouldn't know, but I guess it's too late to stew about that."

"What are you going to do once you run out of vacation to cash in, Dad?"

"I don't know, sweetheart. I've been looking for some kind of part-time gig to supplement what I get at the factory, but nobody in town is hiring."

"Maybe I could get something after school to help out. I know you always say that school is more important, but a few hours a week wouldn't make any real difference when it comes to my grades and it could help out a lot when it comes to paying off our bills."

"No, Selene—"

"You can't just say no and expect that to be the end of the discussion, Daddy. I'm practically an adult now. I deserve to be able to help out—"

He pulled me into a hug. "There's nothing out there right now, honey. I ran through all of the regular blue-collar stuff weeks ago and I've been applying at fast-food joints and anywhere else that still has their doors open ever since then. Even if it was a good idea to let you sacrifice your future in an effort to pay down our bills, it wouldn't matter. There isn't a job to be had in this town for love nor money."

"This is Mr. Conner's fault. If he had a decent benefits package the insurance would have paid for the medical expenses."

I tried to sound reasonable, but I couldn't help myself. The anger I felt towards Sandra and the anger I felt towards her father had all mixed together into one big, messy ball. I couldn't talk about either of them without hatred leaching into my voice.

"You shouldn't talk like that, Selene."

"Why? It's true. Everything bad that's happened to us since Mom was diagnosed can be laid directly at the feet of the Conner family."

"You shouldn't talk like that because words give extra power to emotions and I don't want you to end up a bitter old woman. Not only that, right now Mike Conner is the only thing keeping us from going bankrupt. If he hadn't given me that raise last year we would have lost our house."

"Some raise. It was less than two thousand dollars a year more once you add in the overtime you used to get before he moved you to salaried. When you figure in all of the extra hours you work now you're probably worse off."

"Maybe so, but it has let us survive for this long."

"We should move, Dad. Let's go somewhere else where you can make the money you deserve."

"The whole state is this way right now, Selene. I'll admit I avoided looking outside of this area for a while, but even I couldn't deny the truth when it was staring me in the face like it has been for the last several months. I've been looking for something like I've got at the tile factory, and everywhere I turn it's the same story. The economy is slowing down, businesses are shrinking and going out of business."

"So look outside of Colorado. Look out of the country if you have to. Ari and I will follow you wherever you find work. There isn't anything tying us to Cold Springs anymore."

Dad started to respond, but the sound of footsteps stopped the words before they made it past his tongue.

"We'll talk about this later, Selene. No speaking out of turn, you hear?"

"Yes, Dad."

Dad gave me one more squeeze and then released me from our hug and started up the stairs toward Ari. She absently returned his hug, at which point I realized that I needed to get around to the other side of the car. I was going to have to hurry if I was going to hide Jace's letter before Ari opened the passenger door and Dad saw the simple white square.

I got my door open a split second before Ari opened hers up and started to drop down into my seat, only to be pulled up short by my dad's voice. I slipped my right foot up onto my seat and covered the letter with the sole of my shoe.

"Selene, it was just the one tire, right? And the Tire Shack didn't say anything about putting new tires on, right? Because those tires look—"

"They look black, rubbery, and full of air, Daddy, just like they are supposed to. Can we please go? If we don't get on our way we really are going to end up late."

"Okay, drive safe."

Ari was still waving goodbye to Dad as I slid into my seat, so I managed to keep the note hidden from her too. I didn't want to give her any more ammunition—she was going to tease me mercilessly as it was.

My normal reluctance—and complete lack of skill—when it came to deceiving, had combined with the frank discussion regarding the family finances to throw my emotions into a tangled knot. We'd been driving for nearly five minutes before the muscles in my neck and shoulders finally started to unknot.

As we turned onto Main Street Ari looked over at me. "You've got some serious tells you're going to need to work on if you're going to be successful at this whole lying thing."

"I wasn't exactly planning on making a career out of it, runt."

"Really? You mean you aren't planning on spending the afternoons with Kat and Jaaa-ace?"

Ari once again added an extra syllable to Jace's name, and I blushed again despite my best efforts. There was no way she was going to miss the red creeping up over the collar of Jace's leather jacket.

"That's what I thought. I can count the number of times I've seen you wear that sweater on one hand. You've got it so bad, but it's kind of cute that you're still in denial. Trust me, if you want to avoid a big blowup with Dad, lying to him is the only way you're going to get to spend any time with Jace."

I pulled the car up to the curb in front of Ari's school and pointed at the big red door the other students were entering through.

"Get to your classes, and not a word about any of this to your little friends, or I'll stop coming to get you after school."

"Like that will ever happen. I'm not that lucky."

I tried to shove Ari's shoulder, but she was too fast—she unbuckled her seatbelt and slipped out of the car inches ahead of my hand, then she stuck her head back into the car for one last parting shot.

"I don't need to say anything to my friends, dummy. You showed up at my school in a Dodge Viper with Jace's sister, who happens to be hot enough to make half of the girls in school wish they played for the other team, and you're wearing Jace's jacket to school. Trust me, *everyone* is going to know that you and he are an item."

Ari shut the car door before I could muster any kind of response and skipped into the school without looking back.

She was right; I had it bad. I was going to be so screwed when Sandra found out.

Chapter 4

Only pure willpower let me drive away from the junior high without opening Jace's note first, and even then I broke a few traffic laws on my way to the high school so I would have time to read it before school started.

I pulled into my normal parking spot at the back edge of the main parking lot, and then fished Jace's note out from underneath my butt. It was pretty sad looking by that point. The once clean square of paper had been replaced by a dirt-stained, crinkled mess. I'd been expecting the dirt given that I'd stepped on it, but I hadn't been expecting the heavy paper to mold itself to the curve of my posterior quite so quickly.

Thinking of Jace made my skin flush. It was stupid, I barely knew him at all, but I was definitely not in control of my reactions right then. I cracked my window a couple of inches to help cool down my burning skin, and tore the envelope open. Inside was a single piece of heavy paper.

I'm sorry I let you drive off with Kat—I know she's crazy, but I didn't think she'd be quite that crazy with someone else in the car. As her (slightly) older brother, I hold myself responsible and I hope you'll let me make it up to you. How about dinner at our place? I managed to get our kitchen unpacked last night between putting new tires on your car and dropping it off this morning. I promise not to put you in any mortal danger that you don't want to be put in.

—Jace

I'd been flushed before, but the note seemed to have thrown my system into overdrive. My heart was racing and I knew I needed to get out of the car right away or I was going to start sweating. Actually, I needed to do more than just get out of the car, I needed to get out of Jace's jacket.

I climbed out into the weak morning sunlight and shrugged out of the heavy leather, setting the jacket down on the roof of my car as I stepped around to the back door. The cool air felt heavenly on my now-bare shoulders. I started to adjust the neckline on my sweater, but the lure of finally cooling back down was just too much. Instead of opening the door and grabbing my backpack as I'd planned on, I grabbed the front of my sweater and lifted it away from my skin so the cool air could more easily make its way inside.

It felt so good that I closed my eyes for a second and took a deep breath.

"Wow, the girls in my last school never could have gotten away with wearing something like that. I'm suddenly extra glad that we moved."

I'd only thought I was blushing before then. I recognized that voice and even the gentle, teasing note I could hear underlying the words wasn't enough to stop my face from heating to the point where it felt like I was going to spontaneously combust.

I left my eyes closed for a slow count of three as I steeled myself to turn around and face Jace. "Hasn't anyone ever told you that it's not polite to sneak up on people?"

I was so out of my depth it wasn't even funny. I was pleased that my response came out without having my voice crack, but my tone made me sound like a total witch.

"Hey, it's not my fault that you were so far gone you didn't hear me drive up and park next to you."

I opened my mouth to tell him that he was crazy—only he was indeed leaning back against the same gorgeous, black Viper that Kat had dropped us off in the night before. The same black Viper that even when idling had sounded like an airplane taking off.

"How did you do that?"

"Do what?"

"Teleport into existence less than four feet away from me."

"I swear upon my honor as a Boy Scout that I didn't do any teleporting this morning. And I cross my heart. Twice."

"You've never been a Boy Scout."

"You don't know that."

I narrowed my eyes at him. "Tell the truth, Jace. Have you ever been a Boy Scout?"

He let out a big, melodramatic sigh. "I hate it when you do that. You take all of the fun out of lying. Fine. I've never been a Boy Scout. I would have been a good one though."

"As long as you're coming clean about that you should admit to the teleportation too. It's always best to just swallow all of your medicine at once."

"Really, is that something your mom tells you every time you get sick?"

The teasing, happy feeling instantly turned to ash.

"No. She...she's been dead for almost five years."

Jace's face fell so fast it would have been funny if I hadn't been feeling so crappy. "I'm sorry, Selene. I didn't know..."

I shrugged, pretending that it hadn't affected me even though we both knew it was nothing more than an act.

"It's fine—there wasn't any way that you could have known. She got cancer and she was one of the thirty percent. It's just one of those things, it sucks and then it's over."

I hadn't seen Jace cross the distance between us, maybe he'd teleported again. He was standing with his hand only millimeters from my exposed shoulder, obviously wanting to comfort me, but unsure what was appropriate in this particular situation.

"Stuff like that is never over, Selene. It can't be over because it changes who you are. I'm sorry I stuck my foot in my mouth again, it's basically a time-honored tradition at this point though so maybe I should just learn to accept it."

"Really, it's fine, Jace. I need to learn not to be so sensitive about it. I'm not the only person to ever lose someone—I don't have the corner on grief. Besides, it's been five years, I should have figured out how to move on by now."

He stepped into me and placed one finger underneath my chin gently raising my face so that I would meet his eyes again.

"You don't just get over things like that, Selene. Maybe some people do, but not you. You couldn't just casually let go of someone you cared about and still be yourself. It's okay to grieve, even for years if that's what it takes. Sometimes that is the only way to properly honor someone. Tell me how to make this up to you. Please."

Having him so close to me was making me feel all tingly. I wasn't shaking on the outside, but inside of me there was an eight point nine magnitude earthquake going on. I wanted to reach out to him, wanted to go up on my tiptoes so that I could kiss him, but that felt wrong on nearly every level.

My skin felt hyper-sensitive. I could feel the weave of the fibers in my jeans in a way that I'd never experienced before. The cool, morning breeze seemed to cut right through the weave of my sweater, and the bare skin on my shoulders, back and upper chest seemed to be able to trace the temperature differentials between gusts. It felt like the wind was caressing my bare skin, like Jace was caressing me.

"You lost someone too."

"Yeah. It was a really long time ago though. Practically ancient history. She…well, she's gone now and I need to accept it and move on."

"Isn't that my line?"

That earned me a shadow of the crooked grin that I remembered from the day before. This smile lacked the wattage of the last one he'd thrown my direction, but he was still heart-stoppingly-beautiful. He still looked perfect, but he looked more mature, like someone who had experienced more than any seventeen-year-old was meant to endure.

"I guess it is."

"Tell me about her?"

Jace shook his head. "I wish I could. Maybe someday I'll be able to, but not now, not today."

"You wanted to know how to make every-thing better. What if that's what I want?"

He closed his eyes for a moment, and when he opened them the sheer level of hurt looking out at me sliced slivers off of my soul. Mom had been religious, and I still remembered the story about Adam and Eve being cast out of the Garden of Eden. I used to wonder what that must have felt like; I didn't need to wonder anymore because I could see that exact pain in Jace's eyes. He looked like someone who had seen paradise, who had lived there, and then had it all yanked away from him between one breath and the next.

"Please don't ask me that, Selene. I would love to tell you, but it won't make anything better, not for you, not for me. It would just ruin things."

If I'd had any doubt that he was talking about an ex-girlfriend that would have put it to rest. Talking about a dead mother or a dead sister wouldn't ruin everything with a girl he'd just met, a girl who wasn't even worthy of breathing the same air as him, a girl he was flirting with for no good reason.

"Okay, I won't ask."

"Still, ask me for something. I do want to make up for everything that's happened during the last twenty-four hours."

"Admit that you teleported here."

"Are you saying the thing you want is for me to lie?"

"No, I want the truth. I'm not stupid, Jace. Your car is loud; there is no way you just pulled up and parked right there without me hearing you. I was distracted, but I wasn't that distracted."

I'd made my demand playfully, determined not to let him see just how unnerving his sudden appearance had been. I'd always hated things that didn't make sense—things that I can't explain—and even Jace's devastating looks and rock-hard body couldn't completely distract me from the things that weren't adding up.

Dad had been right, we should have heard Jace drop off my car. Our house was old enough that it didn't even have double windows. We could hear our neighbors yell at each other from inside of *their* house without even cracking our windows.

Even if there was some weird explanation for how he'd driven my car up our driveway without waking any of us up, that didn't explain how Kat could have followed along behind him in his Viper and not made enough noise to wake up the entire neighborhood.

I tore my eyes away from Jace and they came to rest on my tires. Dad had been right, these weren't the nearly bald, weathered monstrosities that Sandra had deflated, they looked brand new. It was one more thing that I couldn't explain.

Despite my efforts to mask how rattled I was, Jace seemed to see through me. He took a deep breath and then nodded. "Okay, I'll tell you, but not right now, not right here. Promise me that you'll come to dinner tonight."

He seemed to be admitting that there was something unusual going on, but I tried not to focus on that. There were probably a hundred perfectly normal explanations. The last thing I needed was to get all freaked out right now. Jace was nice, gorgeous, and inexplicably interested in me. I was not going to screw this up by jumping at shadows.

I needed to focus on safe, normal things. I'd spent the last five years since my mom had died with my feet firmly grounded and my head out of the clouds. I took another deep breath and drew on almost sixty months of dealing with the minutiae of life. "I can't, I need to go get Ari after school."

"Bring her along. Kat hasn't stopped talking about her since the two of them met. I'll cook dinner for both of you. Please, Selene."

"Did you really put brand-new tires on my car?"

"Yeah, sorry, the old ones couldn't be saved. That isn't a problem is it?"

"It's a problem because my dad noticed and was asking about them. It's a problem because it means I'm going to go slam Sandra Connor's head into a wall over and over again until she either apologizes and pays for them or loses consciousness."

REBORN

I was so mad I could barely see straight. A very tiny part of me screamed that it shouldn't be possible for me to get this angry this quickly, but the rest of me dismissed the warning. The anger wasn't new, I just usually did a better job concealing it from everyone—including myself.

The truth was that I existed in a constant state of anger. A new set of tires was what, two or three hundred dollars? That was nothing to Sandra. She spent more of her daddy's money on a single designer handbag. For me it was more than my clothes budget for the entire school year. I did laundry twice a week because I'd splurged on the stupid top I was wearing and didn't have enough other clothes to get through the rest of the week otherwise.

In that instant I hated every single thing about Sandra and if she'd been standing in front of me I would have happily shoved a knife into her chest. I started towards the back door to the school, backpack forgotten, but Jace grabbed me before I could take a second step.

"Let go of me!"

My yell should have brought half a dozen people running towards us to make sure that I was okay, but it was nothing more than a reflex. The truth was that Jace letting go of me was the absolute last thing I wanted in that instant.

He'd grabbed my arm and pulled me back towards him, spinning me so that I ended up facing him with his right hand cradling the side of my neck. His touch felt like fire, and the trembling inside of me had made it to the outside now.

"What an incredible little berserker you are. You can't go slam Sandra's head into a wall, and you know it."

His words pierced the trembling haze that his touch had thrown over me—not all the way, but enough that I tore my right arm free of his grasp. I had a sneaking suspicion that he let me break free, which was validated when he effortlessly recaptured my shoulder just above where my sweater ended.

"I'm not saying that you're incapable of bashing her head in, Selene, I'm saying that I'm not going to let you because she's not worth going to jail over. You're mad now, but before the day is over you're going to remember that the best revenge is living well."

I wanted to laugh in his face. He knew next to nothing about me. He deserved to have me mock him for his ignorance, but I couldn't think past the feel of his hands on my neck and bare shoulder. It was like my universe ended at the nerve endings in my skin. Nothing else mattered, nothing else was real.

I felt like I could have closed my eyes and drawn his fingerprints down to the last arch and swirl. I was that hyper-aware of his touch.

"I guess the joke's on me, because not only don't I get any kind of revenge, I don't get to live well either."

"You've got all the right ingredients to live better than Sandra and her friends can even imagine. You're smart, pretty, talented, and you've got fire. You've kept it buried down deep all this time, but it's there."

"You don't know that."

"Yes, I do. I knew it when you didn't freak out after Kat nearly wrecked my car before the two of you even left the parking lot, I knew it just now when you tried to go put her in the hospital, but most of all I know it because you refuse to let her break you. Let me show you how to put all of the ingredients together. Come to my house tonight. I'll cook dinner, Kat will pick up Ari and we'll plan the best revenge against Sandra this town has ever seen."

His lips were just fractions of an inch away from mine. I'd never been kissed before and I was scared to death that I was going to mess things up, but I wanted him to kiss me with every part of my body. Even my pulse seemed to cry out for him.

"Fine, I'll come."

The lazy, half smile was back, but this time it didn't send my heart racing even faster, it calmed me down. That smile felt like coming home.

"You're going to be late to your first class, Selene, you'd better get going."

"What about you?"

He shook his head. "I got what I came for today. I can always start school tomorrow. Besides, I have a house to unpack and a night to plan."

Jace stepped back, letting go of my arms and releasing me from the paralysis that his touch had inflicted on me, and then opened the door to my car and picked up my backpack, holding nearly thirty pounds of books straight out in front of him as though it were weightless.

I went to take it from him and he moved it just out of reach with a playful smile. "I think you'd better put this on first. I'd hate for the administration to send you home to change."

His other hand was holding the leather jacket that I'd left on the roof of my car. I started to ask him what he was talking about and then looked down at myself. Somewhere during the course of the morning—probably when he'd grabbed me to stop me from bashing Sandra's head in—the neckline of my sweater had gotten stretched out. Luckily it wasn't ruined. It would be fine after I hand washed it, but it was riding much lower on my shoulders than it had been when I put it on this morning.

I'd already been flashing enough skin that it would have been a borderline case, but he was right, there was zero question but that I would be sent home.

I let him help me into the jacket, and then used the heavy weight of the leather across my shoulders and arms to adjust the neckline of my sweater back to something less scandalous.

"I don't think that I ever actually thanked you for fixing my tires."

"Sure you did. Seeing you this morning is all the thanks I need."

It was too good to be true—*he* was too good to be true. As much as I wanted to just enjoy it for however long it lasted, a jaded, cautious part of me knew that the longer I went along the worse it would be when he yelled 'psych' and dumped me on my butt.

"Why are you being so nice to me?"

"You're going to be late for class, Selene."

"No, I'm serious, why are you doing all of this? All it's going to do is cause you and Kat problems here at school. I'm not worth that."

He looked angry for the first time I could remember. "*Never* say that again. You're worth more than all of the rest of the kids in this school combined. They are nothing more than insects. I hate this place for making you feel that way."

I should have been terrified—Jace looked like some kind of avenging Norse deity—but I knew his fury wasn't directed at me. Besides, he'd seen the worst I had to offer and hadn't even flinched. It seemed like it was only fair to return the favor.

We were standing several feet away from each other now, but I could still feel the warmth of his hands on my skin. It was like his jacket had trapped the sensation and bonded it to my skin. I forced myself to stop playing with the neckline of my sweater.

"You're avoiding the question."

His smile this time had an air of resignation to it. "If I tell you, will you get moving so you're not late for school? The last thing I want right now is for you to start getting in trouble and making your dad suspicious that something is going on."

"Fine, you tell me why you're being nice and I'll go to class like a good little girl."

"You remind me of someone I used to know, someone who meant the world to me."

I felt my expression stiffen. It all made sense now. The hints he'd been dropping all fit together perfectly. He'd lost a girlfriend at some point in the past and he still hadn't recovered from that loss, still hadn't gotten over her.

He was being nice to me because I reminded him of her. I was nothing more than some kind of freaky, post-death rebound.

I took a step backward. "I'm not sure dinner tonight is such a good idea…"

He pulled his teleporting trick and was there in front of me again. He captured my hand in his and shook his head at me. "This is why I can't tell you anything. You draw the wrong conclusions and then overreact. I'm being nice to you because I once knew someone very much like you. That means I'm uniquely placed to appreciate all of the things about you that nobody but your dad and Ari notice."

It sounded good, but I wasn't sure there was any difference between what I was afraid of and what he was saying.

"I don't know, Jace. I don't think I'm up to competing with a memory."

"With somebody else that would be the case, Selene, but not you. For you it will never be a competition."

"How is that even possible?"

He smiled at me again. "You know that I'm telling you the truth."

My heart started stuttering as I realized he was right. On some deep, untouchable level I knew him—knew him well enough to know that he was absolutely telling me the truth.

"That's crazy."

"Crazy? Yes. The truth? Yes. Wonderful in ways that you can't even begin to explain? Yes. Say you'll still come tonight. You promised…"

I just nodded, unwilling to trust my voice when my insides seemed so determined to rearrange themselves. It was his hand on mine that was doing it, but I wasn't willing to let go, not yet. I had a feeling that I would suffer through a lot worse than some industrial-sized butterflies for the sensation of his skin on mine.

"Good. Now go to your first class. You promised to stay out of trouble."

Jace let go of my hand and then reached up and guided me through a half-turn with gentle pressure against my shoulders. With his leather jacket between his hands and my shoulders, I couldn't feel anything more than just pressure, and that more than anything else seemed to break the intoxicating spell that he'd cast on me.

I nodded and started towards the school. I wanted desperately to look back at Jace, but I forced myself to watch where I was going. I might very well have already lost my ability to exercise my free will, but I needed to at least keep up the illusion that I could still choose something other than what Jace wanted.

A smile turned up the corners of my lips. At least Jace wasn't completely infallible. There was no way I was making it to my class on time. Not after the amount of time we'd spent together in the parking lot. The simple fact that there wasn't anyone else still in the parking lot would have been more than enough to establish that the second bell had rung a long time ago.

Chapter 5

I wasn't late, and that was pissing me off for more reasons than just the fact that Jace was once again right.

It made absolutely no sense. There were always people who waited out in the parking lot until the last second.

Even more weird, as I walked across the parking lot I realized that everything was eerily silent. No birds were singing, no insects were chirping, there was nothing but the sound of my footsteps to indicate I hadn't gone deaf.

All of that changed as soon as I stepped through the first of the double doors that formed a kind of airlock system to keep out the cold Colorado winters. The first door had been propped open, but as I reached for the next set of doors, the door behind me swung shut of its own accord.

The thump as it hit the metal doorframe made me jump. It was like the door closing had opened up some kind of auditory floodgates. I could hear the hum of conversation and yelling on the other side of the doors and now that the entry-way was a little darker I could see through the safety-glass windows set into the doors ahead of me.

The halls were full of other kids, and as I stepped through the second set of doors I checked the digital clock set high in the wall and saw that I still had three minutes to get to my first class.

I'd never realized before that instant how much I depended on my sense of time to ground me. I'd been a little…distracted…while talking to Jace, but there was no way that our conversation had been less than three minutes long.

I had the nagging feeling I should step back outside and confirm that the parking lot was still empty, but instead I found myself moving towards my English class as though on autopilot. Apparently I wasn't ready to deal with a world where the physical laws I'd grown up with no longer worked like they were supposed to.

I thought about turning around and going out to the parking lot. It was tempting, but if I went out there and saw dozens of kids where just seconds before there hadn't been any, I wasn't sure my mind could stand up to the implications.

Even worse, what if I went back out there and it was still empty and silent? What if I somehow got stuck inside of that weird, isolated version of the world forever?

I knew I was being silly, that there had to be an explanation for everything that had happened so far, but I just couldn't take the chance that I was wrong.

I stumbled into my first class thirty seconds before the second bell and went through the first half of the day in a haze. I was so far gone that I didn't even notice the looks I got from every single girl I passed.

I didn't start putting the pieces together until I grabbed my normal lunch of French fries and slipped out of the cafeteria to go sit in a quiet corner in one of the halls that was full of nothing but vacant classrooms. I'd known that people knowing Jace was interested in me was going to cause problems, and despite all of that I'd stupidly worn his leather jacket through the first four classes of the day.

Even the girls who hadn't ever met Jace were still going to know something was up. The real kicker was that I couldn't do anything about it. Even if I took Jace's jacket off now—which I couldn't, not if I wanted to avoid being sent home—the damage was already done. I was screwed.

I was debating just skipping the rest of my classes when I heard footsteps approaching from around the corner. I had a couple of seconds to worry that Sandra had tracked me down, and then Kat came around the corner with the same devil-may care smile that had graced her face as we'd sped through the town on two wheels.

"Selene, what on earth are you doing out here by yourself?"

"Honestly? I'm trying to keep a low enough profile that Sandra and her friends will forget about me."

Kat started laughing, and then stopped again after a second. "Oh, sorry. I didn't realize you were serious. You can't have really thought you were going to fly under the radar wearing that sweater..."

"Yeah, one of my split personalities was running the show when I got dressed this morning. She's since retreated back under the rock inside my head where she usually lives and now the rest of me is left to deal with the results of her craziness."

Kat sighed. "You poor thing. Rather than keeping the crazy you buried under a rock you should be putting her in charge of the asylum. You're letting Sandra and her pet sluts dictate everything. You should be flaunting the fact that you've got a new rich, hot boyfriend, not trying to hide away like you're ashamed of it."

"Do you call everyone you don't like sluts?"

"Nope, usually I call them whores, but you seem a little sensitive for that, so I thought I'd rein myself in a little—are you proud of me?"

I shook my head in disbelief. "How do you do that? How do you make me feel like none of this matters and that we're both destined for bigger, better things?"

"Well, I just happen to know that *none of this really matters*. I mean seriously, this is just high school. In a year and a half we're both going to graduate and we never have to come back unless we want to. The first reunion is mostly just full of a bunch of posers trying to impress each other, so it's not like we'll be missing anything."

Kat plopped down next to me with her back against the wall and grabbed one of my French fries. "Man, these things are one of the best inventions ever. I still remember the first time I had fries—talk about life-changing. I hope that I never forget that day. Hey, next time you should get some extra salt—you're only young once, right?"

Thinking about the likely retaliation I was going to have to weather from Sandra and her clique had ruined my appetite. I pushed the remaining fries over in her direction.

"I wish I had your confidence, Kat. I just can't stop thinking about all of the different ways that Sandra could screw me over."

Kat scrunched her nose up in thought and then pulled her phone out of her front pocket. "We don't have enough time left before our next class starts to do anything about Sandra, but you just leave her to me. Come on, let's get moving. I want to get to Chemistry with enough time to convince the teacher to put me in the right assigned seat."

I stopped her by grabbing her arm and refusing to let her drag me along behind her. "Wait, you're in my class?"

Kat didn't look up from the last French fry, which she was studying with a kind of sad longing. "Yeah, I'm in all of your classes. I would have been here this morning, but Jace was in full 'oh my gosh, the house is a mess and Selene is coming over tonight' mode. So of course I had to…"

My shock must have been obvious, because as soon as Kat looked up at me she stopped talking.

"That probably sounds creepy, doesn't it?"

"You think?"

Kat plopped the last fry in her mouth. "Look, it's not as creepy as it sounds. Jace is in all of your classes too…"

"Right, because having the Barbie twins stalk me *together* rather than *separately* is so much less creepy."

"This is so not my fault. I'm placing the blame for all of this squarely on Jace's shoulders. Look, you and Ari are the only interesting people we've met in this entire town. We *could* have just left everything to chance and spent most of our days bored out of our minds, but that's not really our style. Why settle for mediocrity if you have the ability to go get what you want and nobody gets hurt along the way?"

"Why do I get the feeling that you really do get *everything* you want?"

Kat's response was too perky to be practiced. "Because I do, obviously. Now that we've got that settled and you're no longer creeped out, let's get to class."

We stopped at our lockers, which were suspiciously close to each other, and then headed off to Chemistry. Mr. Reynolds had flown in the Air Force for twenty years before making the transition to small-town educator, and it showed. He ran his class with a ruthless discipline that made the rest of the teachers look like pushovers.

He was less than five years away from retirement and not afraid to make kids look like idiots if they disrupted his classroom. Kat entered the class and studied Mr. Reynolds with slitted eyes for several seconds before nodding.

"He'll do very, very nicely."

I started to follow her up to the front of the classroom, but she stopped me. "Could you just wait back here, Selene? I'd really hate to have you get caught in this—it's really considered bad form—you know how it is, right?"

"Um, no, you're talking crazy again."

Kat's sigh was melodramatic. "Someday you're going to understand how hard all of this was for me. Fine, you can come, but stay a few feet back behind me."

I gave her a 'whatever, I'm too cool for any of this, but I'll humor you just because I'm that reasonable' look and then dropped back to follow her at a 'safer' distance.

"Hello, Mr. Reynolds. I'm Kat. Could I trouble you for a moment about the seating arrangements? I think we've got some problems that need to be worked out."

It was bold and almost guaranteed to send Mr. Reynolds off. He took a big breath as though getting ready to start yelling, but before he could actually get the words out Kat closed to within a foot or two of him and he did a double-take, almost like he hadn't really seen her the first time he'd looked at her.

"What do you need out of me, Kat?"

There was a note in Mr. Reynolds' voice that I'd never heard before, but Kat acted like nothing out of the ordinary was happening.

"Could I please see the seating chart for the class that will be starting in the next few minutes?"

"Of course, just one moment while I grab it."

He jumped to his feet and hurried over to the lectern he used to hold his notes. Kat drifted along behind him, making it look casual, but staying within a few feet of him.

"Here it is, Miss Kat."

"Just Kat is fine." She pointed towards the seat towards the back where I normally sat. "Am I reading this right? Is that where Selene sits?"

"Yes. Is there a problem? Do I need to kick her out of my class?"

"Oh, no, that is the last thing I want to have happen. Selene is my close personal friend; I hope that you've been nice to her."

Kat shifted around even closer to Mr. Reynolds and I thought for a second his eyes were going to pop right out of his head.

"I didn't know that she was important to you. I promise I'll work harder at being nice to her."

"I'm sure you will."

Kat patted him on the arm and I finally figured it out. Mr. Reynolds didn't just sound eager to please, he sounded like he'd found his own personal grail. He wanted Kat, but it wasn't sexual—wasn't *just* sexual. I got the feeling that he would have done anything for her, right up to slicing his own wrists if she asked.

A few more seconds of silence passed as Kat studied the seating chart and Mr. Reynolds danced back and forth from one foot to the other like a four-year-old who needed to pee. The suspense was killing me.

I stepped forward, quietly, in an effort to get close enough to get the faintest taste of whatever it was she was doing to him. I was almost close enough for her to see my feet without looking up from the lectern when it happened.

One second I felt fine, then all of a sudden I wanted to drop down to my knees and kiss Kat's feet. The urge was so compelling that I couldn't help myself. She looked up as my knees started to bend and swore.

"Damn it, Selene, you were supposed to keep your distance."

I wondered how I could have been so stupid. What had I been thinking? Of course the most important thing was to honor her wishes. What I had or hadn't promised didn't even enter into it for me as I scrambled backwards on all fours in a desperate effort to get back to where I'd been before I'd displeased her.

"I'm so sorry that she disobeyed you, Miss—I mean, Kat. Are you sure that you don't want her punished?"

I found myself nodding. It was only logical, I needed to be punished, the only question was whether she was going to want him to do it or if she would want me to punish myself. I was obviously too unworthy for *her* to punish me.

"No! Let's not get into crazy talk. Selene is going to stay right there for the next few minutes while you and I work through that seating issue."

"Of course, Kat."

"So Sandra Conner sits here and her two friends sit three seats ahead in the rows to either side of her?"

Mr. Reynolds was nodding so eagerly it almost looked like his head was going to come off of his neck. I wanted to jump to my feet and run over to the desks in question so as to make sure that there wasn't any question where Sandra and her friends sat, but I'd been ordered to stay put and I wasn't about to make the mistake of displeasing Kat again.

"I notice the three of them aren't sitting together, Mr. Reynolds. Is that because they have been a disruptive influence?"

"Please, call me Frank. As to your question, I don't know that I would go that far. They talk more than they should, but I've never felt like they were actively trying to be bad..."

Kat looked at him with just the right amount of righteous indignation, and I suddenly realized that whatever had made me want to fall down and worship her must be wearing off if I was actually capable of questioning Kat's motives.

She shook her head sadly. "Frank, you're one of those rare men who are just too good for this life. The mere fact that the three of them could talk while you were trying to teach makes me very sad. Forgiving their disrespect makes you the best kind of person, but it still doesn't make what they did right. Do you think it would be helpful to have someone you trusted keeping an eye on Sandra and her friends, Frank? Someone who could make sure that they didn't get out of hand..."

He looked like he'd just seen the Mona Lisa for the first time. "Of course! I can't believe I didn't think of that. I should move your friend Selene over closer to Sandra so that she can make sure there isn't any tomfoolery."

There was no visible indication that Kat wanted to scream in frustration, but I somehow knew she was almost to the end of her rope. "No, Frank, I think Selene is well-positioned to keep an eye on the three of them from back where she sits. I was thinking that maybe you'd like to use me to solve your problem..."

He looked the slightest bit confused, like he wanted her to just come out and tell him exactly what she wanted, but he gamely tried to put the pieces together through the 'worship-me' fog she surrounded him with.

"I could...move one of the other students and assign you a seat."

Kat bestowed an angelic smile on him and nodded. "I think that's a great idea, Frank. Where should I sit though? Somewhere where I could watch them without having to turn in my seat...after all, *I* wouldn't want to disrupt your class..."

I could almost see the wheels turning in his head. He started towards the seat in front of my assigned spot, and then stopped as though remembering that I was already there and therefore 'keeping an eye on things' from that side of the terrible trio.

He pointed at the outside row, the one on the other side of Sandra's spot from where I would be sitting, but he obviously hadn't settled on a particular seat based on the way that he was watching Kat in an effort to draw some kind of clue out of her as to where she wanted to sit.

She waited until his finger was pointing to the seat just behind Megan's and then she clapped her hand. "Frank, that's the perfect spot. You're a genius. From there I can easily keep an eye on the two friends while Selene watches Sandra."

Mr. Reynolds smiled and relaxed now that he'd successfully passed the test. "I'll make the changes as soon as class starts, Kat."

Kat smiled. "That sounds perfect, Frank. We'll have to be careful though, we won't want Sandra and her friends figuring out what we're planning. If they realize that we've had this little talk it could ruin everything."

His brow furrowed as he tried to process what she was saying. "So you'll come into the class and introduce yourself again?"

"Yes, and I'll call you Mr. Reynolds again rather than using your first name. This will just be our secret."

Mr. Reynolds nodded, obviously relieved that she'd asked for something he was capable of providing and that she hadn't made him come up with the answer entirely on his own.

"We'll be back in a few minutes, Frank. Why don't you make that change to the seating chart and then go sit back down. You'll want to conserve your strength if you're going to have to face this group of ruffians."

I followed Kat out of the classroom and around the corner into another empty hall. "What the crap happened back there, Kat?"

"Well, let me see. First you promised that you would keep your distance while I was talking to Mr. Reynolds and then you broke your promise. It's okay though, I'm sure you feel awful about it."

A tiny part of me *did* feel awful about it, but I squashed the feeling, drawing on some of the tightly leashed anger that had nearly slipped free earlier that morning. My rage was just barely enough to keep me from giving into the residual effects of her worship-me aura.

"The hell I am! You played him like some kind of musical instrument. Seriously, what is going on?"

"I can't tell you right here and now, Selene, but I promise you that I didn't do that for me, I did that for you. You're going to have to trust me. I promise that I'll tell you just as soon as I can."

"What is it with you and Jace and expecting me to take everything on faith?"

Kat gave me a sad smile that wasn't anything at all like her usual devil-may-care expression. "Would you believe me if I told you that this was as hard, or harder, for us than it is for you?"

"And there you go again. Why do I feel like I know you well enough to know that you're telling me the truth?"

"Maybe because you do."

"That's absurd!"

"Selene, how many high-school kids use the word absurd? One in a thousand? One in ten thousand? You feel like you know me because you do, just like Jace and I know you. I can't explain it right now, but the three of us knew each other better than you can imagine right now."

"No, I refuse to accept that on faith."

"When he touches you it feels like it burns, but in a good way. Your skin feels hyper-sensitive—you feel like you could recreate his exact finger print from memory, just based on one touch."

I took a step back away from her, too shocked to respond. I didn't even manage to take a second step before Kat grabbed ahold of my arm with more strength than anyone her size should have been capable of.

"You can't run away from this, Selene. Not now, not when you only know half of the story. You're going to hear me out right now, and then you're going to come to our house and hear the rest of what Jace and I have to tell you. After that you can cut off all contact with us if that's what you want to do, but not before then."

"What if I refuse?"

My heart was racing, but it was more than just fear, more than just her bruising grip. I somehow knew exactly what she was going to say next.

"Then you'll die, Selene. It won't be Jace or I who kills you, but you'll die all the same. You have to see this through. Everything rides on it."

"How did I know you were going to say that? How did you know how I feel when Jace touches me?"

"Because you told me both of those things a very long time ago. You and I have spent more time than I can even explain talking about Jace and how he makes you feel, and once upon a time our positions were reversed. I asked you what would happen if I didn't hear you out and you told me that I would die."

"I don't understand. How can this all have happened and I don't remember it? Is it some kind of weird time-travel thing?"

Kat's laugh was a sharp, bitter thing, but it was her eyes that sent chills racing down my spine. Physically I couldn't have said what changed, but I suddenly got a feeling of immense age, like Kat had seen more years than I could imagine, like underneath the façade of the rebellious teenager was a world-weary being who had less in common with me than I'd originally thought.

"Time travel. That's good—I haven't heard that one before. No, Selene, it's not time travel. I wish it was, but none of us are that lucky. Are you going to trust me and come to our house tonight so that Jace and I can explain all of this to you?"

"I'll really die if I don't listen to you?"

"Yeah, you will. Maybe not in the next twenty-four hours or even the next week, but it will just be a matter of time, and out of every-thing in the world, that is the thing I least want, Selene. You have to believe that I'm telling you the truth. I have nothing but your best interests at heart."

"I do. That probably makes me just as crazy as you, but I do."

"Okay, let's get to class then. You're not going to want to do anything to raise any red flags where your dad is concerned—not with every-thing else that's about to happen."

Chapter 6

I went back to class reluctantly; if I'd known what was in store that day I would have sprinted back to my seat.

There were only a couple of students in our classroom by the time we went back, but apparently that was all the audience Kat and Mr. Reynolds needed. There was something in the back of Mr. Reynolds eyes that seemed to indicate that everything wasn't quite the way it should have been, but Kat played her role perfectly.

By the time the rest of the class had all arrived and the second bell had rung, Kat was sitting in her new spot, a book open on the desk before her and a pen poised over her notebook, ready to take notes. It made me realize how much I'd underestimated her acting abilities. Every trace of the brash young woman I'd been expecting had vanished.

It made me wonder where exactly the act ended and the real Kat began. Actually, it would have been more accurate to say that it made me feel like I should have been wondering who the real Kat was. The same sleepy part of me that felt like I knew her and Jace, that was convinced I could trust them, was positive that the Kat I'd seen over the last twenty-four hours was the real deal.

Class started much like it had every other time that semester. Once Mr. Reynolds was done taking roll he turned off the first row of lights, turned on his ancient overhead projector, and started lecturing.

It wasn't uncommon for Mr. Reynolds to go ten or fifteen minutes at a time without looking up at the class, but we all behaved anyway because he'd scared us all half to death during the first few days of class.

Today apparently was going to be different. Less than five minutes after the first bank of lights went off, Sandra leaned forward and tapped the girl immediately in front of her on the shoulder.

Patricia Jones was the kind of girl who was constitutionally unable to pass up a good rumor. I was not at all surprised when she leaned back in her desk so that she would be able to hear Sandra.

Even before Sandra started whispering, I had a pretty good idea I was going to be the one being badmouthed. I probably could have predicted the general gist of the rumor too, but as it turned out I didn't have to guess because Sandra was talking just loud enough for me to make out about every third word.

"...slut...new guy...totally...whoring..."

I didn't even realize the anger was back and on the verge of escaping until I heard my pencil snap. I turned toward Sandra, planning on letting loose with a stream of profanity that would take the paint off of her manicured nails, but Kat was shaking her head at me.

I wanted to ignore Jace's sister and start an old-fashioned girl-on-girl brawl, but it was like Kat could read my mind. Just at the exact instant when I'd decided to jump out of my desk, Kat gave me a look that told me I was going to regret it if I went through with my plan.

Instead of exploding in a frothing, screaming mess, I closed my eyes and counted to ten. When that didn't do the trick I started over and counted to fifty.

Sandra of course saw the entire drama play out and I opened my eyes to find her smirking in my direction as she finished whispering the same batch of lies in the ear of the girl behind her. What had Mr. Reynolds been thinking? Surrounding Sandra with girls was like stacking dry wood around a leaky container of gasoline. In fairness if he'd surrounded her with boys he'd have had a different set of problems, but this situation was an accident just looking for a spark and I was the proverbial match.

I watched the rumor trickle around the room in slow motion. It was just too good—even the girls who didn't usually get into the gossip game couldn't pass it up. It was creating enough of a quiet ruckus that even some of the boys were noticing and leaning back in an effort to find out what was going on.

In fact, it seemed like the only person in the entire room who *wasn't* about to be told I was a complete whore was Mr. Reynolds. Now that I had my anger more or less under control I wanted to just crawl under my desk and hide.

Kat had been right to stop me from attacking Sandra. The euphoria of having actual friends—despite the odd stuff that was going on—and the heady feeling of having such a gorgeous boy interested in me had been skewing my world view, but the reality was that I couldn't do *anything* to Sandra. She held all the cards and this was just a foretaste of what was headed my way.

As if reading my mind, Sandra launched the second phase of her plan. She looked over at me to make sure that I was watching, and then passed a note up to Patricia. Patricia read the name on the outside of the note and made as though to pass it forward, but before she could make the handoff, the note shot across the aisle and into Kat's hand.

It almost seemed like Kat...flickered...for a split second right after the note landed in her hand. My eyes widened as I realized that Kat was using her powers in view of the entire class. I half expected someone to stand up and denounce her as a witch or something, but nobody said anything.

Given all the carefully-orchestrated drama that Sandra had created leading up to that moment, there was certainly no lack of eyes watching that little corner of the classroom, but it was like everyone else had failed to notice anything out of the ordinary.

Kat sat there motionless for several long seconds as almost every eye in the room turned towards her. I had a split second to wonder if my noticing Kat meant I was somehow unique, and then Kat started unfolding the note.

I felt like my heart was going to explode inside my chest. Grabbing the note and disposing of it wouldn't have stopped Sandra from writing more of them, but it would have been preferable to showing the entire class the nasty things she was saying about me. Now that they'd been prepped with the whisper campaign they'd be predisposed to believe whatever she'd written.

I opened my mouth to yell at Kat, and then remembered that I was sitting in *Mr. Reynolds'* class. Before I could decide whether yelling was worth the extended detention it would earn me, Kat finished unwrapping the note and held it up for everyone to see.

I know I just said that Selene was a skank, but the truth is that I'm the biggest whore in the entire school. Funny, huh? I think I'll sleep with a couple of my teachers next. Then again, maybe some of my dad's friends would be a better choice. They have more money and some of them certainly seem interested...

My lungs were refusing to work. It was impossible. Sandra wouldn't have put something like that in writing. She was all about maintaining deniability, but it was hard to argue with my own eyes. The note was in her handwriting and the entire class had just seen her pass the note to Patricia, who had...dropped it straight into Kat's hand.

The flicker. I didn't know how she'd done it, but Kat had forged a note, put Sandra's name on it, and then switched the original note with her forgery. It was the only explanation for the sickly look on Sandra's face.

"Put that away or I'll destroy you." Sandra's voice came out in a hiss. It was impressive that she could sound that angry even when she was scared out of her mind.

Kat gave Sandra a satisfied look before standing and waving her arms in Mr. Reynolds' direction. "I'm sorry to interrupt, sir, but I'm afraid that one of my classmates is being disruptive."

It was social suicide. The one iron-clad rule of high-school existence seemed to be that you didn't rat out one of the other kids to the teachers. It was stupid, really. The only kids who benefited from everyone keeping quiet were the jerks like Sandra, but that was just the way it was. It was more proof that most high-school kids weren't very bright.

Mr. Reynolds stepped away from the lectern and the overhead projector. "What's going on here?"

"Sandra wrote this note and was passing it to someone in front of her."

"That's a lie!"

I expected Kat to go down in flames as the rest of the kids in the class hurried to defend Sandra. Instead there was a perfectly-cued chorus from the kids closest to Kat, all weighing in to indicate that they'd seen Sandra write the note.

I didn't even realize that I'd joined until the words had already left my mouth. Sandra shot me a dark look, but I was too busy being shocked that Kat had used her worship-me aura to be very worried about Sandra.

Mr. Reynolds took the note from Kat and his expression darkened even further as he read it. Sandra didn't even let him finish.

"I didn't write that note! I wrote a note, but somehow she changed the words when she picked it up."

Mr. Reynolds looked at her with disgust on his face. "You can't really expect me to believe that."

"No, it's true!"

"Fine, what was your note actually about?"

"I...ah...I was telling my friend about a party."

I felt a sudden urge to jump to my feet and yell Sandra down. Apparently Kat had expanded the reach of her aura again because several of the kids between her and I made as though they were going to stand up. They didn't get the chance though because Mr. Reynolds slammed his fist down on the closest desk, silencing Sandra and intimidating everyone else.

"I cannot abide liars, Miss Conner."

"I'm not lying. That's not my note!"

Mr. Reynolds looked around at the rest of us. "How many of you saw Miss Conner write this note and pass it forward?"

More than a third of the class raised their hands—basically everyone who sat behind Sandra—even a couple of kids who couldn't possibly have seen her pass the note raised their hands.

"And how many of you saw Kat pick up the note?"

The same group of kids raised their hands, and I realized for the first time that most of the kids who were supporting Kat's story had been too far away from her to have been affected by her worship-me aura. It looked like there was a lot more resentment against Sandra than I'd ever realized.

"And do any of you believe that Kat was able to write this note and swap it for the note that Miss Conner claims she wrote?"

The only two hands in the air at that point predictably came from Sandra's clique. Mr. Reynolds shook his head at them before turning the paper in his hands so that they, and most of the rest of the class, could read it.

"Is this or is this not Miss Conner's hand writing?"

Jenn shook her head, but she looked miserable. Megan on the other hand looked like she was a small animal caught in the headlights of a large truck that was about to run her over.

Mr. Reynolds got right in Megan's face. "I have a substantial sample of Miss Conner's handwriting sitting in my files. I already know the answer to my question, I'm just giving you a chance to save yourself a very unpleasant trip to the assistant principal's office."

Megan nodded choppily. "That's Sandra's handwriting. I'd recognize it anywhere."

Mr. Reynolds radiated an unmistakable air of satisfaction. "Jenn and Sandra, you're both coming with me. The rest of you stay here and read through the rest of this chapter. There will be a quiz when I get back."

REBORN

Sandra looked for a moment like she was going to refuse to get out of her desk, but apparently she decided that Mr. Reynolds wasn't above picking her up by her arm and physically hauling her out of the room.

I sat there in shock for several seconds staring at the classroom door after all three of them had left. I finally came back to myself enough to look at Kat in wonder, but she just shot me a jaunty wave and a wink before looking down at her book.

I wasn't going to get any answers there, at least not any time soon. That was okay though. For the first time in years I'd come out ahead of Sandra in one of our exchanges and this time she couldn't pin any of it on me. That might not stop her from trying to retaliate, but even she was going to have a hard time explaining that note away.

I couldn't imagine that her dad was going to be very eager to fire my dad on nothing more than her say-so now, not when he was going to be busy worrying which of his associates he needed to keep away from her.

I wasn't going to push Kat for an answer now, not after she'd just saved me like that, but I was definitely going to their house once school was over, and I was going to get my answers then.

Chapter 7

The rest of school flew by. For the first time in recent memory, I was able to watch people pass notes and whisper without worrying they were talking about me.

Actually they *were* talking about me, but this time I featured into the rumors in only a very small way. Sandra's bizarre confession was the talk of the entire school, and more than one person wanted my reaction to everything that was happening, so I got a blow-by-blow account over the next couple of hours as Sandra was marched to the assistant principal's office where she underwent a series of presumably uncomfortable meetings with Assistant Principal Snyder, the school counselor, and ultimately her father, who apparently arrived at the school in his Rolls Royce looking like storm clouds had followed him the entire way.

I enjoyed what was happening. Being the center of attention in PE was nice, and there was no denying the fact that Sandra had had it coming, but a tiny part of me kept pointing out that I *shouldn't* be enjoying this.

Reveling in Sandra's unhappiness would make me no better than her. I could be glad that justice had been served, and hope that it would teach her a lesson, but that was as far as things should go.

Likewise, all of the attention from my peers was pretty worthless when you got right down to it.

They were floating around me like planets pulled into orbit around a star, but the truth was they weren't going to stay. Sooner or later—probably much sooner than I was prepared to admit—they were going to latch onto someone else. A friend who wasn't your friend until you had something that they needed wasn't any kind of friend at all.

I probably should have come to that realization sooner, but at least I came to it before the school day ended. About five minutes before class ended I shook myself free from the cluster of girls who had been following me around and made my way over to Kat, who had stayed close but who hadn't interfered with me talking to all of the gossip girls.

"I thought maybe we'd lost you."

I nodded. "Yeah, that was pretty heady, but deep down I knew they didn't matter. You and Jace were there for me before you made Sandra look like an idiot. I'm not going to abandon you two for that group of mindless lemmings."

"Plus you want to know how I did it, right?"

"Yeah, I guess so."

"You don't sound as eager as you did a little while ago…"

Even as she said it I realized she was right. "I guess I'm starting to worry about what it all means. I have the feeling that once I know what you and Jace are doing, there won't be any going back."

Kat gave me a sad smile. "You're right, but it's already too late for that. You've crossed the Rubicon, Selene. From here there are only two ways forward."

"I don't want to die."

"I don't blame you. I didn't want to die when it was me standing in your shoes either." Kat looked down at the archaic wrist watch and sighed. "I promised Jace I would keep you here until school ended, but I just can't stomach this place any more. You want to get out of here?"

I couldn't get my voice to work; I settled for just nodding.

"Great. Go grab your clothes. I'll meet you out by your car in five minutes. Don't worry about changing—you can shower at our place. Trust me, it's way better than the locker room here at school. I'll go make sure that we don't get into trouble."

Kat turned and started off toward Ms. Stacker before I could ask her what she meant. I watched her for a second, jealous of her confident stride, and then turned and started toward the girls' locker room.

I grabbed my jeans, sweater, shoes, and everything else from my PE locker, but it was kind of a lot to carry, so I ended up just putting Jace's jacket on over my regulation Cold Springs t-shirt and then picked everything else up and slipped out the side door into the hall.

I felt a little self-conscious in my navy PE shorts. Ironically they weren't too short for PE class, but they violated the dress code once I left the gym. I figured that Kat would magically take care of that too though if push came to shove and headed back towards the parking lot.

I arrived at my car exactly five minutes after separating from Kat, but there was no sign of her...until I turned back towards the school and realized she was standing less than two feet behind me.

"Holy crap! I swear you weren't there just a second ago."

"You're not wrong. Also, that is a nice look on you..."

Her smile said that she was enjoying teasing me, but it was hard to get angry with someone who'd just stood up to a bully for you.

I blushed at the reminder that I'd once again ended up wearing Jace's jacket. I started to shrug out of it, but she stopped me, cool hands on mine, before I could complete the action.

"I was serious. Leave it on, it's not like Jace minds, and you've already pissed off Sandra as much as you're going to piss her off. Oh, that reminds me, you should probably see this."

Kat reached inside of her sports bra and pulled out a note that had Megan's name on it in Sandra's handwriting.

I took it hesitantly, although I couldn't have said why. It wasn't like it was going to explode in my hands or anything.

S. is totally going to pay. Get Todd and slip away from your last class. It's time to send a message that she can't ignore. Key her car. If she doesn't break up with the new guy then we'll see how she likes replacing her windshield.

I came back to myself with Kat's arms wrapped around me in an effort to keep me from going back into the school.

"It's not worth it, Selene. She's already going to be in deep trouble with the administration here at the school and with her dad at home. If you go after her directly you'll just give credence to her claims that somebody is out to get her."

There were so many things I wanted to say, but none of them really mattered. Kat already knew that Sandra was the worst bi-otch in the world. Me screaming it at the top of my lungs wouldn't help matters at all. Besides, I suspected that Kat didn't really understand what my car meant to me.

Kat obviously wasn't poor. For her a car was just a car, and if something happened to her car she paid to have it fixed and never thought twice about it.

For me, my car was more than that. I'd never gone to the factory and watched my dad at work, but I didn't have to see him there to appreciate what he was doing for us. I saw the effects every morning when I woke up and on the afternoons when I made it home in time to see him before he headed off to work again.

I saw him wake up to see us off, so exhausted it was all he could do to keep his eyes open. I saw him standing at the door, psyching himself up to go to a job he hated, a job that was slowly draining the life out of him, so that he could continue to put food on the table for Ari and me.

The two hundred dollars' worth of tires that Sandra had so casually destroyed was less than a couple of weeks' worth of allowance for her, but for me it was days and weeks of my dad's life. A new paint job would have been out of the question and a new windshield would have set us back months. It felt like Sandra and her dad were slowly killing my dad.

I still hadn't regained control over my anger, but I didn't want to put it back on a leash. I forced myself to breathe again and then looked at Kat. "Okay, I won't go after her. Why did you show me that note if you weren't going to let me do anything about it?"

"I told you because you deserve to know. You deserve to know what she had planned, and I figured if I told you back at our house that Jace would overreact and help you bury the body. He always caters to your temper more than he should. I think it's because you remind him of... Never mind. The important thing is that you need to know that my little trick today probably just delayed Sandra rather than stopping her permanently."

"Great, that's exactly what I needed to hear."

The bitterness in my voice could have etched steel, but it just made Kat smile. "It is what you needed to hear, but you're going to have to trust me on that. You needed to have time to work through your feelings towards Sandra now while you're less likely to kill her."

"I don't think there's ever been a time when I was more likely to kill her. She's a spoiled brat who needs a healthy dose of reality."

Kat gave me a surprisingly fierce hug and then released me. "You never know what the future may bring, Selene. But in the meantime, just remember that Jace and I aren't going to let Sandra put you in the poorhouse."

It was less reassuring than she'd meant it to be. I didn't want to be beholden to the two of them any more than I wanted my dad to continue being beholden to Sandra's dad, but even I wasn't so far gone as to say anything. I managed a smile as I climbed into my car and reached over to unlock the passenger door.

Kat's laugh was surprisingly kind. "I've got my own ride, Selene. I'd tell you to just leave your car here, but there's no need to provide an even bigger temptation to Sandra and the rest. I'm right over there."

I looked over to where she'd gestured and finally registered the presence of the fastest-looking motorcycle I'd ever seen. It was black and pink and had absolutely no manufacturer's logos on it anywhere, but that wasn't what made it look so fast. It was low-slung and had tires that were even fatter than the ones on my car.

"That bike?"

"Yeah, she's a beaut, isn't she?"

"I guess you'd better give me directions to your house. There's no way I'm going to be able to keep up with you."

Kat laughed again. "Don't worry, I'll go slow—I promise."

I shook my head at her as I took in the bare skin revealed by her shorts and t-shirt. "Slow is a relative term. Here, you'd better at least take Jace's jacket. It won't do anything to protect your legs, but at least it will keep the rest of you from getting as cut up."

"That's sweet, but I don't get in wrecks—at least not on my motorcycle. I'll be fine."

Kat shut my door for me and then jogged over to her bike. She fiddled around with a key at the back of the bike, popping open some kind of cargo area where she'd stored a pair of sunglasses, and then straddled the bike, which roared to life with an only slightly higher-pitched growl than the Viper had the day before.

I started my car as she backed her bike up, and then I followed her out of the parking lot at a sedate pace that I figured had to be making her chomp at the bit.

The ride out to their house ended up being much less crazy than I'd feared it might be. Kat still opened her bike up with a high-pitched whine that left me in her dust on two different occasions, but she always slowed back down within a mile, so I never actually lost sight of her.

Their house ended up being all the way out on the north side of town on an unassuming lot that looked like it was just part of the forest that butted up against that side of town. The driveway was gated, and wasn't even asphalt until after it curved around a line of trees and was no longer visible from the road.

I wasn't Ari by any stretch of the imagination, but I still flinched when I thought about what the gravel driveway would do to Jace's Viper if he drove over the rocks at any kind of real speed. I followed Kat past the gate, which closed automatically behind us, and then once we were on the pavement, she shot away like a bullet.

By that point she must have figured that it didn't matter; it wasn't like I could get lost on the driveway. Only I *was* actually starting to wonder if I'd gotten lost by the time I'd driven for five more minutes without any sign of a house.

When the house finally came into view my jaw dropped. I'd never seen anything like it before, not even in the movies. It was all the gray, nondescript rock that was everywhere in our particular part of Colorado, which meant that parts of the house almost seemed to blend into the countryside.

That meant that my first impression was that the house was huge, and my second impression was that the house was *enormous*. I counted six garage doors on this side of the building, but that wasn't the full story, because one of them was open and Kat was waving at me from inside of a garage that was five or six times as deep as a normal garage. They had room for an entire fleet of cars.

Kat seemed to want me to park inside next to her bike, but I shook my head and started to park out on the asphalt. I looked away from her for just a second as I brought my car to a stop, and when I looked up she was standing at my window.

"Selene, come park in the garage."

"No, my car has an oil leak and I don't want to get it all over your floor."

Kat smiled. "Don't be silly. We've got entire bays in there that aren't being used. I'll open up the shop bay and you can park in there. Fair warning though, I think he's going to try to talk you into a new set of rims at some point over the next few days."

"Yeah, because that's subtle enough that my dad won't notice."

"In case you haven't noticed, Jace isn't always the most subtle guy. Here, pull forward into the far door, I'll go open the garage."

A couple of minutes later my car was parked inside of the 'shop' bay and I was following Kat through the garage, towards a heavy door that presumably led into the house itself. The garage was cool enough that I was glad I still had Jace's jacket on. I honestly didn't know how Kat was enduring the walk through the cavernous building with nothing more than her shorts and t-shirt on. Actually, come to think of it, she'd probably been even colder on her bike.

It was one more question that I'd have to ask once they started telling me what was really going on.

The door turned out to have some kind of fingerprint reader on it. Kat ran her finger over the sensor and then held the door open for me.

"Sorry about this. The previous owner was a paranoid nutjob. Remind Jace and he'll get you entered into the database later so you can come and go as you please. Oh, by the way, can you please take off your shoes? Jace had the entire place re-carpeted before we moved in; he's kind of a freak when it comes to carpet."

Whatever I was planning on saying in response evaporated when I stepped inside and saw their kitchen. Saying it was big didn't even begin to do it justice. The entire back wall was nothing but glass, and beyond that was a solarium that looked like it was set up for indoor-outdoor living. Right now the back of the solarium had been opened up so that Jace could cook on the grill that took up the far corner of the area, but I could tell that once the solarium was closed back up it would make the perfect sun room for the winter months.

I didn't know if Jace or Kat either one were readers, but assuming they were still inviting me over once it got cold, I was definitely going to curl up in one of the hammocks with a good book.

There was a lot more to the solarium, but that was all that I managed to notice before I realized that Jace was cooking with his shirt off.

Wow didn't even begin to cover it. You don't always expect blond guys to tan, but Jace had the tan of a surfer combined with the lean, tight muscles of a gymnast. I could feel myself starting to hyperventilate and had to close my eyes in order to get control of myself again.

"Down, girl."

I opened my eyes and glared at Kat. "You could have given me some warning."

She snorted. "Like I know whether or not he's got a shirt on at any given moment? Please girl, there are days when I'm lucky if I know whether or not *I've* got a shirt on. Nobody could reasonably expect me to keep track of him."

The door between the solarium and the kitchen was closed, so Jace hadn't realized we were there yet. He opened up the grill and flipped the hamburgers that were cooking there with the sure hands of someone who was no stranger to cooking.

I tried to look away from him again, but my eyes refused to budge. The wind had tousled his wavy hair. He looked perfect, like a Greek god, like he'd been carved out of marble.

I let my eyes drop down to his shoulders and biceps, and for a split second my sense of déjà vu was so strong I had to put my hand out to catch myself against the wall. The setting wasn't right—not even close—but him standing there cooking with his shirt off, the sun illuminating his muscles while I watched from a little ways away, that felt right in ways that I couldn't even begin to describe. It felt like something I'd done hundreds of times before.

"I was originally planning on showing you the rest of this wing, but I guess I could just leave you here if you want—you know, let you take in the...scenery. We aren't due back for a little while still, so he probably won't even realize that you're here..."

I opened my mouth, uncertain how to respond to that. In that moment Kat didn't sound very sisterly, but by the same stretch she didn't sound jealous or anything.

"I'm not sure whether I should be grossed out that you're talking about your brother like that or if I should just bow before the inevitable and admit that *any* girl would think Jace was hot."

"Yeah, well, there are brothers and then there are *brothers*. Don't think that I haven't noticed that you didn't answer my question. You're going to want to hurry up and decide though, Jace gets testy when dinner doesn't go as planned."

I took one last long look at Jace and then sighed. "I'd love to see the rest of the house, but you mentioned a shower. Can we start with that? I'm suddenly feeling like the ugly duckling. A shower and changing clothes won't magically put me in Jace's league, but maybe it will keep him from running away screaming for a few more days."

Kat raised her eyebrow suggestively. "Oh, I don't know—I think seeing you in those shorts might convert Jace to being a butt guy..."

My face went hot and I wished that I could make myself invisible, but the universe stubbornly refused to grant my wish.

"Can you please just show me to a bathroom? I don't want Jace to see me like this."

"He's seen you in a lot worse, but whatever. Let's get you showered."

That didn't make sense considering that Jace had seen me a grand total of twice before now, but by that point I was already following her through the house and the great room was so impressive that it took my breath away.

There was a huge water feature on one wall, a torrent of water that disappeared down into the floor, presumably cascading on into the basement before being pumped back upstairs. The décor had an almost industrial feel to it, all black, white and silver, but it fit the massive open space perfectly, as did the tall bay windows that looked out over the front of the house and the skylights that let additional light in.

"Sorry, I told Jace to leave that stupid waterfall off, but apparently he was determined to pull out all of the stops. He still doesn't believe me when I tell him that it's beyond pretentious."

"No, it's fine. It's spectacular—how did you guys end up with this place?"

"It belonged to some dot-com billionaire who ended up losing his shirt when the economy took a turn for the worse a few years ago. Like I said earlier, he was super-paranoid, so he built this place outside the town boundaries and managed to keep it a secret by importing a building crew from outside of the state."

"Wow. Just wow. It's amazing, but not very much like what I would have envisioned a paranoid billionaire building for himself. It doesn't feel very secure."

Kat grabbed my hand and pulled me into a hall that was wide enough for six people to walk abreast. "Yeah, don't let all of the glass fool you.

It's all bulletproof—much thicker than it looks until you get pretty close to it. More than that though, the house is built in zones."

Kat waved at our surroundings, taking in the heated marble floors as if it was nothing out of the ordinary.

"This is one of the low-security zones. When you get to the bedrooms things are even more secure—thicker glass set inside a steel cage and all that. The coolest part is that there are hidden passages from the rooms down into this super bunker underground. It would take an army to dig you out from there if you locked yourself in and refused to come out."

She led me into a large room on the left that was full of every kind of exercise equipment imaginable. "This is the gym—just in case you were curious how Jace manages to keep his figure so studly."

The space had windows along two walls, mirrors on the other two, and a massive skylight that let in even more light than I'd seen in the great room. There were more than twenty different speakers hanging from the ceilings at various points, and half a dozen big-screen televisions mounted on the walls.

Kat gave me a second to take it all in, and then resumed talking. "It's wired for sound and temperature-controlled with a separate thermostat. There is a locker room back over there and as you can see we're looking out over the back of the house again, so the hot tub is just down that path and the lap pool is right here, less than twenty feet away from the exterior door."

"I think I might actually convince myself to work out if I had access to all of that stuff."

"I know, you'd think. Our exercise facilities were almost this good in the last place where we lived though and I gave up after a week or two. I keep telling myself that the exercise bug is just something that you're either born with or you aren't. If I say it often enough I can almost drown out the little voice that tells me I'm just lazy."

This time it was my turn to roll my eyes at her. "You can't seriously tell me that you stay that skinny without working out."

"Yep, sorry—I guess I just have good genetics. Don't worry though, your bod is just as slamming—trust me, it's come up with Jace a number of times already."

I managed not to blush again, but it was a near thing. "Speaking of Jace, I'm just about due for that shower. Do you just want me to use the locker room here?"

"Right, I'll stop showing off and we'll make a beeline to the bedrooms."

We passed more than two dozen more rooms over the next couple of minutes and I nearly stopped her a dozen times despite my desire to make sure I got cleaned up before I saw Jace again. It was like they'd purposely tried to make it hard for me to hold to my resolution.

REBORN

For everything other than the bedrooms and the bathrooms, the doors to the various rooms were made out of glass, which meant I caught glimpses of the rooms as we passed. It wasn't enough to really get the full effect of the massive home theater that was upholstered all in black leather. It was just enough to whet my appetite and make me want to stop.

The same went for the large office space on the front side of the house and the library that adjoined it. The wood shelving in the latter ran from the floor all the way up to a second story and had one of the rolling ladders that I'd seen at the Cold Springs library before they'd started transitioning to electronic devices rather than actual physical books.

Some of the bedroom doors were open, which meant that I saw a guest bedroom that was almost as big as our entire house and which Kat casually mentioned had multiple sets of bunk beds built right into the wall.

It was the massage room with its raised table and folded privacy sheet though that really made my knees weak.

"Oh, you should ask Jace to give you a massage some time. He's forgotten more about rubbing knots out of someone's back than most people will ever know."

The idea of stripping down to nothing and having Jace's hands on my bare body brought back my earlier blush with a vengeance. Kat looked back at exactly the right time to catch my reaction and she laughed again.

"I can stay in the room if you want—you know, just to make sure that the two of you behave yourselves."

"I think my dad would kill Jace and then kill me if he found out that I'd let Jace give me a massage—regardless of who else was in the room."

"Oh, well, it's your loss."

Kat let us through another biometric reader and heavy glass door and then we went up a set of stairs that opened into a large central area that had only two doors leading off of it. The open area didn't have any windows, but the top was nothing more than one huge skylight. I was so shocked that I stopped moving and Kat had to grab my arm so she could tow me along towards the door on the far room of the area.

"The one back there is my room, but I need a shower too so you're going to be using Jace's room."

"Hold on—I just wanted a shower, any of the guest rooms would have been just fine."

"Sorry, Selene, we just moved in yesterday. We had the movers arrange most of the furniture that we had shipped in, but we haven't had time to re-stock every bathroom in this place. Right now the only bathrooms that have toiletries and towels are the two up here. Of course you could always just go back downstairs and wait with

Jace while I shower—I'm sure he wouldn't mind what you're wearing."

"That was a low blow, Kat."

"I know, but you'll thank me for it later."

"All right, lead on."

Jace's room continued the same 'glass as far as the eye can see' theme that had been so prominent in the sitting room at the top of the stairs. Kat had said that the bedrooms were heavy glass inside of a steel cage, but so far I couldn't see very many places that weren't glass, so I wasn't sure where the steel came in. In fact, the baseball-diamond-shaped room was nothing like I'd been expecting.

The door we'd just walked through was set into a wall that was made up of something more substantial than glass. That wall butted up against another wall at right angles which contained a door to the bathroom and closet, but everything else was nothing but open space and a beautiful view.

"The glass all polarizes if a current is run through it, so if Jace wants some privacy he just hits a button on his phone and this all goes opaque."

I nodded, but I was only partially listening. The wooden bed was huge—three people could have slept on it and never bumped elbows during the middle of the night—and it dominated the center of the room. There were small tables on either side of it, but no lamp. I guess that made sense when your entire room was wired and you could turn your lights off from your smartphone.

There were a couple of chairs and a small table almost directly across from us. It looked almost like a little breakfast nook. Off to our right there was a desk and rolling office chair that formed a tidy workspace which featured a computer that looked like it could power all of the space shuttles at once.

Next to the desk was a large bookcase that held a number of slender, leather-bound books. I started towards the bookcase, curious what books Jace valued so much that he kept them in his room rather than down in the enormous library, but Kat grabbed my arm and tugged me towards the other door.

"You're going to run out of time if you don't hurry. Remember, you didn't want to do any more sightseeing until after you were clean and presentable."

I reluctantly followed her. It was one more thing that didn't make sense, but the longer I looked at the bookshelf the more convinced I became that it was somehow important. The carpet was more than amazing. It cradled my bare feet in ways that I wouldn't have believed were possible. If I'd lived in this house I would have never put on shoes again. I could see why Jace was so protective of it.

"Is your room like this?"

"Yeah, mostly. I mean the carpets and furniture are all different and I have a TV, but they are almost the same size. I let Jace have the bigger one because mine has the better bathroom."

I started to ask her what her bathroom was like, but then I stepped into Jace's bathroom and the question lost all meaning.

I'd expected the bathroom to be impressive given the sheer size and luxury of everything else I'd seen up to that point, but I'd still somehow managed to be too conservative in my expectations. The bathroom and closet combined were almost as big as Jace's bedroom, which was as big as my entire house.

Everything from the floor to the sink to the gigantic bathtub was done in black granite, or something that looked like black granite but which was probably several times as expensive. It should have given the bathroom a dark, forbidding look, but the plentiful skylights and the frequent lights kept it looking bright and cheery.

The floors were warm, apparently heated, which was good because Jace hadn't put down much in the way of rugs. The fixtures were all elegant brushed silver, but I took that in as an afterthought as I continued past the giant mirror and further into the room.

I'd initially thought the bathtub was gigantic, but I wasn't sure that I'd done it justice. It was a jetted, multi-level masterpiece that probably would have taken hours to fill if not for the fact that there were four separate spouts.

There was a separate shower that was frosted glass that seemed designed less with privacy in mind than it was to tease. I very carefully avoided thinking about Jace in there all wet and soapy. Given my record so far with blushing, that would probably cause me to spontaneously burst into flame.

The closet portion of the bathroom was set behind a set of double glass doors that Kat opened with a hiss of equalizing air pressure.

"The closet is designed to be temperature and humidity-controlled so that you don't have to worry about long showers ruining your clothes."

I just nodded. I'd never seen so much space for clothing outside of a department store. There were racks and racks of shirts, drawers filled with socks, shelves for jeans and sweaters, and an entire section filled with suits that looked like they'd never been worn before. Jace had more clothes than Ari, my dad and I combined, but he still only filled up a quarter of the available space. There were bags and boxes in piles on the floor still waiting to be unpacked and racked, but I couldn't believe that they would be enough to finish filling up the remaining space.

"Your closet is bigger than this?"

"Oh yeah, almost twice as big."

"And I'm guessing that yours is full, isn't it?"

Kat had the grace to look a little embarrassed. "No, not quite, but it will be once the next load of stuff arrives from our last place."

"Unbelievable. What did you say your parents used to do?"

"Our family is in precious metals." She chuckled, but when I gave her a confused look she just waved my question away. "You'll understand later."

"You do know that's getting to be really old, right?"

"Yeah, don't worry though, you're not that far from understanding it all." She checked her watch and then frowned. "Hmm, this has all taken a lot longer than I realized. I need to get going if I'm going to get showered in time to go back and get Ari. Everything you need should be here. Soap and shampoo are in the shower, towels are in the closet right over there."

"You said there is some kind of secret passage down into the basement from here?"

Kat nodded and pointed at one of the shelves inside the closet. "It's in there, but you don't need to worry about it. It's got a biometric lock on it too. Oh, that reminds me, you're not going to want to close the bathroom door all of the way. It's designed to lock too and then you'd have to wait for Jace or me to come get you out."

"Wow, this place isn't very visitor-friendly, is it?"

"Not up here it isn't. The lower levels aren't like this, but like I said, the former owner was crazy paranoid. Don't worry though, Jace is a perfect gentleman, he won't walk in on you or anything."

That last bit was said over her shoulder as she headed out the door. I stood there in astonishment for several seconds before realizing I was running out of time if I wanted to be done before Jace came looking for me.

I stripped off my shirt and rolled it up so that I could use it as a doorstop. It was probably unnecessary and I felt a little silly kneeling down on the floor in my sports bra to place it between the door and the frame, but I was determined not to get locked out of the bedroom.

My shower went just fine. I'd never actually had a shower with that much water pressure. It was like standing under a waterfall, and I got the feeling that the hot water was the next best thing to unlimited.

In fact, the shower was so nice that I lost track of time and ended up staying in there for a lot longer than I'd meant to. By the time I finally got out, my fingers looked like prunes and even then I only forced myself out of the shower because I was worried that Jace would end up accidentally walking in on me if I didn't.

I hadn't thought to get a towel out of the linen closet before I got into the shower, so I ended up having to cross over all of that black, gloriously slick granite dripping wet before I could pull the largest, fluffiest white towel in the world out of the closet and finally start toweling off. The trail of water puddles was regrettable, but I couldn't just stand there in the shower and wait to drip-dry.

Once I was dry, I wrapped the towel around my body and headed back over to the counter where I'd left all of my clothes. I'd just picked up my underwear when something green and glittery shot through the sliver of space between the bathroom door and the frame and bounced off of me.

I'd never seen anything like it and my natural inclination had been to get away, but it was moving too fast, so all I managed to do was throw myself dangerously off balance on a slick surface that had entirely too much water on it.

My arms had already started flailing; I probably would have fallen over even if nothing else had happened, but the impact from the glittering green spark sealed my fate. Something that small, even moving so fast, shouldn't have been able to hit me hard enough to overbalance me, but there was an odd sense of weight to the spark when it hit me, and I was already so off-balance.

I felt my legs fly out from under me with a flash of panic that superseded all concerns about modesty or anything else. My panties went flying through the air, forgotten as I made a mad grab for the counter.

I didn't realize that I'd screamed until my butt landed on the hard black floor and the green, glittery spark that had caused me so many problems disappeared with a pop.

"Selene! Are you okay?"

I once again wished that I could just disappear into a hole in the ground and pull it closed after me. I wanted nothing more than to just sit there and nurse my wounds, but Jace sounded like he was in a near panic—if I didn't respond soon he was going to come charging through the bathroom door.

"Stay out! I mean I think I'm okay, but please don't come in here."

I could hear Jace shifting around just outside of the bathroom door, but it didn't sound like he was getting any closer.

"Are you sure you're okay? What happened? It sounded like you fell…"

"Yeah, some kind of crazy green insect charged me and it kind of freaked me out. I tripped over my own legs and just about cracked my head open on your beautiful, dangerous floor."

"I'm sorry, Selene. I really should have put down some bathroom mats. I was going to, but all of my old stuff was the wrong color so I didn't even bother having the movers pack it up. I've got some new mats arriving tomorrow, but that's not very useful right now. Are you really sure you don't need any help?"

I double-checked that my towel hadn't come off during the course of the fall, and then shifted around gingerly in an effort to figure out how much I'd hurt myself.

"No. I mean, yes, I'm sure I don't need you in here while I'm sprawled on the floor wearing nothing more than a towel. I don't think that I broke anything. Just a second and I'll try to stand up."

I grabbed ahold of the cabinet with both hands and then slowly pulled myself back up to my feet, wincing at the pain in my butt. I probably hadn't broken my tailbone, but I was going to have some spectacular bruises—at least nobody was going to see them.

"Yeah, everything but my dignity is intact. You can stop worrying. How long have you been standing out there, by the way?"

"Not long. I'd just walked into my room when I heard you scream. I saw your shoes downstairs when I came in to grab some stuff from the kitchen and then I passed Kat on my way up here."

I looked around the bathroom searching for my underwear and then felt my heart sink. They had landed in the single biggest puddle from my trip over to get a towel. I hobbled over and picked them up off the floor, but my suspicions turned out to be right—they were soaked through. There was no way I was wearing them anytime soon.

"Selene, what's going on?"

I closed my eyes and wished with all my might that everything that had just happened was nothing more than a bad dream, but when I opened them again I was still standing there in a towel in Jace's bathroom.

"Nothing much. I dropped my underwear in a puddle, so I'm basically just wishing that I'd never been born."

Jace was silent for several seconds. "Wrap a towel around yourself—I'm coming in."

"What? No, you can't come in here!"

This was already embarrassing enough—the last thing I needed was for him to see me looking like a drowned rat.

"Are you covered up?"

"I've got a towel on, but you're not coming in here."

"If you've got a towel on then you're more covered up than you would be in a swimsuit."

When his hand appeared on the edge of the door I squeaked. "Jace, no! What if it falls down?"

"Hold it up. You're going to have to trust me, Selene."

I opened my mouth to try to come up with another argument, but it was too late. The door was open and he was standing there in nothing but a pair of old jeans that hung from his hips like they were barely winning the war against gravity.

"You're not wearing a shirt..."

"Yeah, sorry about that. I spilled stuff on it while I was marinating the steaks and I didn't want it to soak through and ruin my jeans—these are my favorite pair."

"They are very nice jeans."

What I really meant was that his warm, chiseled body made them look nice, but thankfully I wasn't quite so far gone as to just blurt that out. Jace smiled like he knew exactly what I'd been thinking.

"Thanks—all of the rest of my shirts are in here though so I was waiting for you to finish before coming in to get a replacement."

His eyes briefly traveled down my towel-wrapped form and I inched the towel a little higher around my torso as I valiantly fought off the blush I could feel trying to ambush me.

"How exactly are you planning on saving the day this time, Superman?"

"Follow me and see."

Jace skirted the worst of the puddles as he made his way over to the closet, opening the door with a hiss of pressurized air. I followed hesitantly, worried that my towel was somehow going to slip despite the fact that my arms were pressing against my sides nearly hard enough to leave bruises.

By the time I made it over to the closet, he'd already let go of the door and started moving boxes around. I was going to have to lift an arm up if I wanted to open the door and join him in there. It was just one arm, but it felt like playing Russian roulette. I almost didn't do it, almost just stayed out there in the bathroom rather than going into the closet, but I couldn't resist the lure of being in his presence.

I took a deep breath, grabbed ahold of my towel with my left hand to augment the death grip my left arm had on it, and pulled the door open with my right hand. Jace looked over at me for just a second before returning to his search.

A few seconds later he turned around with a big box in his arms. "This is it. Sorry, I just didn't know how to direct you to the right one."

"So the contents of that box will save me from embarrassment? I didn't realize that they'd come up with portable time machines that small..."

"Ha, ha. Even when mortified you still manage to hold onto your sense of humor."

"Really? How do I let go of that? I could really use another hand to hold onto my towel."

That time I got nothing more than an absent nod—Jace was already focused on something else. "Look, Selene, I need you to promise me that you'll hear me out, that you won't freak out until after you know the full story."

"Wow, that's ominous—I'm not sure that I want to know what's in that box now."

He shrugged. "That's fine with me—it would make things a lot easier if I don't have to have this conversation now. You can always just go commando. I'll leave so you can pull your pants on."

Jace started to walk around me, box still in his arms, but I suddenly couldn't let him walk out on me without finding out what was in the box. The last two days had been filled with nothing but secret after secret and this was the first time that anyone had offered to explain *anything*.

I grabbed Jace's arm. "Stop. I'm not going commando, so go ahead and just come clean about the fact that you collect women's underwear."

I'd said it mostly in jest because I couldn't come up with any other explanation for how he was going to solve this particular problem. The sickly grin I got in response seemed to indicate that I struck uncomfortably close to the mark.

Jace set the box down and then looked back up at me again before he started to open it. "Remember, you promised to let me explain everything before you freak out."

I watched as Jace opened the box and revealed something that looked like a time capsule. Rather than the box of frilly underwear that I'd been afraid he had stashed in there, I seemed to be looking at a random collection of...well, junk.

Jace started pulling things out, stacking them on a nearby box. A leather-bound book similar to the ones I'd seen on his bookcase was first, handled with the reverence of a true bibliophile. That was followed by a couple pairs of jeans, and a toiletries bag.

There was a sense of familiarity to it all, an inexplicable feeling of déjà vu. I didn't know any of this stuff, hadn't seen it before, but I felt like it was familiar in some way.

I reached over to the pants and fished them out from the bottom of the pile. I'd actually wanted to go after the journal first, but something told me that Jace wouldn't have let me read it—not yet, not until after he'd finished explaining.

I unfolded the jeans and shook my head in confusion. It was a designer brand from my mom's era, something I recognized solely by chance. The cut was timeless, but there was no question in my mind but that the clothing I was looking at was older than I was.

Jace had paused for a second while I examined the jeans, but now he pulled out a heavy leather jacket that was a smaller, more feminine version of the one that I'd been wearing for the last two days, the one that he'd loaned me. The jacket was followed by a bunch of tops, one of which caught my eye.

I pulled the blue fabric off of the top of the pile and my heart sped up as I got my first good look at it. Jace pulled several bras out of the box, which should have made me blush and stutter, but I was too focused on the shirt to give anything else much attention.

My sweater had been my unconscionable splurge from last year, the thing I couldn't afford and which I shouldn't have purchased, but which I bought anyway. The year before I'd purchased a blue top that was completely unremarkable other than the fact that I liked the color and it fit me perfectly, making it look like I actually had boobs without hugging my stomach so much that I looked like a fatso.

I'd had to borrow an extra twenty bucks from Ari to buy it and had spent the next three months babysitting and doing other odd jobs to pay her back. I'd worn it so often that it was nearly falling apart. It would have been my go-to outfit this morning instead of the sweater if not for the fact that the last time I'd worn it my dad had told me it wasn't decent any more now that parts of the material had become nearly see-through.

That shirt was still sitting at home in my closet, but this shirt, the one in my hands, was an exact match. Despite my inner turmoil, my hands weren't shaking as I gently placed the blue shirt down and picked up one of the bras.

It was my size—exactly my size—just like the shirt, just like the pants, and just like the panties that Jace had finally pulled out of the box. He at least had the grace to look embarrassed as he offered them to me.

"Here, they are all brand new. They've been laundered, but never worn—there are more in here that are still in the manufacturer's packaging if you'd rather. I don't know what you—"

I cut him off as I reached into the box and pulled out a package of brand-new underwear. "How long have you been in town, Jace?"

"We told you—we arrived yesterday."

"Tell me the truth! You didn't just arrive yesterday, you've been here for years spying on me—it's the only way you could have a box of clothes that was obviously intended for me." I grabbed the blue shirt with my other hand and shook it in his face. "Did you follow me to that store two years ago? Is that how you ended up with this?"

I wanted to close my eyes and slam my head into the wall. I'd been so stupid. Of course any cute, rich guy who was interested in me wasn't going to be well-adjusted. Of course Jace was secretly some kind of stalker pervert. I didn't know how he'd managed to follow me around all these years without me seeing him, but maybe he'd been hiring people to do it.

All I knew for sure was that I needed to get away, needed to get somewhere safe before he realized how big of a mistake he'd made by telling me.

I jumped up to my feet and started towards the closet doors, cursing myself. I should have pretended to be fine with everything so that he wouldn't realize that I was going to run away as soon as his back was turned.

"Selene, it's not like that. Hear me out."

"You're right, it's not like that. I'm sorry, I think my shower was too hot and it's been too long since I had anything to eat. I'm just a little light headed."

I was through the doors and I headed directly towards the counter. I grabbed my clothes—everything but my gym shirt, which I kicked out of the way so that the door would swing shut behind me—and made a beeline through the bedroom.

"Selene, where are you going?"

"It's just so hot in here, Jace. I'll be right back, I just need to step out and cool down a little."

As soon as I crossed into the bedroom I broke into a sprint.

I've never been much of an athlete, but I surprised myself at just how fast I managed to get going across the soft, springy surface of the carpet. As surprising as that was, it was nothing compared to the shock of having Jace appear in front of me less than five feet before I would have arrived at the door out into the sitting area.

When I say appeared I don't mean that he ran really fast and caught me by surprise. There was literally nothing but empty space in front of me, and then he was there filling it as though he'd teleported.

I tried to stop, tried to change direction so that I wouldn't crash into his waiting arms, but I was moving much too fast to have a prayer of doing either. I half expected to knock him over when we collided, but he absorbed all of my momentum without even grunting, and then grabbed me by the shoulders.

I dropped my clothes and tried to hit him, but it was like watching a child try to hurt an adult. I wasn't fast enough or strong enough either one. He grabbed my wrists as my fists headed towards him and immobilized them with a vice-like grip that was only a hair's breadth from being painful.

"You promised to hear me out and that's what you're going to do, Selene."

"Let me go!"

I threw myself toward him, trying to bite him, but he flipped me around so that my back was pressed up against his chest, my arms crossed in front of me and my wrists down next to my waist. It was like he'd put me in a strait jacket.

I lifted my foot to slam it down on Jace's instep, but he jerked me to the side, throwing my balance off, and then tripped me and took me down to the floor. I'd never fallen that fast before. Somehow I landed on the carpet on my back, with Jace straddling my hips and my arms pinned above my head. I never would have expected my towel to weather that kind of rough-housing, but somehow it had stayed more or less in position. That only lasted until I struggled though. The first time I tried to pull my arms free my chest nearly popped free of the towel.

It was probably silly that the imminent threat of nudity was what finally broke through my panic, but that was what did it. I was still scared, but I was now thinking clearly enough to realize that there was no way I was going to get away from Jace.

The sun wasn't setting yet, but it was low enough on the horizon that it cast Jace's chest and abs into stark relief. I'd grown up wrestling my dad and even the occasional neighbor boy until after I turned nine and they couldn't take being defeated by a girl, but that was all years ago and it had never felt like this.

My heart seemed to be skipping every other beat and tendrils of warm energy seemed to be working their way down my arms from my wrists where Jace was holding onto me. I was suddenly aware in ways that I hadn't been before just how big his upper body was. He was so much bigger than me that I'd never had even the slightest chance of throwing him off me even if my towel hadn't been threatening to come off.

The knowledge that I couldn't win combined with the addictive feel of his skin against mine finally calmed me down. It was uncanny the way that he always seemed to know exactly what I was feeling. As soon as I'd calmed down Jace let go of my arms and then he sat back as I reached down and adjusted my towel. There wasn't a ton that I could do while he was still sitting on me, pinning my towel against my body, but I managed to make it so I wasn't in quite such immediate danger of exposing myself.

"Are you finally ready to listen?"

"Do I have a choice?"

"You could put your fingers in your ears and yell at the top of your lungs to drown me out."

I shook my head. "You'd just pull my fingers out of my ears."

"Knowing that you couldn't succeed doesn't always stop you."

I didn't understand how Jace managed to do that. Between one heartbeat and the next he'd changed how I felt. He'd gone from being scary psycho-stalker back to being the guy I'd been so busy falling for.

"Fine, I'll listen. Are you going to let me get up?"

Jace considered the question for several seconds before finally shaking his head. "Sorry, I'd like to, but you might freak out again and I don't think your towel would survive another takedown like that."

That made me blush again, and this time I could feel the heat spreading down to the broad expanse of exposed skin that my towel wasn't up to covering.

"I promise not to run again."

"Sorry, Selene, that ship has sailed. You're going to just have to lie there while I explain things."

My exasperation was strong enough to cut through even the haze his good looks threw over me.

"Fine, please proceed. Explain why you've been following me around for the last few years. Explain why you've been stockpiling underwear for me. What can you possibly say to make it sound like you're not some kind of creep?"

Jace sighed and then took a deep, bracing breath. "I haven't been following you around, and I wasn't stockpiling those clothes. Everything in that box was already yours. You gave it to me a long time ago."

I wanted to laugh in his face, wanted to tell him that he was delusional, but something inside of me refused.

"Do you know how crazy that sounds?"

Jace laughed bitterly. "Considering that this isn't the first time I've had this conversation? Yes, I'm very much aware that it sounds like I'm a lunatic."

"I don't remember meeting you before yesterday, Jace. I might not be the sharpest crayon in the box, but I'm pretty sure I would have remembered meeting you sometime over the last couple of years."

"It didn't happen within the last couple of years. You gave all of that to me a lot longer ago than that."

"That makes even less sense. I was a late bloomer—I wouldn't have even fit into most of those clothes before a couple of years ago."

"I know. You told me that when you gave me the box, told me that if we found you before you turned fifteen I needed to keep my hands off of you until you'd had time to grow up a little more."

I giggled at the thought of *me* of all people telling Jace to keep his hands off of me. The old me would have told any boy to keep his distance, but meeting Jace had changed all of that. In fact, lately I'd had a hard time thinking about anything other than Jace's hands touching me.

There was more than just a touch of hysteria to my giggle, but I figured that could be excused given the circumstances.

"So what are we talking about, time travel?"

"No, not even close."

"What then?"

Jace refused to meet my eyes as if second-guessing the decision to tell me. Part of me was tempted to tell him not to worry. My earlier concerns notwithstanding, I wasn't entirely sure that I was still capable of disbelieving anything he told me.

Talk about scary. I wasn't sure that I would ever be comfortable with that kind of blind adoration, but deep down inside of me something was convinced that Jace would never do anything to hurt me.

"Do you believe in reincarnation?"

"Like people coming back as cows?"

"No, not exactly. More like the idea that some people come back again and again, reborn each time they die."

"I don't know. I guess I never really thought about it. Are you trying to tell me I gave you that box in a past life?"

Jace looked down at me with those gorgeous eyes that I trusted despite everything, and nodded. "That's exactly what I'm saying."

I shook my head, part in disbelief and part in confusion. "That's impossible, Jace. The other version of me would have had to give you that box before I was born. You would have been an infant—you wouldn't be able to remember any of that unless—"

"Unless I'm a lot older than I look."

I licked my lips, unsure if I really wanted to know.

"How much older are we talking exactly?"

"I don't know, not exactly. Can we just leave it at *a lot* and move on? I'm not done blowing your mind and I'd rather not stretch your ability to believe any further than I have to."

"No, I want to know. If you're going to tell me stuff then I want to know it all. How old are you?"

"My best guess is that I was born about five hundred years ago, but it's not much more than a guess, so you should try to avoid getting fixated on that particular number."

I closed my eyes, partially in an attempt to let myself process what he'd said, and partially because I suddenly felt a strong need to protect myself from seeing his face. It was too hard to be skeptical when he was this close to me.

"Okay, let's just say that I believe you for now. You're five hundred years old, give or take a few decades. So what does that mean? Did you find the fountain of youth, or...?"

I trailed off, unable to finish the question. Jace shifted forward, almost as though he wanted to comfort me, but in the end he settled back on my hips without touching my face.

"There is no such thing as the fountain of youth, Selene."

"So you're not human then."

The words were ash in my mouth. It figured that the universe couldn't let me be happy for more than a day or two. I was now faced with the dilemma of trying to decide whether I wanted Jace to be a delusional stalker or if I'd rather be dating outside of my species.

"No, I'm not. I'm something else."

"So what, you ran into me a few decades back, fell in love with that version of me, and then once I died you thought that you'd try to recreate the magic by hunting for me among all of the billions of people in the world?"

Jace cupped the side of my face, not answering until I opened my eyes. "Is that really so hard for you to believe?"

"Well, I did start off by saying that you fell in love with me. Granted, it was previous-life me, but still, that's pretty hard for any rational person to believe..."

Jace opened his mouth to respond, but didn't get a chance to get any words out before Kat's voice drifted up to us.

"I hope you two love birds are decent. Not only do I not want to see that, Ari is here with me now, and I'm not sure we should be corrupting her like that quite yet. Oh, also the burgers seem to be burning…"

Jace swore, looking back and forth between the door and me. "Seriously, Kat couldn't have worse timing."

I gave him my best crooked smile in response and waved for him to go downstairs. "Go ahead. Kat said that you're particular about dinner and I don't want my sister to see us like this. I think that she's on board with keeping all of this a secret from our dad, but there are limits even to what she'd be willing to keep from him. This wouldn't be easy to explain away."

"I owe you an explanation…"

"No, it's fine, Jace. I won't run away. You'll have a chance to explain later. Go take care of the food and tell Kat to stop implanting ideas in Ari's head. I'll stay here and get dressed. You can even lock me in with those fancy locks if that is what it will take for you to feel you're going to get a chance to finish explaining everything."

Jace looked at me, but it wasn't just a look. It was like he'd peeled back the illusion I usually presented to the rest of the world and looked straight into my soul.

"I don't need to lock you up. This time I believe you when you say that you'll hear me out."

"Good, because I really mean it."

Chapter 8

Jace stood and then offered me his hand, which was good because I wasn't sure I could have managed my towel and made it to my feet at the same time.

Jace picked up my clothes and handed them to me with a smile before disappearing into the sitting room. I stood there looking at his door for several seconds before shaking myself and heading back into the bathroom.

I'd almost waited too long to comb out my hair. It always looked better if I combed it out before it had a chance to dry all of the way. I ran my fingers through it a couple of times and was nearly resigned to having a mess once it finished drying when I remembered the toiletry bag that had been in Jace's—my—box.

I bit my lip and debated for a few seconds before finally deciding there wasn't any reason not to use dead-me's stuff. The toiletry bag proved to be a virtual treasure trove. It not only had a comb, it also had a full range of makeup, still in the original packaging, that was perfectly suited to my coloring. Some of it was so far past its expiration date that it wasn't usable, but most of it was actually in pretty good shape.

I snugged my towel back up and then combed my hair out before going back into Jace's closet to pick out the cutest underwear from the offering of nineties options. Once I was dressed again, it only took me another ten minutes to do my makeup and then I put everything back more or less like I'd found it and headed back downstairs.

The neckline on my sweater had tightened back up some while it had been folded up, first in my locker and then on Jace's counter. That was nice because it meant that it didn't ride quite so low on my shoulders. Maybe it was silly to be worried about that considering the fact that Jace had seen a lot more skin than that while I'd been wearing my towel, but somehow it still mattered to me.

I found the others sitting in the solarium behind the kitchen. Jace was cooking again—presumably trying to replace the stuff that got burned while I was freaking out—while Kat and Ari were watching a funny video on Kat's tablet.

Ari took in my wet hair with a suspicious glance. "Where have you been?"

"Sorry, Kat and I ditched school a few minutes before we were supposed to go in for showers, so she said that I could use Jace's shower."

Now it was Kat's turn to give me a suggestive look. "Wow, Selene does it usually take two people to get you showered?"

I wanted to punch her. Instead I managed a sickly sweet smile. "No, actually, it only takes one person to get me through the shower. Once I was done showering I called down for Jace so he could let me into your room—I hope you don't mind that I borrowed some of your makeup, Kat."

I turned to Ari and casually pointed to the kitchen door with its biometric lock. "Has Kat given you the tour yet? It's pretty crazy, they've got those fingerprint locks everywhere, even on their bedrooms and bathrooms."

Apparently my lie held together well enough. I got another raised eyebrow from Kat—apparently she didn't stock makeup in my color—but Ari seemed content to let things drop. I actually felt bad about that. I didn't like lying to Ari.

I tried to salve my conscience by telling myself that nothing had *happened* between Jace and me, but it didn't really seem to be helping. Maybe because I knew how much danger there had been of something happening. Even after thinking that he was some kind of stalker I'd still been ready to jump his bones just a few minutes later.

That was probably a sign that I had some deep, unresolved issues from my childhood, but as hard as I tried to believe that I needed some kind of professional help, I just couldn't quite buy it. Jace's story was crazy, but I couldn't deny the connection I felt to him. Even more than that, it was the first thing that provided a halfway decent explanation for all of the déjà vu I'd been experiencing since I'd met him and Kat.

There was just something about him that made me want to believe him. Besides, I'd known for hours that there was something unusual going on. Between the lost time I'd experienced before school and Kat's worship-me aura, I was pretty primed to believe the unbelievable.

Ari shook her head. "Nope, all I've seen so far is the great room, the kitchen and this area. Just based on what I've seen so far this place has got to be pretty spectacular."

Kat made an 'aw shucks' face and then checked her watch. "I'd give you the grand tour, but I think Jace is almost done with dinner. Let's eat first so that he doesn't yell at us, and then I'll show you the whole place."

Jace flipped the grill back open and prodded the burgers a couple of times before frowning at them. "Yeah, I think these bad boys are done. Sorry, ladies. I'm afraid these are just regular hamburgers rather than the gourmet burgers and steaks that I was planning on offering."

Kat faked a pout. "Now I'm sad. There's nothing quite as disappointing as coming home from a hard day of fighting bullies and finding out that you're going to have to settle for *normal* hamburgers." She looked back at me. "I blame you, you know, Selene. If you hadn't needed to 'put on some makeup' then we could have dined in the fashion to which I've grown accustomed."

Ari shot Kat a look. "Leave it alone, Kat. If Selene says that nothing happened, then nothing happened."

I winced. I appreciated the vote of confidence from Ari—although it did feed my guilt—but the last thing I wanted to do was piss Kat off. I needed her to verify all the crazy stuff Jace apparently still had to tell me.

Luckily, Kat just laughed. "Fair enough, but when the two of them do decide to get all inappropriate don't say that I didn't warn you."

Jace had used the last several seconds to good effect. Not only had he pulled the meat off of the grill, he'd also slapped one of the patties on a bun, along with a host of fixings. He walked over to Kat and shoved the resulting culinary masterpiece into Kat's mouth with an apologetic smile for both Ari and me.

"Sorry, you two. I should warn you that the only way to shut Kat up is to feed her. She claims that I enjoy cooking, but the truth is I've learned out of necessity. It's the only way I've ever been able to get any peace and quiet."

Kat held up a finger while she chewed the bite that Jace had given her, and then sighed. "Everything he's said is a lie, but I'm going to just concentrate on this hamburger so that Jace will continue to cook me good food."

Jace rolled his eyes at her, which caused us all to laugh, and then pointed at the hamburgers. "These are ready for the two of you—do you want me to fix them or do you want to do it yourself?"

Kat paused with her hamburger halfway to her mouth. "Trust me, you want him to do it. Tell him what you want on it, but let him put it together. He always manages to get the ratios just right."

Ari didn't have to be told twice. Jace was still shirtless, so he still looked like some kind of pagan god and I had a suspicion that Ari was more than happy to be waited on by a hot, shirtless, older guy. Although, come to think of it, she might not be quite so eager if she knew how much older he was. Then again, so far it hadn't slowed me down.

I watched as Jace put a massive hamburger together for my baby sister and couldn't help but smile at the way that she just kept having him add toppings. Jace had toppings I'd never even heard of, and seemed perfectly happy to stack them on however high Ari wanted. Yeah, she was definitely enjoying herself.

Once Ari hit the point where Jace told her she was going to have to add in another hamburger patty in order to keep the ratios all right, she finally told him his work was acceptable.

Jace looked at me with his characteristic lopsided smile. "So what about you? Should I start out with two pieces of meat for you so you don't have to limit your toppings?"

I pursed my lips, looked over my shoulder to make sure that Ari was focused on getting everything into her mouth without having it topple onto her lap, and decided to just go for it.

"How many of these have you made for me? Dozens? Hundreds?"

Jace nodded. "Usually I don't have to start over and skip some of the most important steps when it comes to preparing the meat, but yeah. I used to cook for you a lot."

"Then just go ahead and fix it the way that you know I'll like the most."

That earned me another smile. I tried to get close enough to see what all he was putting on there, but he waved me back to my chair. I started to get nervous when it took him so long that Kat was almost finished with hers, but then he brought not one, but two plates over and sat down next to me.

"Here, this one is yours. Go ahead. I want to see the expression on your face when you try it."

I looked at it for a second before obliging him. Some of the ingredients that I hadn't recognized from before had definitely made it onto my hamburger, and there were at least three or four different kinds of mushrooms on it.

"You're sure all of those mushrooms are the non-poisonous varieties?"

"Of course I'm sure—are you going to eat it or not?"

The smile in his voice gave lie to the stern expression he was trying to pull off. I gave him a mock glare and then opened my mouth and took a bite.

It was more than amazing. It tasted better than anything I'd ever eaten before and I suddenly realized that hanging around Jace might be hazardous to my figure. The melody of flavors was unexpected in a couple of places, but it all fit together beautifully. Behind it all was a curiously sweet flavor that was almost like honey, but not quite.

"Oh my gosh, just kill me now. I'll never find anything else this good—life will just be one big disappointment after another from here on out."

Kat was headed back with a plate full of French fries, and Ari snagged one as she walked by and threw it at me. "Melodramatic much?"

"No more than is merited, runt. This seriously is the best hamburger I've ever had. I'm actually afraid to try the version that Jace originally planned on feeding us. I'm going to have a hard enough time going back to our cooking as it is."

Ari shrugged. "You don't have to invite her next time you cook. I'm up for trying whatever you want to feed me. I'm not scared."

"It's a deal, but only if you finish that monster burger you're currently working on."

"Gah, you were a lot sexier when you didn't sound like my dad."

That drew a gasp out of me, but Ari just shrugged. "What? It's not like we aren't all thinking it. Heck, even Kat thinks he's hot. Besides, I'm not the one he's interested in, so it doesn't matter what I say. You on the other hand should keep trying to play hard to get. I hear rich guys like that."

I shook my fist at her. "You do realize that every time you open your mouth you make it harder for *anyone* to like me, right?"

"Whatever. Jace and Kat both love me." She batted her eyes at both of them. "I'm totally that adorable kid sister that people invite along to everything because secretly they like me more than you, but they just don't want to look uncool because they spend all their time hanging out with someone so much younger than them. By the way, what's the plan after this? You know you have to do more than just treat a girl to a nice meal if you want to really turn her head, right?"

Kat shook some extra salt onto her fries and then popped one into her mouth like it was a cigar. "Oh, we've got a little something-something planned."

Chapter 9

A 'little something-something' turned out to be a movie in their home theater. Ari wasn't very excited about that until she found out that they had a pre-release version of some street-racing movie she'd been excited about for months.

In between gushing about how awesome the movie was going to be and needling Kat in an effort to find out how she'd gotten her hands on a movie that wasn't due to be released for more than a month, Ari settled down in one of the overstuffed leather recliners with an extra-large tub of popcorn, two cans of pop, and three candy bars. Apparently the room next to the theater was a fully-stocked concessions booth.

Jace offered to grab something for me when he disappeared to grab himself a glass of water, but I was feeling oddly full after the burger. Kat brought another plate of fries with her, which boggled my mind, but when I asked her why she would eat fries instead of just having another of Jace's burgers she shrugged.

"I'm slumming. You can't just eat only Jace's best stuff or you start to take it for granted. It's all about keeping a proper sense of perspective."

"Right, it has nothing to do with the fact that my fries are world-class, or the fact that I refuse to fix more than one hamburger for you on any given night. You keep telling yourself that."

Jace slid into the chair next to me and put two bottles of water in the cup holders between us. "Just in case you decide later on that you're thirsty."

I leaned in close enough that I'd be able to whisper without Ari overhearing us. "Thanks, but we aren't really going to watch a movie, are we? I thought Kat was going to distract Ari with a tour of the house while you filled me in on everything we started talking about earlier in your room..."

"Yeah, that was the original plan, but you seem pretty worried about not making Ari think anything is happening between the two of us, so we thought maybe it would be best if we kept the two of you together for now."

"Doesn't that kind of make it impossible for the two of us to talk?"

"Just wait—you'll see."

It was cryptic, but I shouldn't have expected anything else from Jace. Still, the promise of a full explanation was enough to make me settle back into my chair as the opening scenes of the movie started playing. We were only five or six minutes into the movie when it happened.

The movie froze between one heartbeat and the next. I started to get up, but Jace grabbed my arm and pulled me back down into my seat. "That was supposed to happen. Just sit back down and try not to make any sudden moves if you see Ari start to look back here."

That made me look down at Ari, which delivered a second shock to my system. "She's not moving! What did you do to her?"

"Actually nothing, everything that's been done was done to you and me."

"That's not an explanation."

"I've changed the passage of time. You and I are still in the same reality as Kat and Ari, but we're experiencing it at about ten percent of normal speed. Ari is moving, she's just moving very slow.

"It's not the best option, it's going to come with a price for me, but it was all I could think of that would let us seem to still be here while also giving us enough time to talk. You're going to want to hold still though because I'm not augmenting your system enough to allow you to really function at this speed."

I started to ask him what he meant, but then it hit me. I was suddenly out of breath and gasping for air. I could feel the air coming in and out of my lungs, but it felt thin, like it wasn't providing me with any oxygen.

Jace reached over and laced his fingers through mine and I finally felt a measure of relief.

"Sorry, setting the effect so that it would let you move at this speed would have dramatically cut down the amount of time I could have maintained it. I amped your systems up enough that you should be able to get enough oxygen to carry on a conversation, but don't expect to be able to do much more than that."

"How is this even possible?"

Jace gave me another lopsided smile. "I'm not human, remember?"

"This is what you did this morning, wasn't it? That's why we were able to talk for so long without me being late for class."

"Yep, that's exactly what happened. It was a lot less expensive of an effect because even though I amped both of our systems up to the point where you could walk around without going into oxygen debt, I only made us function at about four times normal speed. Also, I put us in a cone of silence and manipulated light around us so that you wouldn't be able to see the fact that the parking lot was full of people, all of whom had stopped moving."

I shook my head in amazement. "What about the note? How did Kat do that?"

"Something similar. She waited until those two girls were in mid-handoff and then accelerated herself to something even faster than we're experiencing right now. At that speed she's basically invisible to anyone who is still moving and thinking at normal speed. She grabbed the note, ran off to an empty room, and practiced forging Sandra's handwriting until she had something good enough to convince everyone else that Sandra had written it."

I let out a low whistle. "After which she came back to our class, swapped the notes and then let time speed back up to normal."

"Yeah, that's the basics of what happened, along with some telekinesis to make sure that the note landed in her hand like she wanted it to."

"When did she tell you about all of this?"

"As soon as she finished up her shower. She buzzed down to the kitchen and then we both jumped to ten times normal speed while she explained it all."

"I think my brain is starting to hurt. How do you keep track of when you're talking to someone whether or not you sped time up or slowed it down?"

Jace hadn't ever released my hand, which should have been incredibly distracting, but I'd been so busy fighting for air when he'd first grabbed my hand that I'd missed the normal flush of excitement. Now my system had mostly adjusted to the feel of his skin on mine. It meant that I could enjoy the feeling without being overwhelmed by it.

He gave me a gentle squeeze. "Don't worry about it. You learned all of this before now, which means that you're fully capable of getting up to speed on it all again."

"Pun intended?"

"Yeah, pun intended."

"Okay, I'll stop worrying about my brain coming out of my ears."

Jace looked down at Ari and Kat as though checking something and then turned back to me. "In answer to your question, the proper way to discuss it is to say that we slowed down time, or that we sped ourselves up, but for all practical intents it doesn't really matter because it only works going in one direction. We can slow time down, but we can't speed it up."

"So you just throw out a number like ten times or a hundred times and everyone in the know understands that you're speeding yourselves up to that level."

"Yep, exactly."

"Wow, that must be amazing."

"Yeah, it's a major perk, but it's not without a price, Selene, none of what we do is."

"What do you mean?"

Jace ran his fingers through his hair and then sighed. "What do you know about mythology?"

"What do you mean? Greek? Norse?"

That won me a chuckle. "Just the fact that you know there are multiple kinds of mythology puts you way ahead of most kids these days. You could have added Egyptian, Sumerian, Mayan, and Aztec mythology to your list if you'd wanted to, but that still wouldn't have been enough to really be comprehensive."

"So which pantheon are we talking about?"

"All of them and none of them all at once."

I rolled my eyes at him. "Well, that's helpful."

"Sorry, I think I'm still waiting for you to freak out and try to run away again."

That drew a sigh out of me. "I'm sorry I ran away, but you have to be able to see how freaky all of this is. Go ahead and do your worst, I'm prepared to suspend my disbelief—at least temporarily."

"Okay, the basic truth comes down to this. All of the myths from all of the different cultures are true. Not exactly of course, there are some things that they got wrong, but those people all really existed. Zeus, Mars, Thor, Freya—they were all real beings and they did most of the things that the stories say they did."

"Wait, you're telling me that you're a *god*?"

My voice got so shrill that I expected Jace to shush me, but apparently he had that angle covered too. Ari didn't even budge.

"No, I'm not a god. I'm just part of a group of beings that ancient civilizations believed were gods."

"It sounds like the same thing to me."

The sarcasm dripping off of my voice was probably not the smartest thing considering that I'd just learned that Jace was capable of vaporizing me with a thought, but my tone didn't seem to bother him.

"There's a big difference. People who believe they are actual gods tend to become unhinged over the long run. We already have an unhealthy amount of power, the last thing Kat or I need is to have that going to our heads as well."

That made sense, and ironically the fact that Jace had told me he was only five hundred years old was now a source of comfort rather than being the craziest thing I'd heard yet.

"Okay, so you have all of the powers one would expect out of a god—lightning, pestilence, plagues, that kind of stuff—but you're young as far as gods go, so you weren't around during the fall of Troy or anything…"

Jace gave me a hesitant smile. "Maybe it would just be best if I started at the beginning and worked from there."

"What, like the Garden of Eden?"

"No, the beginning of the explanation that I originally planned on giving you."

I successfully resisted the urge to stick my tongue out at him, but it was hard. "Fine, go ahead, but where do you stand on the whole Garden of Eden thing?"

That question earned me a glare, so I put my free hand up in a gesture of surrender. "Sorry, please proceed, your holiness."

"I'm not the Pope, Selene. You can just call me Jace."

"Yes, your holy Jaceness."

"Now I know you're yanking my chain."

"Of course I am. I expected you to realize that a while ago, based on the fact that you seem to be able to read my mind—wait, can you actually read minds?"

Jace looked like he wanted to put his head in his hands and pretend like he couldn't hear me. Maybe that should have been terrifying, but it actually finished putting me at ease. Apparently I was wired so that I couldn't be scared of someone that I successfully teased without getting vaporized.

"No, we can't read minds. May I proceed?"

"Sure, by all means, oh omnipotent one."

"Fine. So as we've already discussed, those like me are capable of a number of different things that modern science doesn't have any explanation for. Thousands of years ago we used those...powers, for lack of a better term, to set ourselves up as gods to a variety of early societies, but by and large we were anything but godly. Reading about ancient mythology, especially Greek mythology, is uncomfortably close to watching daytime soaps."

"Right people cheating on each other, stabbing each other in the back, dying and then coming back to life after a cheery visit to the underworld. I know, I took the class."

"Yeah, basically, people are jerks and when you give them extra power it just turns them into bigger jerks. That would have been bad enough all by itself, but there is a price for all of the feats we're capable of. Using our power causes a kind of permanent amnesia. The bigger and more spectacular the effect we unleash the more of our memory we lose."

It took me a couple of seconds to process the implications of what he was saying. "Wow, that's terrible. I always thought the Greek myths tended to focus on the most erratic of the gods because that was where all of the stories were, but that wasn't it at all, was it?"

"Nope, the flashiest of the Greek pantheon were so erratic precisely because they tended to walk around with huge chunks of their memories missing. They were the ones who got the most involved with human affairs, sometimes because they wanted worshipers, sometimes because they were legitimately trying to help, but the result was always the same. Eventually they became so disoriented that someone manipulated them into acting against their own best interests."

I opened my mouth to ask how that was even possible and then really thought about what he'd said. I couldn't think of many worse fates than trying to help those around you, but being forced to trade away your memories in the process. I'd always thought that we were mostly a result of our experiences. Jace's theories on reincarnation—combined with how well he knew me—seemed to at least partially invalidate that world view, but even so it would still basically be like trading your soul away every time you used your power.

Then, after all of that, having someone trick you into doing other, probably terrible, things would be even worse. Eventually you wouldn't even be able to remember who your enemies were. All someone would have to do was be nice to you for a few days and you'd be willing to do practically anything for them.

"That's terrible."

"Yeah, it's even worse than you realize. Since it's a combination of strong emotions and memories that fuel us, as we lose more and more of our memories we become weaker and weaker until we're basically no different than normal humans."

"So the gods who don't actually use their powers are the ones who end up being the strongest?"

"Yeah, only like I said, most of us don't call ourselves gods anymore. Other than a small group of psychopaths, we mostly prefer the term Awakened."

"So the more an Awakened uses their powers the weaker they get, but if they can avoid burning up memories they eventually end up more and more powerful?"

"Yeah, we all have eidetic memories, so if we don't use our powers we'd never forget anything."

"Wait, you mean that there might actually be Awakened whose memories stretch back thousands, or even tens of thousands of years?

"In theory, yes. There is a pretty persistent set of legends among our people about Awakened who have resisted using their abilities and therefore have been able to watch history play out over thousands of years.

"The reality is that being one of the Awakened is a pretty dangerous gig. Not only do you have to worry about other Awakened, other pantheons if indeed you're part of a pantheon, you also have to worry about humans trying to use you for their own ends. And through it all you're fighting a constant low-level temptation to use your powers in a hundred little ways to make your life easier or better."

It should have been obvious to me at the start of the conversation, but it only hit me just then. "Oh, no, Jace. You're losing memories right now! Kat too. Because of me you've both lost experiences that you wanted to remember. Stop the time thingy. Put us back to normal speed right now. I believe you—every word. Put time back and we'll talk later when you don't have to use your powers."

I tried to get to my feet, but Jace pulled at my hand to stop me.

"Stay sitting, Selene. You'll go into oxygen debt if you keep this up and then I'll have to amp your system up again. That's going to use up more of my memories than letting the rest of the time effect run its course."

I stopped resisting him immediately. "That's fighting dirty. You've backed me into a corner. If I let you continue to play with time it will cost you, but if I do anything but just sit here and listen *that* will cost you too."

"Welcome to my world. The costs of doing what we want are always unpleasant—it's just a matter of deciding what price we're willing to live with."

There was a double helping of unhappiness in his voice right now, but I wasn't sure what to do or say.

"I'm sorry, I didn't mean to touch a nerve there. I just didn't want you to have to give up bits and pieces of your life when it isn't necessary."

Jace managed a smile for me. "No, you're okay. It's just that after a couple hundred years this can get a little tiring."

"I guess there is a lot more that got left out of the mythologies than most people realize."

"Yeah, like seeing someone you care about slowly melt away right in front of your eyes over the course of just a few days or weeks, until what is left walks and talks like them, but doesn't even remember your name."

"That's terrible."

"Yeah, but most Awakened don't agree because someone like that at least got the full use of their memories. Most Awakened think that the worst way to go is to simply be killed. If that happens then you die with a bunch of memories that you never got to accomplish anything with. 'The great waste of untapped potential' is what one of my fellows called it."

"So you can be killed?"

"Yeah, after a manner."

"What does that mean?"

Jace sighed heavily and I suddenly got the feeling that this was what we'd been circling around for hours now. This was the thing that he was the most worried about freaking me out. "It means that if you cut our heads off or shoot us with a gun our hearts stop beating and what you're left with is only good for burying."

"That sounds pretty dead to me."

"Yeah, but we don't stay dead. Within nine months of our death we are reborn into new bodies. We start off as infants indistinguishable from any other human child, but as we grow, our appearances gradually change. Eventually—often by the time we hit our mid-teens—we look exactly the same as we did before we were killed.

"We think the same way, talk the same way, act the same way. We are the same person, just without all of the memories we had before we died."

I wanted to run away, but I couldn't. Jace had locked me inside of a strange alternate world where running would just result in me suffocating. I looked up at Jace with tears in my eyes and saw the answer to my question even before I asked it.

"But that would mean..."

"I'm sorry to break it to you like this, Selene, but you are an Awakened just like Kat and me."

Chapter 10

Saying it was a shock would have been the understatement of the year. I'd thought I was ready for anything Jace could throw at me. I'd been ready to hear any crazy thing about him or Kat, but I hadn't been ready to have him tell me that I wasn't just another normal teenage girl.

I should have seen it coming. The very first thing he'd told me was that I was the reincarnation of someone else, that he'd known me a long time ago, but somehow that had been overshadowed by everything else. I'd started to assume that this was just going to be some kind of epic love story that included a hot blond god who had spent the last couple of decades looking for me.

That was closer to the truth than I'd realized, but he hadn't just been looking for me. Jace had been looking for a goddess who was ready to join him in this insanely dangerous world where he lived and fought. I suddenly wasn't so sure that all the money in the world was worth the kind of existence he'd described to me.

Only seconds had passed since he'd told me who—what—I was. My heart was racing and I was having a hard time breathing, but that somehow paled in significance to the fact that Jace still had ahold of my hand, that he was clinging to me with the desperate strength of someone who was worried I was going to hurt myself.

"...need to calm down, Selene. If you keep this up you'll pass out, but even that might not be enough to bring you back out from being in a state of oxygen debt. I'll let the time effect lapse if you can convince me that you're not going to freak out and alarm Ari, but you have to get control of yourself first or I'll just let you pass out and tell Ari that you fell asleep."

I wasn't okay, not really, but I was mentally present enough to understand what he was saying and want to respond. The only problem was that I couldn't get anything out around the deep gasps as my body tried to get the too-thin air into my lungs where it could stop me from passing out.

I collapsed back into my chair in the hopes that would convince Jace that I understood him, but I wasn't entirely sure that my collapse was voluntary. The drop down to the leather upholstery seemed to take forever, and by the time my butt finally hit the chair, the sound of my pulse in my ears was so loud that I couldn't hear Jace anymore.

I tried to smile and nod around the near convulsions of my breathing, but I couldn't tell for sure he got the message until I felt the air start to thicken up.

The sound of my gasps brought Ari around with a concerned look on her face "What the heck happened, Selene?"

"She just swallowed her drink funny and is coughing up the water. Don't worry, I'm watching to make sure that her lips don't turn blue."

Jace held up one of the bottles of water as though to underscore the story he'd just fed Ari, but I didn't expect it to work. My gasps didn't sound very much like coughing, but apparently Ari was more worried about not missing the movie than she was about anything else.

"Okay, let me know if you need me to come hold her down while you give her mouth-to-mouth."

Jace had continued to hold onto my hand, and I could feel him doing something, feel tingly energy feeding into my hand. Whatever it was helped, but ironically the first sign that I wasn't going to die was the strong urge I had to strangle Ari. I was pretty sure she was just trying to break the ice, but it was having the opposite effect. At this rate he was never going to invite me back.

Only he didn't have any choice because I was his long-lost Awakened love...who didn't have a single memory of him, but who couldn't deny the bond we seemed to share.

"No need for mouth to mouth here, but if Jace or Kat feels the need to lock you in their dungeon I'm totally not going to tell the cops where you are when Dad reports you as missing."

I was still gasping as I forced the words out, but I got them out despite that.

Ari looked back at me and rolled her eyes. "Whatever, they don't have a dungeon."

I stuck my tongue out at her. "How would you know? You haven't got the full tour yet."

"Even if you're right I'd take their dungeon over sharing a room with you any day of the week. Based on the rest of this place, their dungeon has cable and a day spa."

Kat snapped her fingers. "A day spa! I knew we were forgetting something. Jace, can you please call the contractor first thing tomorrow and ask them to put a day spa in downstairs? I would hate to miss out on our chance to be on the cover of *Better Homes and Dungeons*..."

"Sure thing. The balance in your trust fund has been getting a little too big and it's past time you started pulling your weight around here."

"Hold on. A deal is a deal. You are supposed to pay for all of the boring stuff like cars and houses so that I have enough liquid capital to pay for the necessities of life—you know, shoes and motorcycles."

Ari shushed them both. "You're ruining the movie and I'm pretty sure that the main character is about to jump over two semi-trucks in his Ferrari before bailing out at the last second to hitch a ride on a helicopter."

Kat reached for the TV remote. "Well, that's that. Ari has figured out the ending of the movie—there's no point finishing it now."

"If you touch the stop button I'm going to tickle you mercilessly the next time I'm riding behind you on your bike."

"What makes you think she's going to ever give you a ride again, runt?"

"Because I'm adorable and people can never get enough of me. Besides, she promised to take me camping tomorrow night."

"You don't even like camping, Ari."

"No, I don't like *camping*. This is camping with a motorhome and jet skis."

Kat gave me a repentant look. "Sorry, Selene, I did kind of promise to take her out to the lake tomorrow night."

"Ari, you know that there's no way Dad is going to agree to that..."

"He might if you agree to come too."

"Really, you think he's going to be okay with the two of us heading off into the wilderness with Kat, Jace and no adults? I don't know what bizarro world you're living in, but it's not going to happen."

"So leave Jace behind. There's a chance that he'll agree to it if it's just us girls."

"Ari Jane Jenkins. That is incredibly rude even for you. Do you really think it's right to tell Jace he can't go to the lake and use his own things?"

Kat was making a time-out signal. "Hold on everybody. What if the three of us go to the lake and camp overnight in the trailer, and then Jace can meet up with us the next morning? Do you think your dad will agree to that?"

"Yes—"

"No—"

Ari gave me a dirty look. "Why do you have to be such a negative nelly?"

"Why do you have to be such a brat?"

Jace grabbed the second bottle of water and tossed it to Ari. "You're missing your show. You watch; Kat and I will see what we can do to talk some sense into Selene. You want us to bring you anything back?"

"Yeah, only like a dozen candy bars."

"You're never going to make it through a dozen candy bars before the movie ends, runt."

"Fine. Jace, please get me one candy bar to eat during the remainder of the movie and eleven for the road."

"Roger that, oh tiniest member of the Jenkins clan."

By that point I was spoiling for a fight. I took a step towards Ari, but Jace casually wrapped his arm around my waist and picked me up. With anyone else I wouldn't have let them get away with that, but Jace still hadn't found time to put a shirt back on, and as soon as I touched his bare skin I practically swooned.

I didn't come back to myself until we were outside of the theater and he set me down. "Are you ever not going to be able to shut me up just by touching me?"

Kat shook her head. "No. It's actually pretty sickening. The two of you are practically made for each other. Even after decades together you were still all sugary sweet. In fact you only ever fought about...well, that is to say there was only ever one thing that made the two of you fight."

"Do I get to know what that one thing was?"

Kat shrugged. "Not if I have anything to say about it, but Jace will end up telling you sooner or later despite all of my advice to the contrary. He's just that much of a goody-goody. By the way, you're handling all of this much better than I expected...unless Jace hasn't told you anything other than the whole reincarnation bit yet."

"So the reincarnation stuff is the truth? And the whole Awakened demigods bit who trade their memories in order to vaporize people? That's true too I take it?"

"Yes, but the proper term is smiting. Vaporizing just sounds too New Age and techy. We don't vaporize our unrighteous followers, we smite them."

"And am I really, I mean…"

"You mean are you a little embryonic goddess fully capable of realizing the normal smiting powers gifted to our pseudo-omniscient badass selves?"

"Yeah, all of that."

"Yep, that's true too, which is why we need you to go along with this trip out to the lake, Selene. You've got all of the potential, but none of the practical skills required to keep yourself alive. Ari is acting all cool when it comes to you and Jace—well, mostly cool—but she's not. She's watching the two of you like a hawk and she'd like nothing better than to rat you out to your dad."

I literally saw red for a second, but Kat grabbed hold of my arm with more strength than anyone her size should have been able to muster.

"I'm going to slap her into next week."

Kat shot Jace, who was laughing, a dirty look and then waved her finger at me.

"You're going to do no such thing. Right now she doesn't know that we're onto her and she not only trusts me, she's all wrapped up in fantasies about Jace. That's about as good as things are going to get for us, but it means that we need valid reasons for the two of you to be together, preferably where she can see you both, but while she is distracted by something fast and shiny. This trip is perfect for that."

Jace nodded. "You're right, I should have seen it already. You can keep Ari busy on the jet skis while the two of us sit back at the beach and train. It won't work once we get into the more advanced stuff, but it will at least let us get started."

"Right, especially if you speed yourselves up to double or triple time. I'll keep her at the far end of the lake so she can't register the occasional flicker, and you'll be able to get the better part of a full day's worth of training in."

I held up a hand. "No, I don't want Jace using his abilities. He—both of you really—have already sacrificed too much for me."

Kat gave Jace an exasperated look. "You overplayed the 'these miracles come at a price' card, didn't you?"

"I'm not going to let her go into this blind to the realities of how our gifts work."

With someone else I might have thought they were pissed, but something told me that Kat was just trying to make a point. Of course, if I knew that even after dying and being reborn, then there was a very good chance that Jace knew it too.

"Look, Jace, I get it. You don't want to see the same thing that happened to Kyle happen to Selene. It's understandable, but the only way we avoid using our powers is if we're dead. She's going to have to use and that's the end of it."

I looked back and forth between the two of them and suddenly I wasn't so sure that it was all just for dramatic effect. Kat's face was all flushed and she'd stepped well into Jace's personal space.

Jace still looked calm, but he'd developed a tic above the right side of his mouth. I could feel tendrils of energy reaching out from both of them, but this wasn't the warm, friendly energy I'd come to associate with Jace, it was cold and prickly.

"Hey, who's Kyle?"

"Yeah, Jace, who's Kyle? Are you ready to tell her that yet, or is that another card you were planning on playing close to your vest until it's too late?"

"Don't push me, Kat."

"Somebody needs to push you or all three of us are going to end up dead, Jace, and you know it. This isn't the seventeen hundreds anymore. Kids these days end up with hundreds of their pictures on the internet before they make it out of high school. Even if they don't have a social media account of their own they'll still end up in a picture posted on their friend's account."

"I understand all of that, Kat."

"Do you, Jace? It was sheer dumb luck that none of the others thought to hire a team of programmers to try and hunt her down. Hell, for all we know one of the other pantheons is looking for her already. If so, the mimic effect will slow them down a little, but it's still only a matter of time before they work through the other potentials and arrive here."

"I get it, Kat, now shut your mouth."

"Really? Or what, you'll continue to act like a spineless piece of crap? You need to get it together, because we both know a group like the Chicago pantheon isn't going to just stroll into town and watch her for a little while in an effort to decide whether or not she's one of us. They'll just start killing any girls who match her description and worry about the fallout later. This is our last chance, Jace, if we can't save her now they'll farm her. Every fifteen or sixteen years they'll go through and wipe out every female on the planet who looks like her, and she'll come to a tragic end again and again without ever knowing why."

Jace's expression turned dark, and he raised his hand almost as though intending on hitting Kat. "You're going to scare her."

"Good. I'm terrified. She should at least be scared. Nearly every single scenario we're up against results in all three of us dead or wiped before Christmas."

I knew it was a futile gesture, but I couldn't stop myself.

I turned and ran.

Chapter 11

I only made it to the kitchen before Kat suddenly materialized in front of me, her back against the garage door.

"It wouldn't have worked, Selene. The locks still don't have you down as an authorized thumb print."

I laughed. It came out bitter and with a touch of hysteria, but that wasn't entirely surprising. "Honestly, I never expected to make it even this far."

"Why'd you run then?"

"Because apparently it's all I know how to do. I can't fight back, can't even see the threats coming, all I can do is just run away and hope that will be enough to keep me alive for another day."

Kat winced. "I'm sorry about that. I shouldn't have sprung so much on you so quickly. Jace just made me so mad. He promised he was going to tell you everything, that we weren't going to let another day go by without starting to prepare you for what's coming."

"No, you're right, I needed to know. I'm off with my heads in the clouds, wrapped up in little schoolgirl fantasies while people I don't even remember meeting are hoping to find and kill me before I get old enough to figure out that I'm even more of a freak than I always thought I was."

Kat grabbed my arm and pulled me towards the solarium. "Come on, I need some air and you need some distance from all of this."

"Is it safe? I mean, out there where people are hunting me?"

"Honestly? No, but right now there isn't really any safe place for any of us. It's as safe as anywhere else, and that will just have to be enough for both of us."

I followed her out into the cool night air and immediately started shivering. I'd hoped that she was going to close up the solarium and turn on a heater, but she didn't even slow as she led me out into the darkness.

"How far are we going? I don't even have any shoes on."

"Me neither, princess. Don't worry though, we're almost there."

'There' turned out to be a heated reflecting pool that was surrounded by rose bushes and a few small solar-powered lights. It was late enough in the year that the rose bushes were all bare, but in the pale moonlight there was still a haunting elegance to the scene.

"Wow, this place is amazing."

"Yeah, I'll let you in on a little secret—this place is my absolute favorite spot here. It gets better though. Roll your pants up and put your feet in the water."

"No way, I'm already cold enough as it is."

"Do it, you wuss."

I sighed, but I did it. That was the crazy thing about Kat, it was rare that she couldn't get me to do exactly what she wanted me to. The water wasn't just warm, it was hot enough that I kept thinking it should be steaming.

"This is actually new. We had something like this a couple of houses ago and I've had the same kind of thing put in all of our places since. The details change, but there is just something about sitting in the cold with your feet in a warm pool that relaxes me."

I just nodded. The feeling of all my stress melting out through the soles of my feet was just too perfect to spoil it by talking if I didn't have to.

"Okay, now hold still and don't freak out."

"What do you—?"

Between one heartbeat and the next the water turned hard. Not like a rock exactly because there weren't any sharp edges, more like mud that had dried and become unyielding.

Given my current company, there wasn't any way to know for sure what had just happened, but I had a pretty good guess.

"You just sped us up."

"Yep, somewhere around fifteen times normal speed, which should mean that we have plenty of time to talk while Jace keeps Ari distracted. That's the new plan, by the way. Sorry, it's going to suck for both of you, but you and he are going to be spending a lot less time together for a while. That's actually what I was about to suggest right before he and I got into our big shouting match. Ari isn't going to rat you out to your dad if she's the one who's spending the most time with Jace."

My objections were piling up faster than I could get them out. "No, Kat. First of all, slow us back down to normal speed. I don't want either of you burning up your memories for me. Second of all, even apart from how I feel about Jace, I don't want him playing with Ari's emotions. It would be cruel for him to get her hopes up and then dash them."

Kat gave me a tired look, and I wondered just how long her day had been. My time sense was all kinds of screwed up, but I was reasonably sure that it was past eleven. That was a long day for just about anyone, but she'd been adding to it every time she sped herself up. An hour when she'd forged the note from Sandra, a few minutes when she'd jetted downstairs after her shower to talk to Jace, at some point it added up to a twenty-four-hour stretch without any sleep.

"Jace is right to warn you about the dangers of over using your gift, but the kind of low-level stuff we've been doing for you lately doesn't burn peak memories, it just burns the routine background stuff."

"What do you mean by peak memories?"

"A peak memory could be a first kiss, or bungee-jumping, or drag-racing down Main Street. A peak memory is any time you were feeling especially high or exceptionally low. It's the kind of stuff that most people spend their lives subconsciously chasing, but allow themselves to get so tied down with a job and mundane tasks that they only rarely find. You've been gathering a lot of peak memories over the last two days."

I started to agree and then one of the pieces clicked into place for me. "The drive over to pick up Ari in the Viper—you were purposefully trying to scare me."

"Scare you, no. Create a peak memory, yes."

"How come?"

"Because that's part of what a pantheon does. We help each other create peak memories because that's the bank we draw on when things get really rough and we have to do something major with our abilities. Your power hasn't manifested yet, so you don't have a photographic memory right now, but when it does you'll be that much further ahead because you've been living it up over the last two days."

"The food was part of that too, wasn't it?"

"Smart girl! Yep, the food was definitely designed to be a peak memory that you could burn if it came to that. It helps that Jace really is a good cook, but there was more to that burger than you realized."

"Oh, no. You guys put a drug into it, didn't you?"

I got another eye roll. I shouldn't have been able to see that well in the darkness, but I could. Maybe it was a side effect of being an Awakened, a benefit that came even before my ability fully manifested itself.

"No, we didn't drug you—at least not in the conventional sense. You've heard of ambrosia?"

"The food of the gods?"

"Yeah, that's the stuff. You just had your first taste of ambrosia. It was invented by the Greek pantheon before they were destroyed by the Roman pantheon. It was part of their advantage for a while there. Back then you couldn't go skydiving or bungee-jumping, so mostly the gods had to look for other more dangerous ways to build peak memories. You've heard of the running of the bulls?"

"Wait, that was started by you—by us—too?"

"Yep. Of course it isn't much of a challenge if you can speed yourself up, but I don't think the pantheon that started it had figured out how to bend time. The Awakened who did it later on all swore that they wouldn't use their abilities so as to still create the kind of adrenaline rush they needed."

Kat reached down and put her palm flat on the water, pushing against the warm, perfectly smooth surface.

"Did you know that it's actually possible to run across water if you bend time far enough? Of course if you're moving that fast nobody can see you do it, but it is possible. Anyway, ambrosia was the Greeks' secret weapon because it let them build a store of peak memories without having to put themselves in jeopardy."

It was almost physically painful to ask the question, but it needed to be asked. "Is that why Jace has been the way he's been—you know, touching me and making me feel all melty inside?"

"Melty?"

"Yeah, you know, weak knees, racing heart, a sudden desire to start taking clothes off."

"Ah, melty. I'll have to remember that. Can I quote you?"

"Not to Jace or anyone you think might eventually talk to him."

Kat pouted. "You really suck all of the fun out of life."

"Is that a new development?"

"No, you've always been a fun-sucker. Who knows what it is that the two of us see in you."

Kat studied the palm-shaped imprint that was slowly forming on the top of the pond and then sighed. "No, Jace isn't consciously trying to generate peak memories in you, he's just having a hard time keeping his hands off of you. It's always like this when the two of you are together...unless there are other considerations."

I felt a little thrill of warmth shoot up my center. I already had evidence that Jace liked me, but I still craved reassurance where he was concerned. Craved it the way I craved air.

"Well, you've given me a lot to think about."

"I hope so. It really is important that we get you started training right away. I know you're not comfortable with us bending time to speed the process up, but given that we have perfect memories when we aren't using them to fuel our powers, it really ends up just making us a little more human."

"Meaning it's just like what happens to us—I mean, humans—as they age. They forget the mundane stuff and only remember the high points."

"Yeah, except that humans forget the high points too—it's just part of having a porous mind."

"Does it bother you?"

"Honestly? Most of the time I just accept it as a natural part of life. The past just kind of evaporates and drifts away. Sometimes I can remember back a hundred years, sometimes I can remember back a hundred and twenty. When things get really bad I might only remember eighty years. Individually the memories I give up really don't matter much. It's just boring crap like going to the post office or having coffee with someone while we are both lost inside our own heads."

"But in the aggregate?"

"In the aggregate those stupid, unimportant memories are a big chunk of what defines me as a person. More than that, they are what define the people I've lost. You're here with me now, but I still remember what you used to be like twenty years ago before you were killed. So full of life, so in control, the best friend a girl could ever ask for. I worry that this time you'll turn out differently, and then when I've lost all of the old memories of you, you'll really be dead, permanently dead, but I won't even remember enough to mourn you."

"Do you wonder what else you've lost, things that happened four hundred years ago, things that might have been life-changing at the time?"

"Every damn day."

That nearly succeeded in killing the conversation. We sat there in silence for several seconds, but in the end my knowledge of what it was costing Kat to keep us out of sync with the rest of the world compelled me to ask my questions and get as much benefit as possible out of her sacrifice.

"So what's the deal with the Chicago...was it pantheon?"

"Yeah, pantheon—the proper name for a related group of gods."

"Related like family, like you and Jace?"

Kat's laugh had an edge to it that could have etched steel. "Jace and I aren't actually related. It's incredibly rare for two Awakened to be born to the same family, and even when it does happen, there is a certain amount of debate as to what it really means.

"None of us remember all of the way back to when we were all created, so all it means for two Awakened to be born into the same family is that they start out with a chunk of similar DNA—most of which disappears when they hit puberty and they undergo a more accelerated change back to what they were before they died."

Kat pulled her hand away from the surface of the pond and waited as the water slowly filled back in the impression she'd left there.

"By the time the two of them turn eighteen all they have left in common is some memories of growing up in the same house together, which sounds all warm and fuzzy, but you're a bright girl—you've got a pretty good idea by now just how little value memories have for people like us."

I swallowed, unnerved by the bleak picture she'd painted, but I forced my question out anyway. "You said it's rare, but what does that mean? How many Awakened siblings do you know about?"

I think a tiny part of me must have been hoping that Ari would turn out to be an Awakened too. I was already terrified of the things that were going to happen to me, but it would have seemed less scary if I'd known that I was going to be facing it together with Ari rather than just with Kat and Jace.

That hope died when Kat finally responded. "I only know of one time that it's ever happened, Selene, and being siblings has brought those two nothing but grief and heartache."

Something tore inside of me, and tears started to pool in my eyes as my body began shaking. Ari and I had our share of arguments, but Kat was saying that I was going to have to watch her grow old and die while I remained seventeen until another Awakened caught up with me and managed to put me down.

As hard as it was to think of Ari growing old and dying, it was even harder to think of my dad dying. By the time you're eight or nine you understand intellectually that you're going to outlast your parents, but that doesn't mean that you understand it on an emotional level. That understanding hit me like a wrecking ball and I felt myself start to come apart at the edges.

Kat reached over and put her hand on my knee, somehow calming me with just a touch before I could get worked up enough to go into oxygen debt and start hyperventilating. I would have thrown myself against her shoulder, but my feet were still encased inside of almost a foot of cement-like water.

"How do you stand it, Kat? You must both feel so alone. Everyone you meet comes with a built-in expiration date."

"It's not as bad as that. Don't get me wrong, it's tough. Any kind of relationship between an Awakened and a normal human is generally only good for a few years. After that they start noticing that you aren't aging and things get tricky. Occasionally you run into someone who can handle knowing what you are, and when that happens you can spend decades as friends or even lovers, but eventually they either die or grow to resent the fact that you're still young and beautiful while they've become old and decrepit."

"You're right, that doesn't sound so bad."

Kat just smiled at my tone. "Just because a relationship has an expiration date on it doesn't mean that it can't be fun while it lasts, but you're right, if that was all there was to it, there wouldn't be enough to keep me going. In the end it's our pantheons that keep us relatively sane.

"That's what Jace and I are. We're not family in the sense of sharing blood, but we're closer than most human families ever have a chance to be. Before you died, you were part of our pantheon too."

"So what, a pantheon is just a family that isn't going to die from old age, a family that will maybe even last as long as you do?"

"That's part of it, but it's a lot more than that. For as long as humans have been able to communicate they've realized that forming into groups makes them more powerful than they could ever be individually. We aren't any different in that regard. If one Awakened is powerful, then two Awakened are twice as good. A pantheon provides a measure of protection and safety. Even if sometimes you hate each other, you still know that your group has your back if an outsider shows up and tries to take you all down.

"It's more even than that though. A pantheon functions a lot like a miniature research group. In theory, if we are in the grip of a strong enough emotion, and are willing to burn up enough of our memories, there isn't much that we couldn't accomplish, but it doesn't really work like that."

Now she was messing with the vision I'd started crafting of nearly omnipotent beings who had nothing to fear but each other.

"What do you mean?"

"The reality is that a lot of what we do is knowledge-based. If your power manifested this instant and someone was trying to kill you, you could probably bend time, but you wouldn't be very good at it. You might only get up to two or three times normal speed, you wouldn't know to amp your body up to where it could function at those speeds, and you would have to burn peak memories to do it rather than just the base memories that Jace or I use to power such a minor effect."

"So the more I know, the more efficient I can be with regards to burning my memories."

"Right, and the more power you'll ultimately have access to. Not everyone has the right mindset for research, so most pantheons only have one or two researchers, but they make a huge difference because the things they teach their members can easily make the difference between life and death."

"Wow, that's a pretty hefty responsibility. Anything else?"

"Yeah, pantheons tend to serve as a kind of grounding point for their members. Memories tend to make up a big chunk of who we are, but how our peers react to us also helps to make up our self-image, and that can be incredibly valuable if you've just lost a big chunk of memories and are adrift in the world. Sometimes a member of a given pantheon will be caught separate from the group and be forced to burn nearly everything they have in order to get free.

"Having a pantheon means that when you get back you'll have people around to help you find your way back to being the person you were before you lost your identity. The pantheon's home base also serves as a safe place for an Awakened to store journals that can be used to at least partially piece themselves back together."

"That's what you're trying to do for me."

"Yeah."

"And the leather books in Jace's bedroom are his journals, the records he uses to try to keep himself from drifting into becoming someone else."

"Right again."

The memory of the leather book contained in the box I'd given Jace before I'd died last time seemed seared into my mind. It had seemed so innocuous nestled there in between my old jeans and shirts, but now I knew it for what it was.

A message from my past self, a message from the person Jace and Kat wanted me to become.

Chapter 12

The conversation between Kat and I didn't go much of anywhere after that, so a few minutes later she let the time effect lapse and we headed back into the house.

It shocked me how cold it was once we were back to normal speed. Kat tried to explain it to me through chattering teeth as we walked, but I wasn't sure I really understood. It was something about our temporarily-faster-moving blood drawing heat up into our bodies from the pool at a faster rate than the cold air could suck it away, which kind of made sense, but by that point my mind was getting so stretched and stressed that I just tried to nod in all of the right places.

We made it back into the house as the movie was ending. I expected Ari to ask me where I'd been, but she was so over the moon about having had Jace all to herself that she barely seemed to have noticed that Kat and I had been missing.

REBORN

Before we left, Jace took Ari and me back to the security room and scanned our fingers so that we would be able to get in and out of the house on our own. I thought Ari was going to start hyperventilating, which turned out to be a good thing because it meant that she didn't notice that Jace gave the two of us different levels of access.

Ari was going to be able to get into zone one, which consisted of the kitchen, great room, guest bedrooms and exercise facilities, but not the master bedrooms or garage. I on the other hand was assigned full access to the entire house.

The sheer amount of trust involved in that gesture would have blown my mind even before I'd understood what was going on, but now it left me speechless. They weren't just giving me access to their fabulously expensive things, they were giving me access to their journals, which was the one thing connecting them to the people they'd been hundreds of years ago.

The trip back home went by faster than I'd expected it to. I caught glimpses of a pair of familiar-looking headlights a couple of times, but by the time I turned off into our neighborhood they were gone, so I didn't think anything of it.

We managed to make it home and into bed before Dad came home, but not by much. I was still awake when I heard him open the door and make his tired way upstairs so he could shower.

I fell asleep worrying about what Dad was going to say when we asked him about going camping. I still hadn't come up with a solution by the time I woke up.

Breakfast was an odd affair. Ari alternated between being effusive about how awesome Kat and Jace's house had been and giving me worried looks, like she expected me to turn catty over the fact that Jace had spent the last part of the evening with her rather than with me.

It was going to be a problem at some point, but I didn't know how to handle it. I had a sneaking suspicion that Jace and Kat would have been more than happy to pack me up and take me to some secret lair in order to continue my training, but I wasn't ready to just disappear on my dad and Ari. That meant I needed Ari to go along with me spending so much time with Jace and Kat. As much as I wanted to believe that Kat had been wrong about what Ari was thinking, I was becoming more and more certain that she was right. Underneath all of the suggestive jokes, Ari was jealous of the fact that I had met Jace first.

Dad came limping downstairs a few minutes before we were supposed to leave. Ari and I jumped out of our chairs to go help him, but he waved us away.

"It's fine, I just slipped at work. It wasn't bothering me this bad last night, so it should loosen up once I get warmed back up and moving around again."

Ari seemed to take his explanation at face value, but I wasn't so convinced. "Are you sure, Dad? Is it your leg or your back?"

"Both, but don't worry about me, honey. I really will be fine."

"Maybe you should go see a chiropractor, Dad."

He shot me the same look he'd used the other day, the one that said that he didn't want Ari knowing how dire the monetary situation was getting. I almost kept on despite that, but he was the adult. If he said he was fine I wasn't going to be able to convince him otherwise.

It did get me thinking though. If I'd been alive for hundreds of years before giving Jace that box full of clothes and a secret leather journal—which still terrified me—then there was a decent chance that I'd had money back in the day, maybe even a lot of money.

I wasn't going to ask Jace and Kat for charity, but maybe they knew what had happened to whatever money I'd had before I'd died. I made a mental note to ask Kat today in school. When you added in the fact that I probably needed to know how I'd died last time, and questions about when I could expect my ability to activate, my list for Jace and Kat was getting pretty long.

I came back to the present just in time to hear Ari ask Dad if we could go camping.

"…it wouldn't be a big deal. Just the three of us spending the night out next to the lake with

Kat in her motorhome and then riding their wave runners that afternoon."

Dad gave Ari a suspicious look. "Just the three of you?"

Ari nodded enthusiastically. "Yep, just the three of us, no boys."

"That's an interesting response, Ari, especially since I was really asking whether there were going to be any adults there to keep an eye on the three of you. I have to wonder why you were so excited to establish that there weren't going to be any boys around..."

Ari, the great—expert even—liar, looked like she'd just bitten into something sour. It was the first time I'd seen her at a loss for words in a long time.

Dad turned towards me. "What about you, Selene? What do you have to say about this proposed boating trip? Does this Kat really think she's going to be able to convince her parents she doesn't need any supervision this weekend?"

I was getting so tired of lying to my family, but Kat and Jace had said that this trip was important, so I gamely played along.

"Actually, it doesn't seem like Kat and Jace's parents are around. As far as I know she doesn't need to get permission from anyone to take the jet skis out."

Dad frowned. "That sounds like a recipe for trouble if I've ever heard one. Two young kids on their own with more money than sense. So

Kat is your age, and Jace is the one that's Ari's age?"

The lies just kept piling up, but there wasn't anything to do but plow forward. "Yep. I think Jace is old for the grade he's in, but yeah, he's going to school with Ari."

Dad poured himself a glass of milk while he thought, and then sighed. "I'm sorry, girls, but it's just not safe. I know you'd like to be able to go out on the lake like everyone else, but the thought of the three of you out there all by yourselves just doesn't sit well with me."

Ari looked like she was about to throw a fit, but I beat her to the punch. "Would you be willing to at least talk to Kat, Dad? If you still say no then we'll of course abide by your wishes, but I'd like for you to meet her before you make a final decision."

"I don't know how we'd even make that work, Selene. You've got to stay late so you can pick up Ari from school and I'm probably going to have to go to work a little earlier than normal today..."

"Kat and I will come straight here after school so the two of you can talk, and then I'll go back and pick Ari up."

"Okay, if it means that much to you both, then I'll at least talk to her."

"Thanks, Dad."

A couple of minutes later we were in the car and on our way to school. Ari pouted the entire way there, apparently convinced that I'd given in too easily, but I figured that if anyone was going to have a chance of convincing Dad to let us go camping it was going to be Kat.

I dropped Ari off and headed over to the high school. It wasn't until I was almost there that I realized the reason my heart was racing and my palms were getting clammy. I was going to see Jace again, maybe even spend time alone with him for the first time since I'd found out that he was some kind of semi-omnipotent demigod.

My heart jumped into overdrive when I saw him waiting in the parking lot, leaning against his Viper, which was parked next to my regular spot. It would have been perfect—romantic even—if not for the crowd of more than a dozen kids standing around looking at his car.

He smiled at me as I pulled up two spaces over, and then walked over and opened my door while I was still reaching back to make sure that I'd managed to cram all of my books into my backpack and the tired old zipper wasn't going to give out on me again.

"Hello, Selene."

I would have said that it wasn't possible for anyone to look as good fully clothed as Jace had last night with his shirt off, but he made a valiant effort. I checked him out starting from his feet and working my way up in the hopes that would allow me to acclimatize gradually and avoid swooning.

REBORN

He was wearing unassuming black boots that disappeared into his pants, but which I was pretty sure cost as much as my car. His jeans were the same kind of ripped, designer works of art as he'd been wearing the day before. I didn't know how they managed to be tight and still look like they were hanging from his hips by the slimmest of margins.

I forced my eyes up over his black, studded belt, and up to the tight blue shirt that seemed to be having a hard time containing all of those muscles. It was an almost perfect—albeit more masculine—match for my favorite blue shirt, the one that was still sitting at home in my closet because I hadn't been willing to just throw it away. Over the top of the shirt he was wearing the leather jacket that I'd worn all day on Thursday.

I once again felt like my insides were quivering so furiously that some sign of how I was feeling must be making it out where everyone could see it, but I took a deep breath and forced my eyes the rest of the way up. His blue eyes smoldered as he gave me a slow, confident smile.

"Are you tired this morning?"

My face instantly heated up. I didn't need the catcalls from the peanut gallery to tell me what everyone within earshot was thinking, but that didn't stop Jonas Hemart from whistling. Really it shouldn't have been a surprise. Jonas was one of the biggest guys at school and I'd always been a safe target.

This time Jonas got more than he bargained for. I didn't even see Jace move. One second he was standing in front of me, and then he was back over next to his car with Jonas' throat in his hand. There was a half second of shocked stillness as everyone tried to figure out what had just happened, and then Jonas tried to take a swing at Jace.

Jace easily caught the punch and then began applying pressure against Jonas' hand until tears started streaming out of the bully's eyes. Jonas was big, but Jace was the slightest bit taller and seemed to have more strength than three guys combined. He easily kept Jonas' feet from touching the ground.

"I'm going to say this once, and once only. Selene is a lady and therefore above having to defend her actions to scum like you. Luckily I'm here to take up that task on her behalf. You're going to apologize to her and then you're going to tell everyone you know that you acted like a baseborn cretin. If anyone in the school repeats these baseless lies that Sandra Conner made up, I will make them wish they could trade places with her."

Jace looked around the crowd as he made that threat, and more than one big, brawny football player stepped back in response to the force of his stare.

Satisfied with what he saw in everyone's eyes, Jace dropped Jonas to the ground and then rolled him over onto his back with his boot.

"Lady Selene is waiting for her apology."

Jonas choked out an apology around his coughing and gasping. I couldn't have told anyone what it was he said, but it was obvious that he was very sorry.

For the first time in my life I felt sorry for Jonas. He was the worst kind of bully, but now that he'd come up against someone even bigger and stronger he didn't know what to do other than subject himself to the same kind of abject embarrassment he'd always expected out of his victims.

Jace turned his back to Jonas and the rest of the onlookers and walked back over to my car, where he reached into the back seat and pulled out my book bag. I accompanied him towards the school and didn't say anything until I figured we were out of earshot of the crowd.

"You know he's probably going to key your car, right?"

"Maybe, but if so, he'll be sorry. Besides, like Kat said, that would just give me an excuse to have the paint job redone. I'm thinking something with green highlights this time."

"I'd ask you if you took anything at all seriously, but after last night I know you do."

Jace looked at me with worry in his eyes. "I'm sorry about that, Selene. Kat and I never should have gotten into it like that with you around."

"No, I'd rather know what the risks are and be scared out of my mind than be blissfully headed towards a landmine that I otherwise could have avoided."

"You believe it all? At the rate we've been going I was expecting it to take another day or two for us to convince you it was all true."

"I guess I do. I went to bed scared out of my mind and fighting the occasional worry that this was all just some kind of weird prank. I mean, I knew you weren't just a couple of normal kids—especially after you both stopped time and Kat turned the reflecting pool into some kind of weird, transparent silly putty—but, well, I guess I figured even demigods occasionally find kids to play practical jokes on."

"And now?"

"I don't know. I feel like I should be more skeptical, like I should keep you both at arm's length, but it all just seems right. Something tells me that I should trust you both, that neither of you would ever do anything to harm me. I guess all of the doubts didn't make it through the night."

Jace's smile was still slow, still a little lopsided, but this time it wasn't confident. It was relieved.

"I came prepared with all these plans to convince you that we were legit, and here you've already gotten there on your own. It's going to take me a second to adjust to this glorious new reality I find myself in."

I rolled my eyes at him. "Well, while you're adjusting you can start by telling me what was up with a comment like that back at the cars. Aren't you five-hundred-year-old demigods supposed to be more suave than that?"

Jace winced. "I really am sorry about that. I just wanted to know if you were tired. You got to bed pretty late last night. Most people would be really dragging this morning after something like that…"

"Of course I'm…actually, now that you mention it I'm not nearly as tired as I should be. Do I have you to thank for that?"

"Only very indirectly. Being around Kat and me is going to force your gift to manifest faster than it would otherwise. Nobody is sure why. Some pantheons think it is because you end up catching the fringes of things when we release our power to create effects, and that energy bleed supercharges the ability of the nascent Awakened."

"Some pantheons, but not you and Kat, I'm guessing?"

"No, I think that being around one or more Awakened causes a nascent Awakened's ability to manifest more quickly as a kind of unconscious defense mechanism. Basically, your gift doesn't know whether or not we're dangerous so it's trying to get to the point where it can keep you alive if we come after you."

"Okay, I buy that, but what does that have to do with me not being as exhausted as I should be?"

"As your gift begins to mature, you'll find that you need a lot less sleep than you have up until now. It's one of the perks of being an Awakened."

"How much less sleep are we talking?"

"It depends a little on the individual in question, but most Awakened can comfortably go off of three or four hours a night. We can get by on as little as two hours a night for a week or two in a pinch."

"Wow, that's got to be helpful when you start messing around with time, but doesn't it get boring?"

"Boring is good, remember? Those extra hours every day are part of what lets us build up the base memories to screw around with time and space and not have to always tap into our peak memories."

"You do have a way of making your life sound absolutely thrilling—where can I sign up?"

"Ha-ha. The joke is on you, you signed on the dotted line something like seven thousand years ago. In all seriousness, it's not as bad as all that. The extra time is nice to have, and you'll find stuff to do with it remarkably quickly. You used to read books all the time. I asked you one time what the point was when you were eventually just going to forget them anyway."

"What did I say?"

"You said that was the best part of being an Awakened. It meant that you got to rediscover your favorite books over and over again and each time felt like the first time."

"So the base memories don't actually have to be boring?"

"Nope, and nobody says that that time has to just be filled with base memories—you can always add in peak experiences. Beyond that, most of us tend to spend a big chunk of time going through our journals every day."

"Ah, that makes sense. That way the memories you are building during your downtime are a recreation of what you've already lost."

"More like a shadow of a whisper of what we've lost, but yeah, that's the general idea. It's a way of trying to stay grounded in who we've been up until now."

"Wow, there is a lot to learn, isn't there?"

Jace's smile this time was back to the confident expression that was so endearing. "You have no idea. Way back in the day, you were one of the best researchers around. We only managed to save some of your journals, and I only went through the ones you'd labeled as being technical volumes, but even those just about blew my mind. At first I felt like you'd been holding out on us, but the deeper I got into them the more I realized that neither Kat or I were really ready to learn that stuff. Kat just about killed herself the first time she tried to bend time as far as your notes indicated you'd reached."

It was like being told you were the starting forward in the championship game when you'd never even touched a basketball before that instant.

"Wait, I'm the researcher? We're up against a bunch of hostile pantheons and you and Kat are depending on me to pull fluffy bunnies out of magic hats in new and exciting ways so we don't all end up dead and—what was the term Kat used? Farmed?"

Jace grabbed my arms and pulled me around so that I had to look at him. "It's not like that."

"Really, Jace? That's quite the surprise because based on what Kat told me last night it's the researchers who figure out how to keep their pantheons from getting wasted."

My voice had continued to go up in volume during my rant, to the point where Jace winced and then I felt a gust of cool power blow across my skin.

"Okay, if you need to yell now's the time to do it. I've surrounded us with a vacuum so nobody will be able to hear us."

"A vacuum? Really?" I waved my arms around furiously. "If you put us inside a vacuum then how come I'm still breathing and I can feel the air against my hands?"

Jace grabbed at my arms like I was waving dynamite around or something. "Good grief, Selene, you're like a bull in a china closet. What I should have said is that we're standing inside a sphere of air which is enveloped by a layer that is essentially a vacuum, and if you put your hands in the vacuum you might lose some of your fingers."

"What, so you essentially put us inside a giant thermos bottle?"

"Yes, if the thermos bottle is perfectly clear and made of pure awesomeness. Now are you going to freak out, or did I just waste the memory of my fifth-grade graduation for nothing?"

I stuck my tongue out at him. "You're five hundred years old; you never went to fifth grade."

"Okay, fair point. Are you going to freak out now?"

"No, I don't think so—you kind of took all of the fun out of it. How about if you just get to the explaining part?"

Jace sighed. "Okay, it might be like that a little, but you don't have all of the information. Researchers are vital, and you were responsible for an incredible number of advances for our little pantheon, but you have to understand that we Awakened tend to think in terms of decades and centuries rather than days and weeks.

"You put us on the map with your discoveries, but Kat and I have been very careful to avoid tangling with other Awakened since even before you died. Part of that is because there was only the two of us, but part of that is because we were trying to keep your discoveries as much of a secret as possible. Right now we're ahead of the curve, which means that you're going to have time to get up to speed on all of this stuff."

I shook my head. "I'm not smart, Jace. Maybe you have the wrong girl. Maybe I'm just one of the mimicries that Kat was talking about."

Jace wrapped his arms around me right there in front of everyone. "There's more to being a researcher than just smarts. It requires creativity, a willingness to take chances, and a dogged determination that most people can't even begin to touch. You have all of that in spades, but beyond that, you are smart. You've just never had a reason to push yourself before."

"How can you be so sure that I'm the right girl?"

"Because I've talked to dozens of mimicries over the last two years. They all looked an awful lot like you, but none of them made me feel like this."

Chapter 13

The rest of the day went by in a blur of stops and starts that was like nothing else I'd ever experienced before. Once Jace got me calmed down, we headed toward my first class, which also happened to be Jace's first class. I guess that shouldn't have surprised me.

In the course of finding out what we were currently studying, Jace found out that I'd had homework that I was supposed to have done the night before. Predictably he demanded that I let him bend time and speed us up enough that I would be able to get my homework done before class.

I tried to argue with him, but the best I managed to do was get him to agree to only speed us up to half the speed he'd originally wanted to use. It wasn't a clear victory for me, but as nearly as I could tell bending time wasn't a linear kind of thing. Going from double speed to quadruple speed didn't just use twice as much power, it used a lot more than that.

Keeping the time field down to just eight times normal meant that it would cost Jace a lot less than it would have at sixteen times normal. It was still going to use up a chunk of base memories, but at least it would mean that I wasn't making him tap into peak memories.

I wasn't sure I was going to get even that much of a concession out of Jace, but when I made the point that I could still get my homework done as long as we did a number of shorter studying sessions spread out over the day, that convinced him.

Once we agreed, Jace led me to one of the abandoned classrooms and used telekinesis to unlock the door. He then flipped on the lights and covered the windows with an illusion to make it look like it was still dark and abandoned.

It took me twenty minutes to get ready for my first class, at which point we headed to homeroom and I turned in my homework while Jace went through all of the new student stuff like introducing himself to the class and getting a book.

Jace took the next several study sessions and then handed me off to Kat during lunch to do the next one. I felt less bad about Kat bending time for me because she actually did have homework that she needed to get done. I was pretty sure though that she pushed things up higher than we'd agreed though, because once we were done with our assignments she didn't seem like she was in any hurry to get to our next class.

"So what's the verdict about tonight? What did your dad say?"

"Oh, right, I should have told you already. He wasn't very keen on it, so I asked him to wait to make a decision until after he'd had a chance to meet with you."

Kat sighed. "Okay, what were his objections? Presumably I'm supposed to meet him after school gets out but before it's time to go get Ari?"

"Yeah, sorry. As for the objections, he mainly didn't like that there weren't going to be any adults there and was worried that you had more money than sense."

"Okay. Well, I guess I'm going to be missing PE today."

"Wait, what do you mean?"

She shrugged and gestured at her clothes, which consisted of jeans and a t-shirt from some eighties band I'd never heard of before. "If I go talk to your dad wearing this he's going to see everything he's worried about. I've got to go home so I can change and redo my makeup."

Something was off, Kat wasn't usually this curt. The coward inside of me wanted to just pretend that nothing was wrong, but that didn't seem like a very good way to start off the third day of a relationship that might last for the next several hundred years.

"What's wrong, Kat? If it's about the fact that you have to meet with my dad, I'm sorry. You said it was vital that we go on the trip and I could tell he wasn't going to go for it, so I did the only thing I could think of. Can't you throw a whammy on him or something and make him agree to let us go? You did it with Mr. Reynolds…"

"I hate using the worship-me aura, Selene."

"Wait, that's what I've been calling it inside of my head."

That earned me a smile. "That's what you called it when you taught it to me. You didn't like it very much either, but it seems like we just can't get away from using it."

"So use something else. You and Jace are the next best thing to all-powerful. If you don't want to use the worship-me aura then use something else."

"There isn't anything else, Selene. Mortals have their free will; it's just how things work. Mindreading, compulsion, all of that stuff is just pure fantasy. If one of us wants something from one of them then we either have to trade for it, play upon their emotions, trick them, or threaten them. Our powers can make it easier to do one of those things, but no effect is capable of doing it for us.

"I could amp up my body to the point where I could break your dad's bones as easy as breaking a toothpick, and hurting him might be enough to make him allow you to leave, but once we were gone there wouldn't be anything other than that fear to stop him from calling the police."

I started to stand, fists clenched, but Kat waved me back to my seat. "I'm not going to hurt your dad, Selene, it was just an example."

I hadn't even realized what I was feeling until that moment. The anger had just pushed its way to the front, ready to fight and even die if necessary to protect my dad. I wouldn't have said it would be possible for anything to short-circuit my rage so neatly, but Kat did it without even needing to touch me. It was like she'd known exactly what I was thinking and feeling and that had given her the perfect tool with which to defuse me.

"Seriously, sit back down. If you go into oxygen debt I'm not going to amp you up, I'll just drop the time effect and leave you here to either recover or suffocate. I've used way too much power over the last few days."

I dropped back down into my chair, confused by the way that she was treating me. "I'm sorry, Kat. I don't want you to have to burn your memories like this. Let's be done—we'll go back to class and I'll just not turn in my homework. It won't be the end of the world."

"That's just it, Selene, you don't get it. I don't have any other choice. You'd never go for us taking a fear approach with your dad—not that we'd want to anyway—so that means we either have to trade for what we want, play to his emotions, or trick him.

"No father worth the title is going to trade his daughters for cash, and that includes accepting something in return for putting you in a situation where he doesn't think you'll be safe, so I have just two options to work with. Both those options work best if he isn't suspicious. You need to continue to get good grades and carry on as though everything is okay or my job is going to get even harder."

"This isn't about my dad."

The words came out without me even realizing I'd opened my mouth, and they came out with the kind of bold, unapologetic tone that I'd always admired in Kat, but only rarely managed myself. It was like throwing gasoline on a fire. Kat's energy surged up and this time it wasn't warm and friendly, it was cold and prickly. Her face had gone so hard she almost looked like another person.

"You should keep your opinions to yourself—they aren't wanted."

"Well, tough. If you're going to drag me along behind you without even telling me the full story then you're going to have to deal with me opening my mouth and interjecting my opinions."

"I could kill you right here and nobody else would ever even know."

I actually laughed in her face. It was the last thing I should have been doing, but it was like the other version of me, the one who had spent decades as friends with Kat, was reaching forward in time and controlling me.

"Good luck with that, Kat. Jace would never buy it and we both know it, but that's not even the real reason why you aren't going to kill me."

"Oh, yeah?"

My mind was spinning frantically. Up until now, everything had just exploded out of my mouth of its own accord, but whatever had been motivating me was gone. Now I had to cash the checks my mouth had been writing. I opened my mouth intending to stall, and then it hit me.

"You're not going to kill me because I'm your last hope. You said it yourself last night. The other pantheons are hunting you and Jace as we speak, and the two of you aren't strong enough to stand up to them. Hell, based on how scared you are, there's a good chance that the three of us won't be strong enough to survive against what's coming for us, but at least with me you might have a chance."

"You figure that all out by yourself or has Jace been going off script again?"

"Some of both, but mostly things are just starting to click for me. It's rare that one of us dies in a big blaze of glory, isn't it? I mean it probably happens, maybe that's even what happened to me, but usually conflicts between different pantheons are just long drawn-out affairs where the side with more people wears the weaker side down, makes them burn up all of their memories until they are helpless and they can be dispatched by any idiot with a knife and a vendetta.

"With me in the pantheon we'll be adding memories fifty percent faster. That's a lot of extra power in a pinch. It just might make the difference if we get cornered at some point in the future—and that's not even accounting for the fact that I'm apparently some kind of savant researcher who could tip the scales irrevocably in our direction if I manage to unlock the right secrets of the universe."

We stared at each other, neither willing to blink for several seconds before I raised an eyebrow and tilted my head to one side.

"Well, Kat, what do you say? Am I getting warm?"

"Yeah, you did surprisingly well. For a second there you almost had me convinced I was talking to the old you, the one who wouldn't have let me get away with this kind of crap."

"So what am I missing?"

"You're missing the fact that once your powers fully manifest you're only going to need two hours of sleep per night as compared to my five, and you're missing the fact that Jace would do anything for you. He'd cut me loose in a heartbeat if that's what he thought he was going to need to do to keep you."

It was the last piece, Kat wasn't just scared of the other pantheons, she was afraid that we were going to abandon her when times got tough.

"Kat, I would never—"

"Don't say it, Selene. That's just going to make it worse when you end up deciding to cut your losses. You still don't get it. I have to sleep for five hours a night. Five. That's three extra hours a day spent in a useless slumber that doesn't do anything to generate base or peak memories either one. Even compared to Jace, I need an extra two hours a day of useless sleep."

"That's—"

"No, don't say it. I know it doesn't sound like much, but over the course of months and years it starts adding up. I'm a four-banger in a world of V-8's. I stay in the running by using peak memories to fill in when my store of base memories starts to get low, but the older you get the more jaded you become and the harder it is to form quality peak memories. My time is already running short. Jace remembers almost a hundred and fifty years together with you and me. I barely remember eighty at this point. I fill back in with my journals, but I'm already down in the danger zone. If another pantheon finds us and we have to make a run for it, I could lose twenty years' worth of memories in just a few days."

"Oh, Kat. You poor thing."

"Yeah, poor Kat. I'm nothing more than a pawn. Most pantheons would chew me up and spit me out. They'd drain me dry in just a century or two, and then once all of my peak memories were gone it would only be a matter of time before I'd end up dead."

"Only these aren't the old days, are they, Kat? Back then dying just meant you had to start over with no knowledge of what you'd lost. Now in a world with digital cameras and social media, once you're used up it's game over. You'll never get another chance to have your power awaken. You'll be killed over and over again. Never knowing why powers you can't even hope to understand are out to get you."

She was crying. I got the feeling that didn't happen very often. As quickly as the tears had arrived she started bringing herself back under control.

"It's okay, Kat. If you need to cry then cry. I won't tell Jace any of this if you don't want him to know."

That brought a smile to her lips. "Don't kid yourself; the two of you are incapable of keeping secrets from each other."

"I'd do it for you. I think you're right that it would be hard, but I'd do it anyway."

"No, there's no need. Jace is fully aware of just how much of a basket case I am. I don't know how you do this. It was the same way back before you died. I can count the number of times I remember crying on one hand, and each and every one of them was because you said exactly the right thing at the right time to bring my tough-girl act tumbling down."

"I'm sorry..."

"Don't be—you just helped me form another peak memory. Maybe someday this will be what keeps me alive when my number otherwise would have been up. You always were better at triggering strong emotion in me than I was at triggering it for you. You've always been a better friend to me than I deserved."

I shook my head in protest. "Don't say those kinds of things, Kat. I'm sure that isn't true. Just over the course of three days you've proved that you're a great friend. I can't think of anyone else who would burn a peak memory just to show Sandra up like that."

"Yeah, I've always had a weakness for making that whore look like the idiot she is."

"Wait, you mean Sandra is one of us? She's an Awakened too?"

"Either that or she's a copy—a mimicry. She's a dead ringer for the bane of your existence, of course she went by a different name back then."

It was so obvious I couldn't believe that I hadn't seen it before then. Sandra and I had the same birthday. That meant that we'd died within seconds of each other.

"Kat, I'm going to ask you a question and I want you to tell me the truth."

"Selene, sometimes we're better off not knowing—"

"She's the one who killed me, isn't she? It was Sandra who did it."

Chapter 14

Kat hung her head in shame. "It wasn't supposed to be you, Selene. I was the one who was supposed to die that night."

I felt like I'd been punched in the gut, but I couldn't have said for sure whether it was Sandra, or rather her previous incarnation, killing me that was the biggest shock, or if it was the fact that I'd sacrificed myself to save Kat.

"What happened, Kat?"

"We were being chased by a group from another pantheon. They were hoping to run us to ground so that they could capture you, or barring that get their hands on your research journals. There were three of them and three of us, but they were all known quantities and we were too closely matched.

"You and Jace were more powerful and skilled than any of them, but I was much, much weaker than even their weakest. Jace suggested splitting up as a way of trying to even the odds. He went one direction and we went the other. We figured Jace would be able to overwhelm whomever they sent after him, and then he was going to meet back up with us and ambush the last two of them."

It was surreal to hear someone talking about how I'd died. I couldn't remember any of it, but I could still feel a complex tide of emotions rising inside of me. Sorrow was part of it, but only part, and I couldn't even begin to untangle the rest of the feelings.

"It didn't work though."

"No. Jace ran into problems. The guy following him was cagier than we'd expected and it seemed like nothing Jace tried was sufficient to get the other guy to engage. Meanwhile we were running out of time. Sandra and Mephistoles were closing in on you and me. We went to a safe house and you called Jace...you called to tell him goodbye. I didn't realize it at the time. I thought you were just checking up on him, trying to figure out if there was any chance of turning the situation around, but you were saying goodbye."

Kat stopped talking. The tears were back. It physically hurt me to see her in so much pain, but I had to know what happened next.

"Please, Kat. I need to know."

"You pulled me aside and told me that you had a plan. You were going to engage Sandra and

Mephistoles head on. While I circled around and came at them from the other side. It was risky. Even I realized that. I tried to convince you to trade places with me. It only made sense for me to take the most dangerous spot."

"You knew what I had planned?"

"No. I had some vague suspicions that you weren't telling me everything, but that wasn't anything new. Mostly it was just the fact that you were so much more important than me. You'd been telling us for months that your research was on the cusp of producing something that would change everything for us."

Kat made a fist and slammed her hand into the desk. The blow looked casual, but she shattered the ceramic upper surface and sent her book spinning to the ground.

"I don't know what you were thinking. You should have fed me into the meat grinder and saved yourself. If you'd spent the last eighteen years working on your research you could have finally made us untouchable."

"I expect that I was probably thinking that I loved you, Kat. I saw an option that gave us both a chance to save ourselves, but I knew there was a risk, so I did what I could to make sure that at least you would make it out alive."

"Then you were an idiot. You saved me, but what did that really accomplish? You saved someone who won't even remember your sacrifice in a few more years.

"I'll still have my journals, I'll still know that you died to save me, but I won't know what that felt like. Every time I burn a peak memory I worry I'm going to lose the memory of that day, but in a little while it won't even matter. I'm steadily losing the day-to-day stuff that defined our relationship. At some point it's just going to be a memory of a stranger who threw her life away to save mine."

"Oh, Kat. I finally understand. You're not just scared for your own life, you miss your friend, and you're in mourning for the day when you won't be able to remember her, for the day when her sacrifice will cease to have meaning. Why didn't you just tell me?"

"Because it sounds stupid to say that I miss you when you're sitting right here next to me."

"I'm not really her, and I know it. Maybe someday I'll be someone very much like her, but right now you and I don't even begin to have that kind of history together. It's okay, I don't expect you to feel any different than you do."

Something about that statement calmed Kat instantly. It was eerie, like the way that she'd short-circuited my anger so effortlessly just a few minutes before. The difference was that I didn't have any idea what it was that I'd said to reach her.

"You say that, but sometimes I wonder. Most of the time you're exactly what I expect you to be, but every so often you sound just like her."

"I know, Jace explained it to me. My body has changed over the last few years and now I'm basically a clone. Even my voice."

"No, that's not what I meant. Your voice is the same, but it's more than that. Sometimes the things you say are exactly the same things she would have said."

I shrugged. "You guys keep telling me that kind of thing is to be expected. I'm still her, just without her memories."

"Yeah, I know. It just seems sometimes like the similarities between the two of you go beyond even that."

Chapter 15

We went back to our fifth class and made it through without any problems, but when it came time for my next study session I flatly refused to let Jace or Kat either one bend time. They weren't happy about my intransigence, but I'd managed to get a passable amount of homework done during fifth hour, and I was going to take a 'D' on an assignment before I was going to let the two of them wipe away one more memory that didn't need to be wiped away.

As luck would have it, I managed to get just enough work done in each class to continue to be ready as the next class rolled around. I've always hated working under a deadline, so it made for a stressful couple of hours. I was going to have a lot of catching up to do over the weekend because of all the stuff I hadn't gotten done during class, but that was what the weekend was for.

Kat ditched school right before PE started, which I thought meant I was going to have to fly solo, but apparently Mr. Lake and Ms. Stacker decided it was time to let the two different PE classes mix, so we were playing co-ed volleyball.

Predictably, Jace was chosen as one of the captains. Less predictably, he chose me as his first pick, which caused a round of giggling from the girls and a lot of rolled eyes from the guys.

"You just made a huge mistake. I've got to be the world's worst volleyball player. Our team is going to suck."

Jace gave me another lazy smile. "Oh, ye of little faith."

I hit him in the arm, but it was like hitting warm marble. I was pretty sure that I'd just done more damage to my fist than I had to his arm.

"Biblical quotes are less funny coming from you than they would be from other people, Jace."

"What's that supposed to mean?"

I looked around before responding, but we were far enough away from the other captains that I thought we were probably safe.

"I mean quoting another faith's holy book when you probably had a holy book of your own at some point a few thousand years ago comes off as being kind of mocking."

"So what you're saying is that because I'm not like everyone else around here, I don't get to share their beliefs?"

"Wait, are you trying to tell me that you're a believer?"

"Yep. So were you once upon a time, Selene. Just because we can bend space and time doesn't mean we can't believe in a higher power."

He'd stumped me with that one. I opened my mouth to respond, and then just closed it again and shrugged. "With someone else I'd think they were trying to mock me still, but I think you may actually be serious."

"More than serious, my doubting Thomasina. Watch, I'll show you. Who's the worst athlete here—I mean besides you?"

I stuck out my tongue at Jace, but I pointed at Sally Westernaught, whom he promptly selected for his next pick. That proceeded for the next four selections as we filled out the spots on the floor and selected one more person to rotate into the game.

By the time the teams were formed up it was obvious that we had no chance of winning. We had five girls who were more likely to flinch away from the ball than hit it, Jace, and one other guy who I suspected was going to fake an injury shortly into the first game so that he could sit out and avoid humiliating himself.

The worst part of it all was that each person on the team knew that we were all losers. Jace surveyed the six of us and smiled. "I could tell you that I don't care about winning or that I just want us to all have fun, but that would be a lie. I want to win because a lot of the people on those other teams look like the kinds of jerks who would have picked most of our team last.

"I'm going to make you a promise. If you'll hit the ball when it comes to you, I'll do my very best to make sure that it goes over the net."

Sally shook her head. "I've heard this story before. We want everyone to play, don't just stand there, yada, yada. The truth is that you're going to get pissed if we don't hit it just right to set you up to spike the ball."

"I'll tell you what, Sally. I won't spike the ball until you tell me that it's okay to do so, and I don't really care where you hit the ball as long as you hit it. Try me—hit it the worst possible way you can and I'll bet you twenty bucks that I don't get mad."

"Fine, you're on."

We shook out into our spots and waited while the other team served the ball. As fate would have it, the first serve went straight at Sally, but rather than getting out of the way like she usually did, she got under the ball and bumped it…straight away from the net.

I figured it was going out of bounds and the other team was going to get the first point in what was going to be a very short game, but somehow Jace made it across the court and casually hit it back over the net.

I'd been watching Jace the entire time, expecting him to bend time in order to make it to the ball, but he didn't seem to be moving in-humanly fast, he was just somehow *better* than anyone else I'd ever watched. The other team had started out over-confident and they'd already started turning away from the net when they saw that Sally had hit the ball in the wrong direction. They never even saw Jace's return hit coming.

"Good hit, Sally—that's exactly what I'm talking about."

From someone else the words would have come out condescending, but not from Jace, he was obviously just happy that Sally had hit the ball.

"Dang it, I should have thought to stipulate that you had to keep your cool for the entire game. Okay, you want your twenty bucks now, or later?"

"Keep your money. I really do just want you all to hit the ball."

What followed was the most enjoyable series of games I'd ever participated in. One by one Jace converted us. Initially he had to call out our names to get us to go after the ball, but before long we were all enthusiastically bumping and even setting, something that most of us probably thought would never happen.

It was just too fun watching Jace race across the court and dive for the ball *not* to try and hit the ball when it was our turn. It almost turned into a game to see how far we could push Jace, how bad our bumps could be before he couldn't get them anymore.

That almost cost us our second game, but when the other team started talking trash, we all started pulling together. Once Jace wasn't having to move so far out of position he was deadly. It seemed like the ball always went exactly where he wanted it to go. Sally sent the game-winning serve over the net, and from there on out we were unstoppable. We didn't shut anyone out, but we came close a couple of times. By the end of the hour, we were playing the only other undefeated team and all of the kids from the other teams were gathered around to watch us.

We were losing rather badly despite how awesome Jace was—right up until Jace made it up to serve, at which point he sent one bullet over the net after another. He racked up points like the other team wasn't even playing, and then botched what should have been his last serve.

Sally had long before given Jace permission to spike the ball so we returned the other team's serve with a quick bump, set, spike and then rotated Sally into the server's spot.

She served, the ball volleyed back and forth several times and then I managed to set the ball well enough that Pete Parks spiked it home for the game-winning point. There was a big, cheering hug-fest after that. It felt like the geeks had risen up to destroy the jocks and popular kids—which we had, but we all knew that it never could have happened without Jace.

I drifted over to where he was getting a drink of water.

"You botched that last serve on purpose, didn't you?"

"Of course I did. I played two years of college volleyball a little while back."

"Did you amp yourself up back then too?"

Jace gave me a sheepish grin. "Sometimes. It depended on what the stakes were. Today the stakes were making sure that a bunch of kids got a chance to feel like winners. That seemed worth losing a few minutes' worth of memories that I'll never miss."

"Won't you? I talked to Kat and I understand more of what's going on. At some point you aren't going to be able to remember her anymore."

"Remember Kat?"

"No, the other her—me, the other me. I know how you felt about her, I can see it in your eyes when you look at me. I don't want to be the reason that you lose your memories. They are all that you have left of her."

Jace took my hands in his and ran his thumbs over my skin in slow, almost sensual circles. It made my heart flutter and my mouth go dry, but I wouldn't have asked him to stop for anything.

"I'm going to lose those memories eventually, Selene. It's funny, but that's the only certainty of my—of our—existence. We may not die, but it's only a matter of time before we forget every single thing that's happened to us.

"I'm not going to live in fear, Selene. That may be what Kat chooses, but I'm going to live in a way that lets me be proud of the memories that I'm creating as I create them. I'm not looking forward to losing my memories of the time I spent together with you during your last incarnation, but I am looking forward to spending more time with you in this incarnation."

It was perfect. I could feel myself melting inside, but I tried not to make it too obvious. He might have been madly in love with me in a past life, but there was a part of me that was still worried that my coming on too strong would scare him away.

"I'll go get my clothes and then I'll meet you back here so we can wait for Kat to get back?"

"Sure. I'm not going anywhere, Selene."

The possible double meaning behind his words didn't go unnoticed on my part. Once again, he almost seemed to be reading my mind.

Most of the rest of the class had disappeared while we'd been talking, so the girls' locker room was basically empty by the time I made it to my gym locker. The last two other girls left while I was grabbing my clothes, and then I turned to find that Sandra was only inches away from me.

"I know it was you."

"What are you talking about?"

She gave me a cutting look. "Don't play stupid. You changed the note, rewrote it so that it looked like I was a complete slut."

My heart was racing. It was just the two of us, but I'd never been in any kind of fight before. I took a step back. "I don't know what you're talking about. I didn't do anything to your stupid note, but it would have served you right if I had. You've been nothing but nasty to me since kindergarten."

"It was no more than you deserved. I could always see the real you behind the innocent façade that you tried to fool everyone with. I always knew that you were nothing more than a scheming little slut who couldn't wait to get her hands on any guy I wanted."

"Do you hear yourself? You sound like a crazy person, Sandra. I'm seventeen years old and I've never had a boyfriend. I've never even come close. You've slept with at least half of the varsity football team—in what bizarro world am I a threat to you?"

She hit me. She'd probably meant for it to be a slap, but she hit me so hard that my shoulder hit the lockers. I never even saw the blow coming, and the force of it was shocking.

The old Selene, the one who had let Sandra get away with years of torment without ever standing up for myself, was cowering in a corner of my mind, but the new Selene, the one who was starting to believe she was on the cusp of becoming a demigod, grabbed Sandra by the hair and slammed her head into the closest bank of lockers.

Sandra stumbled away from me with surprise written across her features. I was shocked too—despite years of fantasizing and the incidents of rage lately, I hadn't realized I was capable of that kind of explosive violence. My surprise didn't stop me from stalking towards her though.

"Don't you ever hit me again or I'll do a lot worse to you. I'm tired of your crap. Things are going to be different starting right now. You leave me alone and I'll leave you alone. You screw with me and I will bury you. If you have your friends mess with Ari or if you have your dad fire my dad, then I will come for you and make you sorry in ways that you can't even imagine."

She was beyond surprised now. I could see the fear in her eyes, but I couldn't blame her—I was scaring *myself* in that instant. I could see it balancing on the edge of a knife as she wrestled with her fear. For a second I thought I had her, thought that she was going to be scared enough to finally back off, but something pushed her the other direction and she curled her fingers into claws and practically hissed at me.

"I knew it. You can protest all you want, but now he is here and it's happened just like I knew it would. You stole him away from me before I even had a chance to get to know him. Every bad thing that I suspected about you is true, and you're kidding yourself if you think that I'm going to let you get away with this. Things *are* going to be different because I'm different. Don't say that I didn't warn you, Selene."

Chapter 16

Sandra spun around and ran out of the locker room before I could muster a response. Her threatening me wasn't anything new, but she'd always seemed somehow petty before. This time it felt different.

I was shaking by the time I made it out to the gym where Jace was waiting for me. He took one look at me and dropped into a slight crouch as he scanned our surroundings for a threat capable of throwing me into tears.

He reached up and cradled the side of my face as soon as he reached me, covering the smarting skin with his cool, tingly hand.

"Selene, what happened?"

"It was Sandra. She surprised me in the locker room and started saying all of these nasty things. I basically called her a whore, so she slapped me."

Jace visibly relaxed. Obviously he didn't consider Sandra a real threat. "Do I need to go dispose of the body?"

"What? No, of course I didn't *kill* her. I slammed her head into the lockers, but that just made her madder. She threatened me, Jace. It wasn't like her. Usually she enjoys trotting out all of the nasty stuff that she might do to me. This time she just left it open-ended and then ran out through the other set of doors."

Jace pulled me into a hug. "Well, on the scale of worst encounters between the two of you over the last few hundred years that's pretty far towards the bottom of the list. Usually there are explosions and fire. I'd say a slap and someone being slammed into a locker is almost progress."

I pushed him away, breaking his grip on me. "This isn't funny, Jace. I think she's going to do something to Ari or my dad. I'm really worried."

Jace sobered instantly. "I'm sorry, I didn't mean to make light of your concerns. We'll take precautions this weekend. You and Ari will be with Kat, and I'll make sure that nothing happens to your dad."

"Okay, thanks. She just seemed so different this time."

"Who seemed different?"

I turned around and had to look twice to realize that it was Kat who was walking up to us. She'd said that she was going home to change and touch up her makeup, but this was something else altogether.

Kat was wearing black slacks and a white button-up blouse. It was like something you'd expect a bank teller to wear, and her makeup was suitably understated, making her cheekbones look more prominent and adding at least two or three years to her appearance.

Her hair was pulled back into a messy bun that still looked sexy without looking juvenile. The net effect of all the changes was to make her look like a completely different person, someone older, more responsible and very respectable. It was going to be interesting to see how my dad reacted to her.

Jace got a response out while I was still trying to pick my jaw up off of the floor. "Sandra. She caught Selene alone in the locker room and made threats. Selene is worried that something might happen to Ari or her dad."

Kat frowned at Jace. "Seriously? Can't you even watch over Selene for one hour without letting prissy skanks threaten her?"

"It happened in the locker room, Kat."

She waved away his explanation. "So make yourself invisible. Selene's safety is more important than the privacy of a few teenage girls."

"Jace is not following me into locker rooms, Kat. I'll be fine. Sandra isn't going to try anything in the middle of the day in a public place."

And I wasn't about to go exposing him to all of those young, nubile bodies. I was going to have a hard enough time keeping him interested in me as it was.

Jace sighed. "No, she's right, Selene. I won't follow you into the girls' locker room, but it's getting too dangerous for you to be running around by yourself. From here on out, if Kat isn't around, then you don't go places where I can't follow. I should have had you just wait out here until Kat arrived or you could have just gone home in your gym clothes."

I looked back and forth between the two of them. "I don't get it, what changed?"

"You mean other than Sandra threatening you?"

Jace shot Kat an unhappy look. "Can it, Kat. You're not helping." He turned back to me and ran his hand through his hair. "Your gift is in the middle of manifesting. It's to the point where Kat and I can both sense you from several dozen feet away."

"Wait, you mean the Awakened can sense each other even if they can't see each other?"

"Yeah. The stronger the two Awakened are, the further away they can sense each other. There are things you can do to suppress your signature, but it's always there to some extent. The fact that you are starting to generate a signature means that your gift is manifesting. Kat can start training you tonight assuming we can find a way to distract Ari."

That shaky feeling was back, and this time it wasn't because of my physical proximity to Jace. It was actually going to happen. I was finally going to become one of the Awakened for real. Realistically there hadn't been any going back since the day I'd been born, but this still felt like a big, irrevocable step.

Kat raised her hand in an attention getting wave that I had a sneaking suspicion normally would have ended with flipping Jace or I off.

"This still doesn't deal with a certain loose end that needs taken care of. If Sandra is making threats then we should just get rid of her. It will be easy enough to make it look like an accident."

My blood ran cold. I'd known that Kat had some dark places in her soul, but hearing her talk about casually murdering someone was still a shock to my system.

"No, you're not killing her."

Kat raised an eyebrow. "You'd rather Jace does it? Or maybe you'd like to get your own hands dirty this time?"

"No, nobody is going to kill her. She's just making threats. If she attacks Ari or my dad then all bets are off, but I'm not going to just go around killing people for what they *might* do."

"So instead you're going to expect Jace and me to guard all three of you at once? For being concerned about us burning up memories in your behalf, you're oddly eager to overcommit us."

Jace raised his hand. "That's enough, Kat. We aren't killing Sandra and that's final. Even if you make it look like an accident, the whole school knows that you were the one to turn her in for that note. If she dies right now you're going to be a suspect, and the last thing we want is for the cops to start trying to poke holes in these identities."

"So we take her out and then pack up and leave town before the body is found. It won't be the first time we've done something like that."

Jace didn't get mad very often, but I could see the twitch starting back up just above his upper lip. "That's not the plan and you know it. This is a good place to use as a base. It's far away from all of the major population centers, and it's not on any of the major highways or airline routes. If we keep a low profile there isn't any reason that we can't stay here for years. Moving around right now just makes us more likely to run afoul of another pantheon. That's why we sank so much of our money into the house here."

Kat gave him a cold smile. "You're hoping that Sandra's the real deal, that she's not just another mimicry. You're hoping to be able to recruit her. Are you really so uncertain of Selene's affections that you're already trying to arrange an emotional fallback?"

She looked over at me. "Did he tell you that the two of them used to date back in the day? They were quite the item before you…became available."

"Don't! Don't say another word, Kat. I'm warning you."

I could feel their abilities pushing out against each other and their energy had gone cold and prickly. They were only seconds away from fighting and it was up to me to stop them.

"Jace hasn't told me, but I already knew. Sandra basically said as much just now, but frankly it's a non-issue for me. If Jace says that we need her then I'm not going to second-guess him."

"Of course you're going to side with *Jace*. I should have known."

"We aren't going to abandon you, Kat, and we aren't going to replace you with Sandra of all people—even assuming this one is the real deal and not just another mimicry—but you have to meet us halfway. Stop being angry all of the time and trust us for once."

Kat looked at me for several seconds and then stormed out of the gym. Jace started after her, but I grabbed his arm.

"I'll go talk to her. The two of you are just going to strike sparks off of each other. Besides, I need you to go check on Ari for me. Sandra is a lot more likely to go after someone her own size than she is to go after my dad."

Jace pulled me into a hug. "Okay, but if Kat doesn't respond well to seeing you again just back off and drive to the junior high. We'll regroup and come up with another way to get some teaching time in. If nothing else you can just start sneaking out at night. It's not like you're going to need a lot of sleep in the near future."

I found Kat standing next to a silver Lexus in the parking lot. I stopped several feet away and cleared my throat. "Kat, I know you don't want to have anything to do with me, but if we're going to make it to my house in time to talk to my dad before he has to go to work, then we need to leave now."

"I'm fine. Get into the car and let's get moving."

The drive out to my house went by quickly, which was good because the silence was even more awkward than I'd been afraid it would be. Kat didn't speed, but she didn't waste any time either.

My dad was waiting down in the kitchen for us. "So, Kat—it is Kat, right?"

"Yes, Katherine actually. Kat is an unfortunate childhood nickname that my brother Jace has refused to let die off."

"Very well, Katherine. Selene and Ari say that you've offered to take them camping and then out on some jet skis. I think I can speak for all of us when I say that it's a very generous offer, but I'm just not comfortable with the idea of the three of you young girls being out there by yourselves..."

"I understand your concerns, Mr. Jenkins. Frankly I think in your place I'd probably feel the same way, but I hope that you'll humor me and listen for just a few minutes while I tell you a little bit about my brother and me.

"My father never had a college degree. He dropped out of school when he was seventeen so that he could work full-time to support his family after my grandfather was injured in an industrial accident. He never let that stop him from continuing to learn though. He used to make incredible machines in the shed behind our house.

"As luck would have it, a few years ago he managed to secure a job with one of the few dotcom startups that had a real product to sell. They needed someone who had common sense and the ability to make things with his hands. The job paid even less than the one he'd had before, but he believed in what they were doing and even took out a second mortgage on our tiny house in order to secure extra stock options."

Dad shifted uncomfortably in his seat. "That was risky."

"Indeed it was Mr. Jenkins. I think it scared my mother half to death. The four founders were college kids who didn't have much money, so my dad had provided the bulk of the initial capital and with it got final say on all additional funding. When the venture capital groups started calling, my dad just kept vetoing deals until he finally found one he liked. It came just in the nick of time because the demand for the company's product had been skyrocketing. That was the leverage that allowed my father to secure the deal that he wanted.

"As it turned out, just six months later the company went public, but in the meantime my father had been taking care of the business side of things while the four kids who were the creative force behind things continued to innovate. Everyone involved made an obscene amount of money, but most especially my father. Unlike most people would have expected, his partners never forgot that it had been him who provided the initial seed money and steered them through the negotiations with the venture capitalists."

"That sounds like a fairytale, Katherine."

"I'm not surprised, I've lived it, and that's a very good description of what it has felt like. I can provide you with the name of the company and the phone number of the current CEO if you would like to verify things, but that isn't why I'm telling you all of this.

"I was very young when all of this was going on. We have lived very well for a number of years, but I still remember what it was like to be excluded from the popular crowd because I didn't wear the right clothes and didn't live in the right part of town.

"After we had money everything changed. The same girls who wouldn't even give me the time of day suddenly wanted to be my friends, but I never forgot the fact that it was only my father's money that they liked. When my parents died things became very difficult. It seemed as though everyone around Jace and me wanted to be our guardians simply because it would give them—at least temporarily—access to our family's money."

"I'm sorry for your loss."

"Thank you."

"So you went to a court and asked to be emancipated."

"Indeed, and then we moved to a completely different part of the country and tried to blend in. That lasted for just over a year and then people found out who we were and we had to move again. That has happened several times so far, but we have decided that this will be the last place we live before going off to college. On our first day here it was only your daughters who befriended us, and now I would like to return the favor by taking them on the kind of trip that I always wanted to go on before we had the money to do so."

Dad sighed. "That is a very touching story, Katherine, but it doesn't change the fact that you're still not yet eighteen and you're taking my daughters off into the woods where any number of things might happen."

Kat reached into her pocket and pulled out a driver's license, which she set on the table and slid towards my father.

"Jace and I are both old for our grade in school. My mother was a firm believer that it was best for us to be advanced compared to the other kids rather than being developmentally behind and struggling. I've been eighteen for months now."

"I've seen my fair share of fake ID's, Katherine. You'll have to do a lot better than that."

Kat smiled and pulled out a passport and a birth certificate. "I'm not lying, Mr. Jenkins. Camping was a tradition for my family back when we had very little. If it was just Jace and I, maybe we would be going up to the lake and camping in tents, but given your understandable concern for your daughters' safety, I'll be bringing our forty-two-foot motor coach, which will be locked up all night, and Jace will be staying home and only joining us the next day to enjoy the jet skis."

Dad looked at his watch and then sighed. "I have your word that there won't be any boys or booze or drugs?"

"Absolutely."

"And you really know what you're doing driving a vehicle that big? You know how to stay safe on the water?"

"Yes, of course."

Dad turned to me and gave me the look. "Do I have your word, too, Selene? No boys, nothing that you know I wouldn't approve of?"

"Yes, Daddy. It's just like she said. A girls' night camping followed by some time on the water."

Kat cleared her throat. "I know that you have to work tonight or I'd invite you along, but if you'd like to join us tomorrow on the lake you'd be most welcome."

"Thanks, I just might do that. You can go. Just please be careful. My daughters are all I have left."

"I will personally make sure that nothing happens to them. You have my word."

Chapter 17

I saw Dad off to work, and then Kat and I zipped back into town to pick up my car and meet up with Jace and Ari. Ari was predictably on cloud nine at having been picked up by the hottest boy in the entire town, but I just made another mental note to talk to Jace about not leading her on and tried not to let the gushing get to me.

Ari and I hadn't bothered packing that morning because we hadn't been positive that Kat was going to be able to convince Dad to let us go. We both headed towards our car, expecting that we would need to go home and pack now, but Jace told us that our house was on the way and we could pick up anything we needed on the way out of town.

I should have realized that he was up to something then, but I was too busy worrying about the way that Ari bounded right over to his Viper so that she would be able to ride with him rather than riding with me. I was mumbling under my breath as I put my car into gear and followed Kat and Jace out of the parking lot.

Keeping up with a pair of Awakened who could amp up their reflexes and even bend time with nothing more than a thought wasn't very fun, even when they were making a conscious effort to go slow. I nearly lost them a couple of times, and I was in a bad mood by the time I pulled into their ridiculously long driveway.

All that frustration floated away when I saw Jace waiting for me by himself in the garage. If that hadn't been enough, the surprise he had in store next would have done it. One of the guest bedrooms was stocked with a closet full of brand-new clothes all in my size.

"How in the world—"

"This is part of what I was doing yesterday when I came home to get things ready for you. There are stores you can call with someone's measurements, give them some general guidance and a budget and they will overnight you a complete wardrobe."

I tried to keep my disappointment from making it onto my face. It was still an incredibly generous gesture, and right up until that point I probably would have said that it would be weird having a guy shop for me, but I suddenly realized that I didn't care as long as it was *Jace* doing the shopping. Only it hadn't actually been him, it had been some random store employee.

Jace watched me bravely struggle with my disappointment for several seconds before smiling at me. "You know, it's cute when you're so predictable. I had the store employees send me Ari's clothes sight unseen, but I picked out everything here for you."

My eyes darted towards the dresser despite my best effort to keep them under control. I had a sneaking suspicion that when Jace said he'd ordered up a complete wardrobe that really meant that he'd ordered up a *complete* wardrobe.

It was pretty apparent that he and I had been a lot more than just friends back in the day, and with all the craziness of last night I hadn't had a chance to sneak back up to his bathroom and grab the wet underwear I'd left hanging on his towel rack, so it wasn't like he'd never seen my underwear, but the thought of him picking underwear and swimwear out for me was both alarming and super-hot. The thrills of excitement that were almost a constant staple of being in his presence were reaching new heights.

"I hope I did a decent job. If there's one thing I've learned over the last five hundred years it's that all girls like shopping sprees. I knew we weren't going to get a chance to steal you away from your dad long enough to actually take you on one, but I wanted to do something for you, and this seemed like the next best thing."

I reached out and put my hand on his arm, glorying in the rush of heat it sent shooting through me. "I'm sure you did great, Jace. Thank you—this was an amazing gesture."

There was the slightest pause as we both realized that we didn't know what to do next. I suspected that the old Selene would have at the very least given him a very enthusiastic kiss, but I wasn't sure we were at that spot yet.

Don't get me wrong. I wanted to kiss Jace with a desire that was more intense than anything I'd ever felt before, but I was also scared to death of acting on the urge.

Jace was five hundred years old and even if he only remembered the last hundred years, that was still a lot of time in which to kiss girls. Especially when you were an incredibly gorgeous demigod.

At the very least, I knew he remembered kissing the old me, and for all I knew he re-membered kissing Sandra back in the day too. More than likely he'd kissed dozens, maybe even hundreds of girls, but kissing Jace would be a first for me. I was probably not going to be very good at it, and even if I was, it was hard to compete against a version of yourself who had been rich, powerful and experienced.

The pause could have become awkward, but Jace broke the contact before things got to that point. He patted my hand and then let it drop off of his arm.

"I'll go ahead and let you pack. Kat already showed Ari to her room and based on the squeals of delight I heard before you got here, she's very happy with the choices the personal shoppers made. I should go double-check the vehicles."

I checked to make sure that the door was closed, and then realized with a thrill that this was the first time I'd ever been alone with a boy in a bedroom with the doors closed. My mouth was so dry that I almost couldn't get the words out.

"I'm worried about Ari, Jace. I know the plan is for you to keep her distracted, but I don't want her to get her heart broken."

Jace sighed. "I don't want that to happen either, Selene. I'm being as careful as I can—I don't know what else to do. If I have the friend talk with her then it's all too likely that she's going to go running straight to your dad."

"How do you and Kat know that? I thought you couldn't read minds."

"We can't, but we can amp up our senses. It's expensive, but for short times we can basically turn ourselves into human lie detectors. It's not perfect, but it's generally right, especially when the person in question doesn't realize it's being used on them."

"Have you ever used that on me?"

"Not in this incarnation. I've never needed to. You're so much like the old you that most of the time I already know what you're thinking, even without it."

"Wow, that's awkward."

"It doesn't have to be. It means that I know you're nervous about being compared to the old you."

My face flushed, but when I turned away, Jace gently pulled me back around.

"You don't need to feel embarrassed, Selene, and you don't need to worry. One of the amazing things about kissing you is that every time felt like the first time."

Jace gave me one last smile and then slipped out of my room before I could say anything. He left the door open though so I could hear Ari squealing as she found each new surprise waiting for her inside of her closet.

I stood there looking at my door for several seconds until the sound of Ari packing reminded me that I needed to get started if I was going to be ready to go on time. I grabbed the suitcase waiting for me next to the bed and decided to start with the most embarrassing thing first.

The dresser drawers slid open with the kind of smooth action that you don't get out of the cheap dressers from the places where my family could afford to shop. Inside was a full array of socks, more bras than I'd ever owned in my entire life, and enough underwear that I wouldn't have to do laundry more than once a month if I didn't want to.

Once I'd selected a range of underwear and had it packed away, things went very smoothly. We were only planning on being gone for twenty-four hours, so I could have gotten away with a lot less than I ended up packing, but once I got started pulling clothes down from the hangers it was hard to stop.

It wasn't until I got to the swimsuit section of the closet that I remembered we were going to be in the water. Blah. I'd only *thought* that packing the bras and underwear was the worst. At least they were all going to stay safely underneath my clothes, out of sight, even if they weren't ever completely out of mind.

A swimsuit was something else entirely. I could always throw some shorts on, but there was only so much you could do to cover yourself up in a swimsuit before it became obvious that you would much rather be wearing a tent.

I took a deep breath and started pulling suits out where I could see them. Preliminarily at least, it wasn't as bad as I'd expected. Once again, Jace had been a lot more conservative than you would expect from a teenage guy who was dressing a girl in whatever he wanted. Then again, despite his appearance he hadn't been a teenager in a long time.

None of the suits were one-piece, but that was understandable given just how hard it was to find a suit that fit my ridiculously long torso. Instead they were all tasteful two-piece numbers—mostly tankinis, but even the two bikinis looked like they were going to keep all of the important bits covered up.

REBORN

I picked two of the former out, one blue, one black, and then hesitated before grabbing both of the bikinis and throwing them in the suitcase too. I wasn't planning on wearing them, not since my dad might show up at some point during the day, but I figured if worst came to worst that I'd fit into the bikinis—they were a lot more adjustable than a tankini.

I filled out the rest of the space in my suitcase with a pair of cute black swim shorts and a gauzy white cover-up that seemed like it would help obscure stuff at least a little without making me look like I was hiding.

It was about that time that I realized that Jace might not have even seen the suits that the personal shoppers had picked out for Ari. My little sister has always had more...aggressive taste in clothing than me. It's been a regular source of friction between her and my dad over the last few years. Honestly, I'm not sure how Dad hadn't managed to put two and two together. No girl, regardless of age, was going to battle to wear the kinds of things that Ari routinely wanted to wear unless she was *very* interested in boys.

I decided that I'd better get over to her room and try to head her off from bringing anything really slutty. Unfortunately, by the time I grabbed some pajamas and a pair of flip-flops, Ari was coming out of her room with her bag packed and a big grin on her face.

I knew it might cause a fight, but I went ahead and asked the question anyway. "You didn't pack anything too revealing, did you, Ari?"

"I'll bet you'd like to know. Worried that your boyfriend picked out something really hot for me?"

"No, I'm worried that you're going to embarrass both of us and make Jace supremely uncomfortable by dressing like some kind of teenage hooker."

"Okay, Mom. Would you like to pull out your ruler and go over every single article of clothing in my suitcase? How am I possibly going to embarrass him by dressing in something that he picked out for me? If he bought it, then he'd like to see it on me, and given the amount of money he just spent on us, I'm inclined to make him happy."

I was tempted to point out just how hookerish she sounded, but that *would* have caused the huge fight that I'd been hoping to avoid. Luckily there was another option.

"Jace didn't pick any of this stuff out for you, Ari. He just called up some hoity-toity department store and told them that he needed a complete wardrobe for a fourteen-year-old girl."

Ari suddenly looked uncertain. It was hard to go wrong betting on guys enjoying seeing a little skin, but she didn't want to be wrong, not when it might put her out of the running.

"He at least saw it all when he hung it up in my closet, so I think I'm safe."

"Yeah, *if* he really stopped to look at it all as he was hanging it up, and *if* he was the one to hang it up. Do you see Jace spending that kind of time pulling stuff out of packages? My bet is that Kat was the one to hang it all up."

I had her there. The average guy was extremely unlikely to 'waste' hours hanging up clothes like that. Of course I actually had no idea who had hung the clothes up in our two closets unless Kat had done it when she'd come home to change for the meeting with my dad. Even if she'd been bending time that seemed like an awful lot to try to fit into one hour.

"Fine, I'll stay away from the more whorish stuff that I packed, but don't think that I don't know what you're doing here. You're worried that your boyfriend is going to see something tomorrow that he likes, and that it won't be you."

"Be careful, Ari. I honestly think that Jace is just being nice. I'm not going to lie and say that I'm not interested in him, but I also don't want you to get hurt. Jace is quite a bit older than you…"

"Three years is nothing, Selene. I have plenty of friends who are dating seniors right now."

"And it doesn't mean anything at all to you that *I'm* interested in him?"

"Yeah, it means something. It means that I'm leaving the gloves on. Trust me, Selene, I could be a lot more aggressive than this, but I'm not because we're sisters. But that doesn't mean that I'm going to actively discourage Jace. If he chooses you then he chooses you, but I'm not going to take my hat out of the ring. I'm sorry, but I'm not. I might never get another chance at a guy like Jace. Rich, smart, funny, nice, and gorgeous. He's the full package—if you're going to keep ahold of him, you're going to have to get used to a lot more competition than this."

"Fine, but just don't say that I didn't warn you. The last thing I wanted out of all of this was for you to get hurt."

"Don't worry, Selene, I can take care of myself."

Whatever response I might have come up with for that was preempted by Kat's arrival, towing a suitcase of her own along behind her on oversized wheels.

"Okay, girls, let's get moving."

Chapter 18

We were in for a big surprise when we made it out to the massive RV that we were taking out to Cold Springs Lake. Jace wasn't just getting the vehicles ready and then seeing us off, he was coming along.

"But we just got finished telling my dad that there weren't going to be any boys there." I tried to keep the panic out of my voice, but I wasn't sure that I'd succeeded.

Kat rolled her eyes at me. "I told your dad what he needed to hear, just like I told you what you needed to hear in order to sell it. Like it or not, Jace is coming. There are too many crazies out there—I'm not taking the two of you camping by myself."

Crazies was code for other pantheons. It was hard to argue with that, especially now that I knew Kat was the low woman on the power scale. I would feel a lot safer with Jace around, and it probably wouldn't even be possible for

Kat to train me if it was just the three of us girls, but I didn't like lying to my dad any more than I liked being tricked.

Jace walked over and picked up my suitcase. "I'm sorry, Selene. If it makes you feel better, I'll be in a tent a couple of campsites away."

Ari sidled up next to him, handing him her suitcase as she rubbed up against him like a giant cat.

"You can sleep in the RV with us for all I care, Jace. The more the merrier—besides, this is all your stuff too. It's only fair that you be able to come along."

I had to bite my tongue, but it helped a little that Jace stepped away from her once he'd accepted her suitcase from her. He moved both suitcases to the same hand in a casual display of strength that made my heart skip a couple of beats, and then wrapped an arm around me.

"Please don't be mad at us, Selene."

I sighed. "It looks like I've been outvoted. Just make sure that we don't get caught, please. If my dad finds out that we spent the night camping with you after lying about it, he'll never let us see each other again."

Ari rolled her eyes. I couldn't tell if it was in response to my worries, or because Jace had his arm around me, but in the end it didn't matter. Neither of us was going to be able to do anything about the things that we didn't like right now.

REBORN

We all climbed into the RV, and Jace slowly pulled it out of the cavernous garage. Ten minutes later we were on the road and headed towards the lake.

Chapter 19

I suspected that Jace and Kat had agreed beforehand that he would be the one driving. If they hadn't, they should have, because Ari instantly slipped into the passenger seat next to him and proceeded to talk non-stop.

Kat grabbed her suitcase and gestured for me to follow her back to the master bedroom. I could tell that she'd bent time as soon as the door swung shut because I felt a warm rush of power and instantly started to feel out of breath.

"Kat, I don't want—"

"It's not your call, Selene. Orders from Jace. Anytime Ari starts fixating on him, I'm supposed to steal you away and start your training. She seems pretty occupied now, so that means it's time to get started."

"Isn't she going to get suspicious if we spend all of our time locked away together?"

Kat gave me a look that said I was being dumb. "Maybe, but she'll be a whole lot less suspicious of you and me than if it was you and Jace. Besides, the door is locked so she can't barge in, and if she asks we came back here to talk while I was putting my clothes in the closet and I locked the door so I could change without Jace walking in on me."

"While he was driving?"

Kat slipped out of her black slacks and then started looking around inside of her suitcase. "I didn't say that it was perfect—just the best I could come up with on such short notice."

I turned to the side so that I wasn't staring at her while she was standing there in her underwear—not that it seemed to bother her one way or another. She found her pants and pulled them out with exaggerated care.

"How come you're moving like that?"

"Because we're moving at something like ten times normal speed. The other day when I broke the desk I wasn't amping up my strength, I just amped up my bones so I wouldn't break my hand. Up until now we've been using a special time effect that limited the amount of damage that we could do to each other, but it's time for you to start learning how time bending really works. When you're moving at multiple times your normal speed it's really easy to break things. If the thing you hit is soft then you'll break it, if it's hard then you'll break yourself."

"Gotcha, no more moving around until you tell me that you've got the cushioning thing up and running."

I waited while Kat finished getting dressed, and then carefully sat down on the bed. It was none too soon. I was already starting to get light-headed even though all I'd been doing was standing there. The bed groaned, a low, slow sound, but I seemed to have managed not to break it.

Kat sat down next to me, and took a deep breath. "Okay, let's get started. The key to exercising your ability is to generate a strong emotion. Once you have that emotion in place, then you visualize the effect you want and push the emotion outside of yourself."

"What does that even mean?"

"Hold on, Miss Impatient Pants, and I'll explain. Let's start with the basics. Generate a strong emotion."

"Just like that? Aren't emotions just something that you feel when you feel them?"

Kat looked tired, like she'd been up all night. She rubbed her eyes, and nodded. "Yeah, for most people that's the case, but there is something in your brain called the amygdala that is responsible for switching up your emotions. Most people don't realize that they feel an emotion and then after feeling it they rationalize why they feel that way. With practice you can make yourself feel a certain way, you can even make it so that your amygdala naturally tends to switch you to a given state."

"Okay, so how do I get started?"

"You pick out an emotion that you want to become dominant."

"What was my dominant emotion back in my previous incarnation?"

Kat rolled her eyes at me. "Seriously? You actually need to ask given your recurring anger issues?"

"Right, I guess I should have realized that. Is there a reason to pick one emotion over another?"

"Yeah."

"Are you going to tell me what they are?"

Kat sighed. "I guess I can, but most people don't even bother asking, they just pick an emotion and go for it because they are so anxious to get started trying to create effects."

"Yeah, I'd really rather know what it is that I'm getting into."

"Okay, there are three classifications of emotion: positive, negative and neutral. Love would be an example of a positive one, while hate would be a negative emotion and anger would be a neutral one. The biggest difference between them has to do with the fact that some effects are easier to manage when powered by a certain class of emotions.

"Really, your dominant emotional state will tend to color your outlook for everything in your life. For example, healing effects are relatively easy to work if you're fueled by a positive emotion, but much, much harder to work if you're experiencing a negative emotion."

"I guess that makes sense. It's probably hard to visualize flesh knitting together on someone you're actively hating."

"Yep. Combat effects are the opposite, they are easier to power with negative emotions and very hard to do while you're in the grip of a powerful positive emotion. Most people can't incinerate someone while experiencing a powerful wave of love."

"Most—but there are some who can?"

"Yeah, we commonly call them psychopaths."

Something about that didn't feel quite right, but Kat didn't seem to be in a very approachable mood, so I let it go.

"Neutral emotions are…well, neutral. They don't make it any harder or easier to do a given effect. The most important thing to know is that if you're in the middle of experiencing a powerful emotion that isn't your default setting, it can make it very hard to work any kind of effect."

"How so?"

"We are about to go to quite a lot of effort to create a set of neural triggers. They will make it so that you can wipe your emotional state clean at a moment's notice and stoke the fires of a different emotional state that you can call up with sufficient strength to power any of the effects you could conceivably need."

"Right, but why wouldn't I choose a positive emotion as my default setting? Why wouldn't I want to run around happy most of the time?"

"Because happiness isn't the natural state for most people, Selene. What happens if you pick love as your dominant emotion and you anchor that emotion around your feelings for Jace? Sure, at the start it feels awesome. Any time you want to work an effect, you just think about how much you love Jace, and you get warm fuzzy feelings that remind you just how much you love him.

"Eventually though the two of you are going to get in a fight, and one of the unalterable truths of our existence is that emotions have weight and substance. They don't just disappear, at least the strong ones don't. So there you are, nine different kinds of pissed off at Jace, and then someone from another pantheon jumps you and you reach for those feelings of love, but you can't get past the hurt and disappointment, so you only manage to power relatively weak effects and the next thing you know you're dead and your friends are browsing social media sites for the next sixteen years in the hopes that they'll be able to get to you and train you before another pantheon finds you."

"That's why I chose anger before, isn't it? Pretty much no matter what else is going on you can still find something to be angry about. Is that your default emotion too?"

Kat looked away from me for several seconds before sighing. "It used to be. Back when you and I ran together we both defaulted to anger, but after you died everything started changing for me. I can still work with anger—there's plenty about my life to be mad about—but more often than not lately I find myself defaulting to fear. After eighteen years of running, with every day spent wondering if we were finally going to be pinned down by a bigger pantheon, fear pretty much pops into my head without any effort at all."

The idea of spending decades getting angry at the drop of a hat sounded all kinds of unpleasant, but it was nothing compared to having your every thought colored by terror. I couldn't imagine a worse kind of existence.

"Oh, Kat, I'm so sorry."

"Don't be. It's just the way things are. Now are you going to get on with picking an emotion or are we just going to sit here and yap?"

It was tempting to go with anger. It had served me well for decades, or even centuries, and even now I seemed to be able to conjure up a boiling red haze at the drop of a hat. Despite all of that, something inside of me cringed at the thought of feeding the monster I could feel barely leashed inside of me.

I took a deep breath and then nodded. "Okay, I've got an emotion picked out."

"Are you going to tell me what it is?"

"Not unless it's absolutely necessary."

"Fine. Think of an experience, a recent one if possible, that made you feel that way. If you can't think of a recent experience, then you're probably picking the wrong emotion, but it is possible to use a fantasy to achieve the right frame of mind. The goal is to wrap yourself in the memory until you can feel the emotion as strongly or stronger than you did at the time you experienced the memory. It may be harder right now because you don't have the same kind of clarity you'll have once you're fully awakened, but it should still be possible."

I nodded and then reached for the feeling I wanted. It came with almost no effort at all and was part memory and part fantasy. The feeling was nothing less than pure happiness, the amazing revitalizing happiness that seemed to come hand in hand with being around Jace.

It was the moment when I realized that I wasn't going to have to pay for all new tires, it was finding out that I was special in ways that I hadn't imagined were possible, and most of all, it was the feeling of being safe inside of Jace's arms. I knew that he wouldn't let anything happen to me, not while he was still breathing and had the strength to keep fighting.

It wasn't love or infatuation, despite the fact that those feelings also poured into me whenever I was around Jace, this was something as clear and weightless as sunlight. As tempting as it was to go with love as my default feeling—even despite Kat's warnings—I wasn't going to put my wellbeing that firmly in Jace's hands.

I chose happiness and couldn't help but smile as it filled me up to the point of overflowing.

"Okay, I'm feeling the emotion. Now what?"

"Obviously you've picked a positive emotion, which just fills me with warm tingles of excitement. As if Jace wasn't enough."

"It's not going to work, Kat. I'm still not pissed at you. Can you please stop trying to pull me out of my emotion and get on with the next step?"

"Fine. Open your eyes and look at me. The goal is to stop actively maintaining your chosen emotion by thinking about something else, but not something that is emotionally charged. You want to let your gushy good feelings trickle away rather than actively replacing them with something else."

"So what am I supposed to think about?"

"I don't know. Not Sandra, obviously since she pisses you off to no end."

I shook my head at her. "You obviously know how hard it is to *not* think of something after someone tells you not to think about it. That's a pretty low blow, Kat."

"Hey, you can't blame a girl for trying. Anger served you pretty well in your last life. I don't see why you're in such a hurry to change things up now."

"Because the depth of my anger terrifies me."

"That's good, you want a powerful emotion. The amount of memories that you can burn at any given time is directly proportional to the strength of the emotion you're feeling, Selene. Anger that powerful is going to translate to a heck of a lot of power whenever you need it."

I shrugged. "Maybe you're right and I'm making a mistake, but I don't think that I'm strong enough anymore to keep control over that level of rage. All the power in the world isn't going to do me any good if I can't stay levelheaded enough to use it without laying waste to everything around me."

"Well, if you ask me, restraint is overrated. All of you touchy-feely positive emotion types are the reason that the world is such a mess. You never have the stones to put a fallen enemy down like you need to, and they never thank you for showing them mercy. That type isn't capable of changing. They view mercy as weakness and it eats at them that they were defeated by somebody so weak. They always end up obsessing about taking you down until they finally succeed."

"Noted, Kat. You'll be happy to hear that you brought me back down to earth. My positive feelings have been vanquished and I now feel nothing but an apathetic wish that I could just cut my own throat and never have to deal with another human being ever again."

"Perfect, that's how I feel most of the time. That means we can move onto the next step, teaching you how to cut other people's throats."

"I'm going to assume that's an attempt at a joke because the alternative is too depressing to think about and I'm supposed to not be replacing my positive emotion with anything concrete."

"Suit yourself, but we're past that part—you really should try harder to keep up."

"Past that part?"

"Yeah, usually you're supposed to talk about the weather or something else equally boring for fifteen minutes before you move on, but I think you really have managed to let go of your default emotion, so I'm going to let you move on."

"Great, what's the next step?"

"Now you need to pick another emotion, one that you don't want to feel, preferably one from the other side of the continuum. So in your case since you picked love as your default emotion, you should probably pick hate as the thing that you're going to feel next."

She was trying to confirm her suspicions regarding my default emotion, but I refused to let her needling get to me. She'd told me what I needed to know. I needed the opposite emotion, I needed unhappiness, I needed something that was a cross between sadness and despair.

"So I need to think of an experience that will drive the opposite emotion and wrap myself up in it?"

"Yeah, but make sure that you don't choose anger. Right now that's just going to confuse things. It's going to take you a long time and a lot of work before you'll be able to default away from anger and replace it with love."

"It's not going to work, Kat. I'm still not going to tell you what my default emotion is."

"Fine, let me know when you've got the opposite feeling firmly in place."

I nodded and then reached for the memory I needed. It wasn't hard to find. I tapped back into the precise instant when I'd realized that Sandra had let the air out of all four of my tires. I played those few seconds between realizing I was screwed and Jace asking me if he could help over and over again in my mind.

I didn't just remember the experience, I put myself there. Behind my closed eyelids I could see it happening, and it was so real to me that I immediately began to feel the same emotions that I'd felt back then.

I felt depressed and weak, hopeless in a way that you only feel when you've been kicked around by someone stronger than you for a very long time. I grabbed ahold of those emotions and pulled them over me like a cold, clammy, prickly blanket that was never going to let me go.

"Are you feeling it?"

"Yeah, I'm feeling it. Now what?"

I couldn't leach all of the emotion out of my voice, but I came pretty close. Inside I was a quivering, sobbing mess, but I was pretty sure that I'd managed to keep from giving away what I was actually feeling to Kat.

"Let it sit there for a few seconds, and then throw yourself into the positive memory that you were first thinking about. Feel it, relive it like you were there, and let that memory chase the negative feelings away."

I couldn't have chosen a better pair of memories. All I had to do was just let things play forward a few seconds rather than continuing to loop it. A heartbeat later Jace was there with his hand out, offering to fix my car and show me all of the ways that I was more special than anyone else had ever realized.

The sense of happiness and satisfaction didn't just slowly push the sadness out of me, it crashed into me with enough force that the change was instantaneous. I was at the edge of despair and then suddenly the whole world was opening up in front of me, an endless universe of possibilities.

I couldn't help the smile that tugged at the edge of my mouth, but that wasn't entirely surprising. Kat's gasp, however, was. I opened my eyes and gave her a quizzical look.

"Problem?"

"I don't think that I've ever seen anyone make the transition that quickly. How do you feel right now?"

"Good, I'm still wrapped in the positive feeling that I chose as my default feeling. What does this mean?"

"It means you're a lot further along than you should be. Most people have to practice for an entire week to get such an all-consuming feeling and make the transition that smoothly. The original plan was to have you practice for the next couple of hours until we arrived, but you're basically already there. I have some more difficult exercises for you to run through, but they are designed more to increase the strength of your default emotion and make it easier for you to transition from a wider variety of other emotions."

"Okay, give me those other exercises. The sooner I can pull my own weight around here the better."

Chapter 20

The other exercises basically consisted of variations on what I'd already done. Once every couple of hours I was supposed to practice summoning my default emotion of happiness. Sometimes I was supposed to just overwrite whatever emotions I happened to be feeling, and other times I was supposed to imagine situations that would conjure other, negative or neutral emotions and then overwrite them with my default emotion.

Kat seemed to be prepared to keep time sped up so that I could get a few additional rounds of practice in before we arrived at the lake, but I figured there wasn't much point in making her burn memories if I was really as far ahead as she'd indicated. Besides, I really wanted to know what was going on with Ari and Jace. Apparently I was going to get plenty of practice defaulting away from intense feelings of jealousy.

As it turned out, Kat shared my assessment of the pointlessness of bending time just so I could do something that I didn't need privacy to practice. She agreed to let the time effect lapse after only a minimal amount of arguing, and then we headed back out into the main part of the RV.

When I saw Ari laughing and putting her hand on Jace's arm I didn't feel the flash of jealousy that I'd expected. Instead, I experienced a surge of anger that was nothing compared to the time that Jace had been forced to stop me from running into the school and bashing Sandra's head into a wall, but which still set off all kinds of alarms inside of my head.

Kat had said that I should avoid summoning rage for now, but she hadn't said anything about trying to overwrite it if it showed up on its own, so I turned away from Ari and took a couple of deep breaths as I closed my eyes and put myself back in that instant when Jace had seemed to have eyes for only me.

It was harder this time. The anger lingered, unwilling to be displaced, and flared back up every time I heard Ari laugh, but I refused to give up. I slowly blocked out every other sensory feed until all I had left was the memory I wanted to be experiencing and the sound of my own heartbeat.

When I opened my eyes a few seconds later I'd surrounded myself in a cocoon of happiness so thick that even Ari couldn't cut through it, at least not without being a ton more forward than was possible with someone who was driving a forty-two-foot RV towing an SUV and two jet skis.

Kat leaned forward and whispered in my ear. "That was amazing. I wasn't around the last time you were starting to master your ability, but I'm starting to wonder if there was more to your abilities all along than just curiosity and only needing two hours of sleep each night."

I gave her a non-committal smile and decided that I was going to practice defaulting back to happiness every forty-five minutes rather than waiting for two hours between sessions like I'd originally intended.

By the time we arrived at the lake it was almost dark, but it wasn't like we had to pitch a tent or anything. Setting up camp was as easy as pulling to a stop and then watching as Jace engaged the emergency brake and pushed the auto level button.

"And that's that. Come on, Selene, let's go gather some firewood."

"I'll come!"

Ari piping up was hardly unexpected, but that didn't mean her interruption was welcome. Luckily Kat was on the case.

"Come on, Ari. You can help me start cooking dinner—you've monopolized Jace enough already."

I followed Jace out of the RV and into the twilight-shrouded woods. Part of me wondered if he was going to speed us up to forty times normal speed and slip in another training session, but apparently he didn't have anything more planned than just gathering firewood.

"So are we actually cooking over the fire?"

"Nope, not if Kat has any say. It's her turn to cook and she abhors roughing it. If she had her way we'd spend the entire weekend either inside the RV or on the water."

"Maybe we'll get lucky and she'll manage to keep Ari in there all night."

Jace gave me a knowing look. "I'm sorry, Selene. I didn't expect this to be so hard for you."

"Really? What part of having my little sister compete for your affections while I'm stuck with Kat trying to master my power did you think would be easy for me?"

Jace was suddenly there in front of me, just inches away, his armload of firewood a jumbled mess on the ground.

"As hard as I try, I can't always keep my memories of the old you from influencing my perception of you, Selene. Once upon a time, this kind of thing would have done nothing more than amuse you. Once upon a time, I was the insecure one."

That made me laugh in spite of myself. "You're the hottest guy in the entire world, Jace. How could I have ever made you feel insecure?"

"Because seeing you for the first time changed me in fundamental ways that I never could have believed possible. From that instant forward, there was only ever one girl for me. You knew that as well as I did, and it meant that you never cared who I had to flirt with because you knew it was nothing more than flirting, that I would have given it up in an instant to be able to hold you in my arms."

"Well, I'm not that girl, Jace. This girl is insecure as hell and completely unsure how to proceed without scaring you off."

"You could never scare me off, Selene. Not in a hundred years, and that means much more coming from someone like us than it would coming from any of the other boys you've been interested in over the years."

My face heated up and I was suddenly glad that it was so dark.

"There haven't ever been any other guys, Jace. I told you I've never kissed anyone before, but it's more than that. It was like part of me knew that you were out there and I wasn't willing to settle for anyone else. I—"

The kiss was unexpected. We'd been standing there, only fractions of an inch away from each other, but I still hadn't been able to believe that he was actually going to do it. In between one word and the next, he placed one hand behind my neck and pulled me towards him with a restrained violence that made my stomach jump and my heart skip.

Despite the violence of our approach, our lips met like leaves falling on a pond. Jace gave me a second to decide whether or not this was what I wanted, but I knew from the second he touched me that I'd never wanted anything more in my entire life.

I reached up and cradled Jace's head between my hands as I stepped into him, hungry for more even as my legs started to shake.

My reaction must have been exactly the response that Jace was looking for, because his other hand was suddenly at the small of my back, pulling me up against his body as his lips became firmer and more demanding. Every nerve ending in my body seemed awake for the first time in my life, but the places where he was touching me felt like they were alive with fire.

My lips tingled with a burning heat, and my hands felt like they were holding tame lightning between them, but it was his hand on the small of my back that was sending tiny tremors of anticipation shooting through me. Raising my hands up to touch the side of his face had lifted my shirt up enough that his hand on the small of my back was touching my bare skin, only inches above the top of my low-rise jeans, and the feel of his hand on my flesh was so sensual that I gave up trying to think.

His lips were the perfect combination of tension and softness as he took charge of the kiss, and my body shot to an even higher level of sensitivity as my last vestiges of restraint evaporated. I could feel the hard planes of his body pressed up against me, his rock-hard pecs pushing against my chest, the bulge of his biceps against my back, and his hip against mine.

The shaking was getting worse. I moaned in unhappiness when he pulled his lips back away from mine, but then he pressed them against the side of my neck, and my legs gave out completely. I tried to fight it, tried to lock my knees, but my lower extremities had turned into boneless, tingling mush.

There was no way that Jace could have known that I was about to collapse, but he did. He let go of the back of my neck and picked me up by my hips, pressing me against his washboard abs as he slammed me into a nearby tree.

It was like his mouth had found a switch that sent jolts of pleasure shooting out through my entire body. I wanted nothing more than for him to never stop, but some part of me knew it was too much, that if I didn't stop him now I would never be able to deny him anything he wanted.

The feel of his mouth moving down from my neck to my collarbone combined with his hands circumscribing the bare skin of my waist and even the rough texture of the bark pushing against my back launched me into what felt like another plane altogether.

It took everything I had to force his head back up to my lips, but that wasn't because he was fighting me, it was because I was having to fight the part of myself that remembered this, that had been waiting for this kiss since even before I'd been born.

Jace pulled back for the briefest of moments to breathe and then darted back in for one last kiss before pulling me away from the tree and setting me back down on my feet.

"Don't ever forget, Selene. You've ruined me for any other girl. I'll always be yours regardless of whether or not you want me."

Chapter 21

I went through the next few hours in a daze. We made it back to camp with the firewood and then Jace started a roaring fire so that we could roast marshmallows. Dinner was frozen lasagna that was actually pretty good, but which contained absolutely no ambrosia. We washed it down with soda, and then stayed up talking about nothing until Ari finally started to nod off, at which point Kat and I helped her into the RV and put her to bed back in the master bedroom.

"I was really looking forward to sleeping on that bed tonight, but I never did the dishes, and if I don't do them now I'm going to have a complete mess on my hands tomorrow."

"Don't you have some cool effect that makes cleaning dishes effortless?"

"Nope, not even the Awakened can just make dirty dishes disappear. It's a good thing that dishwashers were invented."

"You know, when you tell me that kind of stuff it kind of ruins my desire to join your exclusive little club."

"Sorry, it's too late, you're already in the club. I think you're just going to have to deal with the downsides."

"You guys are rich, why don't you just hire a maid?"

Kat shrugged. "I'd be all for it, but Jace isn't a big fan. It's never a great idea to let anyone who's not part of your pantheon into your house—there's too much chance that someone will use the help to get at your journals."

It made sense, but it also eliminated one of the main benefits to being rich. That was a pretty big bummer in my book.

"Well, if there are no other options, let me give you a hand."

"Don't be silly, Selene. Filling up a dishwasher is definitely a one-person job. You should go out there and spend some time with Jace while Ari is asleep and unable to spy on you. After all, for you that's one of the main benefits to being in our little club…"

Something about the way she said it told me that she knew we'd kissed. I wanted to play it cool, but I just couldn't do it. I immediately went bright red.

"I knew it. You practically floated back to the RV after picking up the firewood. How was it? That was your first kiss, right?"

If anything my blush got even brighter, but I nodded. "Yeah, it happened while we were picking up firewood and it was my first kiss ever. As to how it was—I can't even begin to describe it. Jace was perfect. Considerate when I wanted him to go slow, and then super-hot when I wanted that."

It was a miracle that I managed to get that much out. I was strangely reluctant to tell Kat about what had happened. She was the closest thing I had to a best friend, and first kisses were definitely the domain of female best friends the world over.

All I could come up with was that I was ashamed. Not of kissing Jace, or even how we'd kissed. Everyone had kept their clothes on, and we'd both kept our hands mostly to ourselves. We hadn't actually *done* anything, but in some ways that didn't matter as much as the fact that I'd so completely lost control that I wasn't sure I could have told Jace no if he'd pushed for more than just a kiss. It was nice to know that Jace was that much of a gentleman, but I wasn't used to feeling so enslaved to my hormones.

Kat sighed. "I know that you didn't do any more than kissing, Selene. You were never the kind of girl to go in for casual intimacy, even back in the day when you were a heck of a lot more experienced than you are now. What's the problem? Were you hoping that it *would* go further than a kiss and now you're disappointed?"

"No—well, I mean I didn't go into the kiss hoping for more. Earlier today I wasn't even sure that I was ever going to kiss Jace because I knew he'd be silently comparing me to the old Selene. It's just that once we started kissing things were a lot more…intense than I was prepared for."

"Ah, I think I see."

There was a twinkle in her eye, but I could forgive her for that as long as she didn't make me spell everything out for her.

"Listen, Selene. You and Jace were together for a long time. He knows you incredibly well, and that includes turn-ons that *you* don't even know about yet. Normal kisses with guys you haven't been married to aren't going to be like that. In a lot of ways, Jace just ruined you because you just skipped past all of the awkward kisses with guys who don't know what they're doing."

"Wait, I'm *married* to Jace?"

Kat flinched. "Crap. I've got to learn to keep my big mouth shut. Don't tell Jace that I told you this, but yes, you are—I mean you were. Things can get a little complicated in our world. In the human world it's just until death do you part. For us death isn't a permanent condition, and you also have to worry about what happens if one of you burns away all of your memories."

"Wow, I never even thought of that. So what are the rules for those situations?"

"Well, it varies a little from one pantheon to another, but generally once you die or are memory-wiped, the two of you cease to be married. Back in the day the world was a lot bigger than it is today, so if someone died there was a decent chance that you wouldn't see them for decades or even centuries."

I found myself nodding. "And for most of us, that's long enough that you wouldn't remember them when you did finally see them."

"Yeah."

I looked away from Kat while she continued to scrub away at the worst of the mess in the sink.

"I don't even know what to think about all of this. I mean, things were already complicated enough as it was. Just knowing that he knew me from before and that we dated felt weird. This is a whole new level of craziness. How am I supposed to act around him now that I know?"

"Just act like yourself, Selene. I don't know how so much of you came through from the last incarnation to this one, but you're still the girl he fell in love with in every way that matters. Besides, Jace is a romantic at heart and he believes in a higher power. That makes him more patient and willing to roll with the punches than most of us.

"He may have said the same words as everyone else, but he believes that there is more to life than this endless cycle of death and rebirth. He believes in eternity and he wants to share it with you, but he won't push you into anything that you don't want one hundred percent. In fact, if I know Jace at all, he's probably feeling guilty for using his experiences with the previous you on the unsuspecting schoolgirl you are now. That wasn't fair to you."

My mind was whirling. I wasn't certain of much anymore, but I was positive of one thing—I wanted to spend time with Jace, wanted to see where things were going with him.

"Thanks for letting me know all of that, Kat. I think I'm going to take your advice and go spend some time with Jace while Ari is asleep. I guess the whole no-sleep thing is starting to happen for me—I don't feel even a little tired yet."

I was almost to the door when Kat spoke up. "Selene, promise me one thing. Don't sleep with Jace yet. I don't think he'll let it happen, not until after the two of you are married again—assuming that's what you decide to do—but if he does lose control of himself, then you need to be the one to hold strong."

She'd tried for casual, but something about her tone set alarms off inside of my mind.

"What aren't you telling me about Jace?"

"What? Nothing important. Why?"

The alarms cranked up in volume by a few decibels. "You've made it pretty apparent that you and Jace aren't on the same page when it comes to the stuff that happens after kissing. Given that, I can't help but think that there is something you're not telling me. Otherwise you'd be cheering me on rather than telling me to slow down."

"Did you ever think that I might just be worried about you two, that I might be concerned that you're navigating into treacherous waters given the history between the two of you and the fact that he remembers most of it but you don't?"

It was a good explanation, but I wasn't sure it was the full truth. Still, Kat seemed like she was going to just get her back up if I got all confrontational about it.

"Okay, Kat. That makes sense. I'm sorry that I doubted you—if you say that's all there is to worry about, then I believe you."

Kat sighed. "Even Jace can't get away with laying a guilt trip on me—at least not very often—but you come back from the dead, lose all of your memories, and still manage it like a pro."

"There's something else."

"Yes, there's something else, but I promised Jace I wouldn't bring it up yet. It's not anything about Jace, but it's relevant. Honestly, I wouldn't even care except that I know the old you cared. I wish I could convince myself that you wouldn't have minded. I'd love nothing more than to be egging you and Jace on, but I can't do that and still be a good friend to the girl I used to know."

"Do you have any idea how cryptic that is?"

"Yeah. Believe me when I say that I wish I could just tell you."

"Were Jace and I not happy together? Did he...did he cheat on me?"

"No, don't be silly. Jace is practically perfect and the two of you were ridiculously happy together. I'm sorry, I just can't tell you more. Now go enjoy your time with him."

It wasn't a very good answer, but I chose to just focus on the fact that Jace and I had been happy and leave it at that. If it had been someone else stringing me along like that I wasn't sure I could have left things alone, but despite her sometimes bipolar behavior, I really did believe that Kat was my friend and that she had my best interests at heart.

I slipped out of the RV and walked over to the fire, but there wasn't any sign of Jace. I considered going out into the darkness to find him, but I knew I'd probably just get lost if I did that so I just sat down next to the fire and threw some more wood on it.

It took a few minutes, but pretty soon I had three-foot-high flames which chased the darkness back almost twenty feet. It was a good thing too because I was starting to get a little freaked out. I could have counted the number of times I'd been out camping on one hand.

Mom had never really been much of a camper—especially back when we'd been younger. Once she'd left us Dad had been too busy working to take us on any camping trips.

The little hollow where we'd parked the RV had looked welcoming and open during the day, but now that night had fallen it felt like the trees were starting to press in on me. Even worse I didn't recognize most of the sounds filling the air around me. The insects, with their two-part humming chorus were especially discomforting, and I had to fight the urge to go back to the RV and take refuge behind the heavy vehicle's locked doors.

I was fighting a losing battle, but Kat was perceptive enough to figure out why I'd flee the great outdoors, and she'd never let me hear the end of it. I just needed to gut it out for a few more seconds, maybe a minute or two tops, and then either Jace would return or Kat would finish doing the dishes and come out.

The sound of buzzing wings brought me around to the left, but when I looked there wasn't anything there. Based on the way the wings had sounded, I'd half expected to see some kind of massive white moth. Moths had always freaked me out a little, but even a moth the size of my fist would have been better than turning to find nothing.

The insect buzzed past me again, now on the other side, and I spun around again. I was acting like a crazy person, but I couldn't help myself. The feeling of someone being out here, watching me was just too strong to do anything else.

I spun around again, and this time I caught a glimpse of something out of the corner of my eye. I'd only *thought* that being strafed by a fist-sized insect would be preferable to not knowing what it was that was circling me.

REBORN

It wasn't a moth, not as fast as it was moving, but it *was* fist-sized, which meant it was the biggest insect I'd ever run into. My skin had started crawling a few seconds before, but that glimpse added a chill to the uneasiness I was experiencing. My skin now felt like it wanted to get up and run away.

I started back towards the RV, wanting to run, but afraid that I would trip on something and that whatever it was would attack me before I could get back to my feet.

Something came at me from the right and I slapped out blindly, trying to swat my attacker out of the air. The edge of my hand connected with a glancing blow against *something*, and then things happened almost too fast for me to follow.

The buzz got louder and deeper as my attacker came directly at my face, and then the night lit up with a glittering green glow that scared me so badly that I tripped over my own feet and fell down.

It was the same bug that had knocked me over in Jace's bathroom, only it was way bigger. My fall had gotten me out of the line of attack, but it looped around, flying erratically and much faster than I could have possibly run.

Escape wasn't an option, but my desperately seeking hands found one of the heavy branches that we'd gathered to use as fuel for the fire. I grabbed the improvised weapon as the insect streaked forward, dive-bombing me in an un-mistakable attack.

I swung the stick with all of my might, hoping to knock the glowing menace out of the air, but it just juked down...and landed on my chest.

I'd been expecting to be stung, or bitten, but it wasn't an insect at all. It was a miniature, perfectly formed girl who was about an inch and a half tall. Oh, and she had glittery green wings.

"Why are you such a hater?"

I was speechless. Her voice had a tiny, high-pitched quality, but other than that it was perfectly understandable.

When I didn't immediately respond she jumped up and down on my breastbone. She wasn't heavy enough to hurt me, but the sensation was still uncomfortable. She obviously wasn't an insect, but my instincts hadn't caught up to what I was actually seeing yet and having her bouncing up and down was still making my skin crawl.

"Can you at least see me now? I've been buzzing around your head for days now and getting nothing. Back then all I wanted was for you to be able to see me. Now that you can see me, you're trying to smack the crap out of me. So much for progress."

"I can see you."

She zipped into the air so fast that she was nothing more than a solid green line. Apparently me finding my tongue was an even bigger shock to her than it had been for me.

"Wait, come back!"

For a second I thought she hadn't heard me, but then I saw a shimmering trail working its way back towards me, zigging and zagging as though to make sure that I wouldn't be able to hit her. I finally realized that I was still holding the branch that I'd been using as a club, and set it down—although not without reluctance. She was too fast to hit, and I wasn't going to be able to make it to the RV before she could land on me again, so all that was left was hoping that she wasn't going to hurt me.

"Are you going to try to hit me again?"

"No! What are you?"

She darted to a stop just in front of my nose and frowned. "Isn't that just the way that it always works? People are all too caught up asking *what* someone is to even care what a person's name is."

I forced myself not to sigh, but it was hard. Even my dad couldn't usually get away with talking to me like that. The last thing I wanted was to be lectured by this little diva.

I pulled myself up into a sitting position. "Hold on there, Tinker Bell. Don't try to act like it wasn't you who strafed me the other day in Jace's bathroom. I nearly cracked my head open because of you. Also, that led a pretty embarrassing incident involving Jace seeing me in nothing more than a towel. Before you go off acting like some kind of Miss Manners diva I think you at least owe me an apology."

She looked a little crestfallen. "I am actually sorry about that. It was the first time you'd ever seen me. How was I supposed to know you'd pick that moment to react when you hadn't noticed me the hundred other times I ran into you?"

"Wait, you used to run into me on purpose?"

She shrugged. "Do you have any idea how boring it is to be invisible? People talk like it's awesome in the movies, and it kind of is, but not so much when everything is built to a scale two hundred times your size and you can't ever turn the invisibility off. Then it kind of sucks."

"So you decided to take your frustrations out on me? What's your name by the way?"

"Bethany—my name is Bethany. But as long as we're pointing fingers, it's your fault that I was in the situation at all. You created me and then you disappeared just like you said you would, but you never told me it was going to take so long for Jace to find you again."

"Wait, I created you?"

Bethany gave me a look that seemed to say that I was being dense. "Of course you created me. Where else would I have come from?"

"I don't know, Bethany, this is all new to me."

I could hear footsteps, but they were coming from the wrong direction to be Kat. Either Jace was coming back, I was about to be murdered, or my hallucinations had just gotten worse.

"Selene, who are you talking to?"

I looked at Bethany, who had just settled on my knee and dropped down to sit cross-legged, and then shrugged in response to Jace's question.

"Honestly, I'm not sure. She says that her name is Bethany and she's about two inches tall and has shimmery green wings. Oh, and she says that I created her."

Jace's eyes went wide. "Is this the first time you've seen her?"

"No, she charged into me in your bathroom yesterday, but she was a lot smaller then. That's why I fell down. I thought she was just some kind of exotic beetle. I take it that you can't see her? Do you have any idea what she is?"

"An unexpected complication."

Bethany jumped back to her feet and shot Jace a dirty look. "I can hear him, you know."

"She doesn't like being called a complication. She's glaring tiny little daggers in your direction."

Now it was my turn to get the stink-eye. "I'll have you know that a person's importance has nothing at all to do with their size."

Jace made a calming gesture in the direction of my knee—apparently he'd figured out at least roughly where she was.

"I'm sorry, Bethany, I spoke without thinking. And Selene doesn't know any better."

"I don't?"

Jace nodded at me. "Apparently not."

"Well whose fault is that, Teacher Smarty-pants?"

That earned me a wince. "Mine, but in fairness I had no way of knowing this was going to be an issue. There are a hundred different things that I need to tell you, and only time to get to one or two of them on any given day."

Bethany seemed to be considering his response. "I'm inclined to allow it. Of course it means I like Jace even less than I did before, but that's no great loss. He's been such a bore. Going on and on about missing you anytime he thought there wasn't anyone around to listen. Like he was the only one suffering because you were gone. I spent eighteen years invisible and dodging flies the size of houses."

"She says that she doesn't like you very much and that you're a whiner. Do either of you want to start filling me in?"

Bethany waved airily in Jace's direction. "He can do it. It's way past time for him to start earning his way back into my good graces."

I gave Jace an expectant look. He ran his fingers through his hair. "So your Greek mythology books didn't just talk about gods, they also included legends about monsters that either helped or hindered the gods and heroes."

"Like Perseus' Pegasus?"

"Yeah, or the Minotaur, or any of a few hundred other creatures."

Bethany sputtered. "I am not a creature!"

"She didn't like being called a creature—I think you just lost a few more popularity points."

Jace was looking a bit like he was wishing he could put his hands on an industrial-sized fly swatter, but he managed a strained smile.

"All of the stories have some kind of mythical beings that aren't gods or heroes, but the legends about fairies are the ones that seem to have gotten the most details right."

It was my turn to wince. "Hey, I'm sorry about calling you Tinker Bell."

Bethany shrugged. "It was an honest mistake. Besides, I've seen her on television and she's really quite pretty and it appears that her favorite color is green too. Tell him to hurry up and get to the part about me being Seelie."

"Hey, Jace, what's a Seelie fairy?"

"Can you please ask Bethany if it would be okay for me to explain where fairies come from first?"

I looked back at Bethany, who gave me a resigned nod. "She says go ahead."

"Okay, so Kat explained to you that there are three types of emotions that can power our abilities, right? Well, as nearly as we've been able to tell, not all of the memories that disappear from inside of our heads are actually consumed by whatever effect we are putting into place."

"That doesn't make sense. Why would we lose more memories than we need to? That doesn't sound very efficient..."

Jace shrugged. "This is more your area of expertise—or at least it was—than it is mine. The best way to think of it though is like a fire. When you burn a log a lot of it is converted to heat and light, but you always end up with some ash left. You can't just put in less wood and avoid getting any ash out, no matter how much or little wood you burn there is always going to be some ash."

Bethany looked like she was getting impatient, but I made 'settle down' gestures at her and she sat back down and started using her wings to spin herself around in circles.

"Okay, so every time an Awakened creates an effect they end up with a bunch of magical ash."

"Sort of. The amount of ash is proportional to the size of the effect and how many of their memories went into powering it. Fairies seem to be nature's way of addressing the 'wasted' memories. Any fairies who are around when an effect is powered automatically absorb some of the unused memories."

"So they are para...I mean symbiotes."

"Yes, exactly. Younger fairies tend to be more than willing to help 'their' Awakened out in return for being allowed to feed on the 'wasted' memories. As fairies age, they tend to be less and less attached to their creators. Once they hit a certain size and power, they can absorb baseline memories from nearby humans, and the most powerful of both the Seelie and Unseelie courts have even been known to attack Awakened, taunting them into using effects so that they can feed."

I was suddenly nervous at having Bethany sitting on my knee. I tried to keep that off of my face, but she looked up at me and shook her head.

"I'm not going to attack you."

"Really? Because you kind of already did in the bathroom and then you were dive-bombing me just a couple of minutes ago."

"Look, I already explained that. I was just bored, and touching you makes me feel more solid. I'm a *Seelie* fairy."

Jace gave me an expectant look, obviously frustrated by the fact that he could only hear half of the conversation, and ready to be filled in.

"She said that she didn't mean to hurt me and that she's Seelie—whatever that means."

"Yeah, sorry, I'm getting to that part next. So nobody is *exactly* sure where fairies come from, but your working theory according to your notes was that fairies exist all around us at all times, and occasionally when an especially large measure of power is expended, it is enough to give one of the embryonic fairies a form that lets them interact with the rest of our world."

"Wait, so when she says that I created her…"

"You must have expended enough power in your faceoff with Sandra's last incarnation to allow her to manifest the form you see right now. Honestly, I'm surprised. To hear Kat tell it, the fight didn't last very long, and the damage to the surrounding area was pretty contained. It's pretty rare for a new fairy to be born without an extended, devastating fight."

I started to respond, but something that Bethany had said earlier was tickling the back of my mind. "I don't think that's what happened at all, Jace. Bethany said that I told her to follow you around because you would eventually lead her back to me. Could I have told her that in the middle of a fight like that?"

"No. Usually fairies don't appear until at least an hour or two after the expenditure of power occurs."

"So I created her before then—probably six or seven hundred years ago the last time that I died."

I looked at Bethany to see if she wanted to weigh in, but she seemed completely engrossed with studying her nails now. Jace was pacing.

"No, Selene, that's not how it works. Fairies only stay invisible like that for the first little while. Once they unite with their creator they lose their invisibility pretty quickly."

"So, she spent the last six or seven hundred years looking for me and never found me?"

"No, fairies are really good at tracking down their creators. Their ability doesn't work until we are Awakened and actively creating effects, but once we are, it usually only takes them a few days to find us. You must have created her a short time before you were killed."

My head was starting to hurt again. "That doesn't make sense. Why would I have burned up a huge chunk of memories just *before* going into a fight for my life where I was probably going to need all of those memories?"

"I don't know. Kat didn't know anything about what you'd done, and that means you had to have worked the effects while she was asleep, to keep her in the dark."

"Maybe that's not it at all, Jace. I'll bet that Kat and I burned through a ton of memories while we were running away from Sandra and the rest of her pantheon. Maybe our combined expenditure of power—along with whatever Sandra and the rest were burning up—was enough to bring Bethany into existence. Doesn't that make a lot more sense?"

Jace stopped pacing and dropped down onto a log next to the fire. "Yeah, except there's never been any record of something like that happening. It's always one Awakened who creates a given fairy. If multiple people expend a ton of power at the same time, then you just get multiple fairies."

"So it's never happened before—that doesn't mean that it's impossible though, right?"

Bethany shook her head at me. "No, he's right. When we first start out, we can only feed off of magic powered by one specific emotion.

Everyone's emotions are subtly different—not by much, but just enough that we can't feed on them until we've had a chance to grow. That's why I'm still this size despite having followed that dolt around for eighteen years. He's burned a ton of memories up, but nothing that I could use."

I looked back over at Jace. "She says you're right, that they can't feed off of anyone other than their creator until they've had a chance to mature."

"Right, all of which indicates that you created her just days, or even hours before you died."

"Okay, so we just have a ton of questions that we don't even begin to have answers for. What's up with this Seelie thing she keeps talking about?"

"The fairies are divided roughly into two groups, the Seelie and the Unseelie courts. Fairies who are born from a massive expenditure of memories being consumed under a positive emotion, all go to the Seelie Court. Fairies who are created by a negative emotion, all eventually end up as part of the Unseelie Court."

The nervousness inside of me amped up to eleven. "What about fairies who are born under the auspices of neutral emotions? What do they go on to become?"

Jace seemed to understand what I was getting at. My old self had been big on anger, which felt awfully dark to me. If Bethany had been born while I'd been using anger to help power my effects did that mean she was going to be Unseelie? I didn't even know what it meant for a fairy to be Seelie or Unseelie, but something was telling me that I didn't want to be around one that belonged to the Unseelie court.

"There isn't a third court, so the fairies created under a neutral emotion end up joining either the Seelie or Unseelie courts depending on their temperaments."

"And the Unseelie court is..."

"It's not very pleasant, Selene. Unseelie fairies take what they want and don't worry about what they have to do or who they have to hurt to get it. They don't have much if any moral code other than just greed and a lust for power."

"What about the Seelie fairies?"

Bethany jumped to her feet and then took flight, twirling around in the air. "We are kind, honorable and loyal. The perfect companions and the staunchest of allies."

"Never mind, Jace. Bethany just filled me in. The Seelie fairies are all sunshine, roses and wet puppy kisses."

Jace cleared his throat. "Actually they are most of those things, but they are still occasionally pranksters, and they aren't usually very big on the concept of mercy—justice seems to wield a big trump card where they are concerned."

"He's right to be nervous. He deserves a severe punishment for ignoring me for so long."

"Chill out, Bethany, seriously, he couldn't see or hear you. It wasn't like he wanted to ignore you, he didn't have a choice."

"Fine, just remember that I don't entirely approve of your choice in boyfriends."

I sighed. The last thing I'd been looking for was a self-righteous Jiminy Cricket to ride around on my shoulder and tell me everything she thought I was doing wrong.

"So how do we figure out whether Bethany is actually Seelie or Unseelie?"

She landed back on my knee and stomped her foot again. It was an impressive display of frustration—I didn't have the heart to tell her that I couldn't even feel her foot through my jeans.

"I told you already, I'm Seelie!"

"No offense, Bethany, but isn't that exactly what you'd tell me if you were Unseelie?"

"Hmm. I guess you have a point. What does your dull, self-righteous boyfriend think?"

Jace waited until I looked away from Bethany before responding. "If you come across a fairy in the wild, so to speak, one who is big enough and old enough to absorb memories from anyone, then there isn't any good way to know for sure whether they are Seelie or Unseelie."

"So you just have to treat them like normal people and hope that if you give them your trust they aren't going to screw you over?"

"Yeah, but with the added complication that it is always possible they've screwed you over in the past and you just don't remember any of it."

"Wow, that's lovely. I'm beginning to understand why you and Kat are such big fans of journaling."

"Yeah, it comes in handy. You'll also get pretty good at sketching things out. Just because a fairy tells you their name, doesn't mean they are telling the truth."

Jace looked off into the distance for a second before continuing. "There are some fairies who are generally known to be part of either the Seelie or Unseelie courts. The Lady of the Lake, for example, is generally considered to be the leader of the Seelie court, and Fenrir is as dark an Unseelie fairy as has ever existed."

I'd only thought that my head was starting to hurt before. The Lady of the Lake was from the story of King Arthur—she'd been the one to give him Excalibur—but I was having a hard time remembering who Fenrir was. The best I could come up with was that he'd been some kind of giant wolf from Norse mythology who was fated to help destroy a bunch of important gods in the final battle when the world ended or something.

I was kind of proud that I'd remember that much, but mostly I was just still struggling with the idea that so many figures from mythology weren't just based on real people, they were actually still alive and running around.

One thing for sure, it was becoming very apparent to me that fairies weren't all bite-sized Tinker Bell clones. They might all start out that way, but the ones that had been around for thousands of years sounded like they could be as big as an SUV.

"But nobody really knows, right? I mean the Lady of the Lake may have been super awesome for the last two hundred years, but if she's actually Unseelie, then she could just be playing a really long game waiting for the perfect chance to screw over everyone who's ever trusted her. Gah! This all sucks beyond belief."

Jace was obviously trying not to laugh at me, but the corners of his lips turned up in just the slightest of smiles.

"It's not quite as bad as that. Firstly, the fairies aren't like us; they don't lose their memories over time, and they don't age physically. That means that the Seelie court is quick to kick out anyone who turns out to be Unseelie, and they are happy to make sure any Awakened who asks knows which fairies can or can't be trusted."

"So they can still screw you over, but they'll only get to do it once."

"Yeah, and it means that even any Unseelie fairies masquerading as Seelie fairies are still going to tell you the truth about who is officially part of the court. Since they are only going to get one chance to betray their supposed friends, they aren't going to blow their cover over something small."

I frowned at him. He was right, and that *was* better than worrying about an endless cycle of betrayals, but it still wasn't reassuring. Frankly I was thinking that I'd just be better off telling Bethany to hit the road—she wasn't worth the risk that she was lying about being Seelie.

"What's the other thing you mentioned?"

"Well, if a fairy grows in response to effects that are being powered by positive emotions, then the creator at least knows that they are Seelie fairies."

"All of which doesn't do us any good since I created Bethany governed by a fit of rage."

"No, you didn't."

I looked back at Bethany. "Beg your pardon?"

"You weren't using anger as your driving emotion when you created me. You were using a sense of happiness."

A chill worked its way up my spine. Kat had been so convinced that my default emotion had been anger, just like hers had been for so many decades. Had I started to change right before I'd died? It didn't make sense, but it had happened to Kat and it strained belief to think that I'd ended up picking my current default emotion simply by chance.

Jace was off of his stump and at my side a second later. "What's wrong, Selene?"

"Bethany just told me that she was created by a positive emotion. All I can assume is that I must have started changing my default emotion at some point before the end."

Jace looked like he'd been hit between the eyes with a large hammer. "No, that never would have happened, Selene. I mean it happens, but only to Awakened who have undergone something traumatic, something life-changing. You weren't in that kind of place; you were at the top of your game.

"There is another explanation though. Sometimes one of us can be overcome with another emotion that is actually stronger than our default feeling. It usually only happens under unique, trying circumstances, but when it does, it's usually so strong that the only limit on the effects that can be worked while in its grip is the amount of memories the Awakened in question has available to them. It's the stuff of legend."

"What do you mean?"

"I mean things like continents shifting, new volcanoes suddenly appearing out of nowhere, or tidal waves that are more than fifteen hundred feet tall. We Awakened worry a lot about how fast we are consuming our memories, but the truth is that in most confrontations it isn't the person with the most memories who wins, it's the person who can immerse themselves in the strongest emotion while still being able to function. Most of us would have to fight all-out for hours in order to burn up even just a few decades' worth of memories. That's the kind of thing that is required to birth a new fairy."

"So you're saying that I didn't die with most of my memories untapped, I burned up most of them the night before and created Bethany while working on *something*. But none of us have any idea what that something might have been?"

"No, one of us has to have an idea what you were working on that night. Ask Bethany what you were doing."

I cocked my head at her. She gave me a lazy shrug. "Yes?"

"You heard Jace, we'd like to know what it was I was working on when you were created. You know, right?"

"Yes, but I'm not going to tell you."

"Hello, I'm your creator, don't you owe me some kind of debt of gratitude?"

"Yes, I owe my creator an immense debt. My creator sacrificed more than I can imagine to bring me into existence—and unlike a lot of her kind, she did it with the *intent* of giving me life—but you aren't her."

"What do you mean I'm not her? I've just spent two days with Jace and Kat telling me that I am her."

"No, you look like her, you act like her, you even think like her, but you aren't her. Usually that is enough, but not this time, not when my real creator asked me to keep it a secret for her."

"She says that she's not going to tell us. She says that the old me asked her to keep it a secret and she cares more about the old me than she does about the new me. Is there anything we can do to make her tell me? Can't I just refuse to feed her if she's not going to be any help?"

Jace shook his head. "No, you're eventually going to start working effects, and when that happens she'll naturally feed off of the excess energies that are released. The only way to stop it would be to kill her, and neither of us wants to do that."

Bethany gave me a knowing look that tapped into the anger that I'd spent so long nursing. It was nearly enough for me to tell Jace that he was wrong, but I knew I'd just be making a hollow threat. I wasn't a killer—didn't want to be a killer, when you really got down to it.

"Fine, I guess she can keep her secret. I wish I knew what it was that I was working on though. If I had access to that kind of power, shouldn't I have just blasted my way out of the trap we were in? I mean, even if it had cost me most of my memories, wouldn't that have still been a better way to go than getting myself killed a few hours later?"

"I don't know, Selene. You weren't the kind of person to make many mistakes. If you decided to burn through decades of memories the night before a big battle then there was a very good reason. I just don't have the foggiest idea why you would have done it."

Chapter 22

The rest of the night was basically a bust. Kat came out a few minutes later and we filled her in with regards to Bethany and the fact that I had apparently been working something very expensive and powerful while she'd been asleep that last night before I'd died. I'd been holding out hope that Kat would be able to explain everything, that the new information from Bethany would snap into place with what she already knew and she would be able to solve our mystery.

Unfortunately, she seemed to be just as stumped as we were. We kicked around one hypothesis after another, but I didn't know enough about the world of the Awakened to even guess and the other two started repeating themselves after the first fifteen minutes.

After an hour Jace finally stopped us and said it was time for us to get back to training. Kat begged off, saying that she needed to get some sleep, which meant that it was just the two of us.

Saying that I was nervous would have been a severe understatement. We weren't alone, not with Bethany hovering just a few feet away from me, but after Jace's first few attempts at getting me to tap into my ability didn't work, she started to pay a lot more attention to her wings than to what we were doing.

I'd been afraid that things would be awkward between us, but I couldn't decide whether I was afraid Jace would try to kiss me again or if I was more worried that he wouldn't. It had all of the classic ingredients for me getting lost inside of my own head, but Jace somehow just short-circuited all of that.

He was all business during our training session, but he wasn't cold or standoffish. He was warm and funny and perfect. Honestly it was still blowing my mind that *Jace* had been married to *me* of all people. Not only that, he'd been married to a version of me that hadn't looked drastically different than I did now. I'd seen her—I mean my—old clothes and we were the same size.

I knew I didn't have all of the knowledge and confidence of the old me, but it wasn't like guys noticed confidence and smarts right off the bat. Jace had said that he fell in love with me from the moment he saw me. That seemed to indicate that I still had a chance with him, that he liked the outside package and all I needed to do was make sure that I spruced up the inside package to the point where I could keep him interested.

Of course, being able to use my ability for something worthwhile was a key component to that. We tried for three more hours to get me to the point where I could create my first effect, but in the end we didn't get anywhere.

Jace didn't seem impatient or disappointed, which was nice. He acted like we had all of the time in the world, but I knew that wasn't the case. Kat wouldn't be so worried if the threat of another pantheon finding us wasn't very real.

By the end of the third hour even my Awakened constitution was starting to fail me. I was yawning every thirty seconds, and getting worse by the minute. After my tenth yawn, Jace chuckled and pointed at the RV.

"Go get some sleep. We'll have tons of time tomorrow to work on this stuff."

"How do you know that?"

"Because it's obvious that Ari loves going fast almost as much as Kat does. I suspect that's the one thing that is guaranteed to pull her away from my side."

"I guess that's true. I can see the two of them spending a lot of time on the lake tomorrow."

"Like I said, plenty of time. Go ahead and go to sleep."

"What about you?"

It could have been viewed as some kind of invitation. In fact, I was pretty sure a lot of guys would have tried to turn it into the two of us spending the night together, but Jace just gave me another easy, slow smile.

"I set up a tent thirty yards that way. That's actually where I was when Bethany was dive-bombing you."

"Okay, I guess I'll see you tomorrow morning, Jace."

He looked like he was debating what to say next and then suddenly he was there in front of me. He took me in his arms and gave me a single, long kiss that made tingles shoot out to my extremities.

My defenses, the walls that I'd tried to put up after finding out that we'd been married, crumbled instantly. If he'd wanted to he probably could have had his way with me right there next to the RV. I wanted him to kiss my neck like he'd done the last time, wanted him to make my head spin and my body melt away, but he didn't do any of that.

When he pulled back a minute later his grin was faintly apologetic. "I told myself that I wasn't going to do that again, not so soon, not after nearly losing control the first time, but you were just so beautiful standing there in the moonlight that I couldn't stop myself. Good night, Selene. Sleep well."

I woke up feeling refreshed despite not having gotten much sleep, which was a good thing because Kat and Ari were even more hyped up than I'd expected them to be. Ari came out in a red bikini and jumped up and down on the pull-out bed until Kat and I finally threw our pillows at her.

Jace knocked on our door a few minutes later, which sent me scurrying for the shower. He'd probably seen me with bedhead at some point in the past, but I wasn't going to put that image back in his mind if I could prevent it.

I got ready in record time. The shopping spree hadn't included any makeup, but that probably was for the best since we were going to be on the water. I pulled on the blue tankini, slid on a pair of cute black board shorts, and then pulled my hair back into a simple ponytail.

Just before I was going to leave, Bethany popped through the door. "Jace has breakfast ready, and he's looking back in this direction five times a minute. If your goal was to make him antsy I think you've succeeded."

"Hey, Bethany. How did you go through the door like that without opening it?"

"It's a fairy thing. It's going to go away once you start working effects and I'm no longer invisible, but I figure as long as I've still got it I should enjoy it."

"You seem like you know a ton about what's going on. Is that just a fairy thing too? Are you born with all of this knowledge?"

"Nope. You—I mean past you—told me most of what I know. I've learned a few things since then. Hanging around Jace hasn't exactly been the highlight of my existence so far, but there have been a few benefits. Most of that stuff didn't stick very well, though. You, however, are something else entirely. I remember every word you said to me, and since Jace found you and I've been hanging out around you things have gotten a lot better in the memory department."

"Wow, that had to be hard—I mean flying around Jace, waiting for him to track me down, not remembering what happened from one week to the next…"

Bethany shrugged. "It wasn't exactly a bed of roses, but I made it work."

She flitted around me, checking my appearance and then nodded. "So are you going to go out there or what?"

"I guess it's time."

"Just don't eat so much that your tummy pokes out above your shorts. I'm pretty sure that's not one of Jace's turn-ons."

"Gee thanks. Remind me to return the favor some time when you're obsessing about some hot fairy guy."

"Yeah, it's not going to be a problem. You'll have probably forgotten all about this conversation by then."

That shut me up instantly. She was right. I suddenly felt a profound need to start writing down everything I could remember about my life. I was about to start burning memories. It could happen any time, maybe even today, and once that started I was going to lose pieces of what made me the person I was. I was going to lose my memories of my mom.

Bethany buzzed around and then stopped on my shoulder. "I'm sorry, Selene. I didn't mean to go too far. I've heard Kat and Jace make those kinds of jokes for years now. I thought it was just what you people do to each other."

"Yeah, I'll bet they joke around like that a lot. Probably someday soon I'll be joking along with them; I'm just not quite there yet. Somehow I never realized that I was going to forget my mom. It was staring me in the face this entire time, but I couldn't see it."

"I'm sorry, Selene. I wish I could have known her. I heard you and Ari talking about her that first night after we found you though. Years from now, after you've forgotten all about this conversation, I'll still be able to tell you what you and Ari said, word for word. I know that you Awakened are fond of your journals, but if there is ever anything that you want to know later on, you can tell me and I'll relate it to you whenever you want, as often as you want."

I felt like crying. Before it had been just because I'd been sad about my mom, but now it was at least partly because I was so moved by Bethany's offer. I tried to tell myself that it was too soon to start trusting her, that I needed to confirm that she was Seelie before I let myself open up to her, but it was too late. I could feel myself latching onto her emotionally, grabbing at the one person in my new life who would still remember things two or even three hundred years from now.

"Would you really do that for me?"

"Of course. That's one of the roles that fairies have served for thousands of years. Even when you forget, we don't."

"But you have no reason to be loyal to me. You said it yourself, I'm not your creator. I'm just a shadow of her."

"When you don't have anything else, even a shadow will do, Selene, but you're more than that. I'm sorry about what I said earlier. I'm not going to betray the secrets that I promised to keep for you so long ago, but I do value you. I'm going to value you forever. All of us Seelie fairies value our creators—we never leave you, but eventually you all leave us. It's just one of those things. Nobody has light incarnations forever. Not even Jace."

Chapter 23

I stepped out of the bathroom with Bethany floating next to my ear, and had the satisfaction of seeing Jace's eyes go wide as he took in my swimsuit and shorts. Mission successful.

Breakfast went by in a flash. Ari agreed to do the cleanup—probably hoping to win some points with Jace—and then frowned when Jace headed outside to pull the SUV off of the trailer. I thought about staying inside the RV to avoid pissing Ari off even further, but then Jace knocked on the window and asked for help.

I'm pretty sure that Jace could have done it all by himself, but I wasn't going to complain about the chance to spend a little time with him, even if it was still crazy cold outside.

As soon as the SUV was down on the ground I jumped inside and turned the heat on full. Jace stowed the ramps back on the trailer and then disappeared inside the RV again. I wanted to follow him, but I wasn't quite up to facing the cold again. When he reappeared ten minutes later he was wearing board shorts and carrying a black hoodie.

A few minutes later Ari was done with the dishes and both vehicles were on their way to the lake. It was a short drive, and once we arrived Kat parked the RV and Jace proceeded to move the trailer over to the SUV while she changed into her suit.

Within fifteen minutes of our arrival Jace was using the SUV to back the jet skis down into the water and Ari was bouncing up and down in excitement. Kat reappeared with life jackets as I was pushing both watercraft into the water. She tossed the second life jacket to Ari and then jumped on the closest jet ski and took off like a bat out of hell. Ari was only a few seconds behind her and Bethany was a glittering green streak zipping around Ari's head.

"I'm sorry you're not going to get much time on the lake, Selene."

"Are you kidding? As cold as it is out there, I'm not in any hurry to get on the water."

Jace grinned. "We are far enough south now that it will warm up pretty quickly, but you're right, if either of them go overboard right now they're going to turn into popsicles. Let me get the SUV parked and then I'll meet you over on the beach."

It wasn't much of a beach, but it was big enough that there was a chance nobody would be bothering us this late in the year. I walked across the cold, wet sand until I found a spot where the sand went up high enough that it was dry.

Jace appeared a minute later with towels, drinks, and a bottle of sunscreen. "I parked the SUV in a different spot so if your dad shows up it will look like I showed up at a different time."

"That's a good idea—I wouldn't have thought of that."

He laid the two towels out next to each other and handed me a bottle of water. "Yeah, well, I've got a few centuries of experience at being sneaky under my belt. I am sorry though that we backed you into lying to your dad."

I shrugged. "I don't like it, but I need to get comfortable with the idea that I'm going to have to do a lot of deceiving over the next little while. As long as I'm unwilling to tell them everything about what's going on with me, there just isn't any other option."

"I'm sorry, Selene. That really sucks."

"Yeah, it feels like every step I take lately puts an even bigger rift between my family and me, but there just isn't a good way to tell them this. I guess I should just be grateful that I have you and Kat. I can't even begin to imagine how much it would suck to be finding this all out through trial and error, all the while not having anyone to talk to about what was going on."

Jace nodded. "Obviously neither Kat nor I remember that far back, but some of my earliest journal entries seem to indicate that was what it was like for me. It doesn't sound like it was much fun. There are however some offsetting benefits."

He pulled a thin silvery bar out of his pocket and dropped it into my hand. "Like this."

"What is it?"

"It's a bar of solid platinum. That particular one is worth about eighty thousand dollars."

I'd had a good hold on the bar, but when he said how much it was worth I nearly dropped it. I tried to give it back to him, moving like it was hot to the touch and burning me, but Jace refused to take it. He seemed amused, which just made the whole thing even more frustrating.

"That's worth as much as my dad makes in two years of working, Jace. Please take it."

"Why?"

"Because I don't want to break it. There's no way I could ever replace it and I don't want to be even further in debt to you."

"You're not going to break it, Selene, it's a solid bar of metal. Besides, it's not mine—it's yours."

I shook my head as his words started to sink in. "No, it's too much. It's a nice sentiment, but I can't accept a gift like this. Really, the clothes were too much, but this is—"

"It's not a gift, Selene. It's yours. It was in the box of stuff that you gave me to hold onto before you died. There are five more in there, but it's a moot point because you're going to be able to make them all by yourself shortly."

I held up the bar and shook my head in amazement. "You're just giving me a half-million dollars' worth of platinum? Do you know how crazy that sounds?"

"It's just money, Selene. How did you think that Kat and I maintained our lifestyle?"

"I don't know. Kat talked about successful stock investments. I guess I figured that was basically right, that you had spent the first part of your lives working and earning money so that you could invest it and then live off of the interest and dividends."

"Yeah, there's a little of that, but mostly we're careful not to tie up too much of our money in stuff like that because no matter how careful you are there is always a way for someone to tie it back to you. Mostly we just transmute clay into platinum, silver or gold, and then sell it on the black market. Like I said, you're almost to the point where you'll be able to do that yourself, at which point you'll never have to worry about money again—at least not in the long term."

For the second, or maybe third time that day I wanted to cry. "I don't even know what to say. You have no idea what this means to me."

"Actually, I do. Kat and I have hired private investigators to look into each girl we found online who looked like you. Nothing too intrusive, but enough that we would know the lie of the land if it turned out that you were...well, you. We know that your dad is up to his eyeballs in debt right now and that he's maxed out his earning potential there at the factory. I was planning on doing something for your family even if you turned out not to be who we thought you were, but this is even better because it's the old you helping you out—so there's no reason not to accept the assistance."

That soured my mood. "What if you're wrong, Jace? What if I'm not really the latest incarnation of the girl you knew? Maybe all the signs that you think point to me being her are just dumb luck."

He grabbed my hand before I could get all of the way to my feet. "They aren't. I knew they weren't all along, but Bethany's arrival seals the deal. Fairies aren't wrong about their creators. Besides, you've stopped sleeping as much and I can feel your gift flaring up from time to time as it tries to make the switch to being fully active."

It was hard to say whether his words or his touch was more calming, but the two combined were more than sufficient to do the trick. I relaxed back down to the beach towel he'd laid out for me and took a couple of deep breaths.

"Okay, sorry for freaking out."

"It's perfectly normal at this stage. It gets easier to accept everything once you use your power for the first time."

"I guess we'd better get started training then. There's no telling how long the jet skis will keep Ari entertained and I'm making us waste time."

"I could always do a minor time bend—something like two or three times normal speed wouldn't cost me much in the way of baseline memories and it would make a big difference with regards to how much time you have to practice..."

"Nope, I've wised up to your tricks now. There isn't any reason to bend time. It would just mean that I'll end up falling asleep at the same time as Ari. We'll probably have to do that kind of stuff later, but not right now—not since my dad isn't expecting us home before he goes off to work again. What do you want to start with?"

"I was thinking we should try a transmutation. We can always change things up later if the transmuting doesn't work. Go ahead and immerse yourself in your new default emotion."

I blushed. Unlike Kat, Jace didn't seem to mind that I'd picked a positive emotion for my new default, but he would mind if he realized that I'd stopped practicing. There had been a lot more excitement and disruption than normal over the last twelve hours or so, but I still needed to hold up my end of the bargain.

I closed my eyes and let the memory of Jace saving me from Sandra well up inside of me until it had pushed the embarrassment away. I felt a surge of relief at how easily the memory came back to me and at how strong the feeling was, but the relief was just a flicker around the edge of the happiness. It didn't interfere—I was ready.

"Okay, I'm feeling it."

"How strong is it?"

"Um…strong? How do you describe the strength of an emotion?"

Jace's laugh was so clear and happy that it actually managed to add to my sense of wellbeing and happiness. The feeling spiked to new heights and for the briefest of instants I almost reached out and took his hand. I was pretty sure that would make me even happier, but there was also a possibility that doing that would introduce other feelings that would overwhelm the happiness I was trying to cultivate. I decided not to risk it.

"What next?"

"Okay, hold the platinum bar in one hand and hold out your other hand so I can put some sand in it."

I waited while Jace picked up some sand and poured it into my palm. Under other circumstances I would have felt silly sitting there with my eyes closed, but with my default emotion surging through me I was perfectly content to just sit there and wait.

"There you go, enough to get excited about, but not so much that it should be a hard transmutation. Now, keep your eyes closed and think about the differences between the two materials."

"What, like one is a bar and the other is a bunch of tiny granules?"

"Sure, that can be part of it, but if that's all you notice, it will just mean that you'll fuse the sand into one piece. You're trying to fundamentally change the nature of the sand—that means that the more differences you notice, the more likely you are going to be to succeed in making the change."

I nodded and started trying to catalogue the differences. Texture, density and color were all easy. I already know what sand tasted like from playgrounds as a child, but I put the platinum bar up to my mouth and carefully licked it. Taste, check; smell check. After that I didn't know what else to try. Did they conduct electricity in a different fashion? Did platinum respond to magnets?

I gently knocked the platinum bar against my other elbow, trying to establish if it carried any kind of vibration, and then shrugged.

"That's all I can think of. Is there anything I'm missing?"

"Probably, but that's okay, it works best if this all comes from you rather than trying to hold a bunch of stuff in your head that Kat or I tell you. Now think about how sand makes you feel."

"Happy, and relaxed. Sand feels like playtime, but a little like I need a shower."

I felt silly saying it, but verbalizing my thoughts was making it easier to keep the sand feelings from knocking my default emotion off of kilter.

"Good, Selene, that's good progress. This is where we started having problems last night. Now try to hold the physical differences in your mind at the same time that you're holding onto your default emotion and your feelings about sand."

"It's difficult, it all just wants to squish together, or barring that my mind wants to think about something else."

"I know, but you're almost there. Now think about how platinum makes you feel."

"Happy, secure, safe—it's like knowing that nobody can ever touch me again. Sandra won't have any power over me anymore, her dad won't be able to force my dad to work himself into the grave, it's like a little piece of heaven."

"Okay, now amp your default feeling up as high as you can and then take all of the platinum attributes and feelings and force them to over-write the sand feelings and attributes."

I felt like my mind was trying to split itself into five different pieces, but I gritted my teeth and yanked on the sand feelings, squishing them into the platinum feelings. The attributes followed almost as if of their own accord, and I felt something break free of my mind, streaming out the front of my head like steam from a kettle.

It was so surprising that my focus wavered at the last second and the sand in my hand went hot for a split second before exploding out of my hand.

Jace yelped in astonishment, and I looked down to see that my entire torso was splattered in white gunk.

"Crap, I thought I almost had it."

"You did it, Selene, that's great!"

I took a sniff of the stuff coating my right arm and made a face. "I'm pretty sure that platinum doesn't stink like this."

"Oh, you're right, that isn't platinum—in fact we'd better get cleaned up in case it's caustic—but you did manage to transform something. That means your ability is fully functional and it's just a matter of practicing."

I started to respond and then realized that he was right, my skin was starting to itch. I jumped to my feet and charged to the icy water, jumping in and scrubbing at my suit and body in attempt to get it all off. Jace followed along at a more sedate pace, chuckling.

"Hey, it's not funny. I think this stuff is burning me!"

"You're right, I shouldn't be laughing, it's just that I've never seen you move that fast. I was going to suggest running back to the RV and having you shower there, but I guess you're right, the water here is a lot closer and this way we don't have some kind of unknown substance trying to eat a hole through the plumbing system."

"Is any of it on my face or in my hair?"

I was already starting to drop further down into the water, but Jace had waded out far enough that he was able to grab my arm and pull me back up.

"You're fine. It didn't get on your face or in your hair."

Jace calmly washed the white splatters off, but even after they were gone there were red spots on his chest.

"I'm so sorry, Jace."

"Don't be, watch, I can make it disappear."

He concentrated for just a second and a handful of red splotches faded away—it was like watching a time lapse sequence of someone healing.

"I'd get rid of all of them, but we should probably change our swimsuits and it's going to be best if we have a reason for that other than the one that Ari's going to assume when she first sees us."

"You're right—I never would have thought of that."

"All right, let's go back to the RV."

Jace had been right. The cold temperatures had disappeared even in just the short time we'd been on the beach training. Now that the sun had made it up high enough to clear the mountains and we were no longer in the shade, it was warm enough that I was mostly dry by the time we made it back to the RV.

Jace offered me the choice of changing in the bathroom or changing in the bedroom. I picked the bathroom just so that I would have a mirror. I'd entertained thoughts of trying to salvage my tankini, but once I was standing in front of a mirror I realized pretty quickly that wasn't going to happen. Whatever I'd changed the sand into had been caustic enough that it had eaten through the fabric altogether in several places, and even where it hadn't made holes in my swimsuit it had still made the material so thin it was almost see-through.

That left me with a difficult choice. I had exactly three swimsuits left, which was two more than I'd usually brought. My first instinct was to just put on the other tankini and my last pair of board shorts, just so I showed as little skin as possible, but that could backfire on me if another transmutation went badly.

I was uncomfortable being around Jace in either of the two bikinis he'd bought me, but I would be absolutely mortified if my dad saw me in either of them. They were pretty tame as far as bikinis went, but they were still way more revealing than anything he would have approved of.

If I put on the tankini and ruined it then I'd have no choice but to wear a bikini and potentially face my dad later on. On the other hand, if I put on a bikini now, there wasn't any guarantee that I was going to be able to change back into my last tankini before my dad showed up—if my dad showed up.

I heard the bedroom door open, indicating that Jace was done, and decided to see if he had any ideas.

"I don't suppose that you have any mystical means of knowing if my dad is going to show up here?"

"Actually I sort of do. I haven't told you this, but I've got Kregor keeping an eye on your dad."

"Who's Kregor?"

"He's my fairy assistant. He's quite a bit older and bigger than Bethany, but he's still not much use in a fight. He can, however, watch your dad and let us know if anything happens to him."

I suddenly felt like the worst daughter ever. Less than twenty-four hours ago I'd been worried out of my mind about my dad and sister, but all it had taken was for Jace to kiss me once and all of that went flying out of my mind.

"I'm sorry, Selene. I meant to tell you earlier that I'd left Kregor there with your dad—I know he's not the best option, but I couldn't think of another way to make everything work. I would have stayed, but that would have ruined any chance of training you this weekend because you and Kat would have spent the whole time babysitting Ari. If Kregor sees something happen to your dad, he'll tail Sandra back to wherever she stows him and then he'll zip out here and tell us so we can go get him."

I took a deep breath and reached for just enough of my default emotion to balance myself out without completely washing away my concern for my dad.

"No, you're fine, Jace. It's like you said yesterday—my dad is the one who's probably the safest right now. Sandra isn't going to be able to overpower him physically. Using Kregor was a good idea. I'm just feeling like crap because I forgot that I needed to be worried about my dad."

Jace was silent for a second before responding. "Maybe you didn't forget, maybe you just remembered that I promised to take care of things."

"I think you're being too easy on me."

"I don't think so. I think that I'm just counterbalancing your tendency to be too hard on yourself."

That made me chuckle. Even through the door I could still envision the earnest expression on Jace's face, an expression that always made me want to believe him regardless of how unlikely his explanation might be.

"Well, thank you for the vote of confidence. It means a lot, even if I don't deserve it."

"I think we're going to have to agree to disagree. Why did you want to know if I had a way of knowing if your dad was going to show up?"

"Because this swimsuit is going to have to be thrown away, which means I have exactly one more swimsuit here that wouldn't give my dad a heart attack if he saw me in it…"

"And you're worried it's going to get ruined too if you wear it now."

"Right."

"Well, Kregor is supposed to let me know if your dad heads this way. He'll follow your dad until he's almost here and then he'll come find me and give me a heads up. Kregor is still young enough that he's a little flaky sometimes, but not nearly as much as he was fifty or sixty years ago."

"So I should be okay to wear whatever then."

"Yeah, but if you're worried about it maybe we should just work on something else instead. Transmutations can be a little tricky to get right the first few times. Usually the failed attempts result in something that isn't hazardous, but there isn't any point in taking a chance on a repeat."

There was a lot of sense to what he was suggesting, but part of me was unwilling to let go of the opportunity of learning how to make precious metals. Maybe I'd just been poor for too long to have a normal sense of perspective, but I just couldn't bring myself to agree with Jace.

"No, I want to learn how to transmute stuff. Hold on just a second and I'll get changed into one of the other two suits."

Once I made the decision to wear one of the more sexy swimsuits it wasn't quite as hard to envision Jace seeing me in it, but it was surprisingly hard to strip out of my ruined tankini when I knew there was nothing more than a thin door between us. It wasn't that I thought Jace would walk in on me or anything, but there was something incredibly sensual and exciting about knowing he was just on the other side of the door, that he might be thinking of me the same way that I was thinking of him.

I was all shaky and nervous, but I double-checked the door to make sure it was locked and then I took a deep breath and slipped out of my clothes. I grabbed a washcloth and scrubbed myself down to make sure that I'd really gotten all of the burning goop off of me, and then I reached into my suitcase and pulled out the dark blue bikini, the gauzy white wrap, and the matching blue board shorts.

A few seconds later I was dressed and looking myself over in the mirror. It wasn't as bad as I'd been expecting. I'd eaten a small enough breakfast that my tummy didn't stick out much at all, and the board shorts hung off my hips in a sexy way I hadn't expected. In fact, it was a lot like the way Jace wore his jeans, like gravity might win and pull them down at any second. Normally that would have made me terrified, but for all they looked like they were about to fall, they actually felt pretty solid. Besides, at least I would still have my swimsuit bottom on even if the shorts fell off.

I debated the wrap for a second, but I knew I was going to end up taking it off as soon as we sat back down anyway, so all I'd be doing was prolonging the moment of truth. Better to just get it all over with now.

I slid open the door to the bathroom and stepped out to find that Jace had moved over to the couch. I found myself oddly disappointed. The thought of him standing just outside of the door had been terrifying, but it had been a strange kind of connection between the two of us, and I hungered for any kind of bond tying me to Jace.

As disappointing as that was, Jace's reaction to seeing me for the first time in my new swimsuit more than made up for it. He was still Mr. Nice Guy, but there was a fire behind his eyes that I'd never seen before. I imagined that was how he'd looked last night when we'd kissed, but it had been too dark to see it then.

He took in all of me with one long look and then stepped forward to within arm's reach of me before stopping.

"You look absolutely amazing."

"If by amazing you mean splotchy, then I totally agree."

I took in the red spots across my stomach and upper chest with a gesture. They'd been mostly covered up by my tankini before, but now they were clearly visible and clearly hideous.

"No, I still use standard English where splotchy means splotchy and amazing means amazing, but if they are bothering you then that's an easy fix."

Jace reached forward and placed his hand on my stomach. I felt his energy reach out towards me, warm and welcoming, and then my skin heated up nearly to the point of pain before cooling in a sudden rush that brought goose bumps out on my arms. When Jace removed his hand the splotch he'd been covering up had disappeared and there was nothing left behind but my normal white skin.

The situation seemed to call for some kind of response, but I couldn't seem to get any words out. If I opened my mouth to thank him I wasn't sure what else would come out. The feeling of him touching me had been beyond euphoric. I wanted to grab his hand and press it against every inch of visible skin on my body, wanted it badly enough to almost disregard Kat's warning about not letting things go any farther with Jace until I knew the full story.

It was crazy. She'd said herself that Jace was perfect, that he was the kind of guy she would normally be pushing me towards rather than cautioning me against.

The silence between the two of us stretched out in long, heavy seconds, weighted down with tension that we both desperately wanted to act on.

Jace eventually took my lack of response as permission to continue and rested his hand lower down on my stomach. Once again, the sensation of heat building and then breaking into a cool wave nearly caused my knees to buckle, but this time he didn't give me any time to recover before he repositioned his hand, again and again.

At some point I kind of collapsed into him and he wrapped his free hand around my waist while his right hand continued to slowly work its way across the warm, bare skin of my upper chest. When he was done only two red marks remained, one high up on my right shoulder and the other on my left arm just above the elbow. More importantly, by the time he was done I wanted to kiss him with every trembling fiber of my body.

The feel of his hard muscles against me as his hand had smoothed away my hurts had been more than enough to make me throw caution to the wind. I wanted it, and he knew that I wanted it, but rather than kissing me he steadied me on my feet and then stepped back.

"I'd like to, more than you can possibly know, Selene, but I can't. Not yet. There are things that you need to know first."

"Then tell me. There's never going to be a better chance than now, because I don't think there is anything you could possibly say to change how I feel about you."

That made him grin in the way that only a guy could, a mixture of boyish pleasure and manly satisfaction at knowing just how desperate you were for their touch.

"It's mutual, but sometimes what you think about one person doesn't make a difference in the bigger scheme of things."

I wanted to demand an answer, or beg for one, but Jace switched gears and the moment passed.

"Sorry, I would have erased them all, but we need something to explain the change of clothing."

"I know. I don't suppose you could have given me a tan while you were at it…"

"I could have, but I love the way you look, Selene. Always."

Chapter 24

I realized something for the first time as we were walking back out to the beach. I was idly thinking back to the two kisses the night before and the near kiss from a few minutes before and noticed that all of my memories were much stronger and more vivid than they should have been.

It wasn't like I was remembering being back at the campsite and kissing Jace, it was like I was reliving it. My knees went weak and my insides got all trembly so fast that I started to collapse. I would have hit the ground if Jace hadn't grabbed hold of me.

"Selene, are you okay? What's going on?"

His voice seemed to be coming from a long distance away. This Jace sounded so small and unimportant that I was tempted to just ignore it and focus on the Jace that had his arms wrapped around me while he pushed me up against a tree.

REBORN

If it had been anyone other than Jace, I would have ignored them. The reality of our kiss was just so powerful, and I'd discovered that time seemed to speed up and slow down perfectly to provide the most amazing experience possible. The high points stretched out so that they seemed to take forever, while the boring parts leading up to the kisses flew by at lightning speed.

"Selene! You have to snap out of it. Those are just memories. They aren't real—I'm out here, not there inside of your head."

I tried to force my eyelids to pry themselves open, but my eyes just rolled even further back inside of my head.

"It's so real. Why would I ever want to leave it behind?"

"You don't have to leave it, it's going to be there for you for a very long time, but you do need to come back out here with me. There are so many incredible things that I want to show you and I can't do that if you stay trapped inside of your own head."

I could feel his breath on my cheek. It was still a distant, faint sensation, but it and the feel of my hand in his provided twin anchors that gave me something to pull against. They slowed my fall enough for me to consider what he was saying. He was right. I could stay inside my head reliving everything that had ever happened to me up until now and I'd be happy, but at some point I would start wondering what would have happened next. I would want to know the next chapter of my story, but unless I came back now, the story might not play itself out the way that I wanted it to. Jace wasn't going to wait by my side for decades.

My eyes flickered back open and I looked up to find that Jace had pulled me up onto his lap. I was cradled in his arms, which wasn't the equal of reliving our first kiss, but it wasn't a bad thing to come back to.

It took me a couple of tries to get my voice working. "What just happened to me?"

"We explained that we Awakened don't naturally forget anything, but that doesn't really cover the sheer strength of our memories. The first time someone experiences a peak memory after they become fully awakened can be tricky, but I didn't expect it to happen so quickly. I knew that what we shared just now inside the RV might turn out to be a peak memory, but usually it takes at least a few hours before someone has enough distance from a memory like that to get sucked back into it."

I shook my head. "It wasn't the memory of just now in the RV that grabbed me. It was the memory of our first kiss."

Jace looked poleaxed again. Apparently it was a banner day—I'd managed to shock him twice in less than twenty-four hours.

"That shouldn't be possible, Selene. All your memories from before your first effect should still be there, and they won't get any weaker, but there's no way you should have gotten sucked into something from before your awakening. Those memories don't have the clarity to do that kind of thing to an Awakened..."

"Look, I don't know how it's supposed to work, but the memory of that kiss was as real as anything I've ever felt. I could have sworn that I was back there reliving it again."

"Are you sure? The specifics should have been lacking."

"I could feel the ridges of bark in my back where you had me pressed up against the tree, Jace. There was nothing lacking about the specifics."

I actually managed to make him blush. It was cute. Don't get me wrong, I like Jace the way he normally was, confident and completely in control of his surroundings, but it was nice to know that he had this other side too.

"I, ah...I'm sorry if I got carried away—"

"You didn't get any more carried away than I did. I'm telling you though, the memories from last night are just as vivid as what happened a few minutes ago. It's like someone went back through my mind and added in all of the details that time had worn away from my experiences. What does that mean?"

"Honestly, I'm not sure. I don't have any record of anything like this ever happening, but it's a big deal. The memories from before someone becomes an Awakened aren't as good for powering effects as the stuff that happens afterwards. They still work, but they burn faster for less result. That means you would normally be a lot weaker than another Awakened, even just one who only had sixteen or seventeen years' worth of memories. If your memories are really all as detailed as it seems they are, then you've already got nearly a quarter of the saved-up fuel that Kat has."

I wasn't sure what to think of that. I liked the idea of being able to hold onto my childhood experiences longer than I otherwise would have been able to, but I wasn't quite as reconciled to the idea of losing them as I'd thought I was. The important thing right now though was to find out how to avoid getting sucked back into them again.

"So how does this work? How do you avoid spending every waking moment in the past?"

"You already know part of it. Living in the past prevents you from having a past or future either one. For most people that's enough to force them to deal with all of the less exciting parts of life. Other than that, it's important to keep the people you care about at the top of your mind. You value your relationships with them, so that will naturally help pull you back to reality because, even when you're immersed in the past, you'll know that spending all of your time in memories will destroy those relationships."

I started to nod and then had a terrible thought. "Jace, what happens if everyone you care about is killed? What pulls you back if that happens?"

His face went cold and expressionless for several seconds, and I suddenly realized that it wasn't just a worrisome hypothetical for Jace. He'd experienced that—maybe not completely, but close enough—when I'd died the last time.

"If that happens you just have to try to think about the future you hope to build and remember that other Awakened are never really gone. They may come back somewhere thousands of miles away from you, they may even come back to circumstances that turn them into a very different person than you remember, but they'll be back. That means there is always a chance that you'll be able to rebuild the future with them that you were hoping for the first time around."

"I'm so sorry, Jace. I didn't mean to send you someplace dark."

"It's okay. In an odd way the dark times help me value my time with you even more than I would otherwise. I've detailed them at length so that they'll always be with me in some form or fashion."

I suddenly realized that I was still sitting on his lap and blushed as I pulled myself to my feet. Ari and Kat were far enough out on the lake that I was pretty sure they couldn't make out any details, but there wasn't any reason to court danger.

"Okay, most brilliant of teachers. What's next?"

Next turned out to be putting our towels down in a new spot several dozen yards away from where we'd been before, and then sunscreen for me so that I wouldn't burn now that the sun was over the mountains.

After that, we took another go at me transmuting sand to platinum. I managed glass one time, something that looked and felt a lot like wood the next time, and then actual platinum on the next try. I felt like a million bucks—even though Jace said that my little mound of platinum dust was 'only' worth about twenty thousand dollars.

Knowing that I never had to be poor again, that I'd always have the ability to make sure we had a roof over our heads and food to eat, was liberating in ways I couldn't even begin to describe. When I poured the silvery-white granules into Jace's hand and he confirmed a few seconds later that I'd created ninety-nine point nine percent pure platinum, I jumped to my feet and let out a whoop of excitement that I was surprised didn't make it all the way out to Kat and Ari.

"Do you ever want to just leave behind everything else? There has to be a temptation to just take all this money and go live the life that most people dream about."

Jace nodded. "All of the time. I'd do it if it was possible, but it isn't. Maybe if our abilities worked differently and there was a way to guarantee that other pantheon couldn't sense us, then it would be possible, but it just isn't. No matter where you go other Awakened eventually come looking for you. And if they didn't, you'd still have to worry about the Unseelie Court fairies coming after you."

"That sucks."

"Yeah, it does."

Bethany zipped over appearing as if from nowhere. "What sucks?"

"The fact that no matter what we do, we'll never be able to get away from the constant battle between the different pantheons."

"Oh, that. Yeah, you told me about that before you died last time. It's the same way for us fairies. The Seelie Court is in a constant state of warfare against dark-incarnation, Awakened pantheons and the Unseelie Court. Basically I'm screwed too."

Jace was looking at me oddly, but I just made some flapping motions with my hands to let him know that Bethany had arrived.

"So what are the two of you up to? Have you managed your first effect yet?"

I nodded in response to her question and held up the handful of platinum dust that Jace had returned to me a few seconds before.

"I successfully managed to transmute sand to platinum, which means that I'll never have to be poor again."

Bethany's eyes got really big. "Does this mean that you're going to buy a bigger television? I've seen the television at your house and it's not nearly big enough. Are you going to get one that's the same size as Jace's? Now that's a television."

"Bethany, Jace's theater room is nearly as big as my whole house. There isn't anywhere to put a projector that big at our place."

Bethany made a dismissive gesture. "So get a bigger house—you're rich now."

Trust a television-obsessed fairy to rain on my parade. The truth was that all of the platinum in the world wasn't going to do me any good if I couldn't come up with a way to get my dad to accept it.

"Things could get a little complicated there, Bethany. My dad is going to want to know what's going on if I start spending thousands of dollars all of a sudden. I'm going to be lucky if I can manage to come up with a way to pay down our existing mortgage—I'm pretty sure he's never going to go for a bigger house, not with money that he's going to suspect came from dealing drugs or something else even worse."

It was depressing to be so close to successfully solving all of our monetary concerns and then still not be able to make a difference. Jace reached over and gave my hand a squeeze.

"Actually, Kat and I have a few ideas where that is concerned. Your dad is probably going to suspect that *something* is up, but he's not going to be able to prove that you're into anything illegal."

"What do you mean?"

"Would your dad believe that you have enough spare cash to scrape together the cost of a metal detector?"

"I don't know—how much do they cost?"

Jace shrugged. "I don't have the foggiest, but we'll buy a brand-new one and then bang it up some so that you can claim that it's an old, used model that you got a great deal on."

"Then what?"

"Then we'll go transmute a sizeable rock into solid gold and bury it on your property. You'll let your dad see you poking around the yard with your metal detector one day, and then on the next you'll dig up the eight-pound nugget just before he leaves for work."

I turned and threw myself at Jace, wrapping my arms around him in the most heartfelt hug I could remember giving in ages. Jace braced himself against the ground with one arm and wrapped his other one around me.

"Thank you, Jace. This is going to make all the difference in the world for us. I know I said that before, but then I started freaking myself out because I couldn't come up with a way to get my dad to take the money. This is perfect."

"You're welcome, Selene. I'm not going to leave you hanging. If that idea doesn't work, there are other options. You could find a stash of jewelry in your attic, or if your dad has some-where he stashes cash inside of the house, then you could slowly add to it. If nothing else, a long-lost relative on your mother's side can die and leave you a bunch of money."

Bethany yawned. "Does this mean that I'm going to get a bigger TV?"

"Yes, Bethany, I'll get you a bigger TV. Probably not as big as Jace's TV, and probably not for a while, but eventually you'll get to watch movies in the style to which you've become accustomed."

"Good. Are you guys going to get back to work now, or do I need to tell the two of you to go get a room?"

That made me blush, which caused Jace to give me a raised eyebrow of confusion, but I just shook my head at him. There were some things I most definitely wasn't going to pass on.

"Bethany thinks it's time we get back to work. I suspect that she'd like to be visible to you and Kat at some point in the not-too-distant future…"

"Don't you know it, sister. I was starting to think that maybe you'd forgotten about me."

"Hardly. You're the one who zipped off to play tag with Kat and Ari."

Bethany gave me an unconcerned shrug. "I just thought that the two of you might like some privacy. If that's not the case though I could always—"

"Behave, Bethany, or I'll stop practicing today and go play on the jet skis instead."

"Fine, fine. No more room comments—at least not once Jace can overhear me."

"Deal." I turned back to Jace and sighed. "The winged slave-driver wants us to get started."

Over the next two hours I practiced transmuting sand into platinum until I could force it into flat bars just like the one that Jace had handed me earlier that morning. It was a process. My first couple of attempts were still just loose grains of platinum, but then I progressed to the point where I could fuse the grains all together so I got a rough little platinum pyramid, and then eventually managed an actual bar, albeit much smaller than the one that I'd bequeathed myself.

The final bar was challenging mostly because I was transmuting a lot more sand than I had before. About the time I managed my first actual bar of platinum, Bethany got bored of hovering in the air around us and landed on my shoulder so that she could get a better view of my results.

By the time I finished and told Jace I was ready to move on, he indicated that I had the better part of a million bucks sitting on the towel between us. I would have happily kept on making platinum for the rest of the day, but Jace said it was hard to liquidate much more than a hundred thousand dollars' worth of precious metal at any one time, and even then you had to go to at least a medium-sized city to do it.

From there, we moved on to amping up my various internal systems. I learned how to reinforce my skin and bones, how to drastically increase the strength of my muscles, and how to make my lungs and circulatory system more efficient so that they could function on thinner, less fluid air.

It was surprisingly easy for the most part. After all of the stresses and difficulties mastering transmuting I'd expected to struggle with amping, but apparently I'd got the worst of the learning curve out of the way because I picked up most of them on the first try, and the one I didn't get first time out of the gate only took me two more tries to master.

Kat and Ari came in to refuel the jet skis twice while we were training, but each time Ari called out for Jace to come join her—preferably on her watercraft so that she could wrap her arms around his muscly chest—he just smiled and waved her off. By the second time, he looked more distracted than sincere as he sent her back out onto the water to play with Kat.

He then had me try to maintain all of the amped-up attributes he'd taught me at the same time, and I really struggled for the first time since transforming sand into white goopy acid. Individually, none of the effects he was asking me to do were that hard, but maintaining them at the same time was a lot more difficult than I'd realized it would be.

At first I tried to implement them all simultaneously, but that failed so badly that I didn't manage to get even one of them to work. Jace seemed to relax slightly, but I cut him off before he could say anything.

"Hold on, I'm trying again."

The second time I layered the effects on incrementally. It was still hard, still felt like I was splitting my mind into eight pieces, but that time around I was able to implement all three effects for a couple of seconds before I lost my focus and they all lapsed.

"Okay, go ahead and tell me what I'm doing wrong. I had them all, but each time I added another effect it got harder to hold it all together. I could still feel my default emotion, but it was weird—it felt like there was a force building underneath the surface. It didn't drain away the strength of my emotion, but once it got to a certain strength it washed all of the emotion away and left me feeling blah and apathetic."

Jace ran his fingers through his wavy blond hair and then shook his head. "Honestly, Selene, I have no idea what's going on."

I felt like I'd been slapped across the face, but I refused to cry in front of him, not over something so stupid.

"I'm sorry, I'll try harder. Just let me catch my breath and try to get my default emotion back in place..."

Jace grabbed my hand. "No, you don't understand. I'm not disappointed in your progress, I'm astonished at it. None of the things you just did should have been possible—not this fast, not without hours upon hours of practice. You aren't failing, you're succeeding beyond my wildest dreams. It just makes me nervous because I don't understand how it's happening."

"You mean most people don't pick it up this fast?"

"Not people who are being awakened for the first time, no. Occasionally someone who gets what appears to be a complete wipe, will manage to pick stuff back up very quickly, but we've always assumed that is because there is a level of habitual memories that can sometimes survive even the most brutal expenditures of power. With someone who's died and been reborn there's never been any indication that it's possible for *any* memories to survive."

"But you and Kat kept saying how much like myself I was..."

"Yes, but that all came down to your mannerisms and personality, not actual memories from your past life."

I shrugged. "I guess I should just be happy that for once in my life I'm exceptional and leave it at that?"

"Exceptional doesn't even begin to cover it, Selene. You're like some kind of prodigy. As of right now you're basically the Mozart of effects. Most brand-new Awakened are lucky if they learn one new effect every two or three days. You've learned, what, four or five today and it's barely lunchtime? Even more astonishing, you managed to chain together multiple effects on your second day of training. That usually takes months to accomplish."

I was finally feeling uncomfortable. What Jace had described went beyond just beginners' luck. "Maybe you shouldn't have told me any of that. Now I'm going to be second-guessing myself."

"I know. I tried to keep it inside, but it's just so incredible. I can't wait to tell Kat."

"Maybe we should hold off telling her, Jace. She's already jealous of me—of us. I don't want to give her another reason to hate me..."

I could tell that Jace didn't agree, could see that he was going to argue with me, but right as he opened his mouth a two-foot-tall man with black iridescent wings came hurtling out of the sky and landed right in front of Jace.

"Selene and Ari's dad is on his way."

Jace nodded. "Thanks, Kregor. How much time do we have before he arrives?"

"About ten seconds."

Chapter 25

My heart didn't just skip a beat, it actually felt like it stopped working for a second. Jace looked equally shocked.

"Kregor, you were supposed to give us plenty of warning."

"You told me the most important thing was to make sure that nothing happened to him."

Jace didn't look happy, but apparently didn't want to say something that he would regret later. "Fine, please go back and follow Selene's dad the rest of the way in. If I crank us up to forty times normal speed I think we can get Selene to the trailer so she can change before he arrives."

I felt Jace's power reach out for me, and knew I had only a heartbeat in which to stop him. "No, Jace. You'd have to burn a peak memory to make that happen for two of us at the same time—it's not worth it, not just to save me a little bit of embarrassment. I've got my wrap, that will just have to be enough to stop my dad from keeling over. Besides, there are people over by the trailer now."

"Are you sure, Selene? At forty times normal speed we'll be moving fast enough that they probably won't even be able to see us."

"You're right as far as getting across the parking lot goes, but once we got over to the RV you're not going to be able to open the door fast enough for both of us to get inside without ripping it off of its hinges."

I was right and we both knew it. As we got faster and faster it just made it harder to interact with our environment. I'd only ever experienced a few times normal speed, but I'd had plenty of time to think about what it would be like to be moving at forty or fifty times normal speed.

At that velocity, using a key to unlock the door to the RV without snapping it off in the lock would be a challenge, and even if we successfully managed that, the door's natural inertia would make it feel like we were pulling against a one-ton stone slab. It would move, and to anyone watching from outside of our time effect it would move very quickly, but to us it would feel like it was moving with glacial slowness.

Of course Jace could always make himself strong enough to make the door open even faster than that, but the hinges probably wouldn't survive the experience.

There just wasn't a way to move fast enough that nobody saw us and still avoid destroying the RV. Besides, now that we'd stopped training, I could feel the gaping holes in my mind where I'd burned away baseline memories.

Running my mind along my memories and coming to a jagged-edged gap wasn't a pleasant thing. One second I was headed in to talk to my mom and then there was nearly a minute of nothing before my memories picked back up as I headed out of her room and downstairs.

I could tell that Jace was still considering trying to get me to the RV before my dad pulled into sight, but I shook my head at him again as I pulled my gauzy white cover-up on.

"I'm serious, Jace. Now that I've actually experienced memory loss for myself I'm even less willing to let you waste your power on something stupid like this."

Jace stopped me as I bent down to pick up my towel.

"What do you mean? Right now is the time when most people go wild with using their abilities. Memory loss outside of anything other than a big, extended use of our powers is so slow it's almost imperceptible."

"I don't know what you mean, Jace. I can feel where I lost memories for each of the effects I've used so far. So far it's only a few seconds here, a few seconds there, but it's easy to see where one memory disappears and turns into nothing before it starts back up."

Jace sighed and then bent down to pick up his towel and the two towels I'd ruined with my first transmutation.

"That's not normal either, Selene. Our memories are vivid, but for Kat and me it's more like the memories we lose result in our experiences contracting. The narrative just kind of gets choppy. We'll remember being one place and then suddenly the memory jumps forward several minutes and we are somewhere else. It's disorienting when you go back and examine a set of memories, but it's not the kind of thing that jumps out at you."

"So I'm even more of a freak than you originally thought."

"No, you're not a freak, but there is definitely something going on that I don't understand—something that has never happened before, which is saying something for our kind."

Jace looked for a second like he was going to hold my hand to reassure me, but then my dad's old yellow pickup truck pulled into the parking lot. I double-checked to make sure that all of the platinum I'd created was either in my pocket or wrapped up in my towel, and then we headed back across the beach.

My dad met us at the edge of the asphalt. He gave me an appraising look and then pulled me into a hug.

"I'm so glad that you were able to make it, Dad!"

"Hi, sweetie. I almost didn't come—it hardly seemed worth it given the fact that I'll have to leave to go back to work again in just a few hours, but the three of us spend so little time together these days that I just couldn't bear not seeing you and Ari today."

Jace waited until my dad turned towards him and then held out his hand. "Mr. Jenkins, I'm glad you were able to make it as well. Ari and Selene have both told me a lot about you and Kat spoke highly of you after your meeting yesterday. I'm Jace."

Dad shook Jace's hand and gave him a nod. "I appreciate the invitation to come join you and your sister, Jace. Where are Ari and Kat?"

"They are both out on the jet skis right now. I'm afraid that Kat is almost as much of a speed demon as Ari is, so poor Selene hasn't even had a chance to get out on the water yet."

My dad rolled his eyes. "Somehow I'm not surprised. That child has had an unhealthy obsession with all things fast for almost two years now. I'm sorry that she's monopolizing your watercraft."

Jace waved away the apology. "Not at all. I'm just glad to see Kat unwind a little. Did you bring a swimming suit? You're welcome to change in the RV. With any luck Kat and Ari are almost out of fuel again and when they come back, if all three of us work as a team we can probably pry them off of the jet skis so that you and Selene can take them out."

"No, that's okay, I didn't come to deprive you of the use of your jet skis—I just wanted to spend some time with Ari and Selene. You and Kat should go out on them."

"I'm afraid that I actually need to start setting up for lunch, sir. Do hotdogs and hamburgers sound okay?"

I pulled on my dad's hand as he nodded in response to Jace. "Come on, Daddy. You did bring your suit, right?"

"Yes, but..."

Jace smiled again. "I think you should probably just quit while you're ahead, sir. I'm starting to figure out that if Selene really wants something she'll probably get it."

"All right, I'll go get my suit."

"Thanks, Dad."

Normally I would have just walked back to the pickup with my dad, but this time I hurried into the RV to straighten up the bathroom. I came back just as Jace was pulling a grill out of the side of the RV. Jace unobtrusively gestured at Bethany, who was once again buzzing around my head.

"Bethany is visible now. You should ask her to go out and signal Kat down."

"Good idea, the busier we keep my dad the fewer questions he's likely to ask."

"Actually, I was just thinking that your dad needed to unwind. He looks like a man with the weight of the world on his shoulders. If it helps keep our secrets then that's just a nice bonus."

I wanted to give Jace a kiss on the cheek, but even that felt like too much with my dad headed back in our direction.

"Thanks, Jace. For all of this."

"It's been my pleasure."

I looked up at Bethany, but she just threw me a jaunty little salute. "Aye, aye, captain. I heard Mr. Muscles. Heading off to flag down the dangerous duo now."

A few minutes later Dad had finished changing and Jace was in the middle of mixing ingredients into some kind of thick paste that presumably would go in with the hamburger when he made the patties. Bethany came streaking back a few feet ahead of Kat and Ari, both of who were flushed and laughing.

"Dad, you're here!"

Ari jumped off of the watercraft and into Dad's arms before it had even finished moving.

"Yes, I am—what's this I heard about you monopolizing the water toys?"

Kat pulled up and jumped off her jet ski so she could grab Ari's before it started floating off. "She's totally fine, Mr. Jenkins. Please don't let Jace convince you otherwise. He hardly even gets on them anymore. The only person who's been missing out is Selene, and I figured there would be plenty of time for her to play around on the water after lunch."

"You should totally take one out, Dad. Selene too. It's the most fun I've had in months."

Dad looked hesitant, but Kat had just finished muscling the front of both jet skis up onto the beach so they wouldn't float away.

"It's really no imposition, Mr. Jenkins. Ari and I will just go grab some fuel and then you and Selene can go buzz around until lunch is ready."

Ari went splashing along the waterline in the direction of the RV even before the words were out of Kat's mouth, which was odd. All I could figure was that she'd finally realized that I'd had Jace all to myself for several hours already this morning and wanted to get some time in herself.

I only noticed that in passing though because I was much more focused on the transformation that had overcome Kat. She obviously hadn't had a chance to redo her makeup or anything out on the water before coming back, and she was still wearing the same light-blue two-piece, but she no longer looked like a seventeen-year-old.

All I could figure was that it was something about how she was holding herself because she easily looked twenty or twenty-one now. I had to hand it to her, I hadn't even began to worry about the complications of Dad arriving without any notice and seeing her as something other than the mature, responsible adult who had convinced him to let his teenage daughters head off on a water trip without any other adult supervision.

Kat gave my dad a brilliant smile and then followed along behind Ari, but even then she didn't scamper or bound like Ari had, she walked like a woman who knew that everyone would wait for her.

When the two girls returned they not only had a couple of gas cans, they also had two more life jackets so that we wouldn't have to put on the wet ones that Kat and Ari had been wearing. I waited until my dad was busy filling up the gas tank of one of the jet skis before slipping off my wrap and into a life jacket. Less than five minutes later Dad and I were pushing off of the beach and racing across the glassy surface of the lake.

It took a little while for Dad to get comfortable enough to really open up the jet ski, and I never quite got to that point, but I still had a good time and really enjoyed seeing Dad smile without the undertone of stress and worry that had seemed a constant part of our lives ever since Mom had died.

We must have been out there for nearly an hour before I finally saw Bethany come skipping across the surface of the water towards us. I cut the engine and waited for her to get close enough that I would be able to hear her.

"Jace says that the food is ready to go, so you're both wanted back at the RV."

I checked to make sure that Dad was far enough away that he wouldn't be able to hear me and then nodded. "Thanks, Bethany. Have you already eaten?"

"Nope, but Kregor has promised to show me a field of wild flowers that he passed on his way here with your dad."

"Wow, I didn't realize that fairies lived off of flower nectar…"

"Selene, the things you don't know about fairies still would fill libraries. Try not to get into any trouble while I'm gone."

Dad pulled up next to me as she zipped off.

"Everything okay, sweetie?"

"Yeah, Dad. I just thought I could see Jace and Kat waving at us from the shoreline."

Dad squinted back in the direction of the RV. "Wow, maybe it's time for me to finally give in and make a trip to the eye doctor. I don't know how you can make out anything that far away. You're right though, we've been out plenty long enough."

We sped back over to the shore and beached the jet skis less than twenty feet away from the picnic table where Jace had set up the food. It only took one sniff for me to realize that he'd gone all-out on the food again.

I could go back and relive that first ambrosia-smothered hamburger at any point, but I still felt my mouth watering for *this* burger. I was exceptionally hungry after spending so long trying to throw my heavy jet ski through turns in a vain effort to keep up with my dad, but I was also excited to see what new flavor combination Jace had in store for us. I still didn't recognize half of the toppings he had laid out and waiting, but I was pretty sure a big chunk of them weren't the same as last time.

Ari bounced over and grabbed Dad's arm. I noticed with relief that she'd had the good sense to put a t-shirt on over her tiny red swimsuit. Dad was a lot more likely to let us do this again if he didn't think that we were spending most of our time with Jace and Kat all tarted up.

"Dad, you are in for a rare treat. Kat has told us at least a dozen times how good Jace's cooking is."

I flinched. It was a good thing that Ari was doing most of the talking—I would have said something about how awesome the burgers had been last time, and promptly ended up in a ton of trouble because Dad didn't know that we'd spent Thursday evening at Jace's house.

Kat looked up from a camp chair where she'd sequestered herself with a textbook. "Indeed I have. My opinion, Mr. Jenkins, is that for your first encounter with Jace's cooking you should let him pick out the toppings."

"Please, call me Peter."

Kat's smile doubled in wattage. "Very well, Peter. Feel free to tell Jace if there's anything you despise, but other than that just trust him to do right by you—my little brother has incredible taste."

REBORN

That last was said innocently enough, but she gave me a knowing look as soon as my dad turned away. I nearly died in embarrassment, but it was an interesting look into what made Kat tick. Even now, when she was playing a role, the teasing undertone that so readily made itself felt in normal conversation was waiting in the wings.

Dinner was amazing—even better than the last time. I would have said that wasn't possible, but apparently there really was some magic to his normal recipe that Jace had been forced to forgo last time because the burgers had burned.

The best part was watching my dad's face as he bit into his burger for the first time. He'd relaxed while we'd been out on the water, but it wasn't until I heard his heartfelt sigh of contentment that I realized even eating had become nothing but another chore for him.

Mealtimes had definitely taken a turn for the worse after my mom had died. Seeing Dad actually enjoy a meal was like watching the last five years melt away and seeing him how he'd been before Mom had died. I wanted to hug Kat and Jace, but there wasn't any hurry, we had all of the time in the world.

Once lunch was over, Kat convinced Dad to head back out on the water with Ari. He tried to refuse, but it was like she knew exactly the buttons to push to bend him to her will. I watched the two of them jet away and then turned and gave her that hug.

"Thank you, Kat. I really appreciate you and Jace making this weekend happen, and for convincing my dad to come here today. I haven't seen him like this in years—it was the best gift that anyone could have given him, which means it's the best gift anyone could have given me."

Jace came up behind us and wrapped his arms around the two of us. "The best part of it all is that this is just a preview of things to come. Once we get you that metal detector and you 'find' that massive nugget of solid gold, your dad will finally be able to relax and enjoy himself a little more. Just don't be surprised if it takes him a while to adjust."

"You've seen it before?"

"Yeah. Based on what's survived of my early journals, I even experienced it for myself when I first realized that I wasn't going to have to worry about money ever again. It's funny how much our jobs and the battle to provide for those closest to us can come to define us. Your dad is probably going to need some time to figure out what he wants to do with his life."

"Well, I guess there are a lot worse problems than that to have."

Jace shrugged. "There is an awful lot that I don't know, but it sure seems like people default back to the same level of happiness regardless of their circumstances. Hopefully your dad is one of the rare individuals who can rise above that and just realize how fortunate he's been."

Chapter 26

While Dad and Ari were out on the lake I took the opportunity to practice trying to maintain multiple effects at once for longer blocks of time. I hadn't expected it to be easy, but I also hadn't expected it to be quite so exhausting.

It wasn't just physically tiring, it was emotionally exhausting. Summoning my default emotion with enough strength to weave in more than one effect and then sustaining that depth of emotion wore me out in ways that it was hard to describe.

Kat happened on me a few minutes after I finally managed to sustain a strength-, circulatory- and skin-strengthening effect for an entire sixty seconds. She looked at me and shook her head.

"Jace told me that you were some kind of savant, but I had to see it to believe it. You really are something."

"Thanks, but I'm having a harder and harder time making stuff work. This last time it was like pulling teeth to get my emotions strong enough to start working effects."

"So take a break. It's not like you're behind schedule or anything. Most people don't realize how much work it is to build up emotional muscle because they are so much more focused on trying to get the effects working in the first place. You're in the opposite situation, you're making effects work left and right, but it's going to take some time before your emotional reservoir gets big enough to spend the whole day working effects like this."

"I guess that makes sense."

"Of course it does, everything I say always makes sense."

That earned her an eye roll, which just made her laugh, but she'd succeeded in making me feel like it was okay to call it a night. I ended up going into the RV for my backpack and then put a camp chair out next to Jace and worked on my homework while he wrote in his journal.

I was way past understanding why Jace and Kat spent so much time writing in their journals, but I'd been reluctant to start myself because it just felt like such a big task. I was starting to realize though that I couldn't afford to put the task off, even if it was incredibly intimidating. I'd already lost a couple of hours' worth of my life after just my first day as a full Awakened.

Jace caught me staring. "Does that mean you're ready to start one of your own?"

"Yeah. I'm just not sure where to start even if I had a journal to start writing in."

"Well, there's a blank journal and your favorite brand of pen waiting for you inside the RV."

Jace looked out onto the water as though trying to make out the details of what was happening with my dad and Ari before finally shrugging.

"As for the other part of your challenge, that's something you'll have to figure out on your own, but a lot of us do one journal that is just the high points of our lives, the most important things that you would want yourself to know if the worst happened and you ended up losing all of your memories. Then once that is done we tend to start two more journals. The first one is a daily record of our lives from the time we start journaling, the second picks up from our earliest memory and works its way forward until it matches up with the other detailed journal."

My mouth went dry as I realized what he was telling me. "Is that what's back in that box that I asked you to give me? Is that the high-point narrative of my life?"

"I don't know—it's been hard not to look at it, but I promised you that I wouldn't. It might be the high-point journal, or it might be your final research journal. I know you're probably hoping for the former, but we never found anything in writing concerning your last set of discoveries, the stuff that you were working on just before you died."

"But you found some of my research…"

"Yeah, like I said earlier, it was so far beyond us that frankly I'm surprised that you decided to continue running with Kat and me. You could have used even just your earlier stuff to bargain your way into almost any pantheon in the world. I can only imagine what must have been in the last journal."

I wasn't sure what to say, so I just nodded and returned to my homework as I made a mental note to grab the spare journal later and get started on the highlights version that Jace had suggested.

A few minutes later Ari and I got the biggest surprise of our day when Dad came back from his time on the lake and told us that we could stay there for another night if we wanted. It happened after a twenty-minute discussion between Dad, Jace, and Kat while Ari was refueling the jet skis and I was inside putting the dishes away from lunch, so there was no way to know what the three of them had talked about, but as I came outside with my new journal tucked under my arm, Dad walked up and gave me a kiss on the forehead.

"I need to go if I'm going to make it home in time for work, but if you and Ari want to stay here for one more night that's okay. Just make sure you're home by two o'clock tomorrow so I can say hi to you both before work."

I wrapped my arms around my dad's chest and gave him a hug. "Thanks, Dad. That sounds like fun, but I don't want to miss our Sunday together."

"It's okay, sweetie. I think that I'll actually get next weekend off for a change and we'll spend both days together then. Jace says that there's a tent and sleeping bag in the SUV he drove up this morning, so he'll be sleeping in that. No spending the night together—you or Ari either one. I want your word."

I nodded. "Of course, Daddy."

"Okay, there will be plenty of time for that kind of stuff later."

I'd already let go of him, but he pulled me back in and gave me a hug that made my ribs creak, just like he'd done when I was little, back before he started treating Ari and me like we were made out of spun glass, before he started worrying that we would disappear on him like Mom had.

"Let's go tell your sister."

Chapter 27

Ari was predictably stoked to be staying with Kat and Jace for another day. Dad went in and changed back into his jeans and flannel shirt and then Ari, Kat, Jace and I stood and waved goodbye as my dad drove away in his tired, old yellow pickup.

Ari wanted to go back out onto the lake right away, this time with Jace instead of Kat, but the three of us told her that there wouldn't be any more jet ski fun until her homework was done. She pouted for fifteen minutes before deciding that it wasn't winning her any points with Jace, and then she finally just buckled down.

Really there wasn't a good reason for her to have been complaining. Sitting in the sun made even doing homework feel like a vacation. Still, I hated to be wasting the sunlight doing homework. For once I was tempted to do a little time-bending myself just because I would have vastly preferred for my extra, non-sleep hours, to have been more sunlight and warmth than cold darkness. Although now that I really thought about it, that still wouldn't have done it because I would have just been going to sleep earlier and waking up while it was still dark out.

My between-class homework sessions from the day before meant that I was further along than Kat. I finished up my homework nearly an hour before she did, so I pulled out my journal and started writing. I started by talking about our house, the one where we'd lived for as long as I could remember. There was something grounding and centering about having always lived your life in the same town, in the same house, with the same people.

A lot of people would say a life like that sounded boring. Maybe they were right, there certainly hadn't been much adventure in my life, but there were offsetting benefits. I'd grown up feeling like I was perfectly safe inside of the four walls of our home.

It was odd, I'd never been much of a writer, but once I got past the difficulty of deciding where to start, the words just kind of flowed out of me.

I ended up writing about the things that were important to me, the places and people that had made my life what it was so far, and when I was finally pulled out of the zone by the sound of Ari slamming her book shut, I was more than satisfied with what I'd written down.

"Okay, I'm *finally* done. Come on, Jace, let's go out on the lake—daylight's a-wasting."

Jace very carefully didn't look at me before answering, but I could practically feel him choosing his words carefully so as to avoid leading Ari on.

"Actually, since we've got all afternoon, tonight and tomorrow morning until we have to go home, I was thinking that maybe we should change up our plans a little."

Kat's right eyebrow climbed up nearly to her hairline—apparently the two of them hadn't had a chance to discuss whatever it was that Jace had in mind. Jace gave all three of us a disarming smile.

"There's a set of hot springs that I was reading about online yesterday morning. It's only two hours each way and they are supposed to be spectacular. They are back further north, so it will be a little colder and they will feel absolutely perfect once the sun drops. What does everyone think?"

Ari barely waited for Jace to finish talking before she agreed. The little hussy was probably already thinking about getting Jace off by herself in the dark. Kat gave the plan a cautious nod, and I wasn't going to be the one to spoil the party, so it was agreed, with just one condition from the runt. First she and Jace had to spend some time on the lake together.

I watched the two of them race away as I reapplied sunscreen for the third time. Honestly, it was tempting to just go back inside and change into some real clothes, but we *were* going to be getting wet again tonight. Besides, I'd seen the way that Jace had looked at me when I'd first come out of the bathroom after changing.

Maybe it was silly to feel threatened by Ari, but things between Jace and I still felt so new and fragile right now. I needed every advantage I could get if I was going to keep him from getting distracted by all of the skin she was showing.

Kat sat down next to me and picked up the bottle of sunscreen that I'd just set down. "It feels like it's been forever since we stopped moving for long enough to sit outside and enjoy the sun like this. It always seems like such a waste to me not to spend as much time in the sun as possible since we can't get skin cancer and our skin doesn't get all leathery and wrinkled either."

"Wow, you're right, that is a big benefit to being an Awakened. So all of us just look like late teens, early twenties kids forever?"

"Nope. Your age freezes at whatever age you were when you were first Awakened. Each of us Awakens at the same age in every incarnation, but for some of us that age is quite a bit older than this."

"I guess that makes sense. Some of the gods were painted as old men or women."

We sat in silence for several seconds, and for the first time in a while, it felt strained. I cast about for a reason.

"Thanks for managing my dad so slickly. I don't know how you do it without even changing your clothes or makeup, but I totally would have believed that you were a couple years older than you look right now."

Kat started a little in her camp chair, and then shrugged. "It's mostly just about posture and attitude. You'd be amazed at the small things that make a huge difference in how people perceive you. It helped that I'd already fixed the idea of me being a mature eighteen-year-old in your dad's mind."

"Well, however you did it, thank you. I haven't seen my dad so relaxed in ages. He really needed today."

Kat gave me a distracted smile, but I could tell that her mind was a million miles away. I waited for nearly a minute before deciding to just jump right in.

"Is something wrong, Kat? Was it something I said?"

"Huh? Oh, no. I was just thinking about your dad. I looked at the fuel gauge in his truck and it looked like he was down to not much more than fumes. I was worried that he wasn't going to make it home without filling back up, and he only had fifteen bucks in his wallet, so I slipped a few extra twenties in there so he won't have to put this trip on his credit card."

I'd started out ready to get all self-righteous about the fact that she had looked inside my dad's wallet, but by the end of Kat's tale I wanted to cry. Apparently my emotions were more obvious than I thought; Kat looked at me and frowned.

"Geez, Selene. It's just sixty bucks. You transmuted at least ten thousand times that much platinum earlier today."

"I know, it's not about the money so much as it is about the gesture."

Kat shrugged. "I'm not like you and Jace, Selene. I've never clicked with another Awakened individual. Usually when I fall in love it ends up being someone normal, someone who has to put in sixty-hour weeks to make ends meet, someone who's never known anything other than a hard life. And all too often they still find an early grave despite my best efforts to hold onto them. I can't save everyone, but I'm not going to just sit by and let someone like him work themselves into the ground, not once I know them."

I shook my head at her. "There is so much more to you than meets the eye, Kat. Did I know all of this stuff before I died last time?"

"Most of it. Nobody knows everything about anyone in their life, but you knew more than anyone else."

"Well, for the third time today, thank you for looking out after my dad."

"Yeah. No problem." Kat stretched and then brought her hand up to her eyes so she could look out over the water. "So what do you want to do now?"

"I'd say that I wanted to spend some more time writing in my journal, but I'm not sure that I could dive back into that again quite yet. I need to write about my mom dying but I just feel so dead inside that I can't bring myself to write. It feels wrong to be reliving that and not feeling anything."

Kat nodded. "Just remember that there isn't anything wrong with you—you're just still emotionally depleted from all of the effects you worked earlier. After a good night's sleep you'll be back to feeling normal again."

"Yeah, I figured as much, but it still feels so weird that I'm having a hard time getting used to it."

"It will take some time—there are a lot of weird things that you're going to have to get used to. That brings me back to my original question though. If not journaling, what would you like to do next? It's kind of early for taking a nap or eating, and I'm fresh out of other ideas."

"Can you teach me how to bend time, Kat? I mean I know I won't actually be able to do it yet, but maybe you could teach me the theory behind it and then I can practice on my own later—like maybe tomorrow night while Ari is sleeping."

"I guess. It seems kind of silly, but if that's what you want I'll play ball." Kat bent down and picked up a small rock off of the beach. "Okay, so the first thing you're going to need is something to tell you when you've managed to successfully bend time. I like dropping a rock, personally. You count how long it takes for it to drop to the ground and that will give you an idea how much faster you are than normal."

"Okay, that makes sense. How long does it normally take a rock like that to fall?"

Kat shrugged. "It all depends on how fast you count. Once we're done here you can drop it and count until you're satisfied that *you* know how long it takes for you."

"Then what?"

"So time bending is one of the more dangerous things we do simply because it's so easy to send yourself into a state of oxygen debt. If you bend time past more than two or three times normal without amping up your system to compensate, you risk putting yourself so far into oxygen debt that you pass out before you realize what's going on.

"Even if you realize what's going on, the first few times you run out of breath can be pretty intense and it's hard to amp your body up even further when you're freaking out like that."

"Okay, so it's dangerous and I should probably wait to practice until you or Jace are around."

"Yeah, I think I can safely say that you just won the award for the understatement of the year."

"Okay, so it's *really* dangerous."

"Much better. This time you only won the award for the understatement of the month.

Time bending is the kind of thing that only a few pantheons even bother learning, Selene."

"That doesn't make sense. Isn't it a massive advantage in a fight?"

"Some. Not as much as you might think because you can't just ramp up to fifty times normal speed and kill your enemies."

"Why not?"

"Because it leaves you without any options if your enemy hits you with something that you weren't expecting. Maintaining a fifty-times time effect doesn't just require a ton of power to make the time bend happen, it also means that you've got to have your system amped up to the point where you can move and fight at that speed."

"How are they going to hit you with something at that speed?"

"By not targeting you, but rather somewhere they know you're going to have to be. Think carpet bombing. If nothing else, as soon as they see you disappear they can always throw down a blanket of fire for hundreds of yards in every direction."

"But wouldn't you already be gone by then? Or even have killed them?"

"Maybe, or maybe they are running a ten-times effect themselves and they have plenty of time to burn you to a crisp on your way in, especially since they don't have to amp themselves up because they weren't planning on moving around."

"Ah, I guess I can see what you're getting at."

"Right, plus when you add in the fact that bending time isn't a geometric kind of cost progression, it starts to make sense for some of those other pantheons to stick with the things that they do best rather than dabbling in stuff that might get them killed."

"Is that the only reason?"

"No, but it's the biggest. You have to remember that not all pantheons have access to a real researcher. Some of them only have whatever information they've been able to scavenge from stolen research journals. They might be able to amp up their strength or make their bones and skin strong enough to withstand the severe stresses created by time bending, but not have the knowledge required to amp up their lungs and circulatory system."

The situation she was describing seemed almost incomprehensible to me. "But once you know one of those things don't the others just logically follow?"

Kat's chuckle was a harsh, humorless thing. "You say that because even now, underneath that unassuming schoolgirl exterior you are still a researcher at heart."

"What does that mean?"

"It means that you make logical connections that the rest of us don't. Whether you realize it or not, you always have some kind of working framework in the back of your mind that you plug each new piece of knowledge into. The rest of us just tend to treat the things we know like a bunch of unrelated information. Even when we do have some kind of framework that we are working from, if something new comes along and it doesn't fit together with the rest of the things we know we don't fret about it too much. You on the other hand..."

"I can't leave it alone."

"Right, you just keep worrying at it until you figure out how to make it fit together."

I shook my head in amazement. "That can't really be that rare, can it? There are tens of thousands, maybe even hundreds of thousands of scientists out there all over the world who think just like me."

"Even if you're right, Selene, what does that really mean? Let's say that there are millions of scientists out there in the general population. Out of a total of several billion people, that just means less than a tenth of a percent of the human race has the right mindset to put pieces together like you do."

I tried to get a word in edgewise, but she wasn't done.

"Even if that's right, how many of those scientists do you think would keep experimenting if each and every mistake they made could get them killed?"

"Probably not very many..."

"Right, and if the rest of the human race was going to try to hunt them down and kill them so they could steal their research, what do you think that would do to the rest of the research pool?"

"Probably drop it even more…"

"Exactly, and that is why people like you are so unique."

I tried from a different angle. "But what about you, Kat? You're not stupid, and there isn't much that you're really afraid of; couldn't you research if you wanted to?"

"Man, if only I had a peak memory for every time you and I had this conversation over the years. Look, Selene, I try, I really do, but the honest truth is that it's all that Jace and I can do to work through the stuff that you show us. We've had your research journals for almost two decades and it's been like pulling teeth for us to learn useful stuff out of them.

"The unfortunate truth is that there are relatively few people in any group who actually make a difference. The rest of us can mostly keep the wheels from coming off, but we aren't the ones that cure cancer or raise the national standard of living. I'm not special, not like you're special."

"Wow, when you put it that way it's no wonder you hate me."

"I don't hate you, Selene. You've kept me alive more times than I can count. Sometimes it was just the stuff you taught me that saved me from the long sleep, but more often than not you did it yourself, just like you did that last time."

I started to nod and then suddenly realized something that I should have realized back at the beginning of the conversation.

"Wait a second. If what you're telling me is true, then my old research journals are incredibly valuable. We never should have left town!"

Kat made a 'calm down' gesture at me. "Yes, your journals are worth more than our entire house, but we didn't bring them with us, at least not the originals. Those are locked away somewhere safe. All we brought with us to Cold Springs was the research journal that Jace has spent the last couple of years trying to decode, and the one from that box that Jace showed you."

"Still, we shouldn't have left them there in the house. If something happens to them..."

"Yeah, we'd be screwed, but we didn't leave them there. Our regular journals are back at the house, locked in the vault, but your research journal and the one you left yourself are hidden inside of the RV."

The wave of relief that crashed over me was so strong I couldn't breathe for a second. "Good, they're safe then."

"Well, safer. It's not like the other pantheons have forgotten that Jace and I are your heirs. They know that you left behind a treasure trove of information, and some of them are probably smart enough to muddle through your notes, so they've been chasing us unrelentingly for the last eighteen years. We were even more careful than normal when we set things up in Cold Springs, but that's still no guarantee. For all we know there's a kill team headed our way right now. If that happens then the best we can hope for is that the hiding spot inside of the RV will be good enough to stop them from stealing your journals out from under our noses, and that we'll be able to beat a fighting retreat out of here with them."

"You're not painting a very reassuring picture, Kat."

"That's good—I wasn't trying to. Did I convince you to hold off learning how to bend time?"

"Nope, from the sounds of it, I need to learn it even more than I realized."

"Okay, close your eyes and try to relax like you're summoning up your default emotion. I know you're too fatigued to do it, but that will help put you in the right state of mind."

I closed my mind and tried to do as she'd asked. She was right, I was too emotionally worn out to summon the all-encompassing feeling of happiness that I'd been experiencing earlier that day, but I did manage at least a weak shadow of it.

"Now what?"

"Once you're really calm, you'll be able to hear your own heartbeat. Actually, now that I think of it, 'hear' may not be quite the right word. It's possible that it will be more like you can feel your heartbeat in your ears."

"Gee whiz, Kat. That doesn't sound at all weird."

"Stop being a smart alec and just focus on hearing your heartbeat."

I took a deep breath, let it out halfway, and then held it. It took a couple of seconds, but I quickly realized that she was right. It wasn't that I could quite hear my heartbeat, but I got to the point where I could feel it thrumming through my entire body.

It must have been obvious that I'd managed to achieve the state that Kat told me I was after, because once I found it, she resumed talking.

"Okay, now that you've found your own heartbeat, you need to find the heartbeat of your surroundings."

"That's stupid, Kat. My surroundings aren't alive, how can they have a heartbeat?"

"Everything has a heartbeat, grasshopper. Listen to the waves lapping up on the beach. It creates an audible marker that signals the passage of time. Something you could, if you didn't have the literary acumen of a toad, call a heartbeat."

"Okay, point taken, this location has a heartbeat. What if we were somewhere else without water?"

"Every place has a heartbeat, Selene. Some are just harder than others. Whether it's the sound of your tires against the pavement, or the crooning of an owl, there is always *something*. You just have to listen for it."

"What happens next?"

"You quit rather than trying to create one of the more dangerous effects known to Awakened-kind while you are the emotional equivalent to falling-down drunk."

"Come on, Kat. I won't try to actually work the effect—just tell me though so I can think about how it would all come together."

"All right, but I've got your word that you aren't going to experiment with this, right?"

"Absolutely."

"Okay, then. All you do is force your heartbeat to speed up at the same time that you slow down everything else. You summon up all of the emotion you can contain, you start off by amping up your circulatory system, and then you push against the two pulses with everything you have."

"That's it?"

"Yeah, but you have to remember not to push too hard to start out with. You don't have the experience required to sustain a deep time-bend. You need to start out using the smallest amount of power possible so that you don't throw yourself into an irrecoverable oxygen debt."

"Okay. Noted."

"I'm serious, Selene. We went to an awful lot of work over the last two decades to track you down—nobody wants you killing yourself off."

I gave her my best 'I'd never do anything wrong' look and pointed out at the water. "How much longer do you think they'll be out there?"

It turned out that Ari and Jace were only on the water for a little longer than an hour and a half. Ari looked like she wished they'd been able to stay out longer, but Jace winked at me as they parked the jet skis on the beach.

It took us another half an hour to get the water craft on the trailer and then move it over to the RV so that we could load up the SUV, but then we were off. Jace was quick to volunteer to drive and Kat sat down in the passenger seat before Ari could make it up there to monopolize him.

I suspected that Kat actually had stuff that she wanted to talk to Jace about, but I still appreciated the effort on her part to keep Ari from getting her hopes up even more.

The drive north was wonderfully uneventful. Ari and I watched a video on the massive flat-screen mounted across from the couch, and once Ari was completely sucked into one of the chase scenes Kat and I swapped spots so I could ride next to Jace and ask him about some of the places he'd visited over the years.

I shouldn't have been surprised to find out that he spoke six languages or that he'd spent more than a decade in Asia immediately after I'd died the last time. It actually made a lot of sense because it meant that a lot of the pantheons were still looking for him and Kat over there rather than here in the States.

Jace was a surprisingly good storyteller, and the rest of the trip flew by. All too soon the sun was on its way down and we were pulling to a stop in a rest area that was hardly worthy of the name.

Ari took one look at the aging building and shuddered. "I'm *so* glad that we brought a bathroom along with us. I wouldn't use the one in there if you paid me to."

Jace appeared with a backpack that was loaded up with water, snacks and towels. "My recommendation would be for everyone to change into real shoes and bring a change of clothes. We're going to want to change into something warm for the hike back."

He handed me the backpack with a wink. "Here, Selene. There should be just enough room in this one for your clothes. Kat is bringing another one, Ari. You can share with her or I can go dig a third one out of the gear in the SUV."

"How come you're carrying Selene's clothes for her?"

"Because poor Selene only got out on the water one time all day, which means that she and I are twinners."

"Kat only went out once." Ari knew she was fighting a losing battle, but she wasn't about to throw in the towel. Kat reappeared at precisely the right time and shrugged.

"It's true, but my one turn was longer than Jace and Selene's combined. Come on, runt. It's a good thing you're small, because I'm not excited about carrying a bunch of extra weight on a two-mile hike."

Ari rolled her eyes and followed Kat inside. "You're only like half an inch taller than me."

I was surprised at the sheer weight of Jace's backpack, but the reason became apparent as soon as I made it over to my suitcase and went to stuff a long-sleeved top, jeans and underwear into the backpack. It didn't just have towels and clothes for Jace in it, it also had two of the nondescript black journals at the bottom packed inside of heavy freezer bags. Jace wasn't going to leave anything to chance—he was making sure that the journals came with us where he and Kat would have the best odds of keeping them safe.

I finished packing the stuff I needed, slipped on some shoes and then headed back outside. Jace accepted the bag with a look that seemed to ask whether or not I'd noticed the journals. I gave him a small nod and a thumbs up, which earned me one of his patented grins.

Kat and Ari reappeared a second later with four flashlights and we headed up the trail. I hadn't historically been much of a hiker—it always felt like too much work for too little gain. This time started out the same way as always, but Ari quickly took the lead and set a much more grueling pace than she needed to.

REBORN

I was pretty sure I knew what she was hoping would happen. Jace was obviously in peak physical shape, but Ari knew perfectly well that I was not an athlete. If she managed to convince Jace to speed up, then I would fall behind and she would get him all to herself.

Ari moved out into the front of the group as we started up the first hill and forced herself not to slow down despite the incline. Jace unconsciously followed at the same pace, and in moments my breathing sped up. She thought that she was going to beat me again, but she was wrong. The difference this time was that I had another card to play.

I tried to summon my default emotion, tried to surround myself with the same happiness I'd felt when Jace had saved me, but that well was empty. The spark of emotion that I managed was barely enough to qualify as such. I watched as Jace and Ari disappeared around a bend in the trail, already more than twenty feet ahead of me, and then looked down to see Kat look back at me.

She took a breath to call out for Jace to slow down, but I stopped her with a look. I wasn't going to be the weak link, not this time. More than that though, I was getting sick and tired of Ari trying to steal Jace away from me.

The anger slipped over me without any conscious effort on my part. For a split second I worried that I was going to lose control and do something terrible, but then I realized that the emotional exhaustion had ratcheted the rage down to something that I could manage, something that was still powerful enough for me to use, but not so powerful that I would try to slam Ari's head into a boulder.

I grabbed the feeling of taking a deep breath and pulled it into existence in exchange for a memory about jumping into the swimming pool when I was three. I could only assume that Dad had caught me—he was there a few seconds later when the memory picked back up. It hurt to lose a little piece of my soul like that, but in that moment I realized that this was no different than my struggle earlier to leave behind the peak memories that had come so close to trapping me forever.

I could either hoard my past to the possible detriment of my future, or I could use my past to get me what I wanted right now, to manufacture the future that I wanted. Once I decided that, it was all just a question of what was worth giving up.

In the next three breaths I went from gasping and lightheaded to breathing normally. I sped up, determined to make up for lost time, but now I could feel the burn in my legs that the pain in my lungs had been disguising.

I checked my anger and found that it was more than sufficient to power additional effects—if anything it had grown because Ari had backed me into a corner where I felt like I had to burn memories in order to compete with her.

I amped up my muscles with another thought and lost a full minute of the time from our swimming outing. I realized that I'd overdone it that time, but it was too late to go back and undo the mistake. Now that the effect was powered it would consume memories at a slower rate and I'd just end up losing even more by releasing it and then re-amping my muscles.

It felt like Kat was practically crawling now. I waited until we hit a wide spot in the trail and then went bounding past her at a jog.

"This is a mistake, Selene."

"Maybe, but it's my mistake to make."

It took me less than a minute to catch up with Ari and Jace, and the expression on Ari's face when she looked back and saw me jogging up the side of the mountain was worth the memories I'd had to feed into the effects.

"You in a hurry, little sister?"

Jace looked back and seemed to realize for the first time just how fast the two of them had been going. He opened his mouth, probably to apologize, but Ari beat him to it.

"Oh, sorry, Selene. I guess I'm just excited to get up to the hot springs before the sun goes down and it gets too cold to be wearing nothing more than a swimming suit."

I gave her a smile just as fake as her apology, and saw Jace start slightly as I got close enough for him to detect that I was maintaining active effects.

"No need to apologize, runt. I'm all for getting there sooner. Are you up for a race?"

I could see the gears turning in her head. I'd taken her off guard, but she *knew* that I couldn't actually beat her. I'd just doubled down on her ploy. By running and catching up with them I'd alerted Jace to the fact that she was being petty. If she beat me though, left me a gasping, quivering wreck on the side of the trail, then I'd look stupid.

"Sure, Selene. All the way to the hot springs?"

"Yep, but it's no fun if there aren't any stakes. What do you say, Jace? Are you willing to be a trophy?"

Jace looked at me for several seconds, obviously not convinced that this was a good idea. He was probably right, but I was tired of playing things safe, tired of pussyfooting around Ari. If we'd taken a more straightforward approach then we could have avoided the whole mess we were in.

"Normally I would say no, but if it means that much to the two of you then I can be persuaded."

I faked a happy smile despite the anger that was still clawing at me.

"Great, the winner gets to spend the time at the hot springs with you. The loser has to hope that Kat will take pity on them and not just leave them all by themselves."

Ari returned my smile with one that was just as sugary sweet as anything Sandra had ever flashed at me. "Just remember, sis, this was all your idea."

"Not going to be a problem, Ari."

She took off like a shot, but soon settled down to something she could sustain for a while. I paced her for a while and then passed her, moving just enough faster that she'd feel motivated to speed up in an attempt to stay with me.

It wasn't a fair matchup. Ari wasn't a runner. She had friends who were runners and occasionally ran with them, but it wasn't the same thing. I smiled when she started breathing heavy. By the time we'd finished the first mile, she was gasping and I was still well out of oxygen debt.

"Here's the thing, Ari. You're my sister and I love you, but you've been terrible to me for the last few days. You knew that I liked Jace, and you knew that I saw him first. A decent sister would have backed off and hoped for the best. After all, there was always a chance that me dating Jace would have meant that you got to meet other hot, rich guys."

She tripped and almost fell down, but I reached out and easily hauled her back up to her feet before she could hit the ground.

"Instead of doing the nice thing, you decided to try to monopolize Jace and risked blowing things for both of us. Some guys love having girls fight over them, but those aren't the kind of guys either of us want to date."

"How are you doing this?"

The words were barely intelligible past the gasps and coughing.

"It doesn't matter how I'm doing it, Ari. What matters is that you don't know me as well as you think you do. I'm done being nice. Stop trying to steal him or I'll really take the gloves off."

"Oh, yeah?"

"Yeah. I've talked to Kat and Jace both. If you keep this up they'll just stop inviting you places. We'll drop you off after school and then I'll go hang out with them."

She shook her head, her face white from exertion. "It's never going to happen. I'll tell Dad everything."

"That's fine. Jace and Kat will back me up when I tell Dad that it was all your idea, that you knew Jace was going to be spending the night last night and didn't tell him. We'll both get in trouble, but you're the one he'll never trust again."

"When did you turn into such a massive bi-otch?"

"When my little sister tried to steal away the guy I had my heart set on."

I sped up and left her in my dust. I didn't slow down until I reached the springs. Ari, Jace and Kat were almost half an hour behind me.

Chapter 28

The response to my throwing down against Ari was mixed. Ari obviously hated me. She was going with the sympathy play and Jace was playing the good cop, which made me want to scream. If he'd had the sense of a termite he would have been nice but distant and let Kat be the one to pull Ari back together.

Kat seemed to think that I'd made a mistake, but as nearly as I could tell, it was a mistake that she was all for. It was like she was enjoying the trip back down memory lane that my rage-fest had triggered for her.

Jace apparently didn't know what to think. He spent a few minutes getting Ari situated in one of the lower pools and then stripped off his shoes and joined me next to one of the upper pools.

The hot springs really were quite amazing. It was a series of gradually descending pools that started out with the hottest water up at the top and then each successive pool got cooler as water cascaded down into them from a higher pool. The pools were deep pockets nearly big enough to swim in, which had been worn into the surface of the granite over the course of thousands or possibly even tens of thousands of years, and the vegetation around us was set back far enough that it wasn't dangling into the pools, but close enough that it shielded the pools from any external view.

"Don't forget to turn off your effects, Selene. There's no reason to waste memories when you no longer need to be amped up."

I nodded and canceled the effects. It was hard to let them go, hard to know that I was returning to nothing more than my normal capabilities, but Jace was right.

"You should have let Kat comfort Ari and try to smooth things over. All you've done is make things worse again."

Jace frowned at me. "She's your sister, Selene."

"Yeah, but she's also been a complete bi-otch for the last several days. She's had this coming in ways that you don't even understand."

That earned me a sigh. "I know that she's been making things difficult, but she's also a lonely little girl who barely remembers her mom."

"I don't care. You're mine and it's time that she understood that!"

REBORN

As soon as the words were out of my mouth I realized they were the wrong thing for me to say. Despite everything else he might have said, Jace was both rich and hot. For guys like that a girl getting all clingy and possessive wasn't a turn-on. Guys like that loved the thrill of the chase.

I wanted to take it back, wished that there was a way to erase the last few seconds, but even we Awakened couldn't do that. It was too late.

I couldn't bear to look at him. I finished pulling off my shoes, slipped into the water and started working my way back to the far edge of the pool.

Jace barely made any sound at all as he slid in behind me, but I was so hypersensitive to his every action that I knew as soon as he was in the pool with me. Maybe it was just the ripples along the surface of the water, but I would have sworn that I could feel a faint electric current humming through the water, connecting us despite the distance between us.

The feel of his hand on my shoulder, turning me around so that I had no choice but to look at him, was like a stronger jolt, one that raced from my shoulder down to the tips of my toes and tightened up everything in between.

"You aren't channeling happiness anymore?"

"No. I was channeling anger. I tried to channel happiness, but I was just too exhausted. I guess you could say that my store of happiness was all used up, but I seem to have an unending supply of rage."

I wanted to turn away again, to run away to another pool, but Jace's wet, glistening body was between me and any kind of escape.

"How badly have I screwed stuff up?"

"I don't know. We'll have to just wait and see what Kat can do over the next couple of hours. It's probably best if you stay away from both of them for a while. The last thing we want is for Ari to start thinking of Kat as your friend—that will make her feel completely alone."

"No, I meant between us."

"You didn't screw anything up, Selene."

"Don't lie to me, Jace. I know how things work. I may not date much, but I've seen how guys like you react when a girl like me gets all obsessive. It never ends well."

Jace's smile was still lopsided, but this time it wasn't lazy. This time there was a heat behind it that took my breath away.

"You've got everything backwards, Selene. I was never the one being pursued in our relationship. I was always the one who pursued you, the one who had to fight for each and every minute of your attention, the one who never knew for sure if you were going to move on to greener pastures. Hearing you say that—hearing you lay claim to me—was music to my ears."

I was in shock. It was the only explanation. I'd been amped up, but I must have still overdone it in the run up to the hot springs. I opened my mouth to tell Jace that I was hallucinating and he stepped forward and kissed me.

I tried to pull back, but with the rock wall behind me there wasn't anywhere for me to go.

"Wait…Ari…Kat…they'll see us…"

"No, they won't, not from down inside the lower pools."

I tried to point out that they might move, but Jace's lips were on mine again and I was having a hard time thinking. This wasn't anything at all like our last kiss, the gentle—almost chaste—kiss goodnight. This had all of the hunger of our first kiss, and this time we were both wearing a lot less.

My hands had instinctively gone back up to cradle Jace's head again; his were resting low on my waist, thumbs positioned just inside of my hip bones, gently pressing on the nerves there. The hot water was making me light-headed and I found myself falling into him, hanging on for dear life with my arms around his neck as he flicked his tongue into my mouth.

He pushed me back against the edge of the pool, hard enough to draw a gasp out of me before he covered my mouth with his. I could feel the rough texture of the rock against my back, pressing against nearly the entire length of my body, nothing between it and me but a few strings around my torso and neck, and the board shorts that felt like they might finally lose their battle and fall at any moment.

The rock against my back was the only distraction I had against the feel of Jace's muscular, naked chest pressing against my mostly bare skin. Jace pulled away from my mouth and pressed his mouth against my neck, even lower down than he had the last time, and once again my knees collapsed.

The stakes were higher this time. I wasn't going to just fall to the ground, I was going to drown, but that still wasn't enough to keep the strength from draining out of my limbs. I should have fallen immediately, but the pressure of Jace's upper body against mine slowed my descent enough for him to realize what was happening and lift me back up out of the water.

"Are you okay?"

"Shut up and kiss me."

I wrapped my arms around his neck and pulled his head back down against my neck.

The feel of his tongue against my collar bone sent little shaky tremors through my entire body. It was like my body was so topsy-turvy that it didn't know how to react to what was happening to me.

Kat's warning echoed through my brain, but it was a small, distant thing and at that moment I didn't care what the possible consequences might be. I didn't want Jace to stop, didn't want anything to break the spell he was weaving around me.

I ran the tips of my fingers down Jace's spine and drew a tiny moan out of him. It was like a sensual symphony. I could feel the sound vibrating out of his body and into mine. He drew back from me and then suddenly his eyes went wide.

His head whipped around at precisely the same instant that a green, glittery blur headed towards us from the trail that we'd taken up from the RV earlier. I opened my mouth to scold Bethany for interrupting, but Jace's hand was suddenly over my mouth.

"Someone is coming, Selene. Another Awakened. They were trying to mask their signature, but I can feel them now."

The languid, trembly feeling that I'd been swimming around in was instantly flushed away by a surge of adrenaline.

"What are we going to do? If there's just one of them, can you and Kat beat them?"

"I don't know. It depends on who we are up against. Kat and I had our signals masked as well, but the fact that I can feel him from this far away probably means that he's very powerful."

Jace was already towing me back over to the other side of the pool. As he lifted me out of the water and set me down next to my shoes, I heard Kat swear.

"Jace, do you feel that?"

"Yeah, get Ari out of the water and into her shoes."

"Holy sh—"

Ari's expletive was understandable given that Kat had just casually lifted her out of the water as if she weighed no more than a child, but it was cut short as Kat set her down on the edge of the pool and covered her mouth.

"You need to be very quiet and do exactly as we tell you. Someone very bad is coming this way and if you don't cooperate all four of us could end up dead."

The sun was so far behind the mountains that it was basically gone, but the moonlight was strong enough for me to see Ari's eyes go impossibly wide. Ironically, it was seeing her sitting there frozen in place that made me realize that I'd stopped moving too.

Jace was out of the water too, sitting next to me as he started rooting through his backpack. "What do you think, Kat? Do we have time to get them dressed?"

I took the towel that Jace handed me and automatically began drying my feet as Kat considered his question.

"If we don't and we end up having to make a run for it, they are going to get scratched all to pieces and probably end up with hypothermia too. We aren't going to have any extra bandwidth to waste on anything but the essentials."

Kat was already out of the water and she was toweling off Ari like my sister was a toddler she'd just finished bathing. I could tell that neither Jace nor Kat had any effects up, but Kat was moving as fast as I'd ever seen her move before. She looked up at Jace and me for a second and then reached for the ties to Ari's top.

"You're going to want to turn around now unless you're hoping to get an eyeful."

Jace turned around and then helped me to my feet. "We don't have much time, Selene. You're going to need to hurry—the only thing worse than having to make a run for it cold and wet while wearing nothing more than you are now would be to be partway through getting dressed when that other Awakened shows up."

I was shaking, more from fear than cold, but I managed a nod as I stepped around to the other side of Jace and tugged on the ties to my bikini top. I was starting to see the wisdom behind Kat switching her default emotion around to fear. The strength of the terror I was feeling in that moment felt like it could power any conceivable effect I could ever need.

The urge to just stand there frozen in place was still intense, but now that I was moving I was able to force myself to remain in motion. The rest of my wet clothes hit the rock shelf we were standing on a split second later and then I was drying off my body and reaching for the dry clothes waiting for me in the pack.

I could feel Jace just inches away from me, back turned to me as he mirrored my actions, stripping off his clothes and then drying himself. It should have been sensuous. Having him on the other side of a thin wooden door while I was naked had been enough earlier to get me all hot and bothered. This should have sent me shooting over the moon, but I was just too terrified for the presence of his hot naked body just outside of my field of vision to affect me like that now.

I heard Jace slip on a shirt, and felt him tense up. He was dressed and the urge to turn around and face the threat he knew was coming towards us had to be intense, but we girls all had an extra article of clothing to put on.

I pulled on my bra and then reached for my t-shirt with trembling hands as Jace shifted back and forth from one foot to the other.

"Are you three dressed yet? I can feel them getting closer, we're almost out of time."

Kat looked at me as she pulled her pants on. She was the furthest behind because Ari was still frozen in shock and she'd had to dress my little sister like a child.

"Ari and Selene are dressed. Go ahead and turn around."

Actually I wasn't dressed, but as Kat turned so her back was facing Jace I realized it didn't matter—all of my important bits were covered up and he wouldn't have been able to see anything from back there even if I hadn't managed to get my bra on.

I pulled my shirt over my head as Jace grabbed both of our suits and stuffed them dripping wet into his bag.

"We can't afford to leave anything behind, not with the bad guys this close. It will be a few hours before the link between us and the clothes dies enough that they won't be able to use them to track us."

"I didn't know that was even possible."

"Yeah, there's still lots you don't know. Think of it as magical DNA."

Kat was fully dressed and pulling on her shoes. I dropped down to follow suit, cursing myself for getting distracted and wasting time. Kat was already done with hers and had switched to getting shoes on Ari.

"What's the plan, Jace?"

Bethany had been streaking back and forth between us and the other Awakened, presumably trying to keep an eye on whoever it was, but Jace reached up and grabbed her around the waist just before she could shoot back in the other direction.

"You need to stop that, Bethany. You're just telling whoever is out there exactly where we are. Stay with Selene. You're still too small to go up against an Awakened right now, but if you keep your eyes open and think fast you may be able to help keep Selene out of trouble."

Bethany sketched a hasty salute and then as soon as Jace released her she spun around twice and then bounced over and landed on my shoulder. Jace was still searching the darkness, muscles tensed up as he tried to think his way out of the trap we could all feel closing in on us.

"I can't believe that it's just one out there, Kat. The number of people who can stand you and me both off at the same time isn't very big and the odds are that most of them are still back in China somewhere."

Kat frowned for a second and then reached out and rested a finger on Ari's forehead. My sister's eyes rolled up into the back of her head. Kat grabbed Ari before she could hit the ground. "You're thinking they have some Unseelie Court members along to help out?"

"Yeah. Whoever is over there will either keep their signature masked until they are right on top of us, or they'll flare their signature in an effort to scare us into running into some kind of ambush."

"So if they flare we charge them, but if they stay masked we make a run for it?"

"Yeah, unless they flare and it turns out that they really are powerful enough to take both of us on at the same time."

"You really do look at the bright side of everything."

Jace shrugged. "It's probably just the result of spending so many years with you."

"Any chance that Kregor will show back up and give us a hand?"

"Nope. I told him to keep an eye on Mr. Jenkins until we got back into town."

Kat nodded, but the gesture had an air of distraction to it. She already knew the answer to her question, she'd just asked it as a way of trying to hide her fear. I wanted to tell her that it was okay to be scared, but if Kat lost it I would probably come completely unglued.

"You'll time-bend and carry Selene, I'll lug Ari along?"

A hint of the terror she was feeling made it into Kat's voice and for the first time I realized just how badly she wanted to leave Ari there. Kat had spent too long running, had been in too many situations where it had been all she could do to make it out alive. She was worried that bringing Ari along would be too much, that she wouldn't make it out this time.

Despite that, she was going to do her best to save Ari.

Maybe some people would have been mad at Kat for wishing she could abandon Ari, but not me. I was nothing but proud of my old friend. I wasn't angry with Kat, but I was furious with whoever had tracked us down and threatened three of the four people in the entire world who meant the most to me.

Less than an hour ago I'd been so pissed at Ari that I hadn't been able to think straight, but seeing her now, unconscious and vulnerable, awoke a protective instinct in me that made me want to hunt down whoever was out there threatening us.

"No."

My voice came out sounding remarkably calm considering just how close I was to losing control. "Kat, you get Ari out. I'll amp myself and then put myself at double or triple speed and follow you out. Jace is the free agent. He keeps himself ready to run interference or go offensive if the opportunity arises."

"You promised me you weren't going to do that, Selene. It's too dangerous."

Kat's words came out as a hiss. She was obviously worried that the other Awakened would overhear us, but her anger was starting to come to the forefront. That was good, I felt a lot more comfortable with an angry Kat trying to get my sister out of here than a scared Kat.

Jace held a hand up, stopping Kat before she could say anything else. "You're sure, Selene? It's dangerous, but it would give us a much better chance of getting out of here."

"Yeah. I'd rather die from oxygen debt than let whoever is out there get their hands on me."

"Okay, do your effects, but get them up as fast as you can. I don't think that they've sensed you yet, but as soon as you start they'll know that there are actually three of us here. Newly awakened individuals are always valuable prizes. Some pantheons pride themselves on being able to corrupt people like you and turn them into virtual slaves."

I was shaking now, and it wasn't just the anger. The fear was back, but it was being forced out to the periphery of my being, bouncing off the solid core of anger that was going to allow me to work all of the effects I needed to work.

REBORN

I took a deep breath and then held onto that feeling, forcing it to become a more pervasive part of my reality. Between one breath and the next a stream of memories flowed out of my mind, but I didn't wait to double-check that I was properly amped before I reached out to the pulse of my surroundings.

The water flowing from one pond to the next was the first thing I noticed, followed quickly by the sound of Bethany's wings humming in my ear as she used them to steady herself. It felt like I was missing an ingredient and then suddenly I remembered what I still needed. My heart was hammering away in my chest, more felt than heard this time, but it would be enough. I grabbed ahold of the pulse around me and willed it to slow down at the same time that I sped myself up.

The first sign of success that registered for me was the way that the sound from Bethany's wings had dropped an octave. I turned around, looking for other signs, and my breath caught in my throat as I took in the water falling over the edge of the closest pool like taffy. Even now, surrounded by the imminent threat of violence, there was still so much beauty in the world.

I forced my mind back onto task and started the next amp. The feeling of strength that flowed through me a heartbeat later was all the sign of success I needed. I amped my skeletal system and then checked my anger. I found a roaring inferno still capable of supporting one final augmentation as long as I didn't overdo it.

I strengthened my skin and then turned to find that Jace was bouncing from one foot to the other, obviously running at double speed as compared to me. Kat had just finished picking up Ari, and then ran over to me, moving easily despite the added weight.

"Let's go, ladies."

Jace took off, heading deeper into the forest. Kat looked for a second like she was going to insist that I run in the middle, but I shook my head at her. She was carrying Ari, I would take the rearguard.

Jace zipped along ahead of us, using his superior speed to check a corridor of terrain on either side of the direction we were running. We'd made it less than a hundred yards before I felt a surge of power from behind us that made my blood run cold.

"He's trying to flush us out, Jace."

"I know, but whoever is back there is much too powerful for us to tangle with. We're going to have to just try to outrun them and hope we can make it past the ambush that they've got waiting for us."

The next several minutes went by in a blur. On the way into the hot springs I'd probably averaged ten miles an hour. I seemed to be operating at about triple normal speed, which meant that in theory I could do thirty miles an hour, up the side of the mountain, through some of the worst terrain I'd ever seen.

The reality though was that my circulatory amp wasn't quite good enough to sustain that kind of effort. Early on in the run I'd nearly put myself into dangerous levels of oxygen debt until Jace had appeared at my side and forced me to slow down.

Once I slowed down, I was only doing about twenty-six miles an hour, which we all knew wasn't going to be fast enough.

"Kat, go on ahead."

"I'm not falling for that again, Selene. The last time you did that I ended up having to explain to Jace that you'd gotten yourself killed."

"I can feel him gaining on us, Kat. You and Jace need to take Ari and the journals and get out of here. I'll run for as long as I can and then I'll throw myself off of a cliff. In eighteen years you can find me and we'll try again."

"Still not happening. You'd better run your little heart out, because I'm not leaving you behind. If that piece of crap back there catches up to you, then he catches up to all of us."

Jace stepped off to the side of the trail, letting first Kat and then me pass and then falling into step just behind me.

"Keep running, Selene. I'm going to drop back and try to slow down whoever is back there."

"No, Jace, I'm not worth it."

"You're forgetting, I have the journals—there's a chance if he takes me down that he'll chalk it up as a win and let the three of you get away."

Jace's hand snuck up and clasped my hand for just a second. The iron bands around my chest loosened up as he temporarily amped up my system to clear out the lactic acid that had been building up in my muscles and flushed a burst of oxygen into my bloodstream.

"No matter what else happens, know that I've loved you for as long as I can remember, Selene."

Jace turned and sprinted back the way we came, gone so fast that I couldn't stop him. I used the strength that he'd given me to catch back up with Kat and Ari, and we temporarily pushed the pace back up to something around the thirty miles per hour that I'd started out at.

We made it another twenty steps and then the sky behind us lit up with a light that rivaled the noonday sun and the ground shook, nearly knocking me off of my feet. I thought for a second that was it, that Jace had been killed, but then the ground shook again three more times in rapid succession, as though a giant was trying to crush a fly with a hammer the size of the space shuttle.

Kat looked back at me for just a second and nodded. "As long as whoever is back there keeps launching those attacks we know that Jace is still alive and kicking. That sounds like a relatively focused attack, Jace is amped up enough that he should be able to avoid that kind of stuff. It's the really big area-damage effects that are the most dangerous for someone who's bending time."

The next attack didn't just make the ground shake, it was accompanied by a blast of light and heat that dried the sweat on my back. I spared a glance over my shoulder and found that the entire mountainside back by the hot springs was on fire.

"Kat!"

"I know, I can see it too. Just remember that nobody can be strong everywhere. The bigger the area of effect they try to hit Jace with, the less absolute strength they'll manage to land on him. Jace is fast and smart, he can deflect most effects."

"So the bad guy has to spread out his attack enough to offset Jace's superior speed, but not so much that Jace will be able to parry the attack."

"Yeah."

"What aren't you telling me, Kat?"

"That attack wasn't actually designed to kill Jace directly. That was all about changing the terrain. Jace needs room to move. Dodging burning trees is going to make that a lot harder. Hopefully he's smart enough to beat a fighting retreat."

I opened my mouth to ask her how likely that was, but before I could get the words out a gigantic shadow detached itself from the darkness and threw itself at Kat. There wasn't time to yell a warning. I pushed Kat as hard as I could, using every ounce of amped strength to send her flying forward.

I tried to change direction at the same time, but a jolt of pain across the bottom of my right foot brought me down to one knee as the piece of darkness clipped Kat in the shoulder and sailed over me. Bethany grabbed onto my hair with both hands as I went down, but she managed to keep from being thrown free of my shoulder.

"Selene, that's Fenrir!"

Kat swore as she threw herself into a tree to bleed off some of the kinetic energy I'd just imparted to her, and then spun around to face the gigantic wolf now standing between us. Ari was still hanging limply across Kat's shoulder, but one of her arms was angled wrong, and Kat was bleeding from her shoulder on that same side.

My hand brushed across a stick that was nearly an inch and a half in diameter as I scrambled to my feet, and I picked it up as Kat forced her damaged arm up and launched a blast of pure golden light out of the tips of her fingers.

Fenrir tried to dodge to one side, but Kat was just the tiniest bit faster and she tracked his movement and managed to connect with his flank for a split second before it flickered out. The trees that the beam had raked across exploded into burning splinters, but all it did to Fenrir was leave a fist-sized hole in his flesh that didn't seem to be slowing him down at all.

Kat ducked to one side, using the trees and Fenrir's ox-like size against him, but he shattered the first tree he hit from the titanic force of his collision, and a splinter the size of my fist took Kat through the outside of her leg.

The next tree in Fenrir's path was big enough to stop him cold, which was all that saved Kat and Ari as Fenrir's teeth snapped shut inches behind Ari's head. Kat tripped and went down to one knee as she launched another blast of light back at Fenrir, but this time he barely moved out of the path of the attack. It left a black, charred line across his shoulder and he pushed the tree in front of him over, toppling it directly towards Kat.

There wasn't any time to second-guess my next move. I yelled for Bethany to run away and then I stabbed Fenrir in the back with my improvised spear.

The jagged end of my branch pierced his flesh and sank in more than six inches before he spun around, snapping at me. I should have died right then. I was fast, nearly as amped up as Kat, but I wasn't a match for Fenrir at close range. The only thing that saved me was the fact that him spinning around slammed my spear into my ribs and launched me backwards down the mountain.

Kat hit him with another blast of light, but it flickered off even more quickly than before this time. Blood loss and emotional fatigue were catching up with her.

Fenrir dodged to one side without even looking back at her and continued to stalk towards me. I heard Bethany come buzzing towards me as I skidded to a stop and realized that the skin over my ribs had torn from the force of the branch hitting me.

"Selene, there's a rock next to your right hand, two inches to the right."

I grabbed it without looking away from Fenrir and started backing away from him.

"You're bleeding, tiny girl-child, and I've yet to touch you. Are your abilities not even up to keeping your skin whole in the face of the stresses you're putting on it?"

In the heat of battle I'd forgotten about the pain in my right foot, but it was as though him pointing out my injuries brought them back full-force. He was right, my skin-strengthening effect wasn't up to the task of keeping the skin from splitting when I used all of my strength like I had when I'd avoided his initial lunge. I was facing one of the biggest, baddest nastiest things in all of Norse mythology, the monster that was supposed to kill the god Odin, with nothing more than a rock. I was screwed and I knew it, but the anger that had been powering my effects hadn't gone anywhere and when I opened my mouth I didn't feel any urge to surrender and beg for mercy.

"You're bleeding too, you overgrown lab-radoodle. It must really smart to have someone whose gift has been working for less than a day stab you like that. What are all of the other dogs in the pound going to say when they find out?"

His eyes were an unearthly yellow that made my skin crawl. He hadn't blinked even once since he'd started stalking me.

"It won't be an issue, because they aren't going to find out."

I felt Kat's effects flicker out and I feinted an attack at the precise instant that she hit him with another blast—one that was white-hot and bigger around than my leg. This time he yowled in pain as he threw himself to the side in an effort to put a tree between him and the worst of the attack.

Fenrir sprang at Kat, but now he was moving around on just three legs. He was slower than he'd been, but that wasn't going to save Kat, not now that she wasn't amped at all. I took three quick steps toward him and launched the rock in my hand at him with all of my might.

Moving as I was at three times normal speed, even my amped body struggled to accelerate the projectile at anything that felt like a decent clip. I could feel the air pushing back against me, trying to resist my efforts. When I released the rock it seemed to crawl across the distance between Fenrir and I, but he was moving even slower than that and he didn't hear it coming until the very last instant.

The rock crashed into him with enough force that I heard ribs break. I'd succeeded in distracting him from Kat, who was pulling herself back to her feet, but now I had two or three tons of angry Unseelie wolf charging back towards me.

I threw myself to one side, narrowly avoiding his jaws again as he streaked past me and landed further down the mountain. I'd gotten out of his way, but that was only because he was hobbling on three legs. I heard a familiar buzzing sound and then something materialized in my hand. It was my spear again, bloody on one end and splintered on the other from where Fenrir had used his jaws to rip it out of his side, but it was perfect.

Bethany zipped away from me unsteadily, obviously exhausted from whatever she'd done to get my weapon back, but I couldn't spare any time to be worried about her. The entire mountain shook again as the Awakened who'd been chasing us took another shot at Jace. I couldn't count on Jace showing up and saving us at the last minute.

Fenrir spun around and started back up the hill, but he didn't seem to be in as big a hurry this time. Probably because he knew it was down to just him and me. Kat had obviously worn herself dangerously thin with her last attack.

"Hey, Kat, what are our options here?"

"I'm good for maybe one more beam of light, but that's like pissing on a bonfire. Fairies naturally absorb a portion of the memories powering any attack thrown at them, so you have to hit them incredibly hard to do any real damage."

"How do we stop him then?"

"There's a reason that most of the old legends have the gods fighting things like him with more mundane types of weapons. When you hit him with a rock, there aren't any memories to absorb so he takes the full damage from those kinds of attacks."

"I've been super lucky so far, Kat, but I don't think I'm going to be able to drive this stick into his heart."

"I know. I've got just enough juice left that I could amp myself and bend time, but I can't survive closing with that monster while I'm carrying Ari. Hell, with this arm the way it is right now and a massive chunk of wood buried in my leg, I'm not sure I could manage to fight him even if I put Ari down."

Fenrir's lips pulled back from his teeth and I knew exactly what he was thinking.

"Don't put her down, Kat. As soon as you do that he'll kill her. As big as he is, there's no way we can stop him from getting to her."

"Okay, well, I'm all ears if you've got any bright ideas, but it's looking like this is the end of the road."

"Run away, Kat. You're not as fast as you were before, but then again, neither is he. You run and I'll do everything I can to slow him down for as long as I can before he rips my throat out."

"That's suicide, Selene."

"Probably, but I prefer to think of it as being heroic. Besides, there's always a chance that I can keep him busy for long enough that Jace will work his way back here. This overgrown mongrel may be able to beat you and me, but Jace will rip his head off and spit down his throat."

Fenrir growled, but I just gave him the finger and stoked what was left of my rage up a little higher. I was trying to talk a good game because I needed Kat and Ari to survive, but the truth was that I was hitting the end of my endurance too. I'd started the fight already emotionally spent and been relying on the echoes of rage from my last incarnation to get me this far. I could feel my anger guttering now—I figured I might have another minute or two before my effects started giving out one after another. It wasn't long enough to run, but it might be long enough to take out another of Fenrir's legs.

Apparently flipping off Fenrir was going too far because he exploded up the slope towards me. I yelled for Kat to run as I tried to dodge to one side at the same time that I aimed the tip of my weapon at his right shoulder. I wasn't going to make it. I'd started moving too soon and he'd started adjusting his course.

I tried to summon a bit more speed, but this time it was my left foot that gave out as I stressed my skin beyond what it could take. My right shoe had gotten wet and heavy and I had an instant as my left knee hit the ground to wonder just exactly how much blood I'd lost already.

I felt a tiny weight land on my shoulder a split second before the impact and I wanted to scream in rage. After everything I'd done to try to get Kat and Ari away, why did Bethany have to throw her life away too? She'd done her part already. She'd gotten me my spear and she'd been clear. She'd been safe.

The rage that had been guttering fanned itself higher at the thought of one of my few links to the old me dying, but it was far too late to do anything about it. I grounded the butt of my spear. It was much too frail to hold off two tons of charging wolf, but at least Fenrir would impale himself on it before he got me.

I wanted to close my eyes, but something refused to let me. Some tiny, iron-willed piece of me not only refused to go to my death with my eyes closed, it summoned my rage and used it to send a stream of memories out into the world.

It all happened so fast that there was no way for me to shape the power into an actual effect even if I'd had any other effects to work. Jace had warned me against unfocused bursts of power, had told me they always ended badly for the Awakened involved, but rather than being engulfed in an inferno of undirected power, I saw the tip of my spear turn silver as it entered Fenrir's shoulder.

The heavy branch should have snapped like a toothpick, but instead I felt it bow slightly as the tip caught on one of the massive bones inside of Fenrir's body. My spear—now completely silver—sank several inches into the hardened ground, and then hit solid rock and Fenrir's course was instantly changed.

He still caught me with one heavy paw as he sailed over my head and slammed into the side of the mountain. The force of the collision sent me tumbling further down the mountain. I didn't stop moving until my head slammed into a rock, but before the darkness claimed me I thought I saw a slender figure drive a sword into Fenrir's throat.

Chapter 29

I was more than just disoriented when I woke back up—I was surprised. I'd never hit my head that hard and part of me hadn't expected to ever open my eyes again. I reached up to touch my head and saw that my hands were both bandaged.

That didn't make sense. I didn't remember Fenrir getting his teeth on me there, but then again it was always possible that I'd just stressed my skin too much on my palms too. I turned my head and started taking in my surroundings.

I was in a windowless room that was more than twice as big as my entire house back in Cold Springs. The lack of windows should have made it feel dark and foreboding, but the bright lighting somehow worked together with the dark wood trim to create something that felt both inviting and elegant.

The bed I was resting on was only slightly smaller than Jace's had been and included a canopy of burgundy velvet that hung down far enough in some spots that it very nearly touched the ground. I reached a hand out to the black wood and got a sense of age from it that I hadn't felt with anything else I'd ever touched.

The room had a curved wall, which made me think of Jace's bedroom, but rather than just being a quarter of a circle, this one was half of a circle. I wasn't surprised to see that there was a heavy set of wooden shelves built into the far wall, or that most of the space was taken up by a series of white-leather books that were eerily similar to the journals Jace and Kat used. Size, width, texture, everything looked exactly the same but for the colors.

Other than the bed and the shelves, the room was largely empty. There wasn't a breakfast nook or a desk. There wasn't even a television. It was a room for sleeping, not for working or socializing. In fact I suspected that the journals were there simply because their owner didn't like sleeping with them more than a few feet away from him.

I was a little nervous that my legs wouldn't work, but I was able to roll to the edge of the bed and when I put my feet down on the carpet I was able to feel the texture of the soft fibers that gave it such a luxurious look.

As I experimentally stood, I heard footsteps coming from the open door on the left. A second later my rescuer stepped into the room and I got my first look at him. In that last split second before I'd slammed into that rock I'd somehow thought it was Jace who had saved me, but Jace hadn't had a sword when I'd last seen him, and if he'd saved me he wouldn't have left me to wake up in a strange place all alone.

I didn't know what to expect when I saw my savior for the first time, but I never could have anticipated what I actually saw.

It was like looking at a dark version of Jace.

The blond hair had been traded for a brown so dark it could have passed for black, and he looked older, mid to late twenties rather than late teens, but it was Jace's incredible bone structure that framed eyes that were the exact same shade of blue as the ones that I'd fallen in love with just a few days ago.

The eyes were the same color, but they looked wrong somehow. It took me several heartbeats to realize that was because there was a brooding quality to them that I'd never seen in Jace. That more than anything else was what told me I wasn't looking at my Jace in some kind of weird alternate universe. My Jace could never have looked so cynical. Not in a million years, not through ten thousand incarnations.

It took an act of will to force myself to look away from those darkly captivating eyes, but once I did I took in the rest of my captor's appearance. He was wearing designer jeans and a silk button-up shirt that looked like it must have cost a few thousand dollars, but it was the sword that was the most shocking. His hand rested on it, but the gesture wasn't so much threatening as it was a reflexive attempt to make sure that the weapon was still there, still attached to his belt.

"Who are you, and why am I here?"

"My name is Kyle. Once upon a time I was your husband and you're here because I have a proposal for you."

Acknowledgements

Nearly all of the usual suspects need thanked again. Writing is a solitary affair—just me alone in a room with my desktop—but once the rough draft of a book is finished an impressive team springs into action to help get the manuscript turned into a book that I can be proud of.

As always, RJ Locksley and Amy Jirsa-Smith did great work on the editing side of things catching countless errors and suggesting subtle changes that ultimately made the book a better, more marketable product.

My team of advance readers continue to be much better than I deserve. A big thanks to Jenine, Janelle, Mei, Heather, Merissa, Mimi, Mom, Dad, Shalese, Matthew, Lachele and Kim.

Finally, I most definitely couldn't have done this without help from my wife, Katie. Not only is she my first reader and cover artist, she also supports me in a hundred other ways. Thank you, Katie!

About the Author

Dean Murray is a prolific author with dozens of titles across multiple pen names and more than half a million copies of his work currently in circulation.

Dean started reading seriously in the second grade due to a competition and has spent most of the subsequent three decades lost in other people's worlds.

Things worsened, or improved depending on your point of view, when he first started experimenting with writing while finishing up his accounting degree. These days Dean has a wonderful wife and two lovely daughters to keep him rather more grounded, but the idea of bringing others along with him as he meets interesting new people in universes nobody else has ever seen tends to drag him back to his computer on a fairly regular basis.

Keep up to speed on Dean's latest projects at deanwrites.com.

Stone Heart

Dani's new home isn't just another stopover in a long chain of places she'll never see again, it's the home of both Caine and Jerek, two guys like nobody she's ever met before. One represents the best friend she's been hungering for, and the other represents something much more.

It should be the perfect recipe for a fairytale, but Caine and Jerek live in a dark, shadowy world and one of them is hiding secrets that will change everything, secrets that relate directly to Dani.

Broken

Adri Paige's arrival in Sanctuary thrusts her into a dangerous, shadowy world most people don't believe exists, and places her in the middle of a war between darkly handsome Alec Graves and charismatic Brandon Worthingfield that threatens to consume the entire town.

On the surface, both Alec and Brandon are nothing more than average high-school guys, but as Adri is pulled ever more deeply into their conflict she realizes that one of them wants to kill her. Adri needs to decide who to trust before her time runs out once and for all.

The Society

People need to be monitored, or they'll repeat the mistakes of the Desolation, a centuries-old war that killed billions of people and destroyed civilization.

Skye is part of the Society, the hi-tech, nanite-endowed group responsible for making sure that the millions of surviving people—grubbers—are confined to the ancient, decaying cities where they can be watched to ensure they aren't redeveloping the weapons technology that came so close to extinguishing life on the planet.

When the Society's monitoring programs pick up troubling developments in one of the grubber cities, Skye is ordered in to deal with the man responsible, but what—and who—she finds once she arrives will change everything.

Frozen Prospects

The invitation to join the secretive Guadel should have been the fulfillment of dreams Va'del didn't even realize he had. When his sponsors are killed in an ambush a short time later, he instead finds his probationary status revoked, and becomes a pawn between various factions inside the Guadel ruling body.

Jain's never known any life but that of a Guadel in training. She'd thought herself reconciled to the idea of a loveless marriage for the good of her people, but meeting Va'del changes everything. Their growing attraction flies against hundreds of years of precedent, but as wide-spread attacks threaten their world, the Guadel have no choice but to use even Jain and Va'del in their fight for survival.

The Greater Darkness:
(Writing as Eldon Murphy)

Something powerful is stirring in the darkness. Something so ancient that even creatures who've been alive for hundreds of years have long since discounted this new threat as nothing more than myth.

Normal humans will be caught in the crossfire, but then that's always the way of things. Geoffrey has no memory of his past life or any idea how to survive in the violent, dangerous world in which he's trapped. Despite his best efforts, he's about to find himself in the middle of a conflict that threatens to sweep away everything, and everyone he's been fighting so hard to protect.

CHET:
Whispers From The Past
By Larry Murray

30 years ago Charles Tucker lost everything that made life worth living. A brutal car accident killed his son. A short time later painful cancer took his wife.

The arrival of the Saunders family casts Charles' life into turmoil, tearing open unhealed wounds. Without his help the Saunders' financial troubles threaten to destroy them, but helping them risks destroying everything Charles spent a lifetime building.

Over all the turmoil looms Chet, the battered old '64 Chevy pickup that carried Charles' son to his death. For 29 years Charles blamed the old pickup for his devastating losses, locking Chet away in an old barn.

The most intriguing mysteries refuse to stay locked up. Solving this one promises an enchanting adventure for the whole family.